PRAISE FOR

IF YOU ASK ME

"A gracefully crafted tribute to searching for the right answer—and to finally realizing that sometimes it doesn't exist. *If You Ask Me* is a heart-mending tale about the importance of being our authentic selves, and the joys to be found in embracing our vulnerability. Equal parts funny and moving, Violet's messy, hopeful journey and her beautiful romance will resonate with everyone who struggles with the unexpected twists and turns of life. Libby Hubscher is a master at creating compelling, relatable characters and heartwarming, emotional stories. I cannot wait for her next book!"

—Ali Hazelwood

"I gasped, I ground my teeth, and I cheered along with Violet as she gathered the smashed pieces of her life and used them to build something better than before."

—Jesse Q. Sutanto

"Full of southern charm and self-discovery. Libby Hubscher brings a light touch to heavy emotions in this witty novel about starting over in life and in love."

—Virginia Kantra

"A funny, feminist, feel-good novel about making mistakes, asking for advice, and writing your own happy ending. I laughed and I cried—this novel is an absolute joy!"

—Freya Sampson

PRAISE FOR

MEET ME IN PARADISE

"A beautifully moving mix of self-discovery, sister bonds, and slow-burning romance that's 100 percent pure pleasure!"

—*USA Today* bestselling author Priscilla Oliveras

"*Meet Me in Paradise* is such a compelling read! By turns heartwarming and heartbreaking. Libby Hubscher truly takes us on a journey as Marin learns to find happiness on her own terms. Her adventures are brought so vividly to life that I want to start a #ProjectParadise of my own!"

—Jen DeLuca, author of *Well Played*

"*Meet Me in Paradise* is a stunning tale of love, loss, and the capacity for wonder. Marin's adventure will touch anyone who has ever felt adrift in a sea of responsibility and decided to swim toward the shore. Hubscher expertly crafts a delicious blend of humor, whimsy, and raw emotion that left me laughing, crying, and unable to put it down."

—Denise Williams, author of *How to Fail at Flirting*

"Both a romantic escape and an ode to sisterhood, *Meet Me in Paradise* made me swoon, laugh, and then sneaked up on me and made me cry. Marin and Sadie are the beating heart of this story—I adored them in all their wild, wonderful messiness. A radiantly hopeful book."

—Rachel Lynn Solomon, author of *The Ex Talk*

"*Meet Me in Paradise* will sweep you off your feet. Marin's leap into the unknown is full of love, romance, and adventure, and I felt like I was right there with her on the pristine beaches of Saba as she climbs mountains, dives for pearls, and learns how to open herself up to the possibilities of love."

—Sonya Lalli, author of *Serena Singh Flips the Script*

"Hubscher's debut novel is the perfect book for anyone longing for family, travel, and romance. Prepare for some tears mixed with the happy-ever-afters."

—*Library Journal*

"A poignant, emotionally authentic story of sisterly bonds and unexpected love. . . . This is sure to tug at readers' heartstrings."

—*Publishers Weekly* (starred review)

"Debuting author Hubscher gently weaves in the more somber story lines, so readers aren't blindsided yet will still feel the full emotional impact. The romance blooms beautifully, and while there are several complex and endearing secondary characters, this is primarily Marin's story told mostly through her own captivating narrative. Tissues should be on hand."

—*Booklist*

"Not simply a breezy romantic comedy, *Meet Me in Paradise* captures the duality of life's highs and lows. This romantic comedy offers tropical vacation mishaps, a burgeoning romance, and an undercurrent of heartbreak."

—Shelf Awareness

TITLES BY LIBBY HUBSCHER

Meet Me in Paradise

If You Ask Me

If You Ask Me

LIBBY HUBSCHER

JOVE
New York

A JOVE BOOK
Published by Berkley
An imprint of Penguin Random House LLC
penguinrandomhouse.com

Library of Congress Cataloging-in-Publication Data

Names: Hubscher, Libby, author.
Title: If you ask me / Libby Hubscher.
Description: First edition. | New York: Jove, 2022.
Identifiers: LCCN 2021035201 (print) | LCCN 2021035202 (ebook) |
ISBN 9780593199442 (trade paperback) | ISBN 9780593199459 (ebook)
Subjects: LCGFT: Novels.
Classification: LCC PS3608.U2524 I35 2022 (print) |
LCC PS3608.U2524 (ebook) | DDC 813/.6—dc23
LC record available at https://lccn.loc.gov/2021035201
LC ebook record available at https://lccn.loc.gov/2021035202

First Edition: March 2022

Printed in the United States of America
1st Printing

Book design by Daniel Brount

To Tom, who loves me despite my mess
(and the coffee mugs I leave all over the house).
And to North Carolina, where we made our life together.

The naked truth is always better
than the best-dressed lie.

–ANN LANDERS

Dear Reader,

This book deals with the issues of infidelity, infertility, miscarriage, anxiety, and alcohol abuse. While I have tried my best to portray such difficult subject matter with as much sensitivity and thoughtfulness as possible, I know this content may be upsetting to some readers. If these are difficult subjects for you, please take care. Anxiety/panic attacks and infidelity occur on the page, infertility and miscarriage are discussed several times and are significant themes.

Too many of us feel we have to suffer alone and put on brave and beautiful faces in public, even when we are deeply hurt and most in need of love and support. If you've struggled with any of these things, you are not alone. I hope you find comfort and solidarity in Violet's journey.

All my best,
Libby

One

My mother always said people who work in helping professions are the ones in greatest need of professional help themselves. She's usually right about most things. After all, I became an advice columnist—imagine the irony . . . Who needs more help than that?

When things started to go awry, I was sitting in a two p.m. staff meeting, politely nibbling a stale Girl Scout cookie courtesy of the real estate columnist's daughter, waiting for the *Raleigh Times*'s owner to arrive and the other shoe to drop. The last time Ed Hastings had been here, half our staff had been let go. Low subscription numbers, lost ad revenue, and all that. Today, he whooshed into the room and the air whooshed out—everyone fell silent. I brushed a crumb from my notepad, straightened up, and squared my shoulders. If I was getting the axe, the least I could do was sit up straight.

"Afternoon, folks," Ed said. "I'll keep this brief."

"The online edition has been doing well," Tyler, the Raleigh Out and About columnist, interjected. "We've had great ad commitment for next quarter."

"Let's not get ahead of ourselves." Tyler straightened his lavender tie. He's a Spring, so he can pull that color off. It would've washed me out. "I'm not here for layoffs. Tyler's right, we're faring fine, for now.

Out and About, of course, has been one of our top features. Actually, I'm here to announce a few pieces of good news. First, as you likely already know, our brilliant editor in chief received the Hillman Prize for her series on corruption in the North Carolina general assembly—kudos again, Kyra. Second, we've got a columnist who, if everything goes according to plan, is about to go national."

He surveyed the room, appraising us, while we all wondered who was about to get lucky. Had his gaze lingered on Ashleigh? She wrote the society pages on top of meaty public interest pieces and looked like a princess in pearls, her natural blonde waves cascading over her shoulders. Or maybe Javier? His coverage of the evolution of the educational system had been insightful, thoroughly researched, with crisp writing to boot. They were the real journalists. I smiled preemptively, preparing to show a gracious response.

Hastings extended his arms. "Our very own Dear Sweetie!"

The small room exploded with applause. Javier whistled. "Way to go, Violet!" Tyler said in a tone that sounded as much of an indictment as it did a congratulations.

"Alright, everybody," Kyra said, saving me from the attention, "it is wonderful news, and absolutely well deserved, but the syndication's not a done deal yet. There are a few columnists in the running—all talented. The next three months will determine what happens. Okay, that's it, great job, you superstars. Back to work."

A couple of people congratulated me as they trickled out of the room. I thanked them, but I stayed put, processing. Kyra raised an eyebrow. I'd thought my face had remained neutral, pleasantly surprised; truth be told, I was flummoxed. And despite my years of practice controlling my expressions, curating them for each situation, she read me like a book, just as she always had when we were college roommates at State.

"You're not excited?" she asked.

"No . . . of course I am. Who wouldn't be excited? I'm just shocked, I guess. You are sneaky. I had no idea."

She shrugged. "I always tell Rox that I would've made a great spy. Keeping secrets, digging up dirty ones, whatever . . . it's one of my many gifts." That was the understatement of the year. Not only was she the paper's first Black editor in chief, she was also the first woman to hold the title.

"Right, well don't look at me. I've got no secrets. I'm just a happily married advice columnist."

"Yeah, yeah. How about *kick-ass-soon-to-be-nationally-syndicated* advice columnist? It sounds more exciting, and less smug married."

"It does have a ring to it," I admitted, finally standing up slowly. My legs still felt like rubber after an unusually brutal boot camp class that morning.

"Why do you look like my grandma getting out of her Barca-Lounger? Tell me you're not still doing that awful fitness class at the crack of dawn."

I ignored her and smoothed down my skirt. "Do you mind if I head home early? I was thinking I'd finally break out that sushi-making kit Sam got me for our anniversary and surprise him with my news at dinner."

"Raw fish . . . how sexy. You're not planning on placing the rolls all over yourself like Samantha in *Sex and the City*, are you?"

I recoiled. "That's an option, thanks to all those sessions at that awful fitness class you keep teasing me about. But, no, I was not planning on turning myself into a naked human platter." Although, it had been a while since Sam and I had engaged in anything other than the standard ten-minute, two-position, perfectly fine sex. I pictured a piece of sashimi on my décolletage. *No.*

"Good. 'Cause if I recall, that did not end well for Smith and Samantha. Didn't they break up in that episode?"

"Unlike some people, I haven't watched that show since we binged it in college. Not to worry. I definitely will not be wearing a California roll tonight, so I guess my marriage is safe."

"In that case, I suppose strategizing how to get your column on top can wait 'til tomorrow."

"Thanks, boss." I grinned at her, collected my leather folio, and power walked out of the office. I couldn't wait to see the look on Sam's face when I surprised him with my big news.

SAM AND I MOVED to Sunny Ridge, a small town nestled between Apex and Holly Springs, ten years earlier, when the few subdivisions being built were mixed in among horse farms like some kind of utopia. It was so charming and perfect; we'd loved it right away, just like we'd fallen for each other. The tiny historic downtown still stood, as picturesque as ever, but there were more communities, fewer trees, and no horses for miles these days.

On my way home, I stopped at the newest addition—a high-end grocery store—and bought some sushi-grade tuna and salmon along with a bottle of prosecco, and then headed toward the year-old firehouse, where a crew was bringing the truck to a high shine in the sun. One guy tossed a soapy sponge like a football. It arced over his target's head and landed in the road ahead of me. I slowed the Jeep to a stop to keep from running it over. The intended receiver, a tall, handsome man, sprinted into the road after the rogue sponge. Once he'd saved it from the street, he flashed me a grin and then loped off, launching the sponge right into the laughing quarterback's face. I was in such a good mood I waved before I continued on.

I hung a left into our neighborhood. It had been the first one Sam and I had looked at when we decided to buy. The only one. We lived in a sky-blue Victorian on a cul-de-sac where I baked Ritz Cracker chocolate toffee bark every Christmas, threw the Labor Day cookout with an honest-to-God bouncy castle, and could be counted on to bring flowers and two bottles of wine—a red and a white—to the community Bunco club each month. It was idyllic. Sam mowed the zoysia lawn in perfectly parallel lines and I planted clematis and azaleas that burst with color along our picket fence every spring. It was the kind of life I'd pictured when I was a girl, watching my mother plan all those fancy weddings for her clients and dreaming about my own happily ever after.

I parked in the driveway next to Sam's car—he'd taken an interest in the environment recently and carpooled most days with one of our neighbors who worked for the same firm—and grabbed the mail from the mailbox. I bounced up the steps, wrangling the giant stack of mail, the grocery bag, and my keys. Inside, I left my shoes beside the door before heading into the kitchen. I dropped the mail on the table. The paper fowarded my readers' letters here, so we got more mail than most people. I ran a hand over the envelopes, debating whether I should open them, start the sushi rice, or get changed. I was dying to get out of my constricting work clothes and into a pair of nice jeans and a tank top, unwind my hair out of the high bun that had become a uniform over the years, but I wanted to make sure I had everything ready by the time Sam came home.

I cooked the short-grain rice until it was tender, fanning it precisely the way the directions specified, adding the rice vinegar, placing it on the cling wrap on the little mat, and then filled it with the fish and cucumber sliced into tiny sticks before I tucked it into the fridge next to the chilling bubbly. Sam wasn't due back for another two hours—plenty of time to shave my armpits, wash my hair with the coconut shampoo he liked, do my hair and makeup, and greet him at the front door.

I made a beeline from the bedroom door straight to the bathroom to turn on the shower before I undressed. I hated to be wasteful, but the water took forever to get hot—the water heater was old, like the linoleum. Maybe we could use the extra income from the syndication to finally redo the bathroom. Even better, Sam could stop working so hard to get promoted, all those early mornings and late nights, and—I dared to dream—his mother might even stop calling my column a "little hobby."

I unzipped my skirt and stepped out of it. I was on my way to the walk-in closet to put my skirt in the bag for dry cleaning when I froze. Among my mother's many mantras I followed to a T was *messy bed, messy head*. Sam must've been in a hurry this morning: he'd pulled the covers up, but he'd left the blanket I used to block the blasting air conditioner he liked at night all wadded and lumpy beneath the duvet. He also hadn't opened the curtains. I left them—with any luck, we'd want them closed later anyway—but the bed had to be fixed. I flung the comforter back so I could grab the blanket and smooth the whole tangled mess out.

I admit it, I screamed when I saw them. At first, I only registered people in my supposed-to-be-empty house. A moment passed—my scream hanging in the air—before the people flailed about searching for cover and I was able to finally process what I was seeing. The tangled mess. *Blankets*, I'd thought. Not Sam. Not my husband. Not my husband, Sam, intertwined with a woman.

Seeing is believing: my mother said that too.

I saw. Sam's pale skin, naked, his face like an Edvard Munch painting, his blond curls a mess, and the woman, her hair blonder than his, her skin a shade tanner, but precisely as nude. She buried her face in his chest.

"Oh my God," Sam said. "Violet. Oh God."

None of us moved. I didn't take a breath for several seconds; I was too busy wondering if I was having some sort of episode or near-death experience that was causing me to hallucinate. Had I actually tripped and hit my head on the footboard? The woman's hand clutched for the covers. She wasn't wearing a wedding ring, I noted.

"What is this?" I managed to squeak.

Sam squirmed. "What are you doing home so early?"

I stepped back. My lip was starting to tremble, so I bit it. I realized that I was standing in a wrinkled blouse and my shapewear and I just *couldn't*. There's only so much humiliation a person can bear; certainly I had exceeded the all-time limit. I skulked back to the bathroom and shut the door. The shower was steaming, so I stepped beneath it, letting the water rush over me. It soaked through my stupid blouse and scalded my skin. Mascara dripped down my cheeks and onto my hands when I wiped my face. I pressed my back against the wall of the shower and slid down to the floor.

That couldn't have been real, could it? Sam with another woman, in our bed? But I'd seen them with my own eyes. All that skin. A perfectly toned ass. The platinum-blonde hair with the telltale postcoital matting. *Idiot*, I thought. I'd jinxed myself with the sushi. And after I was the victim of the worst possible type of surprise, Sam had tried to protect her. *Her*. Like she was the one who stood to be harmed in the situation. A sob rose up in my throat, but I clapped my hands over my mouth. The ability to cry, really cry, without making a sound was a skill I'd perfected over a lifetime, and I was thankful for it now. My perfect world had just imploded while I stood there in my Spanx. No way was I letting the perpetrators hear me have a breakdown in the bathroom.

I stayed in the shower until the water ran ice cold. Surely they weren't still lying there? The mirror was covered with a sheen of condensation, but I could make out my reflection, blurred, like a ghost. A drowned raccoon ghost, with the mascara smeared around both eyes. That wouldn't do, I told myself. I toweled off, washed my face, and reapplied my makeup. Then I got out my volumizing blow-drying brush and did my hair. I once saw a quote on Pinterest that said "If my hair looks good, I can deal with anything." I guessed this was a test of that adage. When my hair was as good as it was going to get, I opened the bathroom door. The bedroom was dark, the bed made so tightly you could bounce a quarter off of it. Sam cleared his throat from the doorway.

"We should talk," he said. I opened and closed dresser drawers in succession, pulling out my nicest underwear, jeans, a black T-shirt. "Violet."

I shook my head. "It's not a good time," I said.

"I need to explain."

I turned to face him. His button-down was off by a button; I resisted the urge to fix it. "I think you should go. I need to get changed." He looked at me. An hour earlier, the eye contact alone would've melted me into a puddle, but now I felt I might spontaneously combust and be reduced to a pile of ash on our carpet, something to be sucked up by our robot vacuum.

I listened to Sam's footsteps on the stairs. The creak of the front door. The turn of the dead bolt as he locked it from the outside. His car started and then it was quiet again. Even with the bed made and Sam and whoever that was gone, and my hair voluminous as all get-out, I could still see them. I retreated to the kitchen, to cold sushi and the pile of my mail. There's nothing better for avoiding your own devastation than a mountain of other people's problems. I choked down a mouthful of spicy tuna—the gelatinous rice sticking in my throat—and chased it with a generous gulp of the prosecco I'd planned on using to toast my big news while I tore open the first envelope, a pink one with loopy cursive on the front. *Dear Sweetie,* it read, *I don't know what to do. I feel like my whole world is falling apart.*

You and me both, pink envelope.

You and me both.

Two

THEN

Sam proposed under the red sails of a schooner he'd chartered from Ocracoke for a sunset cruise. Dolphins had raced alongside the ship, leaping playfully out of the water. I was laughing at them when he knelt down on the deck and proffered up a princess-cut diamond that I recognized as his grandmother's.

Of course my mother insisted on planning our wedding. She'd been planning them since before wedding planners were even a thing. A Wynne Vancott Wedding was a coveted occasion, across not just North Carolina, but the entire Southeast.

We met Mom the next day for lunch at a place in New Bern's historic downtown. While I ate fried green tomatoes with goat cheese, pear chutney, and a balsamic reduction, she extracted a giant binder from her bag and got to work.

"First things first—what do you envision for your wedding?"

"Classic, I think," Sam said. "Trey and Piper got married at the Carolina Inn last fall and it was a fantastic wedding. Or there's also the Washington Duke—like Mark and Ashleigh's—that was nice. Something like that, maybe. What do you think, Violet?"

I'd been thinking of something simple on the beach, Sam in a pair of khakis rolled up past his ankles and an untucked button-down. A pig pickin' and Blue Moon beer in bottles around a campfire. Bluegrass and dancing barefoot in the sand. I had not been thinking black-and-white tile and chandeliers. I swallowed my food and smiled. "Maybe. It's a little traditional. I was hoping for something a bit more relaxed."

My mother looked from me to Sam, who was turning his coffee cup on the table.

"What about Fearrington Village? It's elegant, but there's a barn there with those belted cows. Twinkle lights and gardens and a glass pavilion. It has accommodations for out-of-town guests, excellent food, and it's still quite close for your folks, Sam."

Mom always knew how to smooth things over. Sam nodded thoughtfully. "It *is* nice over there. My parents stayed there a couple of years ago for their twenty-fifth anniversary and raved about it. Yeah."

"Sounds great, Mom."

When your mother is a wedding planner, it's only natural to grow up fantasizing about your wedding. I'd wanted the beach in the Outer Banks at sunset. Antique, mismatched tables and chairs. Cottage roses and big candles and Sam with a gardenia pinned to his lapel, looking at me with that look. The look was the most important piece of it all. The only one that really mattered. It was the look that made all those other things mean nothing. Besides, marriage was about compromise. I knew that. So I compromised.

Sam's and my wedding was beautiful, just as my mother had promised—dogwood branches, a band, and outdoor couches, with belted cows as a backdrop. She even commissioned a wax stamp with our monograms together. S&V enclosed in a C, like a hug, in a bespoke font a famous graphic designer made just for us.

During the ceremony my mother dabbed her eyes with a vintage handkerchief, but her makeup was unscathed. Sam's mother, Lillian, had to touch up her makeup in the room I'd gotten ready in before we could take the family photos. She'd wept openly—at the time, I'd been touched. It wasn't until later that I realized she couldn't contain her sadness that her beloved son had married me.

"How do you always look so perfect, Wynne?" she'd asked my mother. "Your makeup is immaculate. Mine gave up halfway through the vows."

"I use a setting spray. Fix It Forget It. Lancôme. I give it to all my brides. I have some in my purse if you'd like a spritz."

I knew the truth. My mother hadn't actually cried. The business with the handkerchief had been merely performative. Not because my mother didn't care or wasn't touched, but because crying meant losing composure, and Wynne did not lose her composure. This was a secret I'd learned long ago, in the kind of lesson that seared itself into my psyche.

The photographer arranged us all. Sam leaned into my neck. "You looked so beautiful, I nearly needed your mother's makeup setting spray for myself," he whispered.

"Smile," the photographer said.

Three

THE NEXT MORNING, I sat alone at the breakfast table wondering how the quality of the light in the kitchen could be the same as the day before, when everything else had changed. One coffee cup instead of two. An uneaten bowl of Greek yogurt with half a grapefruit. A slice of turkey bacon that I couldn't bear to take a bite of. Where Sam normally had his plate and mug of black coffee, I'd stacked the open letters from the night before in a neat pile. I'd wanted to reply to them, those people who'd reached out to me to help them solve their problems, but I had no answers. Would they want my advice if they knew the truth about me? I'd thought everything had been fine, good even. That Sam and I had a wonderful life together. A beautiful home. Breakfast every morning. *I love you*s before we turned out the light each night. But all of that seemed ridiculous now, like a magic trick I'd fallen for. I was looking at the wrong things over here, while everything was happening over there.

I stared at that pile. I could almost see Sam sitting in his seat across from me, just the day before, while I read him my latest letter. Getting his feedback had turned into a habit. He'd set a steaming cup of black coffee in front of me before settling in his seat. Then he'd taken a bite of toast.

"I'm ready."

"Okay," I said. "I'm not sure about this one. But here goes."

Dear Sweetie,

A couple of weeks ago, my husband said I was starting to look a little chubby and I better do something before my fill-in-the-blank got "out of hand." I'd asked him to help me with a stuck zipper for a bridesmaid dress that was a little snug after an overzealous seamstress had gotten her hands on it. Also, I should tell you we've only been married a few months and I'd lost some weight for my own wedding and was just getting back to normal.

I'm usually a pretty confident person—but I can't get his words out of my head. For reference, my hubby's favorite pastime is CrossFit and for his birthday this year he asked for yet another kettlebell. We met playing soccer in a coed rec league, and while I still play, I'm definitely not as in shape as him or the Xena: Warrior Princesses he spends most of his time sweating next to.

After he said that, we went to the wedding and I felt like he was checking out all the other fitter, younger women there, and while it may have been all in my head, or the fact that I was wearing a truly heinous shade of chartreuse satin, I can't help but feel that maybe him saying I was looking a little chubby actually means he's not that attracted to me anymore. I even bought a new pair of jeans that I felt super cute in and he made a face and told me they made my butt look huge.

He's a sweet guy and I know he cares about me. I don't want to let a couple of small comments ruin our relationship. So last week, I told him I wanted to get in better shape, and he was so excited—we went to the CrossFit gym together and I tried so hard, but I couldn't keep up with him and I hated every second of it. And now the thought of doing another high-intensity interval makes me want to puke. So what do I do? What if the only weight I lose is him?

Sincerely,
Fitness Faker

....

I glanced up over the top of my laptop. Sam was engrossed in spearing a piece of scrambled egg with his fork.

"What do you think?"

He paused, fork in midair. "About the letter?"

"Yeah, it's sad, right? How a thoughtless comment totally eroded her self-esteem—it feels intentional."

"The guy's favorite pastime is CrossFit. Are any of us surprised that he is a douche?"

So he *had* been listening. "I take boot camp," I said.

"That's different. You're taking care of yourself. Did you already respond to her?"

"I think. It's a work in progress."

He gestured at my laptop with his piece of toast. "Let's hear it."

I cleared my throat and began to read.

....

Dear Fitness Faker,

It's completely natural to have fleeting feelings of insecurity, especially when someone whose opinion you value uses a loaded word like *chubby*. (Let's face it, that shouldn't be a negative thing, but still it is many girls' 1980s bullying nightmare.) It's only natural that you'd want to try different things to alleviate your worries. And studies have shown that exercise, any kind, is good for the body and the mind. But here's the thing . . . this isn't good for you. You're doing something you clearly don't enjoy because you fear that your new husband will move on if you don't. You didn't want to try CrossFit. You've probably never wanted to deadlift three times your body weight and do burpees until you drop. That insensitive comment left you feeling inadequate, and you are punishing yourself for your husband's bad behavior.

I don't think you need my advice here, but he does. Bodies are beautiful. All kinds of bodies. Period. Fat shaming alone is a giant strike against him. If I had to wager, I'd say it's not the only one. You are clearly smart and funny and care a lot about him. You were willing to slap on a sports bra and run sprints for him. I mean, that's a kind of love that people should be thanking their lucky stars for. So maybe your fat-phobic man should start showing appreciation instead of critiquing how you look in those jeans, and you should try something new that makes you feel good, like yoga, or a trial separation. Whatever you do, do it for you, and no one else.

Sincerely,
Sweetie

Sam wrinkled his nose.

"What is it?" I asked.

"Nothing," he said, and took a painfully long slurp of coffee. "Did you send it to Kyra yet?"

I set down the piece of turkey bacon I'd been about to take a bite of. "I knew you didn't like it. What's the problem?"

Sam did that thing he does when he's uncomfortable, the one that, if it weren't so adorable, I'd want to punch his face—he ran his hands through his blond waves and pressed his lips together. "You don't think the 'yoga or a trial separation' part was a bit over the top? And 'fat-phobic'? Is that a thing? You're not writing for *Cosmo* here."

I shrugged and bit my bacon perhaps just a little aggressively. "I thought it was fine." I had, in fact, already sent it to Kyra. Reading my advice columns to Sam was more a way to connect with him than seek his approval, though he used to lavish me with it.

"Just think it over," he said. He gave me a small grin, the trademark one that carved out a crease in his right cheek.

"Alright," I said. "I'll consider softening my language." I fired off an email to Kyra asking her to press pause on reviewing my latest and apparently not my greatest and attached another letter I'd written in response to a woman wondering if she could ask another parent to pay for her child's four-hundred-dollar luxury lice removal treatment at the Golden Comb after a sleepover party. Then I brushed a kiss across Sam's cheek. "I'm going to be late for boot camp. See you after work."

"Uh-huh," Sam said, engrossed in his phone.

"Love you."

"Yeah, you too."

I slung my bag over my shoulder and headed toward the door.

It was humid out and already hot, as it often is in North Carolina; the sun wasn't up yet, but the sky was a rich shade of peach and birds were chirping. A picturesque morning, some might call it. There were lights on in a few of the houses in our cul-de-sac—teenagers up for their early start at school. Across the street a dog barked, and my neighbor Shelby motored by in a sports bra and a pair of microscopic running shorts, her long platinum-blonde ponytail swinging behind her.

"Hey, Violet!" she called out, grinning.

"Hi!" I tried to reach her level of enthusiasm, but honestly, it was about two hours too early for that.

The boot camp class was held at a nearby gym in a giant room with fake grass that was called the "functional training room," though "torture chamber" would probably have been more accurate. I set my water bottle and my towel on the side of the grass and took my spot next to one of the setups—a short bar, a stack of weights, two bands, and a set of battling ropes that did not bode well for my morning.

Twenty minutes later I thought of Fitness Faker while I pondered if I was going to die from lactic-acid poisoning in my legs or heart explosion. I squatted down. Hypocrite. And up. Hypocrite. I should have signed *Sincerely, Hypocrite*. I didn't *love* boot camp. I wasn't here doing a body good. They should have called it insurance class. Three months earlier, I'd caught Sam watching Shelby rock her bikini from the clubhouse into the shallow end. Don't get me wrong, she looked hot. I took a rather long glance myself. But there was something about his expression, the heat in his eyes, the way his mouth opened hungrily; I thought I was going to have to wipe drool off his bottom lip. The bottom lip that had been married to me for twelve years. Shelby is twenty-four and sells cosmeceuticals to plastic surgeons. It is not surprising that she resembles an athletic model. She sprints around every day in a formfitting ensemble that makes her look like she's trying to win the NYC marathon and is basically one step more coverage than the bikini she'd been wearing that day. I don't fault her for it. If my ass looked like hers, I'd jog around in a bikini too. Actually, that's a lie. I'd lounge. Jogging isn't really my thing either. Anyway, now I showed up for this torture at six a.m. six days a week. Six-by-six, they call it. Only for the truly hard-core, or desperate. I should have been in bed, sleeping or having sex, but instead I was trying to out-squat Marathon Barbie.

"Violet, where's the intensity?!" Bear growled at me. "Ass to grass, ladies!"

And another thing, Fitness Faker, how come there's only ladies in here? Eight ladies, asses to grass, and a fucking Bear.

One woman named Jen flashed a smile/grimace my way. She was squatting off the baby weight. *Why are we doing this again?* she mouthed to me, in between panting breaths.

"Society, Jen. Society."

She nodded. Her sweet face was turning purple. "You know what, Violet? Society sucks."

Jen was right, I thought, stepping under the powerful jet of the gym's shower a few minutes later. I continued this thinking while I dried my hair, twisted it into a tight bun, applied undereye cream for the dark circles that gave away the two hours of sleep I'd missed every day these last several months, and pulled on my work clothes. Society teaches us these things. Mom always told me happiness doesn't just appear, you have to work for it. Like all those things we're taught should just happen effortlessly, it requires the most effort of all. Bear too had his own saying for it: no pain, no gain.

Now I looked again at Sam's empty seat at the table. I pictured him in our bed, clutching the woman to him, protecting her from me. I could see quite clearly the hair, corn silk through his fingers. I *knew* that hair. It was the same exact color as Shelby's ponytail swinging behind her as she ran past my house. My head throbbed from too much prosecco and too many tears, but I knew. She'd been waiting for me to leave.

Four

THE ANNOUNCEMENT ABOUT THE syndication had made me popular overnight. Someone had tied a bunch of big Mylar balloons to my cubicle. In the hallway, Chad, the sports editor, gave me a high five that practically knocked me off my high heels.

Kyra stopped by around ten. “Nice touch,” she said, tugging on one of the balloon strings.

“This wasn’t you?” I asked.

“Hell no. I’m not a balloon person. Harriet’s obsession with sea turtles means I know all about how those sweet little creatures think that balloons are jellyfish and ingest them and die. No helium death snacks for me.”

“Jeez, that’s morbid,” I said. I cast a glance toward the balloon that looked like a heart-eye emoji and briefly entertained the notion of shoving it into my mouth.

“So balloons, a new look . . . you’re really into this next-level Violet right now.”

“New look?” I asked, turning my attention to my email. I had the feeling she was examining me.

“Your makeup,” she said. “It’s a bit more than you usually wear. I like it though. A plum lip works for you.”

I shrugged.

"Let's talk about your syndication plan in my office."

"Sure." I did not want to go to Kyra's office. We'd been college roommates, which gave us a dangerous history. She was perceptive and she knew me better than anyone. For instance, she was well acquainted with the fact that the worse I felt, the more makeup I wore. And this morning I'd painted my face like someone from *Moulin Rouge*. It wouldn't be long before she figured out about me and Sam, or I blurted it out, and I didn't want that to happen.

She closed her office door behind us. "Okay, tell me what's wrong."

Exactly.

I perched on the edge of the chair in front of her desk and shook my head. "Nothing."

Kyra wasn't finished. "Does that eye shadow have glitter in it?"

I shrugged. I was not about to admit that I'd pulled out my old plastic Caboodle that was hidden way in the back of the cabinet under my sink for this morning's look. I said, "Ashleigh wrote a piece last spring about how subtle shimmer was okay for daytime."

"For a nineteen-year-old maybe. But not Violet Covington. And then there's you sending me your column, then telling me you want to rework it, having me switch it for some itchy and entitled nonsense, and never sending me the revised column. That's not like you. You're off your game here, and you need to be *on* your game."

I glanced at my hands in my lap. I was still wearing my rings. The eternity band and two-carat princess cut spun loose on my finger, shimmering reminders of my failure, like the eye shadow. I didn't say anything. A smile is just contracting some muscles. Fewer than a frown. I was a master at moving muscles thanks to the daily boot camp. I'd trained for this. I squeezed a smile and looked up. "I know. Everything is fine. I'll have it for you tomorrow at the latest. I was a few ahead anyway. As for the syndication plan, I was thinking that maybe I could do some following up with former advice column features, kind of a *where-are-they-now* sort of thing."

Kyra furrowed her brow. "That's a possibility. Let me think about it."

My phone buzzed. I glanced at the screen quickly. It was Sam. I declined the call.

"Do you need to get that?" Kyra asked.

I shook my head. "It wasn't important. Where were we?"

"Wasn't that Sam?"

"I can call him later," I said, trying to sound nonchalant.

"Huh."

"What?"

"It's just that in all the years we've been friends and worked together, I have never seen you decline a call from Sam." She tapped her pen on her desk. "Wait, that's it. The CoverGirl makeup look, that rehearsed smile, the way you're avoiding eye contact. Something's up with you and Sam?"

I looked away. "It's fine. We're fine." I'd rehearsed the line in my head earlier, knowing that eventually someone would ask, but it came out sounding like a question.

"That's some weak tea there," Kyra said.

"Not weak tea, just a little glitch." Tears pricked at my eyes. The trouble with my more-makeup strategy was that as soon as my eyes got a little moist, the eyeliner I'd smeared on irritated them, which made them sting.

"Oh," Kyra said. A this-is-bad *oh*.

I looked up at her through blurred eyes. My shoulders sagged. What had been the point of this act if she'd seen right through me?

"You wore the sushi, didn't you?" she said. "Let me guess. He was not excited about your big career news when he's been grinding for that promotion with no luck for months. He felt emasculated. Typical shit."

"I didn't tell him."

"Come again?"

I shrugged, trying to smile but failing. "I went home early, like I said, made the sushi—I did not wear it, I might add—but the syndication didn't come up."

Kyra's face held a million questions, but she didn't say anything. I twisted my hands in my lap.

"He was already home when I got there. I, uh, interrupted him."

Kyra recoiled. "Interrupted what?" she said very slowly, carefully.

"Interrupted . . . them." The words stuck in my throat like the overcooked rice in the sushi. I coughed once. "Sam and our neighbor Shelby."

"Lycra Shelby?"

"I probably shouldn't have been calling her that. She wasn't wearing any Lycra."

"What? What did he say?"

"Nothing. I told him to go and he did." I looked up at Kyra. "Please don't tell anyone."

She came over to me and pressed her forehead against mine. A move I'd seen her do with her daughter, Harriet. I took a breath that hurt my chest. "I'll never say a word. You want me to kill him? Like I said, I got spy skills."

My phone buzzed again.

"You should get that," Kyra said. "Use my office, I'll go for a walk." She gave my shoulder a gentle squeeze.

I pressed my phone to my ear. "Hello."

"Violet. I've been calling and texting you nonstop this morning. I was so freaked out when you didn't answer, I was about to call your mom."

"Good thing you didn't," I said, voice flat. I was not going to cry on the phone. My hair was *Dallas* big. I took a deep breath. "What do you want, Sam?"

"I just wanted to talk, you know, and make sure you were okay."

I almost laughed. "You didn't seem to care that much about me being okay yesterday."

He was quiet for a long time. I thought about hanging up. I looked around Kyra's office, at the awards on the shelf, the pictures on her desk of her and Harriet when she was a baby, another one of her with her wife, Rox; they had their arms slung around each other, so happy. I made a note to take down the picture of me and Sam from our trip to Saint Croix two years ago that I'd put up in my cubicle.

"I'm really sorry about that," Sam said finally. "We should talk . . . please."

I didn't want to talk. I wanted yesterday to cease to exist. But I acquiesced; I never could say no to Sam. Maybe it was a onetime mistake. That could be overlooked, couldn't it? My mother had overlooked so many. She'd turned her lemons to lemonade, wasn't that what one did? Counseling, maybe. We could fix this. We could hang on to happiness. It would just take some hard work.

I thought back to a letter I'd answered a few months earlier from a woman who said she was struggling to forgive her husband after an affair. He was so sorry, she wrote, but every time she looked at him, instead of wanting to move on, she wanted to break his face for breaking her heart and her trust. *Understandable,* I told her. *You've been betrayed. Of course you're angry and hurt. That means you care. If you truly believe he wishes he could take it back, and you feel the same,* I'd written, *then find a way to start again, at the beginning, and build your crumbled trust from scratch. Make a new foundation. Then, and only then, can you really love each other again. Each of us is capable of causing joy or sadness, and likewise, we all do things that we later regret once in a while. The road back may be long and arduous, but that's okay. Take it slow. Be kind to yourself. Try not to add to your regrets.*

I'd made it sound so simple.

"Meet me at Mitch's Tavern, around seven p.m.?" he asked.

My aching heart swelled a bit at that. He remembered. He was sorry, he'd said so. And he wanted to meet at the place where we'd first met all those years ago, before boot camp and phones at the breakfast table, before quiet had settled in. Before whatever yesterday was. I didn't even know. But I didn't want to add to my regrets, of that I was certain.

"Okay," I said. We'd been together for fifteen years, married for twelve. How could I say no?

Five

I MET SAM AT MITCH'S Tavern on Hillsborough Street after work. It seemed like a lifetime had passed since we'd met when we were both students—me at State and him at Carolina. We should have been rivals, like NC State and UNC Chapel Hill were. The bell tower was practically across the street and Mitch's was an institution. We'd nestled in one of the wooden booths where the movie *Bull Durham* had been shot years before and talked for hours while we ate Reuben sandwiches and drank beer.

The menu, like the bar, looked the same. In fact, it probably hadn't changed at all over the years. I wasn't hungry. I got there first and sat near the back. The booth was less comfortable than I remembered. Its wooden edge pressed sharply into the tender flesh behind my knees. When Sam appeared, he looked as uncomfortable as my pinched skin. I'd expected him to look worse, though, haggard with guilt, maybe, but he was still fresh faced, with those bright blue eyes and blond hair that was just long enough to show a hint of a wave; it irritated me. One of my sparkly eyelids twitched. He slid into the booth across from me. I still remembered what he'd said to me back then—I'd been expecting magic when he walked up, and I'd been struck by disappointment when he led off with, "I've been standing over there forever hoping for a table so I could sit down and order some food."

"You just came over here for the booth?" I'd said, willing the flames of mortification out of my cheeks.

He'd fixed his ice-blue eyes on mine. "No. I fully came over here for you." My defenses had collapsed like an undercooked soufflé.

I wasn't a soufflé now, soft and vulnerable. I was a crusty hull, cavernous and overcooked. Inedible. The table seemed to stretch out endlessly between us.

"You want something to drink?" he asked.

I didn't drink much anymore. Sam didn't like it when I got sloppy—his words. He raised an eyebrow whenever I headed to my Bunco group with bottles of wine. "Not for me," I always assured him. "Think of it as community outreach."

I figured the circumstances warranted a drink. Actually, I wasn't certain I could get through this conversation without one. I clasped my hands together to keep them from trembling. "Sure," I said.

"Two Blue Moons, please," he told the waitress.

"You remember my favorite beer?" I asked.

Sam's eyes locked on mine with a look that could only be described as earnest. "Of course I do, Violet. I remember everything about you." He reached out and squeezed my hand.

My chest unclenched a little and I drew in a shaky breath. Maybe I'd been wrong. Maybe this would be okay. Mistakes had been made. Big, bad, heartbreaking mistakes, but no one had died. I hadn't actually spontaneously combusted and gotten sucked up by the robot vacuum. These kinds of things happened. Often, judging by the frequency of letters from readers with some variation of *my husband poked someone else*, and also the rate of my own father's indiscretions over the years.

The waitress brought our drinks with orange slices on the pint glasses. I reached for mine and some beer sloshed on my hand. Sam watched her leave.

I dabbed my hand with a napkin.

"About yesterday," he began. He ran a hand through his hair. "I—" He paused and took a gulp of beer.

I took a bigger gulp. *Please, let it all be a misunderstanding*, I thought. I closed my eyes, but there was Shelby in her running shorts and sports bra. I picked up my glass and drained it. "I'll have another," I said to the waitress as she walked by.

"Sure thing."

Sam raised his eyebrows, but he didn't speak.

The waitress set a fresh beer on the table. I pulled it toward me. "You what?" I said finally, when I couldn't take the silence anymore.

"I want to clear things up."

"Me too. I really want you to clear things up." I took another swig of beer. My cheeks were starting to warm. What I wanted was for him to clear up the misunderstanding that was happening in my head ever since I'd seen them together. From that moment, I'd convinced myself that it wasn't just a onetime thing, a mistake, but that it was something routine, like Sam's cup of coffee and smartphone scrolling during breakfast, my boot camp class, or me reading him my column . . . that, more than likely, Shelby was stopping by our house to screw my husband midway through her morning run, which she took every day.

"Shelby's a friend," he said.

I let the air bleed slowly out of my lungs. *And?* Tyler was a friend. I didn't hide in his bed naked and burrow into his bare chest when his boyfriend wasn't home.

"And . . . we've been seeing each other for a few months. Look, Vi, I didn't mean for you to find out like this. Shit, I mean, obviously.

You're never home that early. You leave for boot camp and don't come home until six most nights."

Bile rose up my throat, and something else came too, searing my insides as it surged within me. Rage. That's what it was. I squeezed my hand around the pint glass so hard that I was surprised it didn't shatter, and then brought it to my lips. I chugged the remaining beer down.

"This isn't a fling then." It was all so . . . premeditated.

"It's real, Violet. What Shelby and I have, it's special. I've been thinking about it for a while. I want to see where it goes."

I nodded.

Sam was a lot of things. Some wonderful. He loved dogs. He held the door for everyone. Without fail, he'd pull over on the road if someone needed help with a tire. Some not-so-wonderful. He was a mama's boy, and his mom was a real piece of work. He wasn't athletic, but he criticized athletes nonstop when he was watching basketball. He rarely voted. But he'd never been cruel. Until this exact moment, right here, in our booth. He wasn't just destroying our future. He was obliterating our past too. Every single happy memory together—was any of it real?

"I'm fully in love with her, Violet."

I closed my eyes. That did it. *Fully.* Not just he thought he was in love. Or he was falling in love with her. He was *fully* in love. He'd used our word.

I knew something that wasn't full. My goddamn glass. I ordered another beer.

"You sure you want that?" Sam said. "You're not a drinker."

"You're right. I wasn't much of a drinker, but you know, I guess we're both trying out new things. Or not so new. I suppose I don't know how long this has been going on, since, you know, it's not really the sort of thing the cheating husband tells the wife. What *is* a few months, anyway?"

Sam's eyes locked on me while I took the fresh beer from the waitress. When I set it down, a few droplets flew up. One splattered on his cheek; he wiped it off with the back of his hand.

"You always get like this when you have a few," he said.

"Like what?"

"Messy, angry. Take your pick."

"You have such a great memory, Sam. You remember the bar where we met, my favorite beer, the fact that I get a little messy after I have a few drinks. Too bad you seem to have forgotten that you're married."

I had to get the heck out of Mitch's Tavern. Right then. I lost my balance a little as I scrambled from the booth.

"What do you want me to say?" he said. "Something was missing. I didn't do this *to* you."

I nodded. There didn't seem to be anything I could say to that. "Well, that's comforting. I hope it works out for the best."

"That's it?"

I shrugged. "What do you want me to say? You want my blessing? Is that why you brought me here—or were you just looking for closure? You know what, don't answer that. It doesn't matter. Sure, Sam, see where it goes." *Never let 'em see you sweat, baby doll*, my mother had taught me. "Don't bother coming back."

The waitress who'd been hovering nearby stepped toward me. "Hey," I said, "could you get me an Uber? My phone's dead."

"You're not taking an Uber," Sam called. "You're always convinced the driver's going to take you somewhere and kill you."

The waitress looked straight at me, as if Sam didn't exist. "Sure thing, honey," she said. She was younger than me, and that *honey*, so sweet, so loaded with empathy, almost cracked the surface tension that was holding my tears at bay. "I'll have them come right away. You can sit at the bar and use my charger while you wait if you want. Great hair, by the way. You look like a total bombshell." She then turned to Sam, eyes narrowed. "Asshole," she muttered under her breath before she walked away.

· Six ·

Maybe I could blame the Blue Moons that the very nice Uber driver stopped to let me buy and drink in the back of his electric car on the way home. Or the fact that there was a full moon out. Perhaps the answer was simple. My husband had decided to tell me that he wanted to see where things went with Shelby and chose to share this revelation with me at the same bar where we'd met, and now, our fifteen-year relationship was basically shit toast. Not quite sure which, but definitely one of those things sent me over the edge.

There were so many options that night.

"Be safe," the driver said.

I pointed at him.

"You! Are the Uber driver of the year! You're getting a one hundred percent tip." I staggered to the front door. I dropped my keys on the doormat and whacked my head on the metal C hanging in the middle of the wreath; the cotton buds tangled in my hair. I freed myself from the wreath and hurled it into the yard. Stupid monogram. It took a bit of fumbling with the keys to get inside, but I made it into the kitchen, where I sat on the floor, my back against the refrigerator door, and polished off another beer. Then I went to the kitchen table and pulled out my laptop. I was remembering that letter again, the one from the woman who wanted to break her cheating husband's face, and found myself wishing I could print a retraction and tell her that actually she should just go ahead and break his stupid, weak man face. But you can't change that which has already been printed. Bingo. I had another response that *hadn't* been printed. Another woman with a stupid-ass husband who needed advice.

Dear Fitness Faker, I read, It's completely natural to have fleeting feelings of insecurity, especially when someone whose opinion you value uses a loaded word. Ugh.

I glared at the screen. Wiggled my fingers to make sure they were working. And then I rewrote the letter.

Dear Fitness Faker,

I've got two things I need you to know.

First of all, you are not alone.

Second, your husband sucks.

It's not often that I feel so uniquely qualified to respond to a letter. You see, I've probably seen you in boot camp class. Hi there. Fellow fitness faker here. My husband didn't actually say anything. I guess each jerk has their own brand of BS. What he did seemed insignificant at the time. A longer-than-normal glance at one of our neighbors at the pool. She's a runner, long legs, perfect little four-pack, and she came up out of the water like a Bond girl. I didn't blame him. Who wasn't looking at her? But something about the way he stared at her and not me in my somewhat larger, more modestly cut two-piece left me feeling a little threatened. So I did what I thought seemed like a great solution at the time. I said nothing. I signed up for boot camp. And I dragged myself out of bed every day before dawn and suffered through a workout that I can only describe as torture wrapped in sweat-soaked spandex six days a week. It was self-improvement, I told myself. Taking care of me. I was sculpting the kind of butt that my husband would stare at next pool season and getting healthy. I was boosting my self-confidence. It was a total win-win.

I hated every minute of it.

But that's not the best part.

While I put on spandex and dragged myself to my predawn sweat session, my husband was having his very own sweat session with the bikini babe . . . in our bed. I guess the only plus side to me getting in shape was that when I caught them together, I had the strength to tear him limb from limb. (In theory. In actuality, I ran into the bathroom and hid.)

You say your husband is a good man and he loves you. That's great. He still sucks. My husband loves me too. I mean, maybe . . . he said he did. Now I'm not so sure. Here are other things my husband loves: his custom-tailored suits, Michael Jordan, two-hundred-year-old scotch (on occasion). The scotch isn't bad. I think I may have to help myself to a glass right now. Oh, and our neighbor. He wants to see where this thing between them goes.

So. If you enjoy working out, if it feels good? Then by all means, go ahead and do it. But don't do it because your husband's stupid words made you feel less than. And definitely don't do it for him, baby doll. He doesn't deserve that effort, and he sure as heck doesn't deserve you.

Sincerely,
Sweetie

I pasted the column into an email to Kyra with the subject line *Truth Bomb*. My fingers tingled with excitement. *Man, that felt good*, I thought. Who said exercise and sex were the only ways to get endorphins? I was feeling fabulous and I wanted to keep it going because, truth be told, even drunk off my ass, I could sense the presence of something less good, something painful and empty and dark, lurking in the background, under the beer and the anger and the payback. I reread the message and hit send.

Sam did love his super-old scotch, I thought. I never partook, of course, because drunk Violet wasn't Sam's cup of tea. But then, sober Violet wasn't either, it would seem. On that note, I stepped over to the cabinet where we kept mixers and some liquor for guests and pulled out the bottle. I poured some into a margarita glass and drained the contents. It burned on the way down and heat flashed in my cheeks. He was going to be so mad. *How do you like that, Sam? I drank your precious scotch.* It had always irked me that he was so adamant about my not drinking, when it was fine for him. He called *me* messy. Just this past Labor Day he'd gotten so drunk during our party that he'd run around in the backyard with his pants down while his former frat brothers lit firecrackers and tossed them at his bare ass, so pale that it glowed in the moonlight. Fortunately for him, they were equally loaded, rendering their aim terrible. Now I wished they were all here and my aim was true, because Sam had tucked one of those firecrackers into my chest and set it off and I wanted to return the favor in a different anatomical destination.

An idea was blooming, a bad idea, certainly, but one that was sure to get my adrenaline pumping even more. We still had some firecrackers in the garage; I'd seen them a couple of weeks ago when I'd KonMari'd the whole house so I could properly address a letter from someone who said that nothing sparked joy, including her underwear and her husband of forty years, and it wasn't like she could donate those things to the thrift store. I wanted to tell No Joy that she could do just that and become a nudist, but of course, I came up with something else about finding the joy in the things we need. Bullshit. Bullshit.

I found the box that I'd labeled *Misc* in thick, neat Sharpie and rooted around in it until I located the firecrackers. Normally, I wouldn't put my hand in one of those boxes for fear of black widow spiders, but now even the irony of the spider's name was amusing. I tucked the fireworks into my pocket. I was planning on doing a little joy-sparking myself after this completely miserable day.

I ran up to our bedroom, taking the stairs two at a time like a goddamn athlete—*thank you very much, Bear*—and pulled out all of Sam's suits. I tossed them on the bed, onto the exact spot where the very image of Sam and Shelby seemed seared into the Egyptian cotton, and then pulled down the framed Michael Jordan poster, signed, of course, and the jersey out of the custom shadow box from the wall above Sam's dresser. I wrapped everything up in the desecrated sheets and dragged it all down to the street like I was carrying a giant cotton trash bag. I went back for all of his underwear—didn't seem like he'd be needing that—and that favorite chair that he insisted we get. Leather with brass pins. I used every bit of my morning training to muscle that thing out the front door and down to the asphalt. I made a big pile of all of it in the middle of the cul-de-sac and then went back to get the scotch. I pulled up Beyoncé's *Lemonade* album on my phone and turned it up. I wish I'd been wearing that fantastic yellow dress, bashing the windows out of Sam's Beamer, but I didn't have the right coloring to pull off that shade of yellow, and Sam's car wasn't around. Still, this came pretty damn close. I sang along with Queen Bey while I doused Sam's suits with the alcohol. Then I struck a match, lit a firecracker, and tossed it on top of the pile.

Boom.

Seven

Cathy Willis was the one who called the fire department. Her name wasn't really Cathy, but when she'd moved into the neighborhood and stopped by to say hi for a full hour one afternoon, Sam had christened her Chatty Cathy, and no matter what sort of word association I tried to do to make her real name stick, Cathy was the only one that ever came to mind.

"What on earth? Violet, is that you? Are you okay?"

I waved to her. "Doing great!" I called back.

She did not respond, disappearing instead into the house, ostensibly to make that phone call, and minutes later a single engine arrived, red lights, siren, and all. Here's the thing: a bonfire of your cheating scoundrel of a husband's treasured belongings is not nearly as fun when a bunch of firefighters show up and all of your neighbors come out of their houses to watch the spectacle from their porches. Honestly, it's a bit of a buzzkill. Now there's an advice column for you. I probably should have been more discreet and done this out back on the patio in our firepit.

While a couple of firefighters worked feverishly, attaching a hose to the fire hydrant, another one walked over to me. He was tall, but that was about all I could tell. The firelight glowed around him, casting his face into shadow. He reminded me of one of those candles with the saints on it. He said, "I'm going to wager a guess that you don't have a permit for this . . ."

"Bonfire," I offered.

"Do you have a permit for this bonfire, ma'am?"

Yup. That was the cherry on top of this magnificent shit show of a day. *Ma'am.* I glared at him.

"I'll take that as a no. Well then, I'm afraid we're going to have to put this fire out. It's a hazard to the houses in the area, what with the wind and the dry conditions. Next time, get a permit."

"There won't be a next time," I said.

"Okay then."

"Don't you want to know why?"

"If it helps."

"Because he doesn't have any stuff left that he cares about in our house," I said. I tried to laugh, but I sounded like an injured bird. "There's only me. The smoke sure is beautiful, though, isn't it?"

Thick tendrils swirled up, filled with pale moonlight, stark against the dark sky. "I was trying to spark joy," I said. He didn't say anything, but his gaze followed mine. "Didn't work."

"You want to say goodbye before we douse it?" he asked finally.

"Why not?" I stepped closer to the bonfire. He put an arm up in front of me, reflexively. The heat washed over my cheeks. Beneath the flames, I could make out the shapes of hangers, scraps of fabric, a metal zipper glowing orange with heat.

"You got anything toxic or dangerous in there?" he asked.

I shook my head. "No. It's overpriced clothes, mostly. A truly hideous chair. Prada loafers. An autographed Michael Jordan poster and jersey."

"You burned Jordan! Man, somebody must've really messed up."

"You could say that."

A spark floated up between us, an ember rising into the night sky; I watched it until it blinked out. When I brought my gaze back down, the firefighter was watching me. I stepped away from the bonfire. The man waved his arm at the crew and they moved in with the hose and sprayed. The fire went out almost instantly, sending a cloud of steam into the air. The whole thing was rather . . . anticlimactic. The charred remains of Sam's things were spread across the cul-de-sac by the force of the water.

I returned to the house and slumped on the porch steps, letting the cool wooden spindles press into my cheek. With the fire out, the night seemed colder. I rubbed my arms and watched the firefighters coil the hose and then climb back into the truck. The man I'd spoken to earlier squatted down in front of me.

"I'm Dez, and I need to take down some information from you for the report," he said. "First and last name?"

"Violet Covington." But that was Sam's name. Tears flooded my eyes.

"You know what, I can work out the rest," he said. He picked something up from the grass and held it out to me. The stupid wreath. "You want this?"

The fire had burned off the alcohol in my system. "I don't know." I was suddenly acutely aware of what a stupid thing I'd done. Even though it seemed so insignificant compared to Sam's transgression. I could never inflict the same kind of damage on him; that was how it worked when you were with someone who felt that something was missing. You simply didn't matter enough to hurt them. Tears stung at my eyes. I didn't want to cry, but I was overrun with emotions—sadness, fury, spite, devastation.

"Should I be numb?" I said out loud.

"I don't know," he said. "You gonna be okay?"

"Honestly," I said, rubbing my eyes with my fists, "I'm not sure.

I could really use some advice right now. Which is so freaking ironic. I basically need me, only that won't work, because I'm the one with the problem."

"Huh," he said. He took off his helmet and settled on the step next to me. "Well, I don't know much about giving advice. I've seen some pretty hard things, and people always seem to get through them, you know. It's rough, but Glennon Doyle says we can do hard things. We can make it through."

"Are you quoting *Love Warrior*?"

"*Untamed*, actually, but that's not the point."

"How?"

"That I can't tell you. Seems to me it's different for each person. But you'd probably do well with two glasses of water and an ibuprofen tonight before you hit the hay." He rose. "No more bonfires in the street without a permit, okay?"

"Sure."

"That was less than convincing."

"Pinky swear." I forced a smile.

He reached out and hooked my finger. "I love a good pinky swear. Good night, Violet."

Exhaustion settled over me all at once, like the water the crew had used to extinguish the flames. The firefighter started to walk away.

"Am I going to be in trouble?" I called out to him.

"Nah," he said, heading back toward me. "We haven't had a call all day. You didn't keep us from anything important."

I nodded.

I waited for him to tell me I should probably go inside, because it was late and I'd already caused enough trouble for one night, but he didn't. He leaned in and the thick fabric of his turnout coat brushed against me. In a low voice, he said, "For what it's worth, I think you're going to be just fine, Violet."

The perfectly acceptable, polite thing to do would have been to nod and say thank you. I did not do that thing. Nope. I grabbed his face with both hands and stared at him. Up close, I could see he had kind, dark eyes fringed with black lashes, nothing like Sam's glacial blue irises. These were the eyes of someone who busted in doors to save little old ladies and pets from doom instead of shattering hearts, I was sure of it. I lost my balance then and started to fall into him, but he had me back upright in an instant. He placed his hands over mine, giving them a gentle squeeze, making sure I was steady on my feet before he helped me lower them slowly away from his cheeks.

"Night," he said. Then he strode over to the truck, climbed in, and drove away, with no flashing lights this time.

I stayed on the stairs for a moment, staring at the charred remains of Sam's stuff, trying to decide if I wanted to laugh or cry. Both, probably. I dragged myself up and into the house, but I didn't make it upstairs. Sam had probably had sex with Shelby there, in our bed. I mean, that was generally why people would be naked in one, and that sure as hell had happened. I wasn't about to go sleep there. I lay down on the couch and closed my eyes. I was so tired. But every time I let my mind wander, it went straight to a replay. Of her face pressed into Sam's bare chest. The way he'd looked at me at the bar, the disdain there. *I'm fully in love with her*, he'd said. Then there was me: setting his clothes on fire. The fire truck in front of my house. Me drunk and out of control center stage on full display in front of my neighbors. I wondered what they would think, if I'd be the big topic at the bus stop tomorrow morning. Oh God, or worse, at Bunco—which was coming up in two weeks. But maybe I already had been the topic of discussion when I wasn't around. Surely some neighbor had noticed Shelby coming to our house when I wasn't there. I turned on the TV and let the blue light and the lives of strangers wash over me until I finally fell asleep.

· Eight ·

HOW ARE YOU?" KYRA asked when I dragged myself into her office the next morning. "And don't give me any of your sugarcoated bullshit."

"I don't have sugarcoated bullshit," I said, straightening a book that was tilted on her bookshelf.

"Mmhmm. Sure you don't. Violet, that is exactly why everyone loves your advice so much. 'Cause of all that sweetness."

Was that true?

"Did you talk to Sam?" she asked.

My shoulders sank a little.

"So it was *that* kind of conversation."

"They're seeing each other," I said.

Kyra closed her eyes. "Excuse me?"

"It gets worse. He wants to see where this goes. Direct quote: 'I am fully in love with her, Violet.'"

Kyra shook her head and leaned far back in her chair. "Damn. Sam's got some balls."

"Yeah, someone should cut them off." I clapped a hand over my mouth. "I didn't mean that."

Kyra laughed so hard her body shook. She held up a hand. "Don't you dare take that back. I like Rage Violet. She's real."

"Well, you would have really enjoyed last night then. I got *raging* drunk and used a firecracker and a vintage bottle of scotch to burn all of Sam's clothes and his Michael Jordan memorabilia in the street."

Kyra pressed her lips together. It was a valiant effort, but she has the kind of laugh that can't be contained—a beautiful, full, infectious laugh. I'd been serious, but even the corners of my mouth couldn't resist rising a little when she lost it.

"The Prada loafers held up surprisingly well."

"Stop. I can't take it." She took a moment to compose herself and swiped at a tear. "Alright, all that great material aside, how *are* you? When Jared left, I was stages of grief over here. I worked too hard, didn't eat, and ended up needing antidepressants and a twice-a-week therapist regimen."

"I'm not there yet, I don't think. What's the first stage?"

"Shock. Then denial. After that there's anger."

"Yup, that's me. Anger. Definitely anger. I'm moving right through the steps. At this rate, I'll be fine in a couple of weeks." Or notorious.

Back at my desk, I opened my Dear Sweetie email to scan the messages for potential candidates for my column. There were a lot of manner questions this week.

My fiancé and I want to have a small wedding with our immediate family and closest friends at our home and pay for it ourselves. My mom and dad are insisting that we have to invite extended family, since that's how our cousins' weddings were. How do we set boundaries without hurting anyone's feelings? *Why bother getting married at all? It's bound to end in disaster.* Next.

Dear Sweetie, I went on a date with a fantastic girl and I had a great time, but now she isn't returning my calls. I'm thinking that I should stop by her work to ask her why she's ghosting me. *She thinks you're a creep, and, apparently, she is right.*

Hi, Sweetie, A few months ago, I slipped up and slept with a coworker on a business trip. It never happened again, though we do still flirt a lot at work. The guilt is killing me. Should I tell my husband? I don't want to lose him. *Maybe you should have thought of that before you "slipped" out of your clothes and betrayed your marriage.*

"Hey, Violet!"

I whirled around to face Ashleigh and Tyler, who were hovering at the entrance of my cubicle. Tyler and I went to State together, but Ashleigh got her journalism degree from UNC, and she was married to Sam's coworker Mark. They weren't friends exactly, more like friendly competitors, though I wasn't sure Ashleigh knew that. Or Mark, for that matter. Sam kept a lot of things close to his chest.

"I have a sitter tonight, so we're grabbing drinks after work," Ashleigh said.

"I thought we'd hit a new place on Glenwood South I have to try out. That way I can expense some of it," Tyler said. "Wanna come?"

I hadn't been out with them in a while. Most days I was too exhausted on account of boot camp to go out for after-work drinks, and happy hours are illegal here in Raleigh anyway, so it wasn't like I was missing out on any two-for-one margarita deals.

Ashleigh leaned toward me. "Mark says that Sam is staying at a hotel," she whispered. "Everything okay with you two?"

"Everything's great," I said, a little too loudly. "We're having our floors refinished." I was a little relieved that Sam was staying at a hotel. I'd been imagining running into him leaving the neighborhood, him and Shelby in matching jogging shorts.

"Already? Didn't you put hardwoods in not that long ago? Gosh, they don't make anything of quality anymore. What a pain. You know you could have stayed with us—we've got plenty of room."

Mark had made partner last year, much to Sam's chagrin, and they'd had a McMansion built . . . inside the beltline. Sam had made fun of it and gone on about gentrification, but the truth was that Five Points wasn't exactly within our budget, and if it had been, Sam would have been the first to suggest moving there.

"Thanks for the offer," I told her, "but we're fine at the hotel."

"Oh, I get it," she said, turning to Tyler. She dropped the volume. "They want to be alone."

"Delicious. It's like a second honeymoon staycation. I think I might write a feature about that. Get away without getting away."

"I wish I could do that," Ashleigh said, looking wistful. "Mark and I haven't been alone for more than a few hours since we had Tristan."

"Isn't he almost four?" Tyler asked.

"Don't remind me. Or do, actually, I need to get cracking on the party. Y'all are invited, of course."

There was an awkward silence while Tyler eyed Ashleigh as if she'd asked him to hold a dirty diaper instead of extending an invitation to attend what would likely be an elegant event . . . well, as elegant as a preschool soiree could be.

I wanted to get away from the conversation, but unfortunately, they'd blocked the cubicle entrance.

Ashleigh pivoted and returned her attention to me. "You're a yes for drinks then . . . or do you have *other* things to do?" She winked.

"Sorry," I said, fully aware of the implications. I smiled as sweetly as I could. "I guess I do have things to do."

Ashleigh and Tyler exchanged a look that was somewhere between *You go, girl* and *Ugh, you basic bitch bragging about your extravagant sexcapade staycation*. I did not correct them. Of course, by *other things*, I'd meant phase two of my postmarital explosion, which I'd planned over breakfast. Right now, it was trouble-shaped, with the main themes being *wreak some more havoc on Sam's life* and *continue my self-destructive behavior.* Definitely some light binge drinking.

I stopped by the ABC store on my way home—it wasn't really on the way, so I suppose in an effort to be authentic, I should say that I drove seventeen full minutes out of the way and bought a bottle of gin. At the house, I mixed myself a gin and tonic, garnished with a thin wedge of grapefruit—now there was a good use for that, since I definitely wasn't subjecting myself to a sour breakfast any longer—before I pulled down the attic stairs. I never enjoyed going up there since a couple years ago when we'd had a mouse infestation and Natalie, our science and tech reporter, had told me that we could get hantavirus from the droppings, but desperate times called for liquid courage and a trip into the attic. And considering my situation, would hantavirus be so bad?

Sam had an organizational technique for his possessions that rivaled the Dewey decimal system. The plastic totes I was looking for were clearly labeled: *Vintage Star Wars I, II, III.* Did I mention that Sam had the entire collection of original Star Wars figurines? We're talking the giant *Millennium Falcon*, the Darth Vader–head carrying case for the figurine set, and the AT-AT walker, with original boxes. I lugged them down the ladder one at a time, and then laid out the collection on our bed for the photo shoot.

Thirty minutes later I'd finished uploading pictures of the entire collection onto eBay. Reserve, who needed one of those? I sat, staring at the computer screen, cackling to myself. Bids were already starting to roll in. I opened a new screen and ordered some Thai food. Spicy eggplant and drunken noodles and something called Sexy Softshell Crabs that I mostly ordered because they were expensive; the fact that Sam would have hated the name was just a bonus. While I waited for the food delivery, I watched the bids and sipped my G&T and tried to picture Sam's reaction. He'd had an attic fan and extra insulation installed to make sure his collection stayed pristine. But I never saw the point of keeping something you purport to love so much in a box. What did a grown man need with toys anyway, I wondered, especially one with no kids?

I thought of Sam's words back at Mitch's Tavern. Something was missing, he'd said. I couldn't argue with him. Something *was* missing. Suddenly, the whole auction of Sam's prized toy collection plan seemed a lot less fun. I went to the seller page on eBay, canceled all of the bids, and ended the auction. The price for my vindictiveness: a whopping $438, the ten percent fee for the highest bid I'd canceled.

I'd thought all this would make feel better. But instead, I felt so much worse. I tossed the gin and the leftovers into the trash. It turned out spirits and sexy foods made me sad and gave me indigestion.

Nine

THEN

WE MOVED INTO THE house on Valentine's Day. After draining our savings for the down payment, we'd only had enough money left to hire two movers from Two Men and a Truck. Lucky for us, they'd had dates and brought a third guy for free so that they could finish early. When they took off, I opened the box labeled *Linens*, extracted a towel, and headed to the bathroom to wash off the moving day sweat and grime.

I came downstairs in one of Sam's Campbell Law T-shirts; my wet hair fell in tendrils around my shoulders and left damp marks on the shirt. There was Sam in the living room, sitting on an afghan on the floor, with a pizza box from Randy's. I'd wanted Anna's, but Sam didn't like theirs. We didn't have much furniture yet. My mother had offered to buy us a living room set, but that had turned into a process, and Sam's mother hadn't made good on her offer to give us his Gran's dining set.

"It's a little rustic," Sam said.

I shook my head. "It's perfect, babe."

He took my hand as I lowered myself to the floor. He'd gotten out two plates of our wedding china, wineglasses for the merlot, and there was even a single red rose in a glass Cheerwine bottle.

"You may not feel that way after you've been sitting here for a while. My ass is killing me. You were in the shower for a long time." He grinned at me. "Is that my T-shirt you've got on there?"

I reached for a slice. "Happy Valentine's Day, husband," I said.

Sam cupped his hand on my cheek. "Happy Valentine's Day, wife," he said. He kissed me. "One day, when I'm a partner, holidays will be different. I'll whisk you away to Bali or something."

"I like it here," I said. "I don't need to get on a plane, or even sit on a couch to be happy. I'm happy like this. If we want the beach, we can just drive down to Kure Beach or Ocean Isle."

Sam took a bite of his pizza. "That's good," he said, sounding surprised, and I wasn't sure if he was talking about the pizza or my declaration.

I turned to look at the towers of boxes around us. "It kind of reminds me of the Raleigh skyline," I said. "If you look at it just right."

Sam found the Sharpie he'd used to label the boxes and started sketching something on the sides of the boxes. I watched with amusement while I devoured another slice of pepperoni and extra cheese. When he'd finished, he rocked back on his heels. "A Raleigh skyline, for my sweetie on Valentine's."

Sam wasn't much of an artist, but he'd done a pretty good job rendering the cityscape—I suppose it didn't hurt that Raleigh was a small city with only a few big buildings, so its skyline wasn't anything like New York or Chicago. It was one of the things I liked about it. It had the big-city things—amazing museums and food, ballets and musicals and festivals—but it still felt like a small town. Sam and I complained about the inadequacy of public transit, but maybe one day we'd have a light-rail. *If I ever run for office,* Sam'd say, *that's the first thing on the agenda*.

"Two Hannover Square?" I asked, pointing to the drawing on one of the boxes. Sam nodded, looking impressed at my ability to recognize the second-tallest building in downtown from his quick sketch. "What's in that one?"

"Hmm . . . well, it says *Important*, so it's either my Jordan stuff or my Star Wars collection."

I took a sip of wine. "Star Wars collection?"

Sam recoiled a bit. "Tell me you're not about to confess some deep-seated disdain for Star Wars."

"No. I like Star Wars. Although, I will admit that before I knew Luke and Leia were related, I was totally hoping they'd get together. Han was kind of a dick. No, I'm just curious. What is a Star Wars collection?"

A new energy overtook Sam and he ripped into the box. He lifted a giant Bubble-Wrapped disc. "Do you know what this is?"

"Not really."

"It's a mint condition *Millennium Falcon*."

"Was it yours when you were a kid?" I asked. "I don't think I have any toys left from when I was younger that are in mint condition."

Sam nodded. "I even kept most of the boxes. I guess I was planning ahead. They're worth a lot of money."

"You plan to sell them?"

"Not now. I was thinking that someday our kids might want to play with them. Carefully, of course. Then they could sell them to help pay for college or whatever."

A piece of me wanted to ask just how much these toys were worth, but I was still stuck on that phrase Sam'd uttered: our kids. He opened the Bubble Wrap like an enraptured child unwrapping a

Christmas present. "Look at the detail," he said. "They don't make toys like this anymore."

I was still staring at him.

"What?" he asked.

"Nothing." I bit my lip. "It's just you said *our kids*."

He blanched a little. "Is that a bad thing?" His hand went to the back of his neck, the way it always did when he was stressed.

"Are you kidding me, Sam Covington? I'm happy. I didn't want to tell you when we saw this house that I thought it was perfect for a family. I could see our little ones playing in the front yard, or riding scooters with the neighborhood kids in the cul-de-sac. I thought you might think I was getting ahead of myself. We haven't been married that long."

Sam scooted toward me on the blanket. "Don't ever do that, Violet. Don't hold things back from me. I want to hear every thought in that head of yours. 'Cause I want the same thing as you. I know we planned to hold off until we were set financially, but we could figure it out."

He lowered his forehead to mine.

"I can do my column from home," I said. "We wouldn't have to pay for day care."

"My mom would help too, I reckon; she's dying for a grandchild to spoil."

"So," I said, tentatively, "should we try?"

Sam pulled in a breath and ran his fingers over the hem of the T-shirt I was wearing. "Yeah," he said, sliding his hands beneath the fabric. "I think we should definitely try—if you really want to." He kissed my neck.

"I really want to," I said. He smiled, and I ran my fingertip over the crease in his cheek. "I love you, Sam."

"I love you too, Vi. I love you so much."

"So, we're really going to have a baby?" I asked, feeling overwhelmed with another, different wave of desire.

He nodded. "Yeah, sweetie, we're going to try . . ." He pushed the T-shirt up and over my head and leaned me back slowly to the blanket, pausing only to place the *Millennium Falcon* safely back in the box. "And try, and try."

Ten

MOM CALLED ME BRIGHT and early on Friday morning. The scream of her ringtone startled me awake. I rolled off the couch, smacking my cheek against the edge of the coffee table on the way down. Pain reverberated up my cheekbone into my skull

I'd fallen asleep with my laptop next to me on the coffee table, still open to the eBay site. The sleeping screen lit up when I slammed into the table.

"Hello," I practically groaned into the phone. I used my free hand to probe the sore spot on my cheek.

"Hello? That's all you have to say to your mother? Were you still sleeping?"

"Mom, I can't talk right now. I actually did oversleep, and I'm going to be late for work."

"Are you feeling alright, Violet? It's not like you to oversleep. Not even when you were a teenager."

"I'm fine. As long as I'm not too late getting into the office."

"Listen, tell Kyra that you needed to talk with your mother. Lord knows that treasure would drop anything if Katherine needed her. She always was my favorite out of your friends. I'd wager she'll understand. Besides, you don't really have one of those regular office jobs. Why do you even waste the gas driving in there when you could easily work from your house?"

"Did you need something, Mom?" I asked. I pushed myself up to a seated position.

"I called Sam this morning to ask him about my new business contracts and to see if he wanted to have leg of lamb or fried chicken on Sunday, and he told me that he's not coming to family dinner and that he couldn't speak for you as to whether you would be coming. Why can't your husband speak for whether or not you'd be available for dinner on Sunday, and why isn't he coming? Are you two fighting? Is that why you overslept?"

"We're not fighting, Mom." Fighting was what happened when people who were both in a marriage had conflict. Sam had just retracted, leaving damage as he pulled away.

"I don't understand. You two always come to dinner . . . except for—"

"Look, Mom, everything is totally fine. Don't start spinning conspiracy theories. I'll come to dinner. Sam's got something he's . . . working on, so he won't be able to make it this time."

Working on. It wasn't completely a lie.

My mother appeared to accept this answer after a stretch of silence.

"Well how about you, leg of lamb or fried chicken?"

"Whatever you want to make is fine."

"Fried chicken then. And you bring some of that famous banana pudding, will you? It's my favorite."

"Sure thing, Mom. But I really gotta go. See you Sunday."

The last thing I needed was for my mother to know about what had happened with Sam. She'd been so determined that I not repeat her history with Dad. This would destroy her, not that she would show it, but that was almost worse. Seeming fine. It can be the worst burden of all.

There was some dry cleaning hanging in the downstairs closet: one of Sam's suits that I had missed burning and a sheath dress of mine. The loud Lilly Pulitzer wasn't my favorite; it'd been a gift from Sam's mother and was lime green and hot pink, a full size too small for me when she'd bought it, and covered with batik crustaceans. The last time I'd worn it—to an engagement brunch for one of Sam's cousins at the beginning of the summer—Ashleigh's husband, Mark, had made some joke about how Sam had finally given me crabs. It hadn't been particularly funny then, but it was even less humorous now. Had he been trying to tell me? Mark joked around so much that it was hard to tell what the hell he was getting at most of the time.

I thought about calling in sick, but that felt too pathetic, even for this situation, which was, in my calculation, pretty flipping pathetic. Instead, I stripped out of my slept-in clothes and pulled the dress over my head. The good news was, all of the boot camp classes meant the dress was now a perfect fit. The bad news: I couldn't zip it all the way up by myself. A small thing. Something that I probably could have solved with a coat hanger or some contortionist routine. But standing there with my ugly dress zipped a little over halfway, I became acutely aware of Sam's absence. He'd always zipped me up, even when I didn't ask or didn't need his help. I'd grown accustomed to holding my hair up in my fist like a ponytail while he worked the zipper. Who was going to zip me up now that I'd lost him? Maybe I'd list all my dresses with zippers on eBay next, since they were now impractical reminders of my failing as a wife. Sam was probably zipping Shelby up right now, his fingers sliding along the nubs of her vertebrae. My face crumpled. I was tired and sore and wearing a stupid dress I couldn't get zipped. I'd been fiery and furious last night, but now I felt hollow, save for the tide of sadness rising within me, filling my bones like marrow. I was going to cry.

The doorbell rang. "You've got to be kidding me," I said. I shuffled to the door, rubbing my tender cheek, willing the tears not to spill.

After what happened, it took me a moment to work up the courage to turn the doorknob. I took a deep breath and flung the door open, expecting Sam.

"Hey." Not Sam. It was the firefighter I'd talked to the other night.

"The pinky swearer," I said. I couldn't remember his name.

"The arsonist."

"Violet," I said. Although, a sliver of me kind of liked the arsonist label. It had a certain rebellious ring to it.

"Dez." He was dressed in street clothes now—jeans and a thin flannel shirt with the sleeves rolled up to reveal muscled forearms and a tattoo snaking along the inside of his right arm to his wrist. I looked away. He was wearing what looked like indoor soccer shoes. His hair was black, cropped so close to his head that I could almost see his scalp. From a purely aesthetic standpoint, he had a nice face with smooth tan skin and chiseled features. On a different day, in a different life maybe, I would have found him attractive.

"Yeah, so, Dez, I'm not really up for more paperwork right now," I said. My head was throbbing and my cheek still smarted. I touched the sore spot.

"Ouch," he said. "That's quite a battle scar you've got there. How'd that happen?"

"I can tell what you're thinking by the look on your face. Don't worry. I gave this to myself. I was sleeping on the couch and I got startled awake and fell off. I smacked my face on the coffee table on the way down."

"Was it me that startled you? Sorry about that. I don't usually show up at houses that we've had calls at. I know it's been a couple of days, but you've been on my mind. I guess I wanted to make sure you were okay. It seemed like you were having a rough night. Can I come in? I've got croissants and coffee, and here's your newspaper."

Croissants and coffee was basically my *You had me at hello* moment, but the thought of having a stranger, especially a man I didn't know, inside the house without Sam there was so bizarre. It felt wrong. Still, I couldn't be rude. The man had brought snacks and kept me from burning down the neighborhood; it was only right to be hospitable. I opened the door wider and he stepped inside. He headed straight for the kitchen and dropped the newspaper on the counter.

"You know your way around," I said.

"Aren't these houses down here all the same now?" he said, extracting a pastry from the paper bag like he was delivering an infant.

"And you've probably been in a lot of them for work," I filled in.

He nodded, took a sip of his coffee. "Oh, that's good. Ah, yeah, I've been in my fair share of buildings. But I also live in the same model, two streets over."

He handed one of the coffees to me. "I didn't know how you liked it, so it's black, but there's creamer and sugars in the bag."

I dumped out the bag and grabbed up all the sugars. I emptied every single one of them and then all of the creamers into the coffee. I'd been choking down black coffee for months. This tasted like heaven in my mouth.

"You live in this neighborhood?" I said, and took a bite of an almond croissant. *Oh, pastry. So good.*

"Yup. Does that hurt?"

I opened my mouth to ask what he was talking about. Then I noticed he was gesturing to my cheek. "It doesn't feel great, that's for sure, but it's fine."

Dez hopped up and headed toward the fridge. "You hesitated. Hey, do you have a cold pack in here?"

"Yeah, it's in the little drawer thing that pulls out."

He rummaged around for a minute.

"I'll get it," I said.

"Got it." He turned around and pressed the cool pack wrapped in a towel to the side of my face. It didn't hurt. The cold actually numbed my cheek. But the tender act of kindness broke me apart. Fat tears spilled and slid down my face, soaking the edge of the towel. How embarrassing. I usually had such good control.

"Sorry. I didn't mean—"

"It's not you," I said. "I mean it sort of is, but not . . . you're just being really nice to me and—" I sniffed, willing the tears back into my eyes.

"I get it. Actually, not really. But you don't need to explain. I just showed up and then made myself super at home in your kitchen. I don't know why I did that, actually." He ran a hand over his hair. "Do you want me to go?"

"No. I just wanted to be angry—not at you, I mean. I really wanted to stay furious like some sort of strong, powerful, vengeful rage queen. Impervious. It's hard to be irate when someone brings you almond croissants and coffee and gets you an ice pack."

"The bonfire," he said, understanding registering in his expression. "You were burning someone's stuff."

"My husband," I answered. I collected the empty sugar packets into a pile in my hand. "Do I still call him that? I'm not sure anymore."

Dez took a sip of coffee, his brow furrowed thoughtfully. "Do you want him to be?"

I really wanted to say no. I just wanted the past three days to disappear. I shrugged.

"It doesn't matter anyway," I said, picking a sliver of almond from my croissant. "He doesn't want to be."

Dez nodded, seeming to process it all without needing any more information. He opened his mouth and I braced myself for some sort of condolence or ego stroking that would make me want to puke up the croissant. "You need a little help with that?" he asked. He was looking directly at me, his coffee cup lifted slightly as if gesturing at something.

I glanced around, confused. What did he mean by that? He stepped closer, and I wasn't sure if the caffeine and sugar had just jolted my heart into an arrhythmia or if his proximity was doing something to me. I looked up, frozen in place. Then he reached out, swept my hair from the nape of my neck, and gently settled it over my right shoulder. I sucked in a breath. He slid the zipper of the dress up.

Dez lingered for just a moment, close enough that I could feel the warmth of his hands on my skin. If I spun around I could have touched his face again and stared into those kind eyes, but I wasn't drunk or having a moment of temporary insanity this time. When I turned around, I lifted my coffee cup between our faces. "Thanks," I said.

"Sure. I should probably let you finish getting ready for work."

"Well, it was very nice of you to stop by. Thanks for the provisions," I told him. "And the zipper."

"Anytime. I'm just around the corner. So, you know, if something comes up and you need a hand, feel free to reach out. My number's on the to-go-order slip on the bag."

After he'd gone, I opened the newspaper. I still had a few minutes before I truly needed to leave the house, and I knew that Kyra had written an editorial about the problems in North Carolina's court system. Since it was the only state that automatically charged sixteen-year-olds as adults, pleas and proposed legislature to "Raise the Age" were not just political, they were moral imperatives. Kyra's reporting also revealed stark statistical discrepancies in the handling of these cases across racial lines. As usual, she was completely right. It was heartbreaking and emblematic of an all too common injustice. We hadn't come as far as we thought.

I read Kyra's story, a moving, impassioned piece, a call to action; it was full of fury and facts, and I hoped that everyone would read it and sit with it. Kyra had a gift, but it also pained me that she had to bear this burden. I wanted to do more to help, something concrete and meaningful. I flipped to the page where my advice column ran. Maybe I could do something there, I thought. I was in the mood to be extremely blunt with the assholes of the world. But instead of inspiration, something else struck me.

Oh shit. Oh shit.

I guess the only plus side to me getting in shape is that when I caught them together, I had the strength to tear him limb from limb.

· Eleven ·

I MADE IT INTO THE office in record time, passing a couple of people in the hallway who tried to engage me in conversation and giving them a wave and a "So sorry, can't talk" as I motored toward Kyra's door.

I burst into Kyra's office, waving the paper in my hand. "You actually ran it? Are you off your rocker? Did you read it first?"

Kyra shrugged. "Of course I read it. I edited it too. You had a dangling participle in there that I couldn't abide. You're better than that."

"Kyra."

"Violet."

"No, this is bad. This is very bad." I paced back and forth in front of her. "You promised you wouldn't tell anyone. Now the whole world knows."

"Okay, well, you haven't been syndicated yet, so not the whole world, more like the Triangle area. And second, I didn't tell them, you did."

"I was drunk when I wrote that!"

Kyra covered her mouth. Across from me, her cardigan-clad shoulders were shaking.

"You actually think this is funny?" My words came out louder than I'd intended. Kyra's eyes darted to the open door.

Her phone beeped. "Listen, deep breaths, girl. No one outside the paper knows Dear Sweetie is Violet Covington. It's like North Carolina's best-kept secret, and it's going to stay that way. All anyone really knows is that Dear Sweetie is a woman with real problems and a smart-ass sense of humor. I think this is a good thing."

"How could this be a good thing? It's a mess. Just like the rest of my life." I flopped onto the couch.

"Violet, you're spiraling. Pull yourself together. Tell you what, my man at Krispy Kreme on Peace Street just texted me that the *Hot Doughnuts Now* light is about to go on in ten minutes. Come get a doughnut with me. You know, warm, just off the conveyer belt, dripping with glaze. We'll have a serving—which is two, in case you forgot—and have a little chat about this non-emergency."

I was about to decline, but she gave me a *don't even think of saying no* look and picked up her purse. "I'm driving."

FIFTEEN MINUTES LATER, KYRA had polished off her "serving" and was sucking sugar residue from her fingers in a booth beneath the glow of the neon *Hot Doughnuts* sign. Still full from the croissant, I'd merely picked at mine.

"Now this is coffee," Kyra said. "Unlike that sad excuse in the break room."

"I guess I can kiss syndication goodbye."

Kyra pursed her lips.

"It's worse than that, isn't it?" I moaned. "I'm going to lose my job, and I can't afford to be out of work now with everything that's going on. My salary barely covers our mortgage, which I guess I'll be paying now that Sam's decided not to come home, and I had to pay eBay four hundred bucks last night."

Kyra was quiet for a long time. Finally, she said, "Look, maybe it's a good thing."

"What? Me losing my job, or my marriage falling apart? Because it looks like both of those things are happening as we speak."

She sipped her coffee. "All I'm saying is I know what happy looks like, and this"—she gestured to me—"isn't it."

"You're right. I'm *not* happy. I'm shocked and sad . . . and really freaking mad at him."

"That's good. Be mad. But I meant before . . . You were not happy *before.* You were going through the motions. You know, we all do it. We're hustling. Getting up in the morning, working out, slathering on some anti-aging serum—maybe not me, 'cause I've got my mother's genes—"

I couldn't argue with that. Miss Katherine, who was knocking on sixty's door, didn't look a day over thirty-five.

"—eating some sad whole-grain breakfast, going to work, lather rinse repeat. I mean, it fills the time, but it's not soul satisfying. Even I think that, and I'm married to a woman, so I'm already a bit better off just right out of the gate."

I considered this. Had that been what Sam had meant by something missing? Silly me, I'd thought he meant fidelity. Maybe Shelby was soul satisfying. My nose started to sting. Kyra reached across the table and gave my hand a squeeze.

"So okay, the column is maybe a little intense for some folks. But it's real. It's alive and emotional and authentic. And honestly, I think a lot of jilted women out there are going to eat that right up like it's one of these doughnuts, fresh and sweet and exactly what they were hankering for."

"It was rage writing."

"Nothing wrong with that. A lot of great writing comes from rage. I've got a shelf of awards to prove it."

"Well, then I should have plenty of good writing coming. The only trouble is, I don't think that I should be giving anyone advice right now. You have to admit I went a little rogue there."

Kyra shrugged. "The way I see it, you don't have much of a choice. This isn't personal, it's business. Things in your home life may seem pretty bleak, but you haven't lost everything. You still have a great career. The syndication could happen."

"It better. I won't be able to afford our house and all the other bills on just my salary for long."

"Well, there you go. You'll figure it out."

"It's definitely not ideal. But you're right . . . I am coping. I can figure this out. I mean, just last night I almost made four grand."

"How'd you do that?" Kyra raised a dark eyebrow.

"I auctioned off Sam's Star Wars stuff."

Kyra choked on her coffee and had to pound on her sternum for a moment. "You what?"

I shrugged. "I used eBay. He said he wanted to start over, and he didn't take them when he left, so I figured that, like me, they weren't important to him anymore."

"That's one way of looking at it."

"I didn't go through with it," I said, trying to keep the shrill defensiveness out of my voice. "That's why I owed eBay money. Fun fact, they charge a fee if you cancel an auction with bids."

"Good to know." She dabbed her mouth with a napkin. "Those doughnuts are getting cold, Violet. What's with you? Are you in the grief stage where you lose your appetite? You've gotta eat."

"I already ate this morning. Croissant."

Kyra tipped her head. "Why do I feel like there's more to this story?"

You could make the investigative reporter editor in chief, but she'd always be an investigative reporter. There was no point trying to fool her. I shrugged and hid my mouth behind my cup anyway, trying to look unaffected. "The firefighter stopped by. He brought coffee and snacks."

"And?"

"And he's really into helping people, I guess."

"He's like one of those calendar guys, isn't he? Was he wearing the pants with only the suspenders?"

"I thought you weren't attracted to men anymore."

"Look, I think we both know that's not how bisexuality works, so I'm going to pretend you didn't just say that. Besides, suspenders or not is a perfectly legitimate question. Let's stay on topic here. Where did you have this breakfast? At the kitchen table, or did you have breakfast in bed? And more importantly—was it good?"

"I think I'll walk back to work."

"Don't go, Violet. I'm proud of you. An eye for an eye."

I stood up. "Nothing like that happened, I'll have you know. I may have married a philanderer, but I am a proper lady."

"Sit," Kyra said. "I promise I won't ask anything else. I won't even mention his hose." She cackled.

"You are the worst," I said, but I still dropped back into the booth. What can I say? Kyra is probably the closest thing I have to a real soul mate, and you don't leave your soul mate sitting alone in Krispy Kreme even if she was being kind of an ass.

"Yeah. I'm your one real friend, the yin to your yang. We both know that," she said, basically reading my mind. "You better not think I'm judging you, Vi. I'm not."

"*I'm* judging me," I admitted.

"Why? That doesn't make sense, Violet. You said nothing happened."

"That's true. Nothing happened this morning. But the other night when I was drunk and having a bonfire with Sam's stuff, we had a moment."

"A moment? Is that a euphemism?"

I shook my head. A moment was just that, close to nothing, even if it felt a bit like . . . something. I just needed to get myself together and stay away from Dez and his kind eyes and warm hands . . . and touchable face—I didn't need moments, I needed a therapist.

"So," Kyra said. "When are you going to see him again?"

Twelve

I'D THOUGHT IT WOULD be easy to avoid Dez. Even though he lived in my neighborhood, apparently, I'd only seen him once before the fire—that day in the street with the sponge and the flirtatious grin, I realized after Kyra's calendar comment—and I wasn't planning on any additional activities that would involve summoning emergency services to my home. On his end, he hadn't tried to pursue anything, and I'd done nothing other than fold up the receipt with his phone number on it and put it in the drawer in the kitchen next to my take-out menus. I still hadn't reached the emotional state Kyra had mentioned where my appetite disappeared, so I saw that receipt the following evening when I caved in and ordered takeout . . . again. Cooking for one, unless it meant opening a pint of Ben & Jerry's and getting out a spoon, wasn't something I was prepared to face. Not yet. I called in my order, chopped barbecue plate, corn bread, kale slaw—my meek stab at taking care of myself—and a sweet tea, from Big Mike's BBQ in Apex, and then went to go pick it up.

I eyed the fire station as I drove by. One of the bay doors was open, and the fire engine that normally filled it was missing. I wondered if they were out on a call, and by *they*, I meant Dez, which was ridiculous. *It's just the infidelity,* I chided myself, *and the croissants.* My interest in the whereabouts of a fire truck or a certain firefighter had nothing to do with his lovely lashes or his very kind eyes. Coffee and croissants and having someone to zip me up weren't in the cards for me after what Sam had done. I was staring down a lifetime of barbecue for one.

In the shopping center, I parked the Jeep on the front side of the building next to the metal pig sculpture. I peeked at myself in the mirror on my visor. My eyes were a tad swollen and I really could've used a coat of mascara, but I'd discovered, much to my chagrin, that even waterproof formulas have a limit. Unless gray streaks became a new trend or spontaneous weeping ceased to be a regular occurrence, I was on an eye makeup hiatus. I slicked on some lipstick—much better—and then got out and headed toward the restaurant. These days, I moved with a kind of intentional efficiency. Get in, get out, all before I ran into anyone I knew. One look at my swollen eyes and naked lashes and whomever I'd seen would know the whole story. My face practically screamed "cheated on."

The good thing about Big Mike's was that you picked your food up out front, so I wouldn't have to face any of the people sitting in the booths toward the back. One table on the patio near the door was full, I noticed, so I kept my head down while I yanked open the door.

"Violet. Hey," a deep voice called.

Shit. I fixed a teeth-gritting smile on my face and swiveled my head toward the voice. "Hi . . ." I dragged out, bracing for impending doom.

But it wasn't doom. It was Dez, rising out of his chair. He was wearing a navy blue fire department T-shirt and slacks, just like the rest of the crew at the table. "You like Big Mike's?" he said, grinning.

"Yeah." My face relaxed with relief. The rest of his coworkers seemed engaged in conversation. One guy raised his cup a little at me in greeting, but he turned his attention back to his brisket almost immediately. "I'm a chopped girl, but the brisket is good too," I said.

"The whole vinegar sauce business threw me for a loop, but I've been converted."

So Dez wasn't a local, then. I'd practically grown up with vinegar-based barbecue sauce in my baby bottle. "That's good. Y'all are taking a break?"

He nodded. "Mostly we eat at the station, but it's nice to get out sometimes. Plus"—he leaned forward and dropped his voice conspiratorially—"it was Eva's night to cook and—"

"I heard that, Dez," a woman with dark hair pulled into a tight bun at the nape of her neck said teasingly. "Who burned the pancakes last week?"

Dez opened his eyes wide. And they were just as nice (and mesmerizing) as I remembered. "Busted," he admitted, with a laugh.

I was still awkwardly holding the door open. A family with a toddler in overalls over a onesie covered with tiny dinosaurs hesitated at the entrance. "Go ahead," the dad said.

"Oh. I—"

"Right, wouldn't want your food to get cold," Dez said.

I ducked inside, followed by the parents and the child, who was cooing about pudding. I gave my name to the girl at the counter and she procured a large brown-paper bag and handed it to me. "You're all set, hun," she said. "Enjoy."

I thanked her and turned to leave. The family stepped up to the counter. "We'll have two plates of chopped barbecue. That's it," the mom said.

"Puddin'," the child whined.

"No pudding for us tonight. We had cookies at Marbles, Sebastian."

"Oh, ma'am, you forgot your drink," the girl at the counter called to me. I had to lean in past the mother to grab the tea with my free hand. I flashed a sheepish smile at the family as I passed by, cheeks burning, but Sebastian was not reacting well to being denied his pudding. His fussing was reaching a crescendo and both parents were engrossed in trying to quiet him. Neither seemed to pay me any mind. My hands were too full to manage the heavy door, so I gave it a push with my hip, but it didn't budge. This was my life now—hands full, on my own, not able to get out of a barbecue restaurant. My nose started to sting, the telltale warning of imminent tears. Oh *no*, crying in Big Mike's would constitute the bottom of the barrel. *Cool it, Violet,* I told myself. *A damn door is not going to be your social demise.* This situation did not call for being ladylike, it required a little muscle . . . and thanks to Bear and my laughable self-esteem, I had that in spades. I rotated further and prepared to crash butt-first into the door, but just before I initiated my launch sequence, I felt a gust of air on the back of my neck.

"Looks like you could use a hand," Dez said. There wasn't even a hint of teasing in his low voice.

"People must feel very reassured by you when you show up," I said turning to face him. "Is there any time you're not rescuing people?" It seemed an accurate statement. He'd helped me that night, talking to me when I'd wanted to burn my whole life down. He'd gotten me an ice pack and zipped me up. And now he was rescuing me again, in the simplest way possible.

He took up a substantial portion of that doorway, and the grin on his face seemed to fill the remaining space. "Just part of the job," he said. One of his arms was stretched out over my head. He gave me a debonair *after you* gesture, and I got a nice view of his ropy, tanned arms as I ducked underneath.

I let out a little puff of air.

He reached out and took the bag from me. "I can carry this to your car," he said, quickly adding, "or you could join us, if you want. There's plenty of room. And unlike little Sebastian, we're definitely getting dessert." He gestured to an open spot at the end of the table between him and the woman named Eva.

I hesitated. As much as I was not looking forward to eating a meal alone in my empty house with only Jessica Day and her ragtag crew of roommates for company, I wasn't up to a public appearance with a bunch of strangers who had likely seen me doing a drunken fire dance in the street a few days ago. None of them seemed fazed, though, which meant that Dez hadn't told them it was me. It had been dark that night, and they'd been preoccupied with dousing the flames; they probably didn't recognize me. Welp, I wasn't about to give them the chance to connect the dots.

"That's a really nice offer, but I've got some work stuff waiting for me. Thanks, though."

"No worries," he said. Then he followed behind me to the Jeep. He set my barbecue carefully on the passenger seat and put the seatbelt on over it.

"Did you just buckle my food?"

He flashed me another one of those amazing smiles, the kind that was so warm it gave me chills, like someone had clicked the AC up a notch. "Safety first."

"I'm relieved to know my dinner is secure," I said, stifling a laugh. "Thanks again for the helping hand."

"Anytime," he said, and it sounded like a promise.

I cleared my throat. "Well, uh, have a nice night."

"You too. It was good to see you, Violet."

He closed the door firmly and gave me a little nod before he stepped back onto the sidewalk. I turned my attention to the road behind me so I could maneuver out of the parking space. When I glanced over, he was still standing in the same spot, hands in his pockets. I'd expected him to be back at his table already, digging into his food, laughing with his buddies, but he was watching me. I gave him a little wave and immediately felt silly. But he returned the gesture with a lopsided grin that chased away the embarrassment I'd felt and replaced it with something different, something I didn't entirely recognize. I glanced back once in my rearview mirror as I made my way toward the traffic circle—he was still standing there.

· Thirteen ·

THE IDEA OF FACING my mother and her probing was worse than the prospect of running into one of my acquaintances at the grocery store or going back to my six a.m. fitness torture sessions with Bear. Nonetheless, she was expecting me for Sunday dinner, and if I didn't go—well, let's just say that wasn't an option. I would be there with bells, and an extra layer of makeup, on.

It took me the better part of an hour to get ready. In the past twenty-four hours, I'd taken to listening to Kelly Clarkson's old albums at top volume and oscillating between ugly, uncontrolled sobbing on the back roads or in the walk-in closet where no one could see and wanting to smash things, like Sam's face and Shelby's spirit. But now I had to put that all away. I picked a sleeveless blouse with a Peter Pan collar out of my closet and paired it with a long baby-pink tulle skirt Sam had always hated. One has to look on the bright side, Mom always said. I guessed I could wear the skirt now without having to suffer through Sam's thinly veiled irritation. Topped off with pearls, the look didn't scream *woman thrown over*; it was more like *sassy Sunday school teacher*, and that worked.

I grabbed the bananas Foster pudding I'd made earlier in the day from the fridge and headed out.

There was a silver Mercedes in the driveway parked next to my car. I narrowed my eyes for a moment, while Sam's mother, Lillian, exited the vehicle and headed toward where I stood frozen in place on the walkway.

"Violet." She'd probably meant it to sound warm and neutral, but even behind all the effort, I could hear the icy bitterness in her tone, as if saying my name was a tad like tasting ice cream flavored with pickles and anchovies and sour milk. Typical. She'd never been able to be completely nice with me.

"Sam's not here," I said.

"I'm well aware. I thought you'd be at your mother's by now."

What was it with Covingtons sneaking around when they thought that I wouldn't be at home? "Can I help you with something?" I asked.

"Sam asked me to pick up a few of his things," she said, holding up his set of house keys like a trophy.

"If he wants his things, he can come get them himself," I said.

"Oh, well, I'm already here, and it's not much, just a couple of suits and his signed Michael Jordan jersey. I'm sure I can find those easily."

Not likely. Their ashes had been ground into the street by the garbage truck that came through and washed away by the storm yesterday that had flooded the cul-de-sac and knocked power out for a couple of hours. I'd spent that time in the dim light of a candle I'd found, watching the flame dance like the bonfire the night after Sam had shattered my heart.

His mother was smiling at me now like a chimp. People think the chimp is nice, but actually when it shows its teeth like that, it wants to rip your face off.

"Coming here wasn't appropriate, Lillian," I said, impressed with my composure. "What's happened between me and Sam is between me and Sam, and he should at least have the decency to collect his things on his own. I think you should go."

"Fine," she huffed, and turned on her heel. She paused, swiveling back toward me. "You know, I'm sure this is painful. I'm hurting too. Sam made a mistake."

"A *mistake*?" I scoffed, in part because calling a long-term affair a mistake seemed a bit of an understatement, but also Lillian was not the type to acknowledge any wrongdoing on the part of a Covington and I couldn't hide my shock.

"Of course. We all tried to warn him marrying you was not a good idea. But he just would not listen. Imagine how this terrible disaster could have been averted completely if he had heeded me before the wedding. It's not your fault, I recognize that. But the fact that you refused to see that you were never going to be good enough for Sam, Violet, well, that's inexcusable. He's a star. Smart, driven, handsome—he's destined for greatness, just like all the Covington men. He'll be running for state senate before we know it. And you, well, dear—you've tried. You have that cute little anonymous column, but let's face it, you're not a senator's wife. You just don't measure up."

Her sharp words sliced into me. I almost didn't feel it when it happened. She'd cut me into bits and I hardly realized until my hands slipped open and the banana pudding smashed into the flagstone.

"Oh, what a shame. On the bright side, cooking's never been one of your strong suits. Come to think of it, I'm not quite sure what your strong suits are," she said. Then she smiled again, slid on a pair of sunglasses two sizes too big for her gaunt face, and started to walk away.

I stepped through the banana pudding and strode toward her.

"Lillian," I called, my voice shaking with pure blue flaming rage. I snatched Sam's house keys from her hand. "I'll be taking these."

She gasped, and when she turned back toward me, her face was aghast.

"Very classy, Violet," she said.

She got into her car and I climbed into the Jeep. She waved for me to go first, and I wondered if she had another set of keys and was just waiting for me to leave so she could go in and take every valuable out of the house while I was gone. I returned the gesture: *You go first, lady. I am the picture of politeness. No, you.* Finally, I gave up. I didn't have anything important in there anyway. And neither did Sam. I grinned to stop my lip from trembling.

Her words were still burning in my ears, but I told myself not to cry. *That's what she wants*, I thought. She wanted to hurt me. That's what she's always wanted. Every little dig about how I wasn't a good cook and she should host all the holidays. About how Sam's side never had any issues with infertility, and it must be something with me. None of her friends read my column—they preferred the real thing, Dear Abby. How it was probably for the best that Sam and I never had children, since I couldn't even take care of our garden. Years and years' worth of these digs flooded up. She turned and beamed at me. A bright, goading grin, and then she waved.

My heart was pounding. I gripped the steering wheel tight in my hands. On the seat, my phone buzzed. My mother, no doubt, wondering what the heck was taking me so long. I eased the Jeep back, past the end of the drive, watching Lillian's eyes, shielded by those massive sunglasses, staring at me in her rearview. *You were never going to be good enough for Sam, Violet.* I shifted into first gear and slammed down the gas.

· Fourteen ·

Dear Sweetie,

A couple of years back, my wonderful son married a girl against my wishes. I know that makes me sound bad, but this girl is truly not right for him. He didn't listen. He was young and, like a lot of young men, made a stupid mistake. Now, this young lady has disappointed us at every turn. She has a ridiculous little job at an arts center, practically a hobby, while he works like a dog to pay for their home and all the things she seems to buy constantly: a bed for their new house, a double kayak, a trip to London to see her family at Christmas. She doesn't even have dinner ready when he gets home, and . . . oh, don't get me started on her cooking. On the rare occasion that she actually invites us over, we are subjected to things like asparagus and the worst rendition of beef Wellington you've ever had while sitting in the saddest excuse for a garden I've ever seen. And that's not the worst bit. We've been waiting for years for them to start a family—is it so wrong that I'd like some grandchildren?—and every time we bring it up, she changes the subject or gets upset. It's like she doesn't even want to try to have a baby, just to spite us.

We'd always hoped that our son would marry a brilliant woman, a doctor maybe, someone who was his intellectual equal, and that after they got married, she'd settle down and have three children and stay home with them. Is that too much to ask? Every year we take a family vacation to Lake Lure, and this year my daughters and I have decided that we don't want her there. She just ruins everyone's fun. But, of course, I don't want to miss out on special time with my son. How can we tell him that we'd like some family time, and that our family doesn't include his wife? I'm not a bad person, I'm just a good mother who wants the best for her son . . . and she isn't it.

Sincerely,
Misunderstood Mother-in-Law

....

Dear Misunderstood Mother-in-Law,

I don't think you're misunderstood here. Unless there's someone out there who thinks you're NOT a horrible person, in which case, yes, I'd say you've been misunderstood.

To ensure there's no confusion, I'm going to use bullet points.

- You say you want the best for your son.
- You are the actual WORST.

You belittle your daughter-in-law's career choice, preferring instead that she'd spent hundreds of thousands of dollars and years of her life training to be a doctor and then . . . let me make sure I read this correctly . . . given it up to pop out a bunch of babies and make sure dinner's on the table every night before your dear son gets home from work. Wow. There's so much to unpack there in that sexist, 1950s list of expectations, I'm uncertain where to begin.

Did it ever occur to you that she likes her job and it is important for a woman to be fulfilled?

Or how about this . . . maybe she's struggling with infertility, and all this time you've been harassing her and making her feel like trash about something that's already breaking her heart? Perhaps your precious son doesn't want children . . . Did you ever think of that? Maybe the garden is subpar because there's a mole there that she's too sweet to want to kill, or she's suffering from depression, or they were supposed to work on the garden together but your sweet boy was too busy cheating on her to help her with it. And that beef Wellington, well, perhaps she was trying so hard to win your approval that she went with the fanciest dishes she could and just couldn't manage the complicated meal. Maybe the whole time you've been judging her, you've been slicing her into bits.

What she lacks in culinary skills, you make up for in cruelty.

You're right, she doesn't deserve your son. Because he is a part of your family, and she doesn't deserve you. She doesn't deserve your judgment. Your superiority. Your meanness. Your inability to respect boundaries or other people. Or your spineless offspring, who won't stand up to the bully who, I'm just guessing here, breastfed him way too long.

She deserves better.

We can't really pick the family we were born into—but we are free to make a new family. Your son made your daughter-in-law his family when he married her—he chose her. So if you choose to purposely exclude her from this trip and explain why you didn't invite her, you probably will burn this bridge. I say go for it. Burn that bridge, Mama . . . because that's what's best for her. She and your son can paddle happily past the rubble into the sunset in that two-person kayak THEY purchased. On the other hand, maybe you could take a long look in the mirror, recognize the absolute villain you've become, and try to change. I'm not going to hold my breath.

Sincerely,
Sweetie

....

• *Fifteen* •

THE CRUNCH OF THE Mercedes bumper was the most gratifying sound I'd heard in some time. Lillian had her seatbelt off in a flash and was out of the sedan and checking out the damage as she stomped toward my Jeep.

"Are you insane?!" she snarled at me. "This is a brand-new lease, Violet. How could you do that?"

I lifted my shoulders, trying to look contrite. I rolled down the window. "I thought I was still in reverse," I said. "Oops!"

"You are a little monster."

"Oh, c'mon, Lillian. Everyone makes mistakes. Especially me. I mean, I can't seem to get anything right, like you said." I threw the Jeep back into reverse and peeled out of the driveway, waving at her as I drove out of the cul-de-sac. In my rearview, I could see her throw her hands up in the air.

My pulse raced, but not out of pain or fear this time. I felt exhilarated. Huh. I kept doing the wrong thing, and yet, it felt so damn right. There was no way Lillian was calling the insurance company or the cops. She didn't know I knew, but she refused to stop for pedestrians and was about a point away from losing her license and being uninsurable.

I hopped on 540. The tolls were a pain, but I was late already, and it was the fastest way to Mom's place in North Raleigh. I left the window down, enjoying the rush of air on my face and the adrenaline in my veins. Twenty-five minutes later, I rang the doorbell empty-handed with hair that was somewhere between finger in a light socket and Dolly Parton in the late eighties.

Mom pulled the door open. I instantly smoothed down my hair with my hands. Here's the thing about my mother: in my whole life, I've never seen her look disheveled. Not only did she not look close to her age, but her hair was still auburn without any help from a bottle, for God's sake. It fell in waves around her shoulders, and her skin was smooth for her age, a testament to the fact that she'd been so pale as a child that she'd had to avoid the sun completely. She was wearing a green blouse and a pair of seersucker slacks that fit her perfectly.

"I knew Sam wasn't able to come, but no bananas Foster?" she said. "I was looking forward to that."

"Sorry. I had an incident."

She hugged me with one arm. "That would explain the hair. You're not hurt, are you?"

"Not that kind of incident. I ran into Lillian as I was leaving."

She waved a hand at me. "Say no more. I'll throw a peach dump cake together right quick. It can bake while we have dinner. The roast's already resting."

I'd been looking forward to fried chicken, but anything was better than sitting alone steeping in regret and revenge fantasies by myself.

I followed her into the foyer, past a massive flower arrangement of white roses and hydrangeas, probably left over from one of her weddings the previous day, through the living room, and into the kitchen.

"How are you, Mom?" I asked, sliding onto a stool at the marble island. There was another, smaller floral arrangement in the center, with a kaleidoscope of colorful dahlias.

"Great," she said. "I signed amazing new clients this week. He's a Hurricanes player and she's a shoe designer. Just the cutest couple. He's huge, big even for a hockey player, and she's a tiny little thing. You know, I think she went to State, textiles. After you though; you wouldn't know her. She has exquisite taste, and their budget is . . . well, let's just say they want no expenses spared at Fearrington Village. It's going to be absolutely gorgeous. Well, of course you know."

I did. Sam and I had gone back there for our ten-year anniversary, stayed at the inn, and had a custom meal prepared by the chef. We'd browsed the lovely bookstore there, talked about where my books would be if I ever got around to writing them, strolled hand in hand through the gardens. There'd been music outside and we'd gotten ice cream and wine and listened for a while. I'd wanted to stop beneath the huge spheres of fairy lights hanging from the ancient oak trees to dance, but I didn't ask. Instead, we sat in white Adirondack chairs and watched fireflies flit around over the fields where the cows roamed, and I felt as if we were the only people in the world. Now I just felt so lonely. It didn't seem like a memory; it was like a movie of someone else's life.

"Can we talk about something else?" I asked.

"I'm sorry, honey cakes," she said. "You must miss Sam, what with that new lawsuit taking up so much of his time. I can't imagine a good reason to work on a Sunday—it's supposed to be a day of rest."

"It *has* been a little lonely, but that's fine. I have plenty to occupy me. Mr. Hastings told everyone that there's a chance that my column is going to be nationally syndicated, so I need to focus my energy there."

Mom had been opening a can of peaches. She stopped. "You didn't mention that when we talked!" She flung an arm around me. "That's wonderful news. Congratulations, Violet."

"Thanks."

"Sam must've been ecstatic when you told him."

I nodded. This was harder than I had thought it would be. My stomach ached, and I had to squeeze my eyes shut for a moment. "Mmhmm." I forced a smile, but my eyes weren't cooperating with the lie. Fortunately, Mom wasn't paying attention. She was too busy draining the peaches.

"Did you tell Daddy?" she asked.

"Why would I do that?"

"He's still your father, Violet, whatever happened. He'd be proud of you."

I shook my head. "I don't think so."

She eyed me over the glass pan. I felt myself cracking under the weight of her gaze.

"Mom, you don't have to make the cake," I said. "Go relax for a bit. I owe you a dessert; I can finish this up."

"I am not infirm, Violet Alice," she said.

"I know that, Mom. But you did have at least one wedding yesterday. Two, from the looks of the different color schemes in the flower arrangements."

She waved a hand at me. "Three, actually, but the guests took home the orchids from the last one." She sighed. "Fine. I could stand to put my feet up for a few minutes."

I cut up the chunks of butter and put them on top of the mix and popped the whole thing into the still-hot oven. Dump cake. Disgusting name, but sheer buttery perfection with some vanilla ice cream.

"Kyra must be proud to have such an accomplished advice columnist on her staff," Mom called from the living room.

"*She's* the accomplished one, you know that. She won another big award a couple weeks back. Again."

"Brilliant girl, our Kyra. She still with Roxy?"

"Yeah, they're leasing the most adorable house on Pace Street."

"That's a sweet neighborhood."

"Literally," I said, tucking in next to her on the couch. "You can smell the Krispy Kreme doughnuts from her porch. She made friends with some staff there, no surprise, and now they alert her before the light comes on."

Mom smiled, then took a sip of her white wine. "How about you ask the two of them over next time if Sam can't make it? I'd love to see that darling little Harriet of theirs."

"Sure thing."

"Didn't she have a big story coming out this week?"

"Yeah, it's maybe the best thing she's written."

Mom stood up. "I was so busy with the triple-decker wedding weekend that I didn't get a chance to read the paper. I know I've got it somewhere. I'll read it now, while the roast finishes resting."

She headed over toward a stack of newspapers that she'd set on a sideboard. Somewhere in there was the edition with Kyra's story . . . and mine. Panic washed over me. As Kyra had said, Dear Sweetie's identity was a secret. It was not, however, a secret from my mother. I'd known Mom hadn't read the paper yet, because she was a die-hard Dear Sweetie reader and she hadn't mentioned my Fitness Faker column. I could not let her read that paper.

"Mom," I said, louder than I'd intended. I ratcheted myself back under control. "Let's save the reading for later. The roast's going to be cold, and I am positively famished."

She paused. "Oh. Well, no one likes a cold roast. I suppose these aren't going anywhere."

I let out a long breath. *Thank you, Jesus.*

We talked about the usual things. My upcoming neighborhood Bunco game, an estate sale she wanted to attend, the groom who had gotten a nosebleed at the first wedding on Saturday and bled all over the front of the bride's gown. When we finished eating, I cleared the dishes and we washed them by hand, standing side by side.

"That's a nice skirt," she said. "I don't think I've seen you wear it before."

"Let's just say it's not Sam's favorite."

"Ah, I see. When the cat's away . . . On that note, let me make you a plate to bring home to your cat."

I was about to object, but I realized it was the perfect opportunity to steal the newspaper so Mom wouldn't read the column. Though we were online, and my mother was pretty savvy when it came to most things related to her business and electronics, she refused to read the paper in any other form than the one that some kid threw into her driveway every day. She liked the feel of the printed page, she said.

While she cut some meat for Sam and put a large portion of cake into a Tupperware container, I dashed into the living room, grabbed the paper, and shoved it into the waistband of my puffy skirt. The tulle might not have been Sam's favorite—unflattering, he'd called it—but it hid all manner of sins in its elastic waistband. Overindulge in dessert? Check. Stuff a newspaper in your pants? We got you covered.

"See you next week, sweetheart," Mom said at the door, and kissed me on the cheek. Under the layers of pancake makeup, the yellowing bruise from the coffee table smarted. "Give Sam my love."

I desperately wanted to tell her that I had given Sam *my* love and he'd thrown it back in my face. He'd hurt me, just like Dad had done to her. Neither of them deserved to hear my news, or eat our peach cake, or have our love ever again. But I would never confess any of those things to her. Pressing my hands to the newspaper so it felt a bit like armor, I said, "Of course, Mom. Thank you for dinner. Love you."

· Sixteen ·

THEN

WATCHING MY MOTHER PREPARE for one of her weddings or parties was a thing to behold. She danced about like a ballerina, with perfect control and grace, fixing the last details, floating from task to task until everything was just so. She was so beautiful. My mother had been getting ready for one of her famous parties—a fundraiser benefiting a local shelter for victims of domestic violence, maybe? It was so long ago now that I couldn't remember that part. She'd been finishing the last touches on the flower arrangements when an unwelcome guest had shown up early. I'd recognized the woman's voice from the phone even though I'd never seen her before. She'd called a few times in the past month, always treating me with a familiarity she hadn't earned, calling herself a "good friend" of my father. She was nothing like my mother. Her mousy brown hair was styled in two long schoolgirl braids and she was wearing a T-shirt so thin her nipples were clearly visible. I slammed the door in her face.

"Violet Alice," my mother had said, reaching for the doorknob, "that is not how we treat our guests." And then she invited my father's mistress into our home.

I brooded from the spiral staircase while I watched my mother serve my father and this strange person charcuterie. The woman shared with them a book she'd been reading about hiking, which she was sure would be helpful when she took on the Georgia portion of the Appalachian Trail that summer, that detailed how to shit in the woods. She went so far as to stride confidently over to the corner where my mother had placed the hydrangea Dad'd bought her that morning and squatted over it, miming the act. I knew, in some distinct way that I felt in my bones, that she was marking her territory. My mother's face was tight with what looked like embarrassment for the woman's lack of refinement, but she appeared otherwise unfazed. She toyed with the pearl necklace she was wearing.

"You'll have to excuse me," my mother said, rising, when the woman had finished miming defecating on our houseplant. "I'm afraid if I don't get changed now, I'll have to keep my other guests waiting."

"That's right," the woman said, "Edward told me there was a party tonight."

"You must have something she can wear, right, Wynne?" It wasn't a question.

My mother tipped her head. "Certainly."

She glided out of the room and past me on the stairs without saying a word. I tried to make eye contact with her, but her gaze was fixed on the steps ahead of her. I followed her up the stairs and into her bedroom. Wordlessly, my mother unzipped the sundress she'd been wearing and let it fall to the floor. She stepped out of it, in her slip and high heels, went into the closet, and came out in a cocktail dress. My mother had a great figure, and in this green silk gown she looked like she was on the pages of *Vogue* magazine. How could Dad have chosen to be with that braless nature woman downstairs? I watched my mother in the mirror at her dressing table while she exchanged her pearl earrings and necklace for dainty diamonds. *Just a little sparkle*, she'd always told me. *You don't want your jewelry to outshine you. That, and if it's too big, everyone will think it's fake.* She dusted some powder over her cheeks. I wondered what my dad and that woman were doing now—a deep dive into the chapter on how to screw in the forest, maybe. My mother touched a tiny bottle of eau de parfum to her wrist and brought it up to her ear. She stopped for a moment and sniffed. It was just once. A sniff. Insignificant. But I felt the tremor of that one little slip, that sniff, shudder through me. Then she smiled at me in the dressing room mirror, her eyes shining. She blotted her lipstick on a tissue.

"Mom?" I said.

She stood up and walked toward me. My chin trembled. She stooped down in front of me, her shimmering emerald party dress pooling around her; my feet disappeared beneath the fabric. In her slender fingers, she grasped my chin. I looked up at her. A big tear escaped my bottom lashes and slid down my cheek. It landed on her hand. I wanted to ask her if we would be okay, if *everything* was going to be okay, but I didn't. She smiled again, that brilliant, shimmering smile. "I'll see you after the party," she said.

I shook my head. "But what about Daddy?" I asked. "Is he . . ."

"We'll talk about that later when I get home." She let go of my chin, wiped my tear from her hand with a handkerchief. "I better get going. It takes a good twenty minutes to get to the club, and the hostess can't be late to her own party."

"But . . . that lady . . . What if everyone knows?"

She barely acknowledged my comment. Instead, she disappeared into the walk-in closet again and emerged with a plum-colored dress that had a deep V in the front. "Can't wear a bra with this one. It should suit her just fine."

She draped the dress over one arm and held her gold clutch with the other hand in front of her like a shield as she leaned forward, checking her reflection carefully in the lighted mirror one last time. I was struck by how beautiful she was. Perfect.

"Never let 'em see you sweat, baby doll," she said.

Seventeen

When I got home, Lillian was gone, and I was relieved to see that there was no broken fraction of the maimed Mercedes in the driveway. It was almost as if it hadn't happened, I thought, heading up the walkway in the dark. I'd forgotten to turn on the porch light for myself—Sam always flicked the switch on our way out, so I'd gotten out of the habit over the years. All the remnants of the run-in were not gone, as I'd thought. I slipped in the pudding on the walk and skidded a full foot, arms flailing, Tupperware from Mom flying out of my hands, and then landed with a thud on the flagstone. So much for composure. I rolled to the side to push myself off the ground, and a piece of glass pierced my palm.

"Oh. Owww," I said.

I managed to collect myself enough to get inside the house, where I turned on the lamp in the entryway and examined my hand. On the way to the door I'd chastised not only my lack of grace and reaction time, but my weakness. *It's probably a scratch, no need to be dramatic*, I told myself. But under the light, I felt slightly queasy at the sight of my palm, which I had somehow managed to slice from one side to the other on what was probably my love line or something, given how things were going in my world these days. And it was bleeding . . . a lot. I went to the kitchen and grabbed a clean dish towel to press over it, but that was soaked through in a couple of minutes. Clearly, what I had here was not a Band-Aid situation. I was going to have to drive myself over to the freestanding emergency room that had been built a couple of years earlier across the street from the Lowes Foods. On the bright side, there was hardly ever anyone in there. I'd taken Sam last year when he had a terrible stomach flu and needed fluids, and he'd gone straight in and seen a doctor right away.

You're fine, I told myself. A couple of stitches and I'd be good to go.

Ever driven stick with a sliced-open right hand? I can't say that I recommend it. By the time I reached the ER—a whopping three miles from my house—I was practicing what I figured was somewhere between yogic and Lamaze breathing, not that I had experience with either of those things, and my Jeep looked like a crime scene. I cradled my hand, wrapped in the soaked towel, as I walked through the sliding automatic doors. The security guard at the desk looked at me.

"Um," I said. "I think I might need stitches?"

He cast a glance toward the triage nurse who was sitting next to him.

"You think?" she said. "Come here, honey. I'll get your information in the back so we can get something on that hand. I don't think your towel there is going to cut it."

She stood up and walked me through another set of automatic doors, her hand hovering behind my back. "Did you get a look?" she said.

"It wasn't good," I told her.

"We'll let the doctor check it out. I don't care for blood."

"Aren't you a nurse?"

"We've all got flaws. Have a seat here on the bed. I'm going to get a fresh gauze for you to put on that. It might be a couple of minutes . . . we just had the fire department bring in a patient from a fender bender. But someone should be available to get you cleaned and stitched up shortly. Hang tight."

There was a curtain hanging on a rod, but she didn't pull it shut all the way. She came back with a thick gauze pad, which she pressed into my hand. "Hold pressure." I watched her carry my dish towel in a gloved hand to the biohazard bin, holding it at arm's length, and drop it in.

My poor hand was throbbing, along with my hip, which had taken the brunt of the impact in the pudding incident. I hoped the person in the car accident was okay. They only took minor things here, sending major emergencies to one of the medical centers in the area. They even had a helicopter pad, which could be used to evacuate someone if necessary. I didn't hear any rotors; I took that as a good sign. Still, I'd gotten some perspective about my problems. I hadn't come here in an ambulance—that was something to be grateful for.

In front of me, a firefighter walked toward the nurses' station.

"We're heading out," she said. "Thanks!"

"Have a good one," the nurse sitting at the computer said.

"Yeah, you too. Hey, Dez, you coming?"

I sat up a little. He probably wouldn't see me if he walked by anyway, but that didn't stop me from wondering if I had banana pudding in my hair and blood smeared all over me. I considered, for an instant, hiding or jumping out of bed to snap the curtain all the way shut.

"Violet?"

So much for that.

"Hi," I said, holding up my hand for a little wave.

"Uh, you lost your gauze," he said.

I was about to say that it was fine and I was fine, but he was already in the room, pulling on a pair of gloves as he walked toward me. "Ouch. That's a nasty gash you got there." He pulled a drawer open and came out with a packet of sterile cotton, which he placed gently over the top. "Better?" he asked.

I nodded. "Thank you."

He glanced at his watch.

I shifted on the hospital bed. "I guess you have to get back to real people who need help," I said.

His brow furrowed, but he smiled and revealed a perfect dimple in his left cheek. "You're not a real person? Hang on a second."

He disappeared on the other side of the curtain, just out of sight, but not out of earshot.

"Eva, turns out my friend's here on her own. You mind if I cut loose?"

"No problem, boss," the woman said. "Jerry and I got it from here. Our shift ended twenty minutes ago anyway."

He reappeared, grinning.

"Let me guess, you're going to stitch me up?" I said.

He shook his head. "You need to be intubated, I'm your man. But sewing up sliced-open hands is not in my paramedic wheelhouse. You'd probably end up like Frankenstein. I can keep you company while you wait, though. Mind if I sit?"

I didn't. It was nice having someone here, even if it was the guy who knew I was basically an accident-prone arsonist who couldn't open a restaurant door by herself. If he had developed a negative opinion of me from these facts, he didn't let it show. He settled next to me—not too close, I noticed, slightly relieved. My legs dangled next to his long ones, which were clad in navy blue cargo pants, his feet planted firmly on the floor. He leaned back onto his palms.

"I was hoping I'd run into you again," he said. "Not quite under these circumstances, of course."

"It's payback," I said.

"Us meeting here?" he asked.

"No." I held up my hand and gestured to it. "This. I'm being punished for burning Sam's stuff and driving into his mother's new Mercedes on purpose."

"Wait, you actually drove into your ex-mother-in-law's car?"

"Yes. I admit it. Honestly, I think I've gone a little over the edge. I'm kind of a disaster." I dropped my head and waited for his judgment. Considering he'd just had to rescue someone from a car accident and bring them to the hospital, it would definitely be a well-deserved scolding. I waited some more. Finally, I peeked up at him through a few strands of hair sticky with pudding residue. In the bright lights of the emergency room, his gentle brown eyes looked almost copper. I felt strangely captivated, like a crow mesmerized by something shiny. *Stop staring*, I scolded myself. I redirected my attention away from his face, but it did not help the situation, because my gaze fell on his arms, instead of something safe, like the bedpan sitting on a cart in the corner. They were outstretched in front of him, his uniform T-shirt straining against his biceps, and he was pretending to hold a steering wheel in his large hands. "Towanda!!!!" he shouted, with what sounded like pure glee, as he feigned impact. His broad smile gleamed.

I couldn't contain my shock. "You know *Fried Green Tomatoes*?"

"Who doesn't know *Fried Green Tomatoes*? C'mon." He elbowed me softly.

"Oh, great movie," the doctor said, coming in. She dropped onto a stool and scooted toward me. "Let's take a look at this hand."

I leaned toward Dez and whispered, "I thought you might give me a lecture about my choices, being a safety officer and all."

His temple pressed against mine. "Nah. Do I look like a cop?" he said, voice low. "I'm team Towanda all the way."

"Okay, I'm going to go grab a suture kit and we'll get you put back together here," the doctor said.

When she'd left, I turned to Dez. "You don't have to wait. I'm sure you're tired."

He shook his head. "I'll stay. Somebody has to make sure you don't wreak any havoc on the way home."

"Very funny," I said, but I couldn't keep myself from laughing.

· Eighteen ·

IF DEZ THOUGHT ANYTHING about the crime scene in the Jeep, he didn't mention it. My hand was mummified in gauze and numb, and I was worn out and traumatized. I'd handed my keys over without protest and climbed in beside him.

It was odd sitting in the passenger seat of my own car while a man who wasn't Sam drove. It felt strangely intimate, which sounds ridiculous, because I'd touched his face and stared at him, and then I'd let him do up my zipper, an act that was pretty intimate as far as things went for me, especially lately, but still. It was different.

"I feel like I should apologize," I said.

"For what?"

"You've been so nice to me, and I didn't stay and hang out at dinner. It was really generous of you to invite me; it's just that I'm kind of a hot mess right now, if that wasn't already super obvious, and I'm not good with being like that around people. I'm still reeling about my—about Sam, and I don't know how to navigate that."

"No worries. Believe it or not, I get it."

"I don't want you to think that means I don't appreciate you keeping me company tonight or bringing me croissants and keeping me from burning down my neighborhood—I do—I just—"

"Can I ask you something, Violet?"

"Sure."

"Is everyone in your life really judgmental?"

I had to think for a second. "No. Why?"

"Because you sound like someone who is used to being judged. What I mean is, you don't owe me any explanation. I put that fire out because that's my job. I stopped by with food and invited you to join us for dinner because I wanted to. Same reason I hung out with you tonight. I haven't lived here all that long, and since I work so much, I basically only know a bunch of firefighters. You are enjoyable to be around. Nothing more to it than that. And I appreciate the apology, but it's not necessary. You won't get any judgment from me."

Huh. I let the statement wash over me for a bit, while Dez pulled into the driveway. "I guess some people around me are pretty judgy. My mother-in-law is an extreme example. She pretty much hates everything about me and likes to give a running commentary on all the ways that I suck. I have to admit, it felt really good smashing her perfect new car."

Dez cut the engine.

In the past couple of days, I'd made so many mistakes: set fire to Sam's expensive stuff (and possibly my career), committed vehicular vandalism, flat-out lied to my mother.

"I've made a lot of mistakes this week," I admitted.

"Okay . . ."

"Do you want to come inside?"

"I probably shouldn't."

"Oh. Are you seeing someone? I'm sorry, I shouldn't have assumed anything."

"I'm not dating anyone. I'm just not sure me coming in is a great idea, Violet, based on everything you just told me."

"My husband isn't coming back, you know. He's with Shelby now and he's made that very clear."

Dez's brow furrowed.

"Shelby's our neighbor. She lives ten houses down, around the corner. You've probably seen her. She spends a lot of time running around in very little clothing."

"I don't think I've seen her, but I haven't lived in this neighborhood that long, and I work weird hours. I don't know most of my neighbors. What's with Shelby?"

"I guess they were meeting up while I was at boot camp? I mean, I came home from work early the other day and they were here." *And he loves her.* There was that too.

"Oh." He looked thoughtful. "Why'd you come home early?"

I smiled. "I wanted to share my good news. My advice column—I work for the newspaper—is short-listed for syndication."

"You're a writer? Advice column . . . Wait a minute. Hold on." An energy had overtaken him. He turned to me, eyes wide. "Are you Dear Sweetie?"

I nodded.

"That is awesome! I've never met an undercover celebrity before. And syndication . . . I don't know much about it, but I've read *Marley and Me* . . . syndication's a pretty big deal, right?"

"Thanks. Yeah, it *is* a big deal. It's funny. You know, I didn't even think about it . . . you're the first person I've told, other than my mother. I wanted to tell Sam but I found him in bed wi—"

Dez's head dipped. He swiveled it side to side. "No. You are not serious. You walked in on them? I thought that only happened on soap operas and *New Girl*."

"Yup." I cringed a little at the admission, but it wasn't lost on me that we apparently had the same taste in television.

"Now I get why you were burning his stuff in the street. He definitely deserved it."

"I guess I'm a little . . . traumatized, maybe? Twelve years of marriage, over just like that. I haven't even been able to sleep in my bed since it happened. I just hate the idea that they were there, you know, betraying me. It's like I should have burned the bed too."

"Don't do that. McElvaney is on duty tonight and he's an asshole. I wrote off the fire in the street as a training exercise. He's not going to do you any favors." Dez opened the door of the Jeep. "Listen, just for the sake of clarity, I wasn't saying that I don't want to come inside. I just don't want to put you in an awkward spot. But if you're up for it, I'll hang out for a little bit. I have an idea."

He was bouncing with helpful energy. I didn't have the heart to tell him that there was no way whatever he was thinking would work. Shattered worlds were not something you could just smile at and wrap some gauze around, even if it was a very nice smile. I didn't say any of that though. I let him unlock the front door for me and we both went inside.

The wine I'd bought for Bunco was sitting on the entryway console. I picked up the red and headed toward the kitchen. Dez took the bottle opener from my hand and poured us each a glass.

"For the pain," I said. "Now what was this idea you had?"

"C'mon," he said, heading toward the stairs. "I'll show you." I followed him up, my heart pounding with trepidation. I didn't know what he had in mind: half of me wanted to find out, and the other half wanted to flee. Maybe not quite half. One-fifth. Just shy of twenty percent of me wanted to flee. The remainder was very curious about what a man who brought coffee and rescued kittens and watched *New Girl* could come up with . . . and also mesmerized by that interesting tattoo on his forearm and, heaven help me, the way he was wearing the heck out of those pants.

Dez paused for a moment in front of the wedding photo of me and Sam on the wall just inside the door of our bedroom.

"Didn't feel like burning that one?"

"I haven't looked that good in twelve years."

He eyed me. "You look good now. Even with that old shiner on your cheek and the right hand of King Tut."

"You're just being nice." But I didn't want him to take it back. I couldn't remember the last time someone had complimented me. Even if it was a pity compliment, it felt good.

"Nice guys don't lie to women," Dez said, and winked. "You're stunning. Plus, I love your energy. I never know what's going to happen when you're around."

Well, that was a revelation. I paused in the bedroom doorway; after everything Sam had done, it felt disquieting to be in here, especially with someone who made my stomach somersault when he looked at me. Dez pulled out his phone and fiddled with it; then he set it on the nightstand. Sam's nightstand. I braced for some sort of sexy soundtrack, but instead music started to blare, an old hip-hop number that I remembered from parties way back when I was fun.

"What are you doing?" I asked.

"What are *we* doing, you mean?" He put his foot on the edge of the bed frame, then turned back to me and extended a hand. I hesitated.

"Is this House of Pain?" I asked.

He nodded. "Appropriate, don't you think?"

"You won't get any arguments there. But I still don't—"

He opened and closed his hand, beckoning. "You'll see, Towanda."

I put my good hand in his, and the sensation was so overwhelming I almost pulled it back. But he closed his fingers around mine, his grasp warm and gentle, and helped me up.

We stood on the mattress facing each other while House of Pain played. Energy crackled between us and I held my breath. Dez did a small hop. "We are clearing the energy of this thing." He took another one, lifting his eyebrows, cajoling me. Then the chorus came, the one I'd heard at frat parties on campus and half the weddings I'd attended over the years (not mine, of course, thanks to a very controlled set list provided by Lillian). I took a tentative hop, right where Sam's arms had cradled Shelby's head to his chest. Huh, that wasn't half bad. I jumped again. My tulle skirt lifted around me, floating up after I reached the top of the leap. *Take that*, I thought, as my feet collided with the mattress.

Those guys yelled "Jump" and we *jumped*. Over and over, until I was cackling with delight and struggling to catch my breath. My thighs and calves burned with exertion. I looked over at Dez, whose eyes were gleaming. A thin sheen of sweat had formed on his forehead and I had a fleeting thought about the dewiness of my own skin. But then Dez squeezed my hand, which was still clasped in his, and brought me back to the present. As I bounced higher and higher, like a kid on a trampoline, a frantic, almost gleeful feeling bubbled within me, building with each jump, like I was a can of Cheerwine about to burst. A little voice chided me to stop, but neither of us did; we both jumped as hard as we could. That's when it happened. A loud crack resounded over the music, and the mattress gave way as the bed frame fractured beneath us. The force hurled me back toward the footboard, but Dez, who seemed to have the reflexes of a cat or a superhero, landed on his feet, absorbed the impact of the collapse, and redirected me forward, straight into him. I did not move. I stood completely still, my cheek pressed to his firm chest, listening to his heartbeat, like the soundtrack to a different kind of life, a happy one. Finally, I pulled back and we both stared at each other in stunned silence.

"Holy shit," he said finally. "I'm so sorry, this was not what I had in mind when I—"

I bit my lip. Dez raised a fist to his mouth; his shoulders started to shake.

I tried to maintain my composure, but Dez's building laughter was contagious. "Oh my God," I cried out as I dissolved into hysterics. "We destroyed the bed."

I doubled over, laughed until I was wheezing, tears streaming down my cheeks. My sides ached.

"We really did!"

Our laughs slowed and I straightened up. I found myself a bit breathless, looking up at Dez. "I haven't felt this good in—" *How long* has *it been?* "It feels like forever."

Dez brought my hand to his chest. "I'm glad," he said. He wasn't laughing anymore; his expression had turned serious. He pressed his lips together. "You deserve to feel good."

"I do," I admitted. "Thank you for helping me."

"My pleasure." The intensity of his gaze changed, deepening, and I couldn't help but bask in its heat. My skin tingled in anticipation. "It's not my place to say anything," he said, "but your husband is a fucking idiot."

I shook my head.

Dez hooked his thumb under my chin. "I mean it. You're incredible, Violet. And I don't just mean that you're beautiful, which you are, but it's beyond that—you have this charisma about you. You're sweet, kind, sassy . . . and you're completely unpredictable."

"I think they call that a loose cannon."

"Well, I'm an adrenaline junkie who loves rock climbing and skydiving and intentionally runs into burning buildings for a living, so you can guess how I feel about cannons." His gaze did not waver. I gulped.

The same kind of excitement I'd felt when I decided to start the fire in the street rose up within me. It was probably the glass of wine or the laughter; maybe it was the fact that the two of us had just decimated whatever ghosts of Sam and Shelby having sex in the bed had lingered. Perhaps it was being called incredible by Dez. I could smell his soap and the faintest aroma of smoke. Firecracker and scotch. He liked that I was unpredictable. *Did he predict this?* I wondered.

"So," I began, "you know how you said earlier that I deserve to feel good?"

"I seem to recall something like that." His voice was low and rough. I glanced down at his hand; it hovered only inches away from my hip. He tipped his head just a little, and there was that dimple again.

"It would be completely ridiculous if I asked you to kiss me, right?" I blurted.

He shook his head. *Of course* he did. Mortification burned beneath my bruised cheek.

"No," he said.

"I get it. I'm sorry. That was . . . I don't know what I was thinking, I'm not—" I stammered.

"I meant *no*, it wouldn't be ridiculous." His face was so earnest, but the intensity of his expression when his gaze met my eyes practically did me in. In the streetlight slanting through the blinds into the bedroom, his eyes looked different than at the hospital. His irises were practically the color of amber, like the mysteries of the universe were suspended in them. "I just don't want to be one of those bad decisions you were talking about. Or like a bright idea that I think will help and ends up breaking something." He gestured toward the carnage of the bed.

I closed the distance between us. My breathing was rapid and my pulse thrummed. "I don't think this is a bad decision," I whispered. "I want to feel something else. I want to feel good."

"I'm all for making you feel good," he rasped.

I planned to kiss him. To take control, to take his face in my hands like the night of the bonfire; I'd stare into his eyes and press my lips gently to his, like a sensual loose cannon. Did I remember how? I knew how to kiss. It's just that I hadn't actually thought about a kiss in so long; with Sam it'd been automatic. I hesitated.

Dez did not hesitate. He threaded his hand into the hair at the nape of my neck and then circled my waist with the other and pulled me tightly to him. I lost my breath. He leaned down and brought his mouth to mine; his lips, tender and firm, melded with my own. His breath became my breath. I threw my arms around his neck, drawn in by his hunger. Dez tasted different than Sam. Sweeter, somehow, like he'd eaten a chocolate bar while he was on shift. My skin was electric with heat and anticipation. He pulled back for a moment, pressing his forehead to mine, and then he kissed me again, slower this time, gently, languidly, as if he planned to kiss me until the end of time. And, I won't lie, in that moment, I would've been okay with it.

When he finally pulled away, I had melted, my mind erased so that the only thing that remained was that kiss, and the shimmering sensation in the places where Dez's lips had been moments earlier.

"For the sake of full disclosure," he said, his voice deep and smoldering, "I've been wanting to do that all night."

I couldn't answer. That kiss hadn't so much made me feel good as it had been a revelation. I bit my lip.

"So, uh, what are we going to do about the bed?" he said finally, rubbing the back of his neck. He helped me down to the carpeted floor and we surveyed the damage. "There's no saving this, I'm afraid."

I looked over at him, unable to keep my lips from curling into another smile. "It'll make good firewood," I said.

"Hey now."

"For my firepit," I added. "On the patio. No funny business, I swear."

He leaned over and pressed a kiss to the crown of my head. "I've got a chain saw if you've got marshmallows."

Nineteen

WHAT HAPPENED TO YOU?" Kyra said when she saw me at my desk Monday morning.

I pecked at the keyboard with one hand. "Nothing. I dropped a glass bowl and cut my hand a little trying to clean it up."

"You've got a giant bandage on it," she exclaimed. "Doesn't look like nothing. Walk with me."

I got up and followed her to her office. "I needed a couple of stitches. They probably put all this gauze on here just to keep it dry. I'm thinking I'm going to take it off in the bathroom later. By the way, Mom wants you to come to dinner next time, if you can," I said.

"How is Wynne?" Kyra closed the door behind us.

"Good. Busy. You know how she is. She was excited about the syndication."

"I take it you didn't tell her about Sam, then?" Kyra said.

I shook my head. "I can't. Maybe when the time is right, but it's only been a few days."

"Please tell me that you aren't in denial about this and thinking that if you give him a little time to get it out of his system he'll come around," she said.

"I am not thinking that."

"That's good."

"In fact, I even got rid of the bed."

"Okay, I like the symbolism. That's good too. That's a start at processing."

"Then I cleared the bad energy from the house."

"How'd you manage that? I'm pretty sure I've got a negative spiritual situation going on in the new house. Did you call one of those ladies with the crystals?"

I rubbed the back of my neck. "Uh, not exactly."

Kyra fixed me with an elementary-school-principal look. I wanted to twist my fingers together and hide my guilty eyes, but the gauze mitten put the kibosh on that.

"It was sexual sage," I muttered.

"Come again?"

I repeated myself, a fraction louder this time.

Kyra's coffee cup stopped inches below her lips. Her expression was bemused. "Excuse me, did you just say *sexual sage*?"

My whole body burned with a mix of memory and mortification all at once. Kyra leaned across her desk. From her expression, I could tell I wasn't getting away without answering. I picked at a thread that had come loose from the hem of my skirt with my good hand. "I met that fireman from the bonfire last night at the ER when I was getting stitches."

"Please tell me you did not rebound with some kind of a creeper, Violet—you're too trusting."

"No, he was there dropping off a patient."

"That doesn't mean he's decent."

"He was working. But he was just finishing a shift and so he kept me company." He'd made me laugh and kept me distracted from how bad my hand hurt. He'd made me feel beautiful.

"Okay."

"And then he drove me home. It was a little hard to drive stick with this paw."

She nodded along with my story, but her brow was still furrowed, I noticed. "And then?"

"And then we broke the bed."

Kyra sprayed the coffee she'd just taken a gulp of across her desk.

"Not like that!" I screeched. "I knew this was a mistake," I said. "We kissed, that's all."

"Must've been quite a kiss to break a bed," Kyra snarked.

"We were fully clothed and jumping, okay? I'm in uncharted territory here."

She held up her hand, taking a moment to collect herself. She shook her head side to side.

"I'm the worst, I know," I admitted, covering my face with my hands. "I don't know what's come over me."

"Are you kidding me? I salute you, Vi. You had the human doormat routine pretty well perfected. But look at you, getting a spine. I honestly thought you were going to say you two slept together. Kissing? That's reasonable. I celebrate you."

I peeked through my fingers. "I should go."

"Why? I want details. It must've been some kind of a kiss for you to call it sexual sage."

"Okay, I have a column to write. I guess. I mean, who wants advice from a woman who lost her husband to a neighborhood jogger and made out with a veritable stranger after breaking a bed to a House of Pain soundtrack? It is entirely possible that I've come unhinged."

I'd been digging for reassurance, but Kyra was tapping away on her clipboard. I headed toward the door. "Wait, Violet." *Here it comes*, I thought, Kyra's words of wisdom, dished up warm, like berry cobbler. She would know just how to set me back on the right path.

"What's his name? I'm gonna google him."

Twenty

KYRA FOLLOWED ME OUT of her office and over to my cubicle. "We'll discuss this later," she said. "And we *will* discuss. But that's not why I was looking for you this morning. I had actual work to talk about."

My heart dropped into my stomach and settled next to the breakfast that seemed to want to come back up. "Oh God," I moaned. "The column. I knew this would blow up in my face. How bad is it?"

"Oh, it blew up," Kyra said.

"I knew it. I'm done, aren't I?"

"I said it blew up. I didn't say that was a bad thing. You really have no idea about this? I want to show you something." She leaned over my shoulder and typed something on my computer. A website opened. I squinted at it. There was my column—nothing out of the ordinary.

"Look at the view count."

I scanned to the bottom of the page and blinked. I looked again. "Eight hundred?" I said.

"Wow, you really are out of it," Kyra said, poking the screen. "This little letter right here—it's a K. That says eight hundred *K*. As in your rage column got eight hundred thousand hits. Look at the comments."

I was still staring at the screen, dumbfounded. "Never look at the comments," I said. "That's like our number one rule."

"Don't be a baby," she said. "Look."

I scrolled down. And kept scrolling. There were thousands of comments. Some were negative, but most weren't. I saw words like *Refreshing. Real. Honest. About time. Smash the patriarchy.*

"That's only our website," Kyra went on. She pushed her phone in front of my face. "You're trending on Twitter." I looked at the list of hashtags Kyra had pulled up. There it was, number seven on the list: #DearSweetieGoesSour.

The phone rang on my desk. I picked it up in a daze.

"Dear Sweetie," I said.

"Sweetie! This is Tamara Hamilton with ABC11. I'd love to interview you about your column."

"Um. Sorry, Tamara, I don't do interviews. Thank you for your interest."

The phone rang again.

Kyra was grinning. Ashleigh appeared in my cubicle. "Is it true? You've gone viral, girl!"

Going viral meant that the whole world had read what I'd written about my failed marriage when I was shit-faced and about to burn Sam's prized possessions in the street. Oh my God.

"Be happy, Violet," Kyra said. "Safe to say syndication is almost in the bag."

I nodded. "I'm delighted!" I said. "I just had a huge Starbucks on the way over and need to use the restroom. Back in flash."

"We're taking you out after work to celebrate. Don't even think about saying no," Tyler said, appearing over the top of my cubicle wall.

TYLER AND ASHLEIGH WOULD not be denied, even after I hid in the bathroom for what seemed like enough time for them to lose interest. They were taking me out to the newest, hottest club in town and there was nothing I could do about it. Once again, Tyler had to cover it and promised that with comped drinks he could get me as sauced up as I liked. Ashleigh had a sitter again for Tristan and wanted to party. Me going viral was the perfect excuse.

After work, I turned down Hillsborough Street and headed toward City Market. Ashleigh and Tyler took a Lyft, but as much as I hated to admit it, Sam was right . . . car services always gave me the creeps. And I wasn't planning on staying long anyway. Besides, driving in the Jeep was the perfect way to ensure I would stick to the one-drink limit I'd vowed in front of half the office. One, two drinks max.

It was strange being down in City Market again. When Sam and I first started dating, he used to take me out here. I liked the standard Irish bar next door, Tir na Nog, and some of the places with dancing, but Sam didn't dance and preferred the piano bar. I always hated that place. One time we went there and the piano guy made me sit next to him while he sang a lewd and humiliating song featuring me and Sam. There wasn't enough room on the bench, so I sat there trying to smile while his thigh pressed against the thin skirt of my sundress. My cheeks blazed with embarrassment the entire time. Sam kept his eyes on me, grinning with pride, or amusement maybe, even whistling at one point. He didn't seem to notice my discomfort.

"Look, Sam," one of his friends had said when I sat down, "she's so into you she's glowing."

I found a parking spot and headed toward the club, a place called the Night Market. Taking a deep breath, I readied myself for socializing and yanked open the door. Inside there were fountains and a lot of purple neon, a DJ with his setup on something that looked like a fire escape, people breakdancing below him. I wished I could do that, even if my mother would have clucked her tongue and declared it undignified. In the center of the space, sofas were placed haphazardly among small stations that featured painted and illuminated signs in a variety of different styles.

"It's supposed to be inspired by a Singaporean street food marketplace." I jumped. I'd been so entranced by the club setting that I hadn't noticed anyone near me. "Jesus, Violet. You are wound up. Did you see that, Ash? She jumped." Tyler laughed. He took his sunglasses and hung them on his shirt.

"Shut up, Tyler. You shouldn't just get in a woman's space like that," Ashleigh said.

Tyler held up his hands. "Sorry. Point taken."

"It's okay," I said. "I was just in my own world checking this place out. There's a lot going on."

"Fabulous." Tyler clapped his hands together. "I'm ravenous, and I see some people over there I know. Let's make the rounds."

I had no desire to make the rounds, but I plastered on a slight smile and prepared to fall in behind Tyler. The good thing about him was that he loved to talk, so I could just blend into the background until he decided it was time to eat.

"I need to hit the restroom first," Ashleigh said. "Wanna come with, Violet?"

"Sure."

We found the bathroom and Ashleigh dropped her purse in the sink and extracted a makeup bag. She rummaged around until she found a lipstick.

"So," she said, eyeing me in the mirror. "What's really going on? The floor thing is bullshit, obviously. I mean, if it were my house, I'd get it, Pickle has done a number on them. That's what Mark gets for insisting we get a Great Dane. But y'all don't have any pets. The last time I went to your house for the Labor Day picnic, your floors looked amazing." She turned to me. "You could use some bronzer. You're a bit ghostly."

"Oh, you got me," I began, taking the compact she held out to me. "Sam and I got in a little tiff and he wanted to cool off. Nothing big."

"I hear you. Mark and I had a little tiff last week ourselves. I spent a whole Saturday afternoon making this elaborate meal while he was out golfing with his boss—flat dumplings from scratch, a roast chicken—and he spent the entire time on his phone. I wanted to cram it down his throat. I was like, Mark, what the fuck are you teaching our son? I'm not raising some prick who thinks it's okay to ignore his little wife after she made a fancy meal. We sorted it out."

"That's good."

"Want to know our secret?" she said. "It's better than sending him off to a hotel. We have angry sex. Like really angry. Then everything's fine." She dotted on some undereye concealer she didn't need.

"So, has he stopped with the phone?" I asked.

"Huh? Here, take some lip gloss too."

TYLER HAD ORDERED US drinks while we were in the bathroom—a *lot* of drinks—and settled in with a group of fashionable people on a set of couches. I slid my lip-gloss-coated lips into a beauty pageant smile and joined them.

"I'd like to make a toast," he said. "To our very own viral Sweetie!"

Ashleigh whooped, and I grinned.

"Oh my goodness," a drunk girl cooed, "did you just say Sweetie?! As in Dear Sweetie?"

Uh-oh.

"What?" the guy next to her yelled over the music. "Who?"

She whacked him. "Dear freaking Sweetie," she said very slowly. "You know, from the paper? She's got the perfect answer for everything! I read your column every week. Babe, here, take my phone. I want a photo. Can we take a picture together?" she asked. I was trying my best to come up with an artful yet polite dodge—or even better, say, *No, sorry, it's just a pet name, I'm definitely not* the *Dear Sweetie*, but "Babe" was already in the process of raising the camera. I was glad Ashleigh had given me a makeover in the bathroom, despite the grilling and the overly intimate detail sharing about her and Mark's sex life. I told myself this would be fine.

"You are such an inspiration!" This girl was still going.

I reached for a neon-green drink that looked like antifreeze, and I sort of wished it were. I gulped it down.

"Kamikaze!" Tyler shouted. "V, you just did like six shots; that was a group drink." He seemed to think this was hilarious.

"A *group* drink?" I asked. "That's revolting."

"Alcohol kills germs," the fan said. "Gosh, that reminds me, you really went off on that last column about the mean mother-in-law." She turned to Babe. "She ripped off her cheating husband's arms!"

"That's not exactly what I wrote," I said, but they didn't seem to hear.

"No way! That's hard-core," he slurred. "Let me get in on this action."

He handed the phone to Tyler, who, like the social media maestro he was, was already raising it to get our best angles.

"I don't really—" I started, but Tyler cut me off.

"Oh, come on, V! It's just one picture."

I'm going to need an exit or another one of those group drinks if this goes on much longer, I thought.

"I pictured you different," the drunk girl said. She was very close to my face.

Sometimes it's important to learn when to hold your tongue. I closed my eyes and pulled a deep breath in through my nose. *You can do this, Violet. Difficult people allow us to practice tolerance and compassion*—that was on a desk calendar I'd gotten at the office white elephant exchange last Christmas. "I mean, no offense," she went on in the dreaded lead-in that somehow always meant something really unpleasant was about to be said, "but I thought you'd be prettier. Or younger, maybe."

I didn't respond.

"Mark!" Ashleigh called, waving a hand.

Ashleigh's husband was hard to miss even in a crowd. He'd been a quarterback for the UNC football team, and even though they sucked at the time, he was a bona fide giant, and somehow managed to be just as big as he had been in college; the seams on his suit looked like they were about to burst. I hadn't seen him since Labor Day, when he'd gotten plastered and grabbed my ass so hard it'd left a bruise.

He cocked his head at me. "Hey there, Violet. Sorry to hear about you and Sam. I always thought you guys were an odd match, but I never pegged him as a cheater." He grabbed the olive out of Ashleigh's martini and tossed it into his mouth. "You got a divorce lawyer yet? Obviously our firm can't take care of you—conflict of interest. You understand. But Ashleigh's cousin's supposed to be great. A real ball-buster. I'm sure she'll make sure you get your fair share of the Covington money."

Ashleigh's eyes widened. Tyler spit out some of the group drink he'd been slurping from a straw.

"Holy shit!" the drunk girl said.

The reaction was not particularly surprising, since it seemed as if the white, middle-of-the-road faction of the state of North Carolina was still mourning the death of the honorable Samuel Covington III, senator from Raleigh, North Carolina. Babe, who was still holding the phone, blinded me with the camera flash. I picked up a double shot glass filled with glowing hot-pink liquid and downed the contents.

"Violet Covington?!" the drunk girl screamed. She was remarkably astute, given her state of inebriation. "I can't believe it. I know the secret identity of Dear Sweetie!" She was squealing and then turned to her companion and gave him a kiss that almost looked like she was trying to devour his face.

"Thanks, Mark, I'll keep that in mind," I said, my voice as sweet and smooth as custard. "This DJ is amazing. I'm going to go dance. Anyone want to join me? No? Alright then. Party of one, on the move." One of Juvenile's songs, a throwback to my college kegger days, came on. "I love this song," I said. "So, yeah, I'm going to go back that azz up by myself. Good chat." I took one more shot for the road and I headed for the dance floor.

I'd faced a lot of challenging situations in my column over the years. People who were hated and people who did the hating. Sad people. Lost people. People who wanted to feel superior. People who just wanted to throw a good dinner party. Total humiliation in a club with neon group drinks with coworkers and a strangely mean fan looking on? That was a new one. I didn't have an answer. I always had an answer, but now, when disaster was at my doorstep, *again*, I didn't have even the hint of a notion of what to do. What I had was humiliation, stinging hot on my skin, and the beat of the music.

I'd stopped dancing after Sam and I got together because he had preferred to sit on the sidelines, nursing a beer. Now I surveyed the dance floor. Couples were grinding, girls were twerking, and a pair of truly talented guys in T-shirts, jeans, and high-tops looked like they were rehearsing for a music video. I watched in awe for a moment, nodding along to the beat, before I stepped out into the crowd. I had a good buzz going now, and as soon as I was out there moving, everything else just sort of faded away.

Twenty-One

I AWOKE TO THE SOUND of an alarm and my head and hand screaming at me, alternating in digital pulses and throbbing pain. I flung my good hand out, feeling for my phone so that I could start the snooze timer and stop that dreaded noise. Last night's celebration at Night Market had gone horribly wrong and then morphed into a blur of music and dancing and . . . calling Dez for a ride home when I realized that, despite not having another drink and sweating out most of the group drink, I still shouldn't drive myself home, and Kyra was probably home asleep with little Harriet while Roxy closed the restaurant. *Shit.*

Before I went to college, my mother had told me not to ever drink past tipsy. *You don't want to ever get drunk, honeybun*, she'd told me. *That's a* sign *of a problem and an* actual *problem at the same time. Always stay in control.* Pretty sure the only thing that had stayed in complete control last night was my Spanx.

The number of times Dez had helped me pressed heavily on my pride and filled me with guilt. I'd probably woken him up on his day off. Had I kissed him again? I thought back . . . No, let's see, he'd walked upstairs with me, getting me a glass of water while I dropped down to the mattress on the floor, pulled off my shoes, and climbed under the covers, but no kiss. A strange mixture of disappointment and relief filled me as the alarm continued to assault my ears.

"Sorry about the alarm," Dez said. "That's mine."

I looked over to where he was propped on one elbow atop a folded comforter on the floor next to the mattress, fiddling with his phone to silence the alarm.

"I'm so sorry," I said, rubbing my temples. "I'm really embarrassed."

A wave of nausea hit me—those damn Technicolor drinks—and I folded onto the bed.

"No worries. The music was pretty loud at that club, so it was hard to hear you clearly—but I caught something about not wanting to be stuffed in a trunk and a *Bone Collector* reference."

He moved onto the side of the mattress, and now I caught the full experience of Dez in the morning. He was shirtless and wearing only a pair of fire department sweatpants. The muscles in his back flexed as he stretched. I would've thought he looked amazing, if I hadn't been so preoccupied with not puking on him. I dropped down and put a pillow over my head. "I can't believe you drove all the way to Raleigh to pick me up after I drunk dialed you. Why am I the worst?"

"No worries. I didn't want to chance you driving home like that."

"I am so sorry. I don't even know what to say."

"It's fine, Violet. I'm glad you called."

"Okay, no. I am so mortified that I inconvenienced you like that. We hardly know each other."

"First, I wouldn't say we don't know each other. And second, I am glad that you called me. I don't love the idea of any woman alone in a hired car when she's vulnerable, especially one I like. I mean, some of my buddies drive for Lyft, so most people are good, but still, you should trust your gut. And the alternative is what, you driving drunk?"

I shook my head. "I would never do that."

"A lot of people do though. I've seen what it can do to a family—smash it to bits."

I thought about his work. What he was saying made sense—still, I felt beyond awful that I'd exceeded my one-drink limit in the first place, let alone troubled Dez with it. Sam was right. I was a horrible and messy drinker, how unlikable . . . Except Dez had said he liked me. What was that?

"Long story short, I will drive anywhere to pick up anyone. Plus, I have a couple days off, and on the scale of possible passengers, you are pretty cute."

I bit my lip, thinking of the kiss we'd shared the other night, the one that'd been on my mind since, the one that I really wanted a repeat of right now—after I'd spent twenty minutes brushing my teeth, of course. "Thank you," I said, wrangling my thoughts. "But I can't believe you did all that and I made you sleep on the floor." A horrifying thought occurred to me. I tried to clandestinely sniff my hair. Had I thrown up and was too gross to sleep near? No. After the drinks, I'd mostly been dancing. I was worn out and a little tipsy, too tipsy to drive, but definitely not trashed.

"You didn't make me. I stayed to make sure you were okay. And . . ."

"And?" I said gently.

"The circumstances were not exactly what I had in mind for *that*."

"Oh." For *that*. Pondering what exactly he meant by that statement was both extremely appealing and unsettling at the same time. He glanced at his phone.

"The alarm. Do you need to go?"

"Nah. I usually teach sunrise yoga on Tuesdays, but a pipe broke in the studio, so it's closed for a couple of days. I just forgot to turn it off."

I must've made a face, because he said, "What? You don't like yoga?"

"I've actually never tried it," I admitted. "I guess you just didn't strike me as the yoga type. I thought you said you were into rock climbing."

"Yeah, I also play rugby and love musicals."

"And you've read Glennon Doyle's books and *Marley and Me*," I volunteered.

"Yup. I'll read anything my sisters recommend. And *Marley and Me* made me cry. See, Violet, I contain multitudes. Besides, yoga is for everyone. You know, you should try it sometime."

I shook my head. "Yoga is something I suggest to stressed-out people in my advice columns, not something I do. It's just not for me."

"It's funny you say that. Because you've got kind of a tense energy. I think it might be exactly what you need."

I swiveled my head toward him. I suddenly had a flash of acute remembrance from the previous evening. Even though it was awash with Day-Glo drink colors, it was clear that at least some part of my consciousness had hoped Dez might tuck me in and kiss me good night after he'd safely escorted me home. My shoes weren't the only thing I'd taken off while he'd been fetching me some water. My work clothes were in a heap on the floor next to the mattress, and a quick glance under the sheet confirmed, to my horror, that I was only wearing my underwear. This was a new low. He gave me a disarming half smile and brushed his fingertips over my bare shoulder. The tension and embarrassment melted away, leaving behind a shimmering sensation on my skin and a full-fledged craving in my core. "All I mean is you could try it sometime. You might really benefit from the yogic practice."

Right now what I thought I would benefit from was a bagel

smothered in cream cheese, about a gallon of coffee, and a reset button for my entire life. I wasn't sure about another early-morning fitness class—even if it came with a side of mindfulness and a much cuter instructor than Bear. The last one hadn't turned out so well. "I guess I should get ready for work," I said, putting a little distance between us.

"Okay, well, if you change your mind about yoga—the studio's over in the Beaver Creek shopping center, in the new part by Big Mike's. You're welcome to drop in . . . once the pipe's fixed."

I smiled. I knew all about yoga from Kyra and was two hundred percent sure I'd never be able to get into it. For one thing, according to her, you spent half the time with your ass in the air or trying really hard not to fall over. One woman in Kyra's prenatal yoga class had been wearing pants that were a bit more see-through than she'd planned, and Kyra had gotten a pretty good impression of that woman's vulva. Then there was the farting. There was literally something called the wind-relieving pose. Kyra had called prenatal yoga a festival of flatulence. And I was never going to be relieving my wind around anyone, let alone the man who was serving as a very attractive temporary distraction from the breakup of my marriage and my growing list of problems.

I did not say any of this to Dez, of course. He was pulling on his T-shirt, which was sort of a shame, because his job (and okay, maybe his yogic practice) had carved him quite a lovely torso, rippled with muscles. He disappeared into the closet for a moment and returned with my robe. It was peach silk, covered with watercolor birds.

"Thanks," I said, taking the robe and shrugging it on. I'd bought it for myself when Sam and I had visited the island of Saba a few years earlier. An unwelcome pang of sorrow arrived. I grabbed my toothbrush and brushed my teeth aggressively to distract myself. "Do you want some coffee before you go?" I called into the bedroom.

"That's okay," Dez said. "I'll probably catch a nap before my shift starts."

"I'll walk you out then," I said.

I followed him downstairs, running through what I'd say at the door. Should I hug him? Say thanks? Both seemed very odd. I opted for *Have a good day.* It seemed polite but not pathetic. Appropriate, if there even was an appropriate way to handle such a situation. I pushed the storm door open. Dez glanced at it, but he didn't move. The sun was just announcing its presence; birds chirped at each other in the crepe myrtle.

"I'm deeply sorry about last night, and thank you for being there for me, even though it was a lot of trouble," I said. Dez looked down at me. My body thrummed with nervous energy over what he was about to say. "Have a good day," I squeaked.

Dez pressed his lips together like he was trying to hold in a laugh. He was always doing that, I realized. The few times we'd spent together, he was always laughing or smiling. Nothing seemed to shake him. What was that like, I wondered, to not have a worry in the world? It made me a tad uneasy, or jealous maybe. I spent most of my time overanalyzing.

He was full-on grinning now, and damn if his smile didn't cause my stomach to do a strange flip-flop that was nothing like the swirling doom of group drink alchemy. It was nice.

"Good thing I like trouble," he said.

"You do?"

He nodded. "Mmhmm." Then, in a motion so swift I didn't even have a chance to respond, he swooped an arm around my waist and brought me up to him. I scrambled to reunite the seams of my robe that I'd lost hold of in surprise. But Dez's mouth was already on mine. I could hear the birds, tweeting loudly; *The neighbors, the neighbors,* they seemed to call at me, but my shoulder was still tingling where he'd touched it minutes earlier, and his arms were so powerful—I simply surrendered. *I don't care*, I told the birds in my head. *Shut up*. It was the kind of kiss that made the birds, the neighbors, the front porch—heck, the entire town—blur around us and disappear. I lost track of place and time.

At some point, Dez pulled back. His teeth pressed into his bottom lip.

"You have a good day too, Violet. I'll see you around."

He left me, speechless and a little out of breath, if I'm telling the whole truth, in my silk robe in the doorway. I watched him walk away, a bounce in his step, like a tan Fred Astaire with muscles. Completely carefree. I'd caught a glimpse of that feeling when he kissed me and I couldn't think of anything else except the sensation of his skin on mine, his strong arms around me, and how amazing I felt. I didn't care about anything then. I wanted more of that feeling.

But it wasn't right. It wasn't the proper thing to do. That feeling that was so good, so alluring, and that man who gave it to me, the one who seemed to like me, inexplicably, and who (if my fluttering heart was any indication) I might like too if I wasn't careful—each of them was its own slippery slope; together, they were like Everest. What I needed was to start using my head and get my life back on track before it spun completely out of control. I clasped my robe a little tighter, reaching for the doorknob with the other hand to close it. I'd made mistakes, yes, but today was a new day. What was the saying? Fresh with no mistakes in it. And no one needed to know.

Except someone did.

Because there, across the street, was Cathy Willis, fully dressed in a pair of teal leggings with tiny hot-pink animals on them and a striped tunic in the same colors, holding a watering can over the petunias in her porch boxes and glaring straight at me.

· Twenty-Two ·

IF SOMEONE EVER WRITES me a letter about needing to avoid a confrontation with a nosy neighbor, I would have a lot of suggestions. One, take an obscenely long shower. Spend a good hour trying to select the ideal conservative and capable-looking professional attire. Sear your hair straight to perfection. Eat a hearty breakfast. (You may need the energy to run.) Do this even if cooking is a huge literal pain because you have stitches in your hand and look like you have a giant panda paw and the previous evening you consumed beverages that closely resembled concoctions college freshmen pledging some horrible fraternity would have been forced to imbibe back when hazing was allowed. When all of these tasks are complete, check through the curtains a couple of times to make sure that the bus has already come for the middle schoolers and that the elementary kids, which your neighbor surely has, are not yet outside. She's probably packing backpacks and is not available to chase you down.

Except Cathy Willis. I'd misjudged her. I should have figured that a woman who was completely dressed and taking care of her plants at six in the morning clearly either packed backpacks the night before or had her offspring so well trained that they packed their own. Instead, I was caught completely off guard when she appeared in her door the moment I turned around after locking mine. While I shouldered my purse, she motored down the brick steps of her white Craftsman and started across the cul-de-sac at a speed that looked like she was gaming for a gold medal in power walking. I had less ground to cover to make it to the Jeep, so I was already closing the door when she made it into the driveway. She wasn't even out of breath, but her face was a little red. She knocked on the window. I had to roll it down—that's how old the Jeep was—so I only cracked it.

"I'm really late," I said. "Sorry I can't talk right now."

"This will only take a moment," she said. "There've been some strange things going on at your house, and I have concerns."

"Gosh, thanks for looking out," I said. "We're fine though. Wish I could chat, but I'm so late for work."

"Violet—"

"Better step back," I said. "I wouldn't want to drive over your toes."

She retreated from the drive into the edge of the grass, but her hands were firmly planted on her hips. I waved.

"YOU'RE LATE," KYRA SAID when I skulked in at nine thirty a.m. still wearing my sunglasses. "Everything alright with you?"

"Everything's fine. I'm late because I was avoiding a neighbor. Rather unsuccessfully, I should add."

"Not *the* neighbor?"

"No, not Shelby. Cathy—well, not Cathy, I can't remember her actual name. But the lady I call Cathy, you know, the one who sells the leggings we hate."

"Why's she interested in you? Does she know about Sam?"

"I told you she called the fire department on me."

"Yeah, but that was over a week ago."

"She might have seen something this morning."

Kyra raised an eyebrow. "Something . . . or someone?"

I shushed her. "Someone, okay?"

"Either you're messing with me or you took Firefighter Dez home and converted that kiss into something worth talking about."

I gave her a wide-eyed look. One that said *If you were not my boss, I'd be telling you to shut the hell up right now*. It only lasted a moment because I was too hungover to maintain it longer than that. I sank back into my desk chair. "More like he took me home," I admitted. "I may have overindulged last night."

Kyra was quiet for a beat. "Should I be worried about you, Violet?"

I pulled my sunglasses off and set them next to my keyboard. "No. I promise, I'm on the upswing. I didn't realize what a lightweight I've turned into, that's all."

She leaned in. "It's okay to admit that you're not okay. You know that, right?"

"Of course I do. But in this case, it's true. I swear. I'm fine, Kyra."

And I was. Hungover? A bit. Slightly mortified, yup. Very confused by this really kind—and okay, gorgeous—man who kept showing up for me over and over with no judgment, absolutely. But fine. Until Ashleigh popped into my cubicle. She looked almost as bad as I felt.

"I am so sorry about last night," she said. "We were supposed to be celebrating and Mark had to blow it with his big mouth. I'll have you know he did not get any when we got home on account of that."

I squinted at her, trying to piece it all back together. "It's okay. I'm the one who told the world about Sam in my column. It's not like it was a secret, like my identity."

Ashleigh gave a pained smile. "See, that's the thing, Violet. Mark said your name during his big moment of idiocy and that fangirl and her boyfriend posted on Insta and Twitter about it, and so your identity as Dear Sweetie isn't a secret anymore."

"Oh, I hadn't realized. Well, that was bound to happen at some point," I said. "Now if you'll excuse me, I had a giant Starbucks on my ride in again and I really need to use the restroom." I rushed past Ashleigh and fled down the hall to the bathroom. I locked the door and flung myself toward the toilet just in time to throw up my entire hearty breakfast.

I wrote a column a few months earlier to a woman who had posted something on a website only to be met with vitriol and hate. She said that the things she'd read kept her up at night and made her afraid. It's simple, I'd told her. People say whatever they want on the internet, without any filter or niceties, because they lose their inhibitions. I cited some science. Then I said, it all boils down to this: don't read the comments.

Reader, I read the comments.

I read thousands of them while the phone on my desk rang and rang. Someone in the news had caught the posts and suddenly *I* was a story. By the time Ashleigh had explained to Kyra what had happened and she'd rushed over to me, I was sweating profusely and very close to vomiting again, this time in my trashcan.

Kyra rubbed her hand over my back for a minute, while I closed my eyes and tried to pretend this wasn't happening. But that out-of-control spinout I'd been so afraid of wasn't something I could avoid anymore—it was already underway. Kyra squatted down next to me. "Take the rest of the day off, Violet. We'll sort this out together tomorrow, okay?"

My eyes were brimming with tears when I looked at her.

"How?" I asked, voice trembling.

Kyra's face was resolute. "Since when have I not had a solution to a problem? I promise. I got you. We will figure this out."

I nodded. I had one hundred percent faith in Kyra . . . The rest of the world, not so much.

"Go home. Put your feet up, get some Ben and Jerry's and Chinese takeout. Watch *Sense and Sensibility* for the thousandth time and cry at the part when Elinor Dashwood finally breaks down. And do not, under any circumstances, cut bangs."

"Okay," I acquiesced. "Should I write a statement? Or talk to the reporters who keep calling?"

"Not today."

My phone buzzed and we both eyed it. "You don't need to answer that," she reminded me.

"But I do," I said, after reading the caller ID. "It's Sam."

Twenty-Three

"I should sue you for defamation," Sam seethed over the line. "I just might. What the hell were you thinking, Violet?"

I was at home on the couch, with a cool washcloth over my face, heading into minute forty-five of Sam flipping his lid about my identity being revealed after I'd said my husband was a cheater in the newspaper.

"What was I thinking, Sam? Really? You threw twelve years of marriage in the trashcan like it was nothing. You cheated on me with that . . . runner . . . and then you say you want to talk and you pick, of all possible places, the bar where we met and fell in love to confess that you want to 'see where things go' with her. I'm not the one who wasn't thinking." I had the moral high ground and he would have to pry it from my desperately-in-need-of-a-manicure fingers.

"Yeah, well, at least I was discreet!" he snarled. "You told the whole damn world our problems. You should see the glares I've gotten at the office."

I tried to pull in a deep breath, but my chest was tight. Was this what having a heart attack felt like? I put a hand over my sternum. "Look, I'm sorry. I was not in a good place when I wrote that. I never thought it would see the light of day, okay?"

Sam had always been so sedate; right now he was anything but. There was a nasty edge in his voice when he replied. "You realize everyone is talking about this, right? All my work colleagues, my clients. They're not happy. Did you even think about how this makes *us* look? I come off like some kind of trash human, and, well, you look insane. But then, I'm starting to wonder about that. I assumed you'd hit the Mercedes by accident, but Mom told me you hit her car intentionally. This is the irrational behavior of someone who's lost her damn mind, Violet."

I closed my eyes. How had I turned into the villain in this situation? I wondered. The doorbell rang. Great, just what I needed.

"Sam, I can't talk about this right now. Someone's at the door."

I shuffled into the hall to open it, my head tipped back so the washcloth wouldn't fall off, while Sam protested in my ear.

"I think you could just ignore the doorbell. This is important. We are going to talk about this. I want to know how you're going to fix it," he said.

"Fine," I told him. "Hang on." I unlocked the door.

I opened my mouth, ready to share some polite brush-off, but Cathy Willis thrust a plate of cookies into my free hand—ignoring the bandage completely—and pushed her way into the house. I winced.

"They're burnt," she said, "but that's about what you deserve. You know, I thought I'd seen it all back in New Jersey." She paced the room like an animal at the zoo, gesticulating wildly. "I was under the impression I'd moved to a nice quiet neighborhood where Rick and I could raise our children in peace, with good Christian values. I never imagined we'd be living across the street from a couple of swingers, never mind one who also has pyromaniac tendencies. So let's discuss how we fix this, shall we? Because it's a buyer's market right now and I'm not taking a financial loss because of you people."

I am well aware that I am a professional fixer of problems, but suddenly everyone in my personal life seemed to think that my job was to resolve every issue that sprang up. Worse yet, it seemed that I had turned into the problem itself. I will admit my behavior had been a bit less than ideal, but I'd had quite the shake-up in my life. Wasn't a bit of acting out warranted? This was uncharted territory for me. I resisted a sudden urge to reapply some lipstick.

"Violet!" Sam's voice came from the speaker. "Is that Chatty Cathy?"

The washcloth fell onto the plate of cookies.

"What did he just say?" Cathy snapped.

Something strange was buzzing beneath my skin, a chill that was spreading and seeping deeper. I started to shiver. *I'm turning into an iceberg*, I thought. The kind that brought down the *Titanic*—or maybe I was both iceberg and *Titanic*.

"Sam. I gotta go."

I tried to pull myself together and turned to Cathy. I listened for my mother's voice in the sound of my teeth chattering. *Composure, that's what you need*, she said.

"I'm not sure what you mean," I said to Cathy. "Sorry about the yard waste bonfire mishap. I should have asked first, but I don't think we need to overreact. It won't happen again."

"Sure. Yard waste. Okay. What about the revolving door of people at all hours of the day?"

I lowered myself onto the couch and crossed my ankles reflexively. I would have tried to look perplexed, demure even, but all I could think of was the tight ache in my chest and getting this confrontation over with as quickly as possible. "Hmmm . . . I'm at work much of the day, so I'm not sure what you're referring to. Should I be concerned about vagrants?"

"Not that kind of visitor," she said through clenched teeth. She was clearly not amused.

"Hmmm . . . I'll have to think. We talked about getting one of those camera doorbells but didn't get around to it. A mistake, in retrospect. There's never time for these home improvements. *You* seem to have a lot of free time to make observations about your neighbors, though," I said. "What do you do for a living, Cathy?"

"My name is Cindy, not Cathy . . . and I sell KiKiCo leggings."

Okay, so we hadn't been too far off with the name. "Isn't that a pyramid scheme? I feel like we did a story on those."

"Are you judging me now? It's a good job. I make money for my family and can still be the room mom for all my kids' classes. What do you do that's so much better than me?"

I wanted to drape the washcloth over my head again. Perhaps if I were as sweet as actual sugar, the moisture would dissolve me then and there. "I write a column for the *Raleigh Times*."

Cathy, no, Cindy laughed.

I realized that when we met, the subject had never come up. In fact, I'd avoided sharing personal information with her. *Make sure you keep your business your business*, Mom'd told me when I was young. Cathy had a big mouth—I could tell right away; everyone could (hence the moniker)—better not share too much. I hadn't kept Dear Sweetie's identity a secret all these years by having loose lips.

"Oh, you're serious."

"Yeah, I'm serious. I'm Dear Sweetie; you may have heard."

She shrugged. "I don't do the paper. Or the internet. Way too much fake news out there."

Oh dear Lord in heaven. Cindy was still staring at me. It was quite clear from the intensity of this look that she was not leaving without an answer. I felt sorry for her children. None of them was ever going to get away with anything with her as a mother.

"I did have a friend at the house this morning. I hurt my hand last night and had to go to the ER." I was an honest person, but desperate times sometimes called for a tiny white lie of timing and a bit of pity. I held up my bandaged hand as evidence. "My friend brought me home from the hospital. Sam and I are going through a bit of a rough spot . . . To be quite frank, we're separated right now, so my friend stayed to make sure that I was okay. That's all. I assure you it's very aboveboard. Just a misunderstanding."

Cindy was quiet, but the flare of her nostrils said it all.

"If you don't mind," I said, "I'm still feeling a bit under the weather. I hope I've put your concerns to rest for the time being."

She stood up and started toward the front door. I was about to praise Jesus under my breath, but she stopped and turned back to me, a saccharine smile on her face. "I didn't realize you and your husband were separated. I guess that makes sense, since you seem to be cheating on him with that *fellow* from around the corner. If you could refrain from taking your show of sin to the front door, that would be wonderful."

I narrowed my eyes. If my hand hadn't been mummified in a giant bandage, I'd have been tempted to ball up a fist and use it to punch Cindy right in her massive mouth.

She was still talking. "Anyway, divorce is a terrible thing, so hard on the children. I suppose it's a good thing that you and Sam don't have any."

That ice sensation was back, along with a sheen of sweat. A strange pressure crushed my sternum. I tried to pull in some air so I could answer her, but I couldn't get a deep breath. My phone buzzed in my hand. "Sam," I rasped into the phone.

"You can't just hang up on me, Violet," he said.

My breathing was fast, shallow breaths, rapid sips of air. I slumped back on the couch.

"Enjoy the cookies," Cindy said, "Don't forget about our chat."

"Say something, dammit," Sam snarled.

The room started to spin.

"I think . . . I'm having . . . a heart attack," I said.

THE FIREFIGHTER I'D SEEN the other night at the ER, Eva, was on duty when Sam called 911 and summoned an ambulance. Cindy looked like she couldn't decide if this was divine retribution or if she should start mouth-to-mouth. Fortunately, she'd sort of frozen, kneeling a few feet away from me, and once the emergency workers arrived she was basically boxed out and ended up retreating to the porch to watch the drama unfold.

"I know you," Eva said. "You're Dez's friend, right?" I recognized her from the other two times I'd seen her. She had beautiful black curly hair that wanted to spring out of its ponytail and perfect, pinpoint freckles all over her cheeks. Her eyes were a rich brown, much darker than Dez's, but just as friendly and kind. She had the lovely sort of face that felt like it was a good one to see as your last. Lucky for me.

While I forced back tears, I managed to tell her about my symptoms. She put an oxygen mask on me and then I was loaded onto a gurney and wheeled to the ambulance.

On the ambulance, she took my blood pressure and attached some kind of sticky pads to my chest while she talked to me. "Didn't get enough of the ER the other night?"

Did she not understand that I was dying? I couldn't find words, but she must've read my panic, because she took my hand. "I know this is scary. But all your vital signs and your heart rate and rhythm look good. I think it's going to be fine. Besides, Dez outranks me, and I get the impression that if I don't take perfect care of you, my life at work would be a living hell."

I tried to speak, but she shook her head. "Keep breathing that oxygen, okay? That's your job right now. That's it. Nothing more or less."

A FEW MINUTES LATER, an ER doctor who looked a bit too much like my father for my liking looked over my EKG results. "Not a heart attack," he declared. "I think we do need to have a chat about your stress levels though."

"Why?" I asked, propping myself up a bit in the hospital bed.

"I believe what you had was a significant panic attack. It can manifest a lot like a heart attack. Shortness of breath. Sweating. Cold. Chest pain. Which leads me to believe you have something going on that we need to address. Are you under a lot of pressure right now? Personal, work, or otherwise?"

All of the above. Under other circumstances, I would've brushed it off, assuring everyone I was fine, apologizing for the inconvenience, rapidly applying some lip gloss when no one was looking. But that would've been a moot point. My hair was flat, and not in a good way, and I'd literally arrived on a stretcher. I nodded.

"I think you need to come up with some strategies to reduce it. While this wasn't a heart attack, chronic or acute stress is actually not good for your heart health."

"What do I do?" I asked. It came out a bit more plaintive than I'd intended.

"It'll look a bit different for each person. You might want to consider talking to a psychologist. Some people have great results with meditation; others benefit from medication. There's no right or wrong answer—except trying to ignore it."

"What about yoga, Doc?"

I looked up to where the curtain was parting, and there was Dez.

"Gentle yoga, yes, that is another option. Whatever works well for you to reduce stress and help you develop better coping strategies is fine. But find something. And do it soon."

I pressed my lips together. "Thank you."

The doctor left, and Dez sat on the stool he'd vacated and rolled it over toward me. "Fancy meeting you here. Again."

He tipped his head to the side. "Rough day?"

"Let me guess, Eva called you. Isn't that breaking the Hippocratic Oath or something?"

"Depends?"

"On what?"

"Whether you're glad I'm here."

"I'm glad you're here." I meant it. When I'd heard his voice, relief had swelled in me. I'd been acutely aware of how alone I was up to that point. I had no one. He reached for my good hand. "I might even try your yoga suggestion."

Dez smiled. "You know, I wasn't always into it either. Growing up in Baltimore, I played these really physical sports, football, lacrosse, rugby, like I was telling you this morning." His smile faded. "I went through a pretty rough time a couple years back. It made me feel disconnected from the world and my body, and I didn't like that feeling. I was running one day in Canton Waterfront Park and there was this yoga class going on . . . I don't know . . . I just felt drawn to it. You ever feel drawn to something like that? Like the universe is sending you toward the exact thing you needed?"

I swallowed.

He stroked the skin on the back of my hand. "It made me feel grounded and gave me a tiny bit of peace. After that, I was hooked."

It was a strange sensation, having someone describe a set of emotions you barely understood yourself. I smoothed the thin hospital blanket over me. "Why were you having a hard time?" I asked.

Dez cleared his throat, and for a second, I thought, *I shouldn't have asked him this.* "I—"

"Where is she? Violet!" Kyra burst into the hospital room, completely missing Dez and practically flinging herself onto me. Her words came out in rapid succession. "Thank goodness you're alive! Sam called me. He said you were having a coronary. Are you okay? What did the doctor say? I knew I shouldn't have been encouraging you to eat all those doughnuts!"

"Kyra, I'm fine," I said. "It's not the doughnuts. Apparently, I had a panic attack. It's no big deal. I just need to de-stress, that's all."

"Oh, thank God. I was beside myself."

Kyra finally caught sight of Dez. She looked from him to me and back again, slowly, like it was all sinking in. "Have I been replaced as your emergency contact?"

"Not at all," Dez said, rising to his feet and extending a hand. "I was in the neighborhood."

"Sure," Kyra said. She reached out and shook Dez's hand, hard. "Nice to meet you, sexual sage. I'm the best friend."

Twenty-Four

I WAS DISCHARGED WITH A printout of local therapists and a tentative promise that I'd at least think about trying out one of Dez's sun salutation morning yoga classes. Kyra drove me home.

"Thanks for coming," I told her. "I know it was probably a pain to race all the way over here for nothing."

"I'm just glad you're okay. When Sam called me out of the blue and said you were on your way to the emergency room, it really freaked me out."

"He was worried?"

"Not that I'm trying to win that piece of junk any points, but yeah, he was. I've never heard him sound like that."

I mulled it over for a moment. With everything that had happened, it seemed hard to believe. But somehow the knowledge also made the constant brutal sting I'd been feeling almost all of the time since I found out just a little less intense.

"Don't you start feeling sorry for him," Kyra said. "He didn't come himself, did he? No. He sent me. That man deserves no mercy from you. What happened anyway? He said he was just having a perfectly normal conversation with you and this came out of nowhere. Like I'm supposed to believe that. He probably was frantic because he knew it was his fault. What did he say to you to upset you that badly?"

I shrugged and ran a finger over the smooth surface of the passenger-side window. "He's mad about the column . . . unsurprisingly. I think I was just overwhelmed. My neighbor barged in and accosted me about the bonfire and seeing me and Dez making out in the doorway this morning. And then Sam called and wasn't happy. It was *a lot*."

"I guess it's not totally unbelievable that Sam would be upset. The whole world knows what he did now."

"I know the column went viral, but really, how many people in Sam's circle pay attention to that kind of thing? A few Twitter shares don't mean anything."

"Violet—and I say this professionally, okay? So heed my words—you're basically a cultural phenomenon now." She bit her lip.

"What?"

"The *News and Observer* ran a story on Sam in the online edition."

I closed my eyes. "How was it?"

"Not great. Let's just say that if Sam wanted to go into politics, he probably will need to wait until everyone either forgets about it or dies."

Every time we went to the University Club, there were murmurs about Sam running for state senate. His dad had been a senator, and his mother had high hopes of Sam taking over his father's old seat. I'm sure that in her mind, getting rid of the lackluster wife who hadn't birthed a namesake and had no accomplishments other than her "cute little hobby in the paper" was a big step in that direction. As for Sam, he never said much when I brought it up, but I had seen a campaign registration website in his browser history last spring.

"That would definitely explain why he had such a strong response."

"I can tell you're not telling me everything. Kind of like how you conveniently left out the fact that Firefighter Dez is smoking hot. Don't think I missed you dropping the whole *Cindy caught us making out this morning* . . . You told me that kiss was a onetime thing. Not that I'm judging; if I was available and had someone that fine bringing me coffee and offering to butter my biscuits, you bet your ass I'd be partaking on the regular."

I pretended not to hear her. My very biscuit-buttering, kind-of-wonderful, wholly confusing relationship with Dez wasn't the only thing I'd kept to myself. Kyra still had no idea that Sam was threatening to sue me unless I fixed the damage my column had done to his reputation. I'd also failed to tell my best friend the real trigger—the worst thing Cindy had said. Her words had cut much deeper than the glass shard that had pierced my hand the other night, but that wasn't anything anyone needed to know about.

· Twenty-Five ·

Dear Sweetie,

I'm a thirty-four-year-old woman with no children. My husband and I have been together since college, and everyone just seems to expect that we should have our two-point-five kids by now. I can't tell you how many times I've been asked when we're finally going to start a family or why we don't have any children. It seems like not being a mother makes me a bad wife, a selfish woman, or a left-out friend.

When my husband and I got together, we both agreed that we didn't want to have kids. We like children, but they just weren't our dream. Recently, he brought up the idea of trying to have a family. The truth is, as much as I want to make him happy and satisfy all the people in my life who think I should be a mother, I just don't want a baby. I have a great career and a fulfilling life and am happy as I am, as we are, the two of us.

I guess my question is, how do I tell all the people who want me to have a baby, including my husband, that I don't want to without ruining everything?

Sincerely,
Childless and Content

....

Dear Childless and Content,

The whole notion of nosy people always asking about the status of a woman's uterus is a classic advice column conundrum. It's simple. With the exception of your husband, your decision to have a baby or not is none of their damn business.

Now, I think we've all realized recently that I'm certainly not the best advice source when it comes to marital relations, but I'll still give this my best shot. You and your husband had a deal—neither of you wanted kids—and now he's changed his mind. That happens sometimes. People evolve; their dreams change. Their tastes change. Sometimes for the better, sometimes not.

It sounds to me like you didn't talk to your husband after he announced his change of heart. I get it. It's super awkward, and marriage is full of all sorts of little things that we don't disclose for the sake of harmony and happiness, right? I know someone who hid onions in her husband's beef stroganoff for years because he claimed he didn't like them, but it doesn't taste right without them, and he scarfed it right down none the wiser. That sort of thing. In fact, that's why right now, all across America, and probably the world, people are faking orgasms. We wouldn't want to hurt their feelings, right? Especially when they are trying So. Damn. Hard. Seriously. Maybe too hard in some cases, ahem, and a little to the left.

But this isn't faking an orgasm—this is a baby, a joint decision. It's not like waiting until your partner hops into the shower and finishing the job yourself. A baby is a lifelong commitment, something akin to the one that you and your husband made when you got married and vowed in good times and in bad. And despite the fact that I know all too well that plenty of people don't honor those promises, you both should. And it starts by being honest with your husband. If I'm not reading too much into it, you're in a good place and don't want things to change. That's okay. You don't need to have an explanation. You do need to be honest though. Try something like this: *Honey, I love you. But I still don't love the idea of trying to have a baby.* Maybe y'all could get a puppy? See where the conversation goes. And as for those other nosy people, next time someone asks you when you're having a baby or why not, you can tell them that unless they've become your gynecologist in the last two minutes, they should mind their manners and their own damn body parts.

Sincerely,
Dear Sweetie

....

Twenty-Six

KYRA HAD TOLD ME to take a few days off to de-stress, and for once I'd taken her up on it. I think she probably had envisioned naps and deep-breathing exercises, but I'd never been great at either of those things, so after I slept Wednesday away, I turned to cleaning. Cleaning was a good coping mechanism, I wagered. It made me feel in control and it would leave the house sparkling in case any more unpleasant neighbor pop-ins occurred. Could Cindy see her reflection in her baseboards? I thought not.

I'd read somewhere that the chemicals used for cleaning could damage the metal and precious stones in rings, so I'd stood in front of the sunny kitchen window and slid them off over the sink. I turned my hand over in the light, taking in its strange nakedness, the indent where the platinum bands had deformed the skin below for twelve years. Those years had changed me too. I used to be afraid that I'd drop my rings down the drain, accidentally, and never see them again. Now I thought how relieved I'd feel if they happened to fall into the unknown depths of the garbage disposal. I settled for dropping them into a mug hidden way back in a cabinet, which I had to stand on a chair to reach, and then I got to work.

I'd finished the kitchen and moved on to the living room when my phone buzzed. I stopped scrubbing to glance at the display and smiled. Dez.

"Hey there," he said. "How's the patient? Feeling better, I hope."

"I don't anticipate needing to go on an ambulance ride anytime soon," I said.

"I have mixed feelings about that."

I laughed. "How's that?"

"Well, you not needing medical assistance is a very good sign. But then again, it's one less chance for me to see you. Guess that means I'll have to get creative."

I dropped the sponge I was holding. "Oh . . ." I had a light feeling in my chest, a bouncy castle sensation that was the opposite of the crushing pressure I'd felt the day before.

"What are you up to right now?"

Angst cleaning did not seem like a good answer; what I needed here was to sound breezy and well adjusted. "Just tidying up. Nothing really."

"Good, because I have two tickets and a real hankering for a fried Oreo."

"Fried Oreo? Didn't the doctor say I needed to protect my heart health?"

"I've got a plan for that, and an extra ticket. So, what do you say, Violet? Will you go to the state fair with me?"

Dez's request, which sounded a lot like a date—a notion that filled me with equal parts glee and nervousness—was impossible to resist.

"Yes," I said, and as soon as we'd made a plan for him to pick me up, I scrambled upstairs to do my hair.

AMONG THE THINGS THAT North Carolina does real well, other than barbecue, friendliness, and pollen (thanks to our bounty of beautiful trees), is its state fair. I hadn't been in ages, but it was just as delightful as I remembered, bursting with color and lights, the smell of funnel cakes and fried Twinkies, and a sea of people who were, let's face it, pretty fun to watch. There were horse shows and rides galore; the state's biggest pumpkin and a world-record-holding cow; and some kind of weird lumberjack competition that I was fairly certain Dez could've won based on his physical prowess, if he hadn't been totally preoccupied with the plush panda that he'd won me at an extreme toss game under one arm and a powder-sugar-covered funnel cake on a grease-soaked paper plate. He alternated the dough between us, taking giant bites, then holding it out for me to do the same.

"What next?" he asked, sucking some powdered sugar from his thumb. "We've hit the games pretty hard, we've had snacks . . ."

"I thought you said you had some sort of plan on the phone."

"It's early. We'll get to that."

"Bumper cars?"

"I know about you!" Dez laughed. "Can't resist ramming people with cars, can you?"

I gave him a playful whack on the arm and took an extra-large bite of the funnel cake. He stopped.

"What?" I said. "I'll eat the rest if you make another comment about my driving."

He shook his head. "You got a little powdered sugar there, Vi." He brushed his thumb over my bottom lip, and my knees nearly buckled. I ran my tongue over the spot he'd just touched.

"Did I get it?" I asked.

"Not quite." His thumb pressed gently into my chin, and then he dipped his head in and kissed me. "Sweet," he said, pulling back.

Lord, grant me strength. My heart was racing and I was pretty sure it wasn't the sugar overload. We stood there for a moment, looking at each other while people moved around us, blurring into streaks of color and sound. Calliope music, a bluegrass band, and . . . crying. Dez's brow furrowed.

"You hear that?" I asked. "Someone's crying."

He nodded. "Sounds like a kid." His head swiveled, searching the crowd. A few feet away from us, a child stood wearing a Hurricanes jersey that was about five sizes too big for her. She had a mop of curly red hair and her face was crimson and slick with tears. Dez jogged across the crowd and I followed.

When we reached the child, Dez knelt down so he was at her level. "What's wrong? Are you lost?"

"I can't find my mommy!" she wailed.

"It's going to be okay," he said calmly. "I'm Dez. I'm a firefighter. Can you tell me your name?"

"Milly," she said hiccupping.

"Hi, Milly. This is my good friend Violet. We're going to help you find your mommy."

She looked at him, her little lip trembling.

"Isn't that right, Violet?"

I nodded and crouched down. "We sure will. Do you know your mommy's phone number?" I asked.

She shook her head. Dez looked at me. "I'm sure there's a safety booth somewhere around here. They can help locate her mom. I'll go find it."

"Hang on a second," I said. I looked at the little girl. "I like your backpack. Is that Mrs. Wuf on it?"

She nodded.

"She's my favorite. I went to NC State, so I got to meet her. I miss her so much. Do you mind if I take a look?"

She slid the tiny furry backpack off and I unzipped the front compartment. I held it open in front of Dez, nudging him with my shoulder. There was the name *Milly* and a phone number inside. Dez already had his phone out and was dialing. "See, Dez is calling your mom right now, okay? It's going to be fine." Milly continued to sob, unconvinced. I eyed the panda tucked under Dez's arm. He caught my eye and we had a quick, silent exchange. He winked at me.

"I know you like wolves," Dez said. "But how do you feel about pandas?"

He held the stuffed animal out, and Milly's face brightened. "I love pandas," she said, reaching out tentatively. Once the panda was in her hands, she sniffed a few times, clutched it tightly to her chest, and then stopped crying. A few minutes later, a woman with flaming red hair and a giant turkey leg in her hand came running through the crowd.

"Milly!" she yelled. The little girl's face brightened and she grabbed on to her mom's leg. After a tearful reunion and enough thanks to make us all uncomfortable, Dez turned to me.

"Nice work there," he said.

I tried to smile.

Dez looked at me. He smoothed a hand over my hair. "Do you want me to win you another panda?" he asked gently. But I could tell that wasn't what he meant. He was asking why I seemed so sad suddenly. I shook my head.

"Maybe we should go," I said. "I'm kind of tired. I probably shouldn't have eaten that funnel cake."

"How about this? Can we try one more thing, and if you don't feel better, I'll take you straight home?"

I pulled in a deep breath; I could do this. I was the queen of being a good sport. "Okay, I'll try your thing, whatever *it* is."

"I was hoping you'd say that." Dez reached over and threaded his fingers through mine. He'd touched my hand before, but this was the first time without my rings. I still wasn't used to the empty space there, but Dez fit it perfectly. I hesitated for a moment before I closed my hand around his. He gave my hand a squeeze and then took off at a jog.

I found myself deeply regretting agreeing to try Dez's plan a few minutes later when I stood, breathless, staring up into the sky at some massive metal contraption called the Tower of Doom. "I take it back," I said, ducking behind him.

Dez sidestepped and then circled an arm around my waist. Over my shoulder he said, "But then you won't be able to do the thing that will make you feel better."

"And what is that, exactly? Vomiting?"

"No . . . screaming."

I looked back up at the tower. It was plummeting down, and blood-curdling screeches filled the air. I didn't see how that was going to help. He must've sensed my skepticism.

"I told you I went through a really tough time a while back, right? Well, the thing that got me through was Six Flags."

"Really?" I turned to face him. "I thought it was yoga."

"This was before the yoga. I was full of hurt and so much anger; I just couldn't get out from under it. It sat on my chest all the time. One of my sisters, Amber—she's the oldest and the wisest—got me a pass to Six Flags. She told me to get on the wildest rides and scream my heart out until my throat was raw and my lungs burned. Over and over again. She called it scream therapy."

I raised my eyebrows at him but said nothing.

"I know it sounds completely bonkers," he said. "But it helped. After a while, I felt unburdened somehow. I thought maybe it would be good for you to have a safe place to scream. And look at it this way: no one will be looking at you. They'll all be yelling too."

I glanced back up at the tower. Dez leaned toward me. "I'll be honest with you," he said in a low voice. "I know I told you I'm a bit of a thrill seeker, but actually this ride freaks the hell out of me, so I wouldn't do it if I didn't think that it would help. I promise, I'll be right there with you."

I sighed. When he put it that way, it was very hard to say no. And there was a part of me that didn't want to. There was another part of me that was deeply concerned about what the ride was going to do to my hair. But I let him give the attendant our tickets, help me with my harness, and hold my hand again. I squeezed my eyes shut while some sort of chain system raised the apparatus to the top.

"You've got this, Violet!" Dez said.

I shook my head. I'd opened my eyes and seen how high we were. "No, I really don— Ahhhhhhhh!" The bottom dropped out and we plummeted and I screamed. I screamed until my ears rang, until I ran out of air, until my throat ached, and my chest was on fire, and I felt lighter than air. I screamed for every time I'd held my feelings in and faced them alone while they festered inside of me. At the bottom, I turned to Dez.

"So," he shouted, "did it work?"

"Can we go again?"

DEZ AND I RODE the Tower of Doom until we ran out of tickets. The sky turned dark against the bright lights of the rides. I bought us those cheesy graffiti T-shirts from a vendor booth. I picked *Hot Stuff* for Dez's T-shirt and he picked *Screamer* for mine.

"Screamer?" I said. "Don't you think people might take that the wrong way?"

"Who cares?" he said, pulling it over my head and the long-sleeved shirt I was wearing.

"What is that like?" I asked.

"What?"

"Not caring what people think? I can't even imagine it."

"It's not that I don't care—I just only care what the important people think, like my family, or my crew . . . or you. Random fairgoers, not so much. You should give it a try."

People did give me some looks, but I was trying not to pay any attention. Besides, people-watching was part of the fair experience. It was just that now, I was one of the people being watched. Finally, hoarse and not wanting to face the port-a-potty experience, we called it a day. A great day. Dez drove me home, opened his truck door for me, and walked me up to the porch.

"Thank you," I said. "I had a really good time."

"Same to you, screaming Violet. Thanks for my shirt."

"It's the least I could do after all the things you've done for me."

He shook his head. "Don't say that. Caring about someone isn't a bank account. There's no balance sheet. Besides, I get something out of helping you."

"What's that?" I said, not entirely convinced.

Dez looked down at me, his gaze soft. I leaned against the doorjamb. "Time with you."

"Not sure that's quite the prize you're making it out to be."

"I'm guessing somewhere along the way someone taught you that lesson, but it's not true. I can assure you, Violet, I know exactly how I feel when I'm around you."

I looked down. Dez brushed his thumb over my cheek. "Maybe it's too soon, and you're not ready, and if that's the case, I accept that. I won't bring it up again, but if there's a chance . . . I'd really like to show you."

"Show me what?" I said, my hoarse voice barely a whisper. My heart hammered against my rib cage.

"How you should be treated." He stepped closer and smoothed

my hair away from my face. His strong hands, which were capable of breaking down doors and wrestling people from fiery infernos, still surprised me with their tenderness. He leaned down and kissed me. It wasn't the kind of searching passion that left me weak. It was a question. And in that moment, I wanted to be the answer. I wrapped my arms around his neck and pressed myself to him.

"I want you to stay with me tonight," I said.

He pulled back, just a fraction. "Are you sure, Violet?" he asked. "I know what I said, but we don't have to rush this."

I nodded. There were so many things I was unsure of—what the hell I was doing with my life, for one. What tomorrow would bring. But in this moment, I was certain that I wanted to be with him. I waited for him to say something. In the quiet, I could hear my own breathing.

He swept me up into his arms. Just like that. Like I was nothing. Like I was everything. Like he was rescuing me from my inferno of heartache. "Wait a minute," I said. "Are *you* sure?"

He laughed. "Why do you think I didn't want to sleep near you that night? I didn't think it was smart to be within arm's reach of you." He lowered his voice. "You're like a force of nature."

I bit my lip. It had been a long time since I'd desired anything more than a baked good. Wanting things was a path to getting hurt. Wanting Dez should've been scary, but it wasn't. I'd been so careful, tiptoeing through my own life, shoving my own desires down, making sure things didn't blow up in my face, and they did anyway. And in Dez's strong arms, my whole being felt like a firework about to go off.

He carried me upstairs and lowered me onto the mattress. Then he glanced down at my new *Screamer* T-shirt. "I love the sentiment," he said, "but if you don't mind, I'm going to have to take it off of you." And with that, with his bright smile and powerful arms holding me, I forgot about every single bit of pain, about my messed-up hair and my messier life. It was just me and him. He settled himself over me, dragging his lips over my bare collarbone, and his fingertips lowered, awakening every nerve as he went, and I let myself go.

I WOKE SOMETIME AFTER dawn. I'd heard the even breathing, felt the warmth radiating from the body beside me, and for a moment, I thought everything that had happened had been a dream. A strange, confusing dream. I turned toward the sound, heavy-lidded.

It wasn't a dream. There was Dez, his face peaceful, his lips slightly parted. I watched him for a moment, following the line of his jaw with my gaze, stopping for a moment at a small scar on his chin. I hadn't noticed it before. I wanted to trace it with my fingers and ask him its origin story. I wanted to mold myself against him until I no longer existed on my own. He stirred a little and the reality of the situation descended on me like a blinding slice of light that illuminated my tangled hair and smeared lipstick in the mirror across the room. It was the funnel cake and the screaming. I quickly slid out from beneath the covers and started crawling toward the closet so he wouldn't see me.

"Hey," Dez said, sleep in his voice. I froze.

"Heeeyyy," I said, my voice so high-pitched, neighborhood dogs probably were covering their ears with their paws.

"Did you get some rest?"

"A little. I was just about to get dressed for work."

"Oh, I thought you were taking off for a few days."

"I probably shouldn't," I said. "I don't want to get behind right now. It's a critical time with the syndication and everything."

"Makes sense. I should get going too. I promised Eva I'd help her husband assemble some elaborate storage unit in their playroom."

My phone dinged on the nightstand. Dez turned toward the sound and I used the opportunity to scramble into the closet and throw on a robe. I hadn't bothered to fix the hangers in there since I'd ripped all of Sam's clothing off of them. It looked like we'd been robbed. I reminded myself there was no reason to feel guilty about what happened with Dez. I'd given myself willingly too—we'd been two forces of nature, magnetism and heat, swirling around each other, and as a result I looked like a person who'd been spit out by a tornado.

I should've run into the bathroom, I thought, considering my exit strategy. At least there I had makeup and styling tools, which were sorely in need in my current state. I took a couple of deep breaths, smoothed down my hair, and then opened the closet door. Dez was standing about an inch back from the doorway. I gasped.

"Thought you might want this," he said. He held out my phone in his palm.

I took it from him. "Thanks."

He grabbed his jeans and tugged them back on in one smooth motion. I turned my attention to the phone screen and the missed message there. It was from Sam.

I'm out of work clothes. And since you took my keys, leave the door unlocked. I'll be over at 7:30 AM.

I clapped one hand over my mouth.

"Everything alright over there?" Dez asked. He'd just finished tying one of his shoes.

I glanced at Dez and then back at the clock on my phone. It was 7:21. "Oh my God."

"Seriously, Violet, are you okay, or are you panicking? 'Cause you look a little like you're about to set fire to something."

"Too late," I said.

There was no time for talking about what had transpired the previous evening. For one thing, I didn't have the faintest idea what to say about it. It was amazing and complicated, and I really hoped it wasn't a mistake. For another, Sam was on his way over to discover that I'd destroyed all his stuff. I did not need him to see what else I'd done—especially since it'd only been two days since he was hollering about suing me. He was going to be devastated about Michael Jordan. Losing that autographed jersey was a tragedy. Losing me, not so much. But that didn't mean Dez and I could just sit down to breakfast and wait to greet Sam. That would be disastrous. I had to think fast. I snatched a shirt dress from a hanger and threw it over my head.

"You want to talk about it?" Dez asked on the way downstairs.

"No. It's nothing."

"This isn't about last night, is it? Are you having regrets?"

I had so many regrets. I wasn't sure if last night was one of them yet, and I didn't have time to decide. I shook my head. "It's not, I promise."

We'd reached the bottom step. Dez turned and tucked a rogue strand of my hair behind my ear. "Glad to hear it. I'd feel like a real asshole if you weren't okay with it by the light of day. Actually, I guess that would make me worse than an asshole, because I let you go through with it." He didn't sound entirely convinced.

"Rest assured, you're not. If anything, I'm the cad in this situation. But an actual asshole is going to be here in about four minutes. And it's a bit of a fiasco because he's coming for his work clothes that you had to spray with a hose that one time, so I don't have them, and to top it all off with a cherry, it's morning and you're *here*."

Dez held up his hands. "Say no more." He kissed my forehead. "I'm not about to complicate your domestic situation. I'll cut through the backyard."

He headed to the kitchen, pausing only to wave as he opened the back door and flashed me a warm smile. "I'll call you," he said.

My heart lifted a little at that.

But there was still the issue of the missing clothes. I had a flash of inspiration—the hall closet! I'd seen some dry cleaning in there when I'd pulled out the Lilly Pulitzer dress the other day. I raced over and flung open the door. Please. Please. Bingo. There were two pairs of dress slacks, four shirts, and a nice tie in the plastic garment bags. I glanced at my phone screen: 7:28. I headed to the porch and dragged over one of our rocking chairs, which I hooked the coat hangers on. Then I planned to drive away. I wouldn't see Sam on my way out of the cul-de-sac, because the universe would finally cut me a break after the infidelity and the Lillian run-in and the cut hand. Maybe Dez's scream therapy had finally set me free from all the things that hurt me.

It was a good thing that my column wasn't about avoiding an unpleasant run-in with your estranged spouse, because wishful thinking was not an effective evasion technique. I was just locking the front door when I heard a car in the driveway. I squeezed my eyes shut for a moment, retrieved the hanging clothes, fixed my posture, and started down the steps.

"Violet," Sam said.

"Here are some clothes," I said. "I'm just leaving."

"You're out of the hospital then."

I twisted the keys in my hand. "Yeah, they didn't keep me. I'm fine."

"I see that. That's a relief."

I stifled a haughty laugh. "Is it?"

"You know what I mean."

"Actually, I don't."

He nodded, lips a tight line. "Mind letting me into the house?"

"Yes, I mind. This should be enough stuff to get you through until your dry cleaning is ready."

He thumbed the hangers. "This is it? I really wanted my pink shirt, and I need some ties. I know you're pissed, but can't we be civil? I won't take anything that's not mine. I just want my Jordan stuff and my work clothes."

I eyed him. He resembled the man I'd loved, but he was changed somehow. Hard where he'd once been soft. Mean. He used to fill me up, and now I felt deflated. I tried to force my shoulders back, but I might as well have been wearing a white flag instead of a pinstripe dress. I muttered, "They're gone."

"Come again?" he asked, his tone so sharp I felt an instant surge of adrenaline.

"I said"—raising my voice and finally straightening up just a bit—"they're gone. Your fancy clothes, your Jordan memorabilia . . . all those things that were more important to you than me. I burned them all. I dragged them out in the street with the bedsheets and poured your precious scotch on the heap and set them on fire."

"You're shitting me," he snapped. "Stop messing around and give me my stuff."

"You're not listening to me. You *never* listen to me. Your stuff is gone."

Sam's expression clouded. I started to shiver. "How could you do that, Violet?!" he seethed.

"You broke my heart!" I yelled. "Don't you get it? You betrayed every promise we ever made, you made a fool out of me, and then you left me all alone in this house. What did you think would happen, Sam? I wanted to hurt you like you hurt me. And that was the only way I knew how to do it."

Sam dropped into one of the rocking chairs. "I can't believe this.

When I heard about the column, I knew you were off the rails, but I never thought you'd truly snapped."

"I didn't snap, you broke me!" There was a tremor in my voice, but I didn't cry.

"Sure, don't take any accountability, Violet. It's not like I lit the match."

I thought of myself on the Tower of Doom. There it didn't matter what I sounded like: I had a voice and I was damn well going to use it. I filled my lungs with air, coiling myself like a spring. "It wasn't a match! I used a goddamned firecracker!" I screamed. At his stunned expression, I lowered my voice. "It could've been worse. I almost sold your Star Wars stuff, but I decided not to."

"Oh, well, thanks very much, Violet."

"You know, I'm just starting to realize, I don't owe you a damn thing. So you're welcome, Sam. Now get off my porch."

· Twenty-Seven ·

I DROVE TO WORK, GRIPPING the steering wheel tightly to keep my hands from trembling. A strange mix of adrenaline, fear, and elation seemed to be coursing through my veins. I could just imagine everyone I knew wondering what the hell had come over me, and I didn't really have an answer. All I knew was that I was *awake*.

I met Kyra next to the coffeemaker. She was wearing a gorgeous magenta-and-yellow A-line dress that made her brown skin look radiant. She eyed me while she added packets of sugar and Coffeemate to her *Boss B!itch* mug.

"Good morning," I said. "Cute dress."

"Someone's in a good mood."

"More like in shock."

Kyra leaned her back against the counter and took a sip of her coffee. "Do I want to know why you're in shock?"

"Eventful morning," I squeaked out, but it sounded unconvincing, as if I were posing it as a question.

"You are not an artful dodger, Violet. And I have a meeting with some board members in a few minutes, so spill."

"Sam showed up at the house."

Kyra raised one of her perfectly arched eyebrows.

"He needed his work clothes. You can probably imagine about how well that went, seeing as I burned most of them."

"Okay then. That *is* an eventful morning—and you're supposed to be avoiding stress. Did he flip?"

"Sort of. Not as much as *I* did though." I took a gulp of my coffee and burned the roof of my mouth.

"Violet Covington flipping her lid? Now that's somethin' I'd love to see. What exactly did you do?"

I turned my attention to stirring my coffee vigorously with a spoon. "I may have screamed in his face."

"And what, may I ask, led to this empowering transformation? In all my years, I don't think I've ever heard you raise your voice. I didn't know you had other volume settings."

"The Tower of Doom."

"I don't follow."

"Dez took me to the state fair yesterday and he gave me scream therapy."

Kyra sputtered when she tried to respond. She set her coffee cup down on the counter and patted her chest a couple of times. "Let me get this straight." She paused to clear her throat. "You and the sexual sage firefighter did . . . scream therapy . . . at the state fair."

"Yeah. We rode the Tower of Doom."

"Is that what you call it?" Kyra dissolved into giggles.

"Oh my God, Kyra. I shouldn't have told you."

"No, sorry, Violet. I'll be good. I just want to hear more about his Tower of Doom."

My cheeks flamed. I rotated away from Kyra.

"Wait. Why are you hiding?" Kyra grasped the sleeve of my blouse. "I was just teasing . . . Did I, *no*, he doesn't call—"

"There's nothing doomlike about it," I said, hiding my face in my hands.

"Okay, I want to hear more about this extremely interesting development later. I'm taking you to lunch." She glanced at her watch. "I need to head to my meeting, and you, Dear Sweetie, have a message on your desk that you're going to want to read."

I drank my coffee in the break room, afraid that everyone in the newsroom would be able to tell my whole scandalous story by my pink-stained cheeks when I walked by. When I couldn't put it off any longer, I scampered to my desk and practically flung myself into the safety of my cubicle walls. There was a note scrawled on a pink Post-it: *Check your email. She called me when she emailed you.* I logged in and went straight to my inbox.

Dear Violet,

We're reaching out to you with an exciting opportunity. Our team has been *completely* absorbed in your story, and we're thinking that it might make for an interesting feature for our readers at *Gloss* magazine. We'd like to run an article in the December issue of *Gloss*: 1,500 words on "Life After Love." You can pull from your own experiences and write a "how to get over heartbreak" for readers. If the response is good, we can talk about making it a regular column.

The timing to go to print is a bit tight, I'm afraid. We'd need your story by October 23 at the absolute latest.

All the best,
Olivia Hazelwood
Editor in Chief
Gloss magazine

I leaned back in my chair. Holy shit. *Gloss* magazine was a top-five women's mag; everyone I knew read it. I even subscribed. And they wanted me—not Sweetie, but Violet Covington—to write for them . . . if this trial worked out, that is. I could write about getting over heartbreak, sure—get mad and move on? That could work. I mean, yes, I now owned a graffiti-style state fair T-shirt and a hard-earned case of laryngitis and had memorized the inside of the emergency room . . . but I also had a very kind, very sexy firefighter who liked being around me and thought I had charisma. Except I couldn't tell anyone that. I'd sent him out through the backyard this morning to avoid one judgmental neighbor and my probably soon-to-be ex-husband. I could just imagine the entire state clucking their tongues at me. No problem, I could go with something else, another angle entirely. I just needed to relax and let the ideas come to me.

I peeked at the calendar. October 23 was three days away.

THAT NIGHT, I ORDERED pizza from Anna's and ate it with a glass of red wine while parked in front of my laptop at the coffee table. Except for a two-minute phone conversation with Dez during which his voice had turned me into a pool of melted honey-butter and I'd shamelessly agreed to attend a morning yoga class with him, I'd spent the majority of my day brainstorming ideas for the "Life After Love" article, typing out two-hundred-word false starts, and pacing. I folded a large slice in half and took a bite. Why had Sam not liked this pizza? I tried to remember. It was delicious—the perfect ratio of cheese, sauce, and salt.

I planned to finish the column tonight so I'd have the rest of the weekend to edit, but everything I'd come up with sounded ridiculous or so trite that the idea of having my real name on the byline was more embarrassing than thinking of how I'd given Kyra the post-fair play-by-play at lunch and our waiter, who had overheard, winked at me and said, "Someone's a lucky girl."

I hoped the wine would loosen me up a little. But so far, I'd consumed four slices of pizza and one-and-a-half glasses of wine and I had nothing. What the heck was I going to do? This was the biggest break of my career, and I was not about to let it slip through my fingers. So, I did the thing only the most desperate of writers do when on deadline and stuck: I googled the article I was trying to write, for inspiration only of course, and ended up in some strange rabbit hole called Men's Guide to Divorce—a website that advocated finding healthy crutches such as sports versus unhealthy ones like pornography and drinking. I side-eyed my half-full wineglass.

My phone rang. "How's the article coming along?" Kyra asked. "I ran into Olivia at a luncheon a couple of weeks ago and might have dropped your name. So you'd better deliver."

"How did you get over your marriage ending?" I asked. "Because all I know is I'm doing a bang-up job writing a whole lot of nothing. Help."

"It's different for everyone. Me telling you my messy story over again isn't going to help you write something that's authentic to you."

"Being authentic is not necessarily my strong suit," I admitted. "I'm more used to putting on lipstick and a smile."

"That's your angle then."

"Maybe."

"Think about it. But I believe in you. Now get back to writing."

"What if I'm blocked?" I shrieked before she hung up.

"Change your font to Comic Sans and lady up then, Violet."

"That does not work," I said.

"My shelf full of awards says otherwise, friend."

I went to my document and switched the font, cursing Kyra's name as I typed out the first few hideous words.

To an outside observer, my marriage seemed to end in my bedroom, while I was locked in the bathroom putting on a layer of lipstick called Luscious Paradise.

Twenty-Eight

"I changed my mind about the yoga," I groaned into the phone. Writing the article had taken me through the full range of my emotions and most of the night. When I finally did get to bed, I wrestled with the memories of all the things I'd written, all my experiences that seemed to be on an endless loop, and now my body felt like some grass that had been ruminating in a cow's stomach chamber overnight.

"That's okay," Dez said. "I wasn't going to take you to class anyway. I heard the undercurrent of hesitation in your voice."

"Right. Hesitation." You know, or lust. Let's be real.

"I'm not sure you're ready for yoga just yet. Definitely not on a Saturday when the studio's jam-packed."

I rolled onto my back and stared up at the ceiling. "You just called to check on me then?"

"Actually, no. I'm here to pick you up. I'm outside your house."

I leaned over so I could peer out the window. There was Dez, clad in cargo shorts and a black T-shirt that was pulled taut over his broad shoulders, looking like a tall, beautiful desert mirage in the middle of the yard.

"Wait, if you're not taking me to yoga, where're you planning on taking me at the crack of dawn?"

"Come out and you'll see."

"I'm worn out," I confessed. "I barely slept last night. Writing for a magazine was a lot more work than I expected, especially since I had to sort through a lot of bad history to do it."

"There's a cure for that, you know."

"Oh yeah?" I said. "What's that?"

"Making some new memories. Now get that fine ass out of bed and get down here." The crease in Dez's left cheek that came out when he smiled was visible even from my bedroom window. In fact, that dimple was probably signaling Cindy from whatever telescope she seemed to have fixed on my house.

"It's not fine anymore; I quit boot camp."

"Agree to disagree."

"Come back in an hour. I need to get ready."

"Just throw something on."

I shook my head. "No can do. I have to take care of my hair."

"Not for me, you don't."

While I found that hard to believe—he probably couldn't see what we were dealing with from his vantage point—I gave in. I pulled on a pair of jean cutoffs and a pale pink V-neck, then slid on a pair of silver flip-flops. My hair was practically matted from my fitful night and in desperate need of a good washing, but I figured I had one of two options—a ballerina bun or a hat. I reached for my old beat-up Costa hat; it was hanging on a rack next to Sam's belts in the closet. He'd bought it for me years ago when he went on a fishing trip with Mark. Had he really gone with Mark? I wondered. Who knew? I set it back down. I went to wrap my hair into a bun but my bandage got in the way. I uncoiled the gauze over the bathroom sink. It stuck a bit to the stitches and the dried blood around them, but I finally got it all off. It wasn't pretty, that pinched line of skin, but at least I was able to twist my hair up into some semblance of a hairstyle that didn't look like I'd spent the night in jail sleeping one off. I put on some lip gloss and headed downstairs.

"I was beginning to wonder if you were coming," Dez said when he saw me.

"What can I say," I said. "*I* was hoping you brought croissants again."

"I'll take the joking as a good sign."

Behind him, long wisps of cloud were turning peach in the sunrise light. A mockingbird screeched from its perch in the crepe myrtle. He handed me a coffee. "You look great."

"Flattery and coffee," I said, raising an eyebrow. "You really are too good to be true. Don't get lost in my undereye circles."

"Only if you don't get lost in *my* undereye circles. I haven't been sleeping much lately, thanks to an adorable arsonist I met on a call who I can't stop thinking about. And I object to that characterization—I'm not flattering you, just speaking the truth. You always look great, but you without makeup is nice. It's different."

I scrunched up my nose. "Yeah, right."

"I'm dead serious. I don't think it's possible for you to look bad."

"How is it possible that you are single? You always say the right thing to make me feel better. You must've had a lot of girlfriends to be so wise."

"Not really. You might be surprised to know that I don't date that much. I've actually only had a couple of relationships since I graduated."

I gave him a skeptical look. "Sure."

"Seriously. Dating-wise, I pretty much peaked in high school. Jenny Tremaine, captain of the debate team, was my girlfriend for a semester and a half senior year." He flashed a playful smile. "Truthfully, all of my insights are thanks to my sisters and their training. Anyway, you up for a ride?" Dez asked.

"I guess so."

I had no idea what a ride was supposed to do for me, but the thought of getting away from here—from the house; from the prying, judging eyes of neighbors; from everything—did not seem like a bad idea at this point. "I'm over here," Dez said, tipping his head toward his Toyota 4Runner, which was parked in front of the picket fence. He held the passenger door open for me. I climbed in, feeling the closeness of him in my bones in a way that was visceral. My body deflated with disappointment when he closed the door and jogged around the front of the SUV. He got in and leaned toward me, swiveling to reach behind the seat.

"I did get croissants, by the way," he said, producing a bag from the back. "Maybe I am too good to be true. If I wasn't so into you, I'd be a little bit smitten with myself right now."

My eyes widened. Dez was *into* me. I had not been expecting a confession like that, let alone so casually, as if he'd said it a hundred times already. And even though I'd had fun with him at the fair and that night we'd spent together, I definitely had not been expecting to like hearing him say that as much as I did. I practically vibrated with giddy excitement, except there was also a piece of me that was remembering what it'd said on the Men's Guide to Divorce website about bad crutches. Right after porn and drinking was jumping straight into a new relationship. *Think the easiest way to get over someone is to get under someone else? Not so fast*, it'd said. Was that what I was doing? I took a croissant and held it out to him. He took a giant bite while I was still holding it. "So good," he said, and then resumed his chewing.

Screw the website. I had never wanted to be a croissant so badly. A tiny buttery flake was stuck to his lip and the sight of it there, just begging me to lean over and take it, was so tantalizing that I had to force myself to look out the window. The azaleas needed watering; I made a mental reminder for when I got home.

"Do you have other things going on today?" Dez asked.

I shook my head.

"No new columns to write?"

"I probably should rewrite the one I turned in yesterday, but I'm not up for it. Kyra can always run one of my old columns. We do that sometimes."

"Why should you rewrite it?"

"Well, for starters, I'm not anonymous anymore. And I told a woman who discovered she and her husband weren't on the same page about starting a family that not telling her husband she didn't want to have a baby wasn't like faking an orgasm."

Dez choked a little on his croissant. He had to thump his chest with the edge of his fist a few times.

"Sorry," I said. "I don't know what's come over me. I'm usually more polite and presentable. My mother would die if she knew I'd just said that aloud. Are you horrified?"

Dez smiled. "Not horrified . . . unless the faking bit is a hint, in which case, I have a lot of questions about what I can do to rectify that situation immediately," he said, but mercifully, he did not follow up . . . not that he had anything to worry about in that department. He most certainly did *not*.

He rested his arm on the console between us while he drove, and I could feel his heat on my bare skin. We drove east on what used to be called the outer beltline until it had been changed some years back because people found it confusing. The whole east/west they'd changed it to was even less clear for a circle, I'd thought at the time. The sun crested over the horizon in front of us, blazing and golden, promising a beautiful day. I still had no idea where we were headed.

Dez took 64 East toward the coast. "Are we going to the beach?" I asked.

"Why not?" he said. "You need to relax, right? What's more relaxing than a quiet day at the ocean?"

I opened my mouth to argue, but he was right.

"Back in Maryland, I used to love walking around the Inner Harbor, and going over to Calvert Cliffs and just feeling the sea. It's a good place to take your troubles and let them wash away."

"You don't strike me as a man who's troubled," I laughed.

"Yeah, 'cause my problems are resting with all those fossils at Calvert Cliffs. Someday an archeologist will stumble upon them." I wondered if I shouldn't have asked, but Dez smiled and put me at ease. What's more: after I ate the croissant, I leaned my head against the window and fell asleep for the rest of the ride.

WHEN I AWOKE, THE truck was parked next to a dune and Dez was already outside. I climbed out and then perched on the bumper. He was crouched next to a tire, airing it down.

I yawned and walked over to him. "Where are we?"

"Corolla," he said. "I was planning on Kill Devil Hills, but you were fast asleep, I figured you could use the extra rest. Besides, we might see some wild horses up here." Excitement flashed in his eyes.

"They're mean, you know."

He trapped my hand in his. "They're just protecting themselves."

Once the air pressure was down in all of the tires, we got back in, and Dez navigated the passage through the dunes and onto the beach. There weren't any other trucks out there—too early and not high season—but the tracks from the previous day were still visible. Despite owning a Jeep and living in North Carolina my whole life, I'd never been out driving on the beach before. My muscles braced and I gripped the handle over the door with my good hand while we slid into the track.

"I'm not sure this was a good idea," I told Dez.

"Don't worry."

"I'm not," I said. "It's just, should we be sliding around like this?"

"Isn't it fun?" He grinned.

"I think you and I might have different ideas of fun, you know, since you run into burning buildings and all."

Dez rested his hand on my thigh and gave me a look; he only took his eyes off the beach for an instant, but that moment, that eye contact was so full of intensity that I flushed.

"I don't think our ideas of fun are that different," he said in a low voice that set the ninety-eight percent of my body that was composed of water to a pleasant simmer.

The next stretch of beach was packed a bit harder, and the sliding subsided. The last holdout of tension in my body unwound with relief. Dez parked and we both got out. I pulled a deep breath of ocean air into my lungs. It was sweet and damp. There was a stiff breeze; it licked at the tendrils of hair along the nape of my neck that had escaped from my bun while I slept. Dez clasped my hand and together we jogged straight toward the waterline, chasing the waves as they receded from us and running from them when they came back. We let go of each other's hands, racing in different arcs. I'd played this game as a girl, every time, when I'd come with my mother. When I was very young, Dad had joined in on the fun. Later, Mom and I would come, just the two of us. She'd watch me from under the brim of a big hat, grinning at me. *Don't be too loud*, she'd say occasionally, if the volume of my delighted squeals exceeded appropriateness, but she never stopped smiling. I paused for a moment to catch my breath. A wave caught me, and cold foam sloshed up and soaked the hem of my jean shorts.

Dez laughed. "You should've seen your expression," he chortled, doubled over. A wave slammed into his shins and some water splashed up and hit him in the face. I dissolved into giggles.

"In some places, they'd call that karma," I called. I'd been walking toward him, I realized, because I was now in arm's reach. He was grinning at me, wiping the salt water from his chin with his forearm. I wanted him to kiss me, long and slow, so that our feet sank into the wet sand and eroded away, deeper and deeper. But he was already moving, jogging along the waterline. I chased after him, my lungs burning from the exertion and laughter and longing.

Dez spotted some horses in the grasses a ways away, so we dropped into the soft, dry sand above the high-tide line and watched them. I raked my fingers through the sand, finding a piece of a Scotch bonnet, a tiny lady's slipper that I tucked into the pocket of my shorts. The horses came nearer; a small one cantered a few circles around its mother.

"They're amazing," I said, surprised at how moved I was.

"Yeah," Dez agreed, his tone reverent, "they are." I turned to him and found him looking at me instead of the horses. He reached out and tucked a loose strand of hair behind my ear.

"Is it helping?" he asked me finally.

I nodded. I figured I should probably tell him how it was uncanny that he always knew how to make me feel better, but instead, I turned my attention to the waves. "It's hard to imagine there are probably a bunch of great white sharks out there feeding right now," I said. "It seems so innocent. If it were warmer, we'd be swimming in it and have no idea."

"I'm actually obsessed with the OCEARCH Shark Tracker. Ferg, the almost-twelve-foot great white, likes to hang out in Corolla this time of year, right?"

I nodded. "I remember going to the aquarium one time when I

was younger . . . probably a Girl Scout trip or something . . . and the staff person asked us what we thought the biggest predator in the ocean was. Of course, we were all like, what a ridiculous question—obviously, it's the great white shark."

Dez picked up a tiny tulip shell and held it out to me on his palm. "That's not the right answer." His tone was somewhere between a question and an answer, deep, soft, and knowing.

"It's man," I told him. "I was just thinking how this ocean is like life. You look at it and it seems so nice on the surface, cool and inviting, shimmering in the sun, but there's all these things lurking underneath; you can't see them. I keep wondering if I should have known. Like maybe I should've seen it coming. People say that it's never just one person's fault."

"I don't know much about what happened," he said after a moment. "But I know enough about you to know that it isn't your fault."

I shook my head. "I'm not so sure. What if it's like the shark . . . everyone thinks they're the problem, but really it's us that's the biggest predator."

Dez was quiet for a long time. The wind undid my bun and blew my hair into my face. He reached over and smoothed it back. "You're not the shark, Violet. You're not a predator. You may not be perfect; who is, right? I know I'm not. But you are kind and sweet. I think it means a lot that you're even asking yourself these things, but no good comes from blaming yourself for something that is out of your control. Take it from me."

I crossed my arms over my chest and nodded. The wind made my damp shorts and shirt chill against my skin.

"Are you cold?" Dez asked, rubbing my arms. "I forgot how windy it is out here."

"I should've thought to bring a jacket," I said. "I don't want to leave just yet. I'll tough it out."

Dez wrapped his arms around me. "Or, and I know this might sound like a wild idea, we could just go buy something for you to put on, and then come right back. I know you're a strong woman, but you don't always have to tough it out."

"How do you do that?" I asked, leaning my head against his neck.

"What?"

"Make everything better."

"Well, now you're just flattering me," he said, beaming.

WE HEADED BACK TO the truck, where Dez filled the tires back up and then took me to Kitty Hawk Surf Co., where we picked out sweatshirts and I bought a new trucker hat, which I put on over my wind-tossed hair.

"Very cute," Dez said, tapping the brim. I peered up at him. His mouth twitched, but he cleared his throat and sidestepped. "Now this. This is what we need." He held up a kite shaped like a paper airplane with black and rainbow stripes and a long streaming tail. I looked at him holding that kite, like a giant kid in the very best way, his eyes shining, his free hand tucked into the pocket of the new sweatshirt, and for an instant I thought, *This is* exactly *what we need.* I pushed the notion away.

Afterward, we got baskets of fried shrimp and hush puppies, Cheerwine in glass bottles, and slices of key lime pie from a restaurant down the street that stayed open year-round, then took it all to the beach and ate in the back of the truck, facing the ocean. When we'd had enough food, Dez set up the kite. He held it out to me. "You do the honors, Vi," he said.

"I've never been very good at kites," I told him.

He shrugged. "Give it a try. It's not magical. Just run for a bit and let the wind do the work."

Begrudgingly, I accepted the spool from him. I ran along for a few discouraging seconds, during which the kite bumped along the sand and nearly took out an unsuspecting sandpiper, before the wind snatched the kite high into the sky; I watched it swoop and swirl in the stiff breeze. Dez stood next to me, his hip bumping against mine. Wordlessly, he took the kite string from my hand and tied it to the open hatch of the truck. I sat in the bed of the truck, and he stood between my legs.

"You're an advice columnist," Dez said in a low voice. "What kind of advice would you have for a guy who really wants to kiss a woman who's maybe feeling ambivalent? Should he hold back like he's been doing all day, even though it's killing him? Or should he go for it?"

Hold back, that little voice in my head, that proper prissy one, screeched. But I wasn't listening to that voice right now. I should have shoved her in that Caboodle with my sparkly eye shadow in the way-back depths beneath the sink. "Who says she's ambivalent?" I said.

Dez slid his hands around my waist to my back, just under the hem of my sweatshirt. They were warm and slightly rough against my skin. He brushed his lips over mine. We tasted of citrus and salt, and he kissed me slowly, hungrily, unyielding. I lost myself in those kisses. I wrapped my legs around him and grabbed the front of his shirt, pulling him to me. I clung to him so tightly that I could feel his heart beating against me. The sun dipped low behind him, that last little bit of golden warmth washing over us dissipated, and finally we broke apart, heaving.

Our day at the beach had come to an end. We drove home in silence. I had things I wanted to say, but no right to say them. I had feelings that I should not have been feeling—or maybe I was drunk on the beach and the kite and the key lime pie. Maybe I was a woman who had had her heart broken and Dez was a distraction, a very kind, very handsome, very sexy distraction, but a distraction nonetheless. This couldn't be real . . . in the context of not knowing someone I'd been with for fifteen years, two weeks seemed like an instant. How could I be certain of anything right now? I did know one thing, and this I *was* certain of: Dez was good and I did not want to burn him. But none of that stopped him from reaching across the console to take my hand, or me from interlacing my fingers with his. I traced the inked skin on the inside of his forearm with my gaze, wondering about its significance, imagining myself doing the same thing with my fingertips in the light of morning and asking him.

When we got back to our neighborhood, I didn't want the spell to break.

"You know," I said, "we've been living so close for months, and I don't actually know which house is yours."

"I can fix that," he said, turning right before he reached my house. He hadn't been exaggerating when he said he lived two streets over. After another left, he pulled into the driveway of a modest Colonial. The yard was neat, with manicured boxwoods and grass mowed on the diagonal.

"Can I come in?" I asked, feeling bold. Despite the warning signal flashing, I wanted to know Dez better. When I imagined his house, it was full of pictures of his sisters and bookshelves. But I wondered about what color the walls were, what kind of sheets he slept on, if he had pets. I was desperate to learn about him, peruse his books, and just be in his space. I wanted that first-time excitement when you step into the home of someone new, who you like, and it's as if you share this secret. I was learning the muscled hills and valleys of his body, the spots that made him groan when I touched him there, the scars, and I was keenly aware of how he made me feel, but I knew little about his life other than his work.

He opened his hands on the steering wheel, but he didn't answer. I eyed him.

"You don't want me to come in?"

"It's not that." I started to regret my boldness. Maybe I'd misread things. "You know what . . . sure, why not?"

I hesitated. I trusted Dez, but the delay, the change in his demeanor, the way he'd avoided looking at me, and the fact that I'd been so tacky and basically invited myself over gave me pause.

We walked toward the house in silence, save for his jingling keys as he fidgeted and my own inner voice, which was giving me a full dressing-down about being so forward and naive. He turned the key and opened the door, and I stepped inside.

I stopped just past the threshold and turned back to him. He had a pained grimace on his face. "I know," he said. "It's bad."

The small entry table was covered with piles of mail; cardboard boxes littered the room. I nearly tripped over a duffel bag as I made my way farther inside.

"You're a slob!" I said, unable to keep the glee out of my voice. I hurried over to a stack of boxes. "Wait, how long ago did you move in? You haven't unpacked yet?"

"Eight months. I keep meaning to do it, but I'm always at the firehouse or the yoga studio, and when I'm here, I just want to sleep or watch TV."

One of the boxes was open and I peeked inside. "Dez, is this *laundry*?"

He was still standing on the porch, just outside the threshold. "Now do you see why I didn't want you to come in? My crew hasn't even been over here," he said sheepishly. "You're my first visitor. In all fairness, I would've stuffed all this in a closet if I'd known you were coming in."

I abandoned the box full of laundry and walked over to him. "Would it've fit?" I said, stifling a giggle.

"I told you I was flawed," he said.

I reached out and grabbed his hand. "You wanna know what I think?"

"I'm afraid to ask. Especially since your house looks like a *Southern Living* photo shoot. Are you horrified?"

It occurred to me that Dez's house was a bit like the inside of my head—a complete mess—and that connection between us filled me with joy. I'd wanted to share something with him, something only I knew, and here it was.

"I think . . . it's fantastic." I grabbed his hand and pulled him inside. "Finally! I get to help you with something."

· Twenty-Nine ·

After we'd worked late into the night hanging photos—several featuring his sisters; he had four, I learned—filling bookshelves with books (he favored detective novels and nonfiction), and folding laundry, we watched a movie on the couch. He wrapped his arms around me and I rested my head on his strong chest.

"What is your tattoo?" I asked, running my fingers over his forearm.

"It's part of a Dylan Thomas poem," he said. He pressed his lips to the top of my head and held me a bit tighter.

"And how about the scar on your chin? Is it from rugby? Or work?"

"That one is courtesy of Jessie, my favorite sister. Let's just say that when she thought it would be fun to put on a circus and rigged a high wire from our tree house, I should've trusted my gut and told her no."

"So you've always been a daredevil then."

"Not really. I fell off because I was shaking so bad." He chuckled. "Don't tell anyone."

"Your secret's safe with me," I said.

We didn't talk much after that. The film played and we fell into a comfortable silence. I fixed my gaze on the television screen, but my attention stayed on the rise and fall of his chest beneath me with every breath he took, and the sound of his heartbeat, slow and steady.

At midnight, Dez walked me home. He had a shift, so he did not spend the night, which was a blessing, because I was on a strict no-overnight-guests/upsetting-the-neighbors policy. Plenty of disappointing things were blessings, Mom always said, and I *was* disappointed—after the beach and the glimpse of the real Dez at his house, the hours spent so close to him, I really wanted him to stay. I wanted to twine our bodies together again until I couldn't tell where I ended and he began, and prove beyond any question that the "faking it column" had not one darn thing to do with him.

I passed most of Sunday on a social media blackout, debating whether going to Bunco was advisable. On one hand, there was the obvious: I'd show up and have to deal with everyone's perfectly plucked eyebrows going sky high at the sight of me and those not-so-secret glances silently communicating their reactions to the column, to Sam, to me going off the deep end. I knew firsthand that a few of the ladies of Bunco would be reasonably sweet and polite to your face but were ten times as vicious if you weren't around. All that sweetness hid a nastiness that was unparalleled—you know, sort of like when it came out that saccharin was carcinogenic.

Dez and I had opened the red the other day, so I had to run down to the supermarket to pick up another bottle. For good measure, I debated buying a bouquet for the hostess, but it seemed to scream *trying too hard*, so I settled on a simple bunch of white hydrangeas in the three-for-twelve-dollars bucket. While I curled my hair, just tight enough to look like I hadn't spent a full hour on it, I tried to recall the last time there'd been a big drama at Bunco. It'd been a good while. Things had been somewhat peaceful since talk of politics had been banned a couple years back, when everyone discovered that we had an honest-to-goodness liberal in the group. Her name was Hannah and she hailed from a little town on the Massachusetts–New Hampshire border. She had an accent that curled my toes and volunteered for the Obama campaign—both times. I did not confess my own similar leanings. I'd been pretending to be a centrist independent for eight years and it'd been working for me just fine. Never talk about your sex life, your bank account, or your politics; I'd learned that lesson young. Anyway, Hannah worked at the EPA in Research Triangle Park and hung in with the group for a season, until the night Belinda Gill asked if we all thought that her feeding her sons soy formula would make them gay—dreaded phytoestrogens—and Hannah had called her ignorant. Even I knew it was ludicrous, and I got a C-minus in biology.

"It was just a question," Belinda'd said, and a few people consoled her. *Of course it was, honey.* Secretly, I'd loved it when Hannah exploded; she was so bold and brave. Most of us, including me, didn't say anything. We were too afraid of the fallout, of being rude, of causing a scene of our own. It simply wasn't done. When Hannah saw the group's nonresponse, her face turned pink with anger beneath the abundance of freckles, and her black hair fanned out behind her in slow motion as she whirled around and headed toward the door. After that, I'd given her a polite smile whenever I'd seen her walking her golden retriever, asked her how work was going, gifted her a tin of my special chocolate bark at the holidays, but I never mentioned that evening and I didn't ask her to come back. I was too ashamed that I hadn't spoken up like she had. After all, silence in a situation like that, something so wrong, doesn't mean you're not saying anything. It gives the impression you agree.

Later I'd brought Ashleigh into the group as Hannah's replacement. We were down a player—you needed an even number for it to work right—and Ashleigh was in dire need of an excuse for a monthly night out. Mark had never been one to help out much with the child-care. "He just wasn't raised like that," she'd confessed once, "but I get tired. I fell asleep getting my highlights done the other day."

Tonight, Ashleigh arrived at the house at 6:55 p.m. on the dot with brownies. "They're shit," she said. "That's what I get for trying to make something from scratch."

I peeked at the sunken brown mass in the dish. "They're chocolate," I said. I held up the bottles of wine. "Besides, everyone will be too tipsy to notice."

Ashleigh smiled. "So . . . Mark said Sam was on a real tear at the office this week. The other partners are not happy."

I tried to keep my face relaxed. "He wasn't pleased when he called me after my name got leaked. I think his exact words were 'I could sue you for defamation.'"

"That's ridiculous," Ashleigh said, jostling the brownies as she tried to set the flowers on top of the lid. "To hit the burden of proof for that he'd have to show you made a false statement in the first place. Did you?"

"What do you think?"

"I think Sam's a son of a bitch."

We headed out into the evening. The sun had already gone down, but it was still light enough out to see the way to Meghan Pruitt's. Meghan lived in a dove-gray Craftsman-style house that was on the next cross-street over, not far from the community pool. Every window was lit, and the group, congregated around the kitchen island, was visible through the storm door. Ashleigh went in first. "Hey, y'all," she called. "We've got the wine and chocolate!"

I said a silent prayer of thanks for Ashleigh's extroversion and followed her inside. Meghan came bustling out of the kitchen.

"These are for you," I said, handing her the hydrangeas.

"Oh, bless your heart. Come on in." In the kitchen, she deposited them in their plastic wrap on the counter and went back to mingling.

"It's good to see you," Charlotte Palmer said, hugging me like I was a piece of garbage she didn't want to contaminate her. I wanted to tell her that having an adulterous husband wasn't contagious, but then again, she'd scarfed down Belinda's whole horrible soy-formula theory, so there was no reasoning with someone like her.

"It's great to see you too," I mirrored. "You look wonderful."

"Thank you. Dave gave me a spa day for our anniversary. It was magical; I feel like a new woman."

I was pretty sure that a spa day meant a Brazilian wax and several units of Botox, neither of which sounded relaxing, but I nodded. "That's fantastic. What a thoughtful gift." I turned away. "Hey, Meghan? Where would you like me to put the wine?"

Meghan was trying to artfully arrange Ashleigh's brownies on a platter. She looked up. "Oh, um, well, we have some open already, but you can put yours over on the sideboard."

I entered the dining room and found the sideboard, where I placed down the bottles next to the box of wine that had already been set up. It was strange. For the past four years, I'd always brought the wine. It was my thing. Everyone loved what I chose. Ashleigh even joked when we walked home alone the first time she'd come to Bunco that if things didn't work out with my advice column, I might have a future as a sommelier.

I frowned at the box of wine and pulled on the tap to put a splash in my cup. I glanced around to make sure I was in the clear and then gave the wine a sniff. Rebecca Glynn came up alongside me and gave me a squeeze. "Glad you came out," she said. "I've been meaning to stop by, but Murph's mama's in the hospital again, so I've been back and forth. Maybe we can grab a glass of pinot at that wine bar that just opened sometime when things settle down."

"I'd like that," I said. Rebecca was one of those sunny people who was kind to everyone. I liked her. I took a deep breath.

"I'm going to grab some of those fried green tomatoes before they're gone," she said. "I'll be back."

"It looks like we're all here," Meghan announced.

I headed toward the doorway and raised the wineglass to my lips. It was a bit sour and had an empty taste, but I was going to need it, I told myself, based on the range of greetings I'd gotten when I'd come in. "Thanks for coming, everybody. So, as some of you already know, Camilla is currently on bedrest for baby number three, so we have a new neighbor taking her place tonight. This is my good friend Shelby!"

I choked on the wine.

"Oh dear, are you alright, Violet?" a woman called Jessica asked. I'd always liked her; she was a bona fide sweetheart who taught preschool, but she talked to adults the way I imagined she spoke to the kids in her class. I wondered if she was going to ask if I should go potty before we got started.

"I'm fine," I said, and cleared my throat. "Thanks."

"This must be hard," she said. "Sorta like the whole group has read your diary."

I didn't know whether it was a mercy or a curse that I had not named Shelby in my column. The Bunco babes could be mean from time to time, but they weren't cunning. I told myself that they did not realize the connection between us and that her being here was just a coincidence, however cruel.

Shelby was standing next to Meghan, and I took the opportunity to eye her for a moment. She was not wearing her usual running clothes and instead had on a pair of ripped jean capris and tall ankle boots with a hunter green peasant blouse that would have made anyone else look pregnant, but managed to make her look like a celebrity. Her trademark ponytail was down, and her pale blonde hair fell around her shoulders like moonlight-colored silk. Thank God I'd taken the time to put together the perfect outfit: dark gray skinny jeans and a black silk camisole with a thin cardigan over it. The cardigan was cashmere with shiny antique buttons, something Mom had bought but hadn't loved the fit of and gifted to me instead of returning. Paired with a shiny pair of ballet flats, it was the ideal mix of understated and elegant. I had so much flexible-hold hairspray in my curls that I looked like I'd just left the hairstylist's chair. And my makeup I knew was on point, because I'd watched three YouTube videos before attempting the look called "Smokin' Hot." Smoking pile of rubble was more like it. Shelby looked over and caught my eye. It was fleeting, but it left me wishing that I was the runner in the scenario, so I could sprint out the back door and hurdle over the picket fence in Meghan's backyard and make it back to the safety of my house before anyone noticed I was missing.

Even though I did not look like a woman whose life was a complete disaster, the wine swirled in my stomach and I felt like I might be sick. I steadied myself. I was not going to make a scene. We each dropped our five-dollar bills into the cash bowl in the middle of the island, next to a plate of fried green tomatoes with crème fraîche, bacon, and green onions that was clearly not homemade and I was willing to bet came from Lucky 32 in Cary, and then drew scorecards. I pulled mine and got one with a star that indicated I'd start at the head table, along with Meghan. Shelby drew hers next.

"Oh, a star!" Shelby exclaimed. "What's that mean?"

"It's perfect," Meghan said. "You'll sit at the head table with me, Ashleigh, and Violet."

Shelby appeared to waver.

"I was new not that long ago too," Ashleigh said. "Don't worry; it's easy. Truly. The whole thing is really just an excuse for us to drink and gossip—kind of like a book club, but without the homework and the guilt for not reading."

Maybe I needed to find a book club. "I need to visit the restroom before we start," I said, and dashed off.

I turned on the light and the fan and gripped the sink. I just needed a few moments to breathe. *You are not going to do anything, Violet,* I told myself. *You're going to smile and roll the dice and pretend like you don't know Shelby. You're going to be polite and cordial and not lose your shit. You will not burn anything, hit anything, or mess up this perfect fucking makeup. Deep breath in.* I practiced a smile in the mirror, which looked almost passable for a real one, except that my hands were shaking. I flushed the toilet and then washed my hands with pungent lavender soap, dried them, and went back to join the group.

Shelby did not make eye contact with me. She answered Ashleigh's questions and rolled three buncos. I learned that she was originally from Ohio and had moved here for work. She had wanted to be a PE teacher, but instead she had ended up in cosmeceuticals; not a dream job exactly, but the money was good. She had a big family with six brothers and sisters, and she missed being around them. She told us this all in her high-pitched voice, which was a little nasal for my taste.

"So . . . dish, Shelby, are you married? Or looking?" Ashleigh asked. My chest squeezed.

"Not married."

"You know, my son's soccer coach is single," Ashleigh said. "He's from Ireland and really cute. I could get you his info."

Shelby winced. "That's okay, I'm not really in the market."

I took the opportunity to visit the box of wine for a very large refill, which I drank next to the sideboard, before filling my glass again and returning to the table. I could feel my makeup starting to shift on my face. I rubbed my eye.

"How old's your son?" Shelby was asking Ashleigh when I returned.

"Three." Ashleigh looked at me, brow furrowed. "You've got a little smudge there, Vi," she said in a loud whisper, while she gestured to her own eye.

Goose bumps pricked up on my arms. There was the cold panic I'd grown accustomed to in these new situations of high stress. *Yoga is no match for this*, I thought, as I converted into an iceberg. I swiped my napkin under my eye. "Better?"

Ashleigh nodded.

"Do you have any other children?" Shelby asked.

Ashleigh shook her head. "Mark wanted more, but I had terrible preeclampsia. The doctor recommended I not get pregnant again, so I had tubal ligation."

I hadn't known that.

"Oh," Shelby said. "I'm sorry.

Ashleigh waved her hand. "It's fine. Honestly, one is enough. Tristan's wonderful, but he can be a real handful."

Meghan passed me the dice.

"How about you, Shelby? Do you want kids?" Ashleigh asked.

I rolled them, trying not to listen for Shelby's answer.

"Oh gosh, yeah—a whole houseful," she said. "I can't wait to be a mom."

I didn't even look at the dice landing. I stared at her. Something inside of me burst. There was a strange tearing sensation in my chest.

"BUNCO!!!" I shouted.

Meghan frowned. "No. You didn't roll three threes, Violet. You've got a one, a four—"

The whole room had gone quiet and everyone, it seemed, was staring at me expectantly. I was sweating now. "I just realized I left the stove on," I said. "So sorry, everybody, I've got to go! I've got to go right now and turn it off before the house goes up in flames." I stood up abruptly and my folding chair flipped over. I stumbled on it, but didn't stop to right it, instead heading with purpose toward the kitchen. I snatched one of my bottles of wine and the entire platter of Ashleigh's crappy brownies and speed-walked out of the house.

· Thirty ·

I WAS TEMPTED TO SEND a text to Dez, but I already felt pathetic enough, so the idea of telling him about what had happened, how I'd turned cold again like the other day when I'd had the panic attack, was too much. I wished I was back at the beach with the kite string in my hand and the ocean breeze cool and refreshing on my skin.

Instead, the only sensation that I had was a stinging in my nose like I'd snorted that wine in the box and a chill that seemed like it was planning to settle in my bones. I went to the bathroom and took my makeup off. It smeared across my face as I swiped with a cotton ball, and I was struck by just how awful I looked. That smoky eye streaked down my cheeks and out toward my hairline; my eyes, rimmed red with tears and irritation, seemed to reflect my inner state. Shelby wanted a houseful of children. What if they'd already been trying?

Something was missing.

I considered calling Kyra but remembered she and Roxy were at *Riverdance* at the Durham Performing Arts Center tonight, so I wouldn't have been able to reach her anyway. My mother was an absolute no. She'd been in Bimini attending to what sounded like the wedding of the century for the last week and had been too busy to talk—or to find out about me and Sam and my identity being revealed, which was a gift from God himself.

I clutched my hands around my core. The tiles seemed to call me to press my mascara-streaked cheek to them, but I resisted the urge to curl up on the floor and cry. I had a limit to just how pitiful I was going to be, and that limit had been reached. Besides, I'd cried in the bathroom enough for a lifetime.

I remembered my spoils from Bunco, which I'd left downstairs. I could eat every last brownie. The divorce recovery website hadn't mentioned brownies. While not strictly acceptable, it was better than the alternative. I lowered myself into a chair at the kitchen table in front of my laptop and shoved a brownie into my mouth. Oh God, Ashleigh had been right. They were awful. I should've grabbed the fried green tomatoes. I washed the cocoa glop down with a swig from the wine bottle. I texted Ashleigh.

Sorry about running off on you like that. Long story. Didn't burn the house down, but think I'm going to have another one of your delicious brownies and call it a night.

At some point, I called it quits on the chocolate fest and was contemplating walking over to the fire station to see Dez and either tell him every excruciating detail of how horrible my night had been and how I was so full of fault lines at this point that I was pretty much about to shatter *or* try to convince him to have sex with me on top of the fire truck like that hot scene in *Backdraft*. It was a toss-up. Then I decided that was all a terrible idea. I felt wretched and raw, and so very ambivalent, to use Dez's word. I wanted to be ready to move on and be with someone who didn't expect me to tough out the cold and offered me a sweatshirt instead. Someone who was kind and made me feel safe to be myself, someone who didn't expect me to be perfect or hide my feelings, but how could I do that when every good moment I experienced these days was eclipsed by the memory of what Sam and Shelby had done to me? I'd had a perfect Saturday with Dez, and then Sunday felt like Shelby stomping on our sandcastles with her words. Everywhere I looked, she was there.

What was it Dez had said the other day about pain—you had to give it a voice and let it out? I'd jumped and screamed and yelled at Sam on the porch, but it wasn't sufficient. He hadn't broken my heart alone. Shelby knew Sam was married. She'd sat across from me at Bunco and said those things instead of leaving. In terms of heart-smashing, Sam may have gotten in the first couple of licks, but Shelby had wielded her own hammer, even if it had been cute and pink and baby-powder scented. I needed to admit that. But I wasn't about to go back to Bunco to scream in her face in front of all of those pretty, polished vultures. Over my dead body was I going to give them more material.

There was a deep ache inside of me, beneath my ribs, radiating down—it felt like a gaping wound. I needed to fill it with something powerful instead of this quiet void, this helplessness and despair. Writing always had been a respite for me, a place where I helped, where I was powerful and respected.

I walked over to my laptop and opened it. Shelby's statement about children had ripped through me. I thought if I could let my anger and anguish pour out and fill the hole with my own words, naming what she'd done to me, that somehow would give me the catharsis I so desperately needed. I wanted to move on, but I couldn't until I was whole.

I took a breath and tried to piece myself together. I typed what I couldn't say when I'd run away.

Thirty-One

Dear Sweetie,

My name is Shelby. I guess you already knew that. I live a few streets over from you in Sunny Ridge; surely you've seen me running laps around your house in my super cute running shorts and sports bra, flirting with your husband. If not, you definitely know me from that time you caught me with him in your bed when you came home from work early to surprise him with big news about your column. I should be sorry about that, I guess, but I'm not. I took your husband away and now I think I'll take your friends too. These Bunco ladies are a lot of fun. I love telling them about how I wish I were a PE teacher. It's super important to be fit, girls. That's what men like, especially if they're already taken. It was so fun too, talking about all the babies I want to have with your husband. I suppose you found that hurtful given your situation. Oops.

I guess I don't really need advice from you. I'm pretty sure advice is the one thing of yours that I wouldn't take.

Sincerely,
Shelby

Dear Shelby,

You're right. You should be sorry that you came into my home and took everything from me. The fact that you're not doesn't make you a winner.

You may not want my advice, but I'll give you three pieces for free anyway.

One: My mother taught me to do unto others as you would have them do unto you. You won't always be shiny and new like you are now . . . so snagging a man based on his desire for those things also gives you an expiration date. When your shine wears off the way mine did, you'll wish you'd been kinder, and you better hope that Sam's next new thing is a tad more considerate.

Two: He probably told you our marriage had problems; something was missing; somehow I brought this on myself. You'll never know our real shared history, the things we went through, the joys and sorrows. Maybe there's some truth to the things he told you, but it's only part of the story, and no matter what you've chosen to believe to make yourself feel better, it's no excuse for your behavior.

Three: Don't read the comments.

Sincerely,
Sweetie

· Thirty-Two ·

When I finished, I did not send the column to Kyra. For one thing, I'd written it as a therapeutic exercise, a diary entry never meant to see the light of day; for another thing, I'm not completely deranged. If mentioning my marital un bliss in the paper had caused such an uproar, something like this would be earth shattering. Besides, I'd written it for myself and no one else. I reread what I'd written out loud, took a deep breath, and moved the cursor over the *Delete Post* button. My stomach grumbled loudly and then an abdominal cramp hit me so hard I folded into myself.

It turned out that my unhinged thieving of the brownies actually had been an act of charitable self-sacrifice instead of selfish gluttony. They'd seemed a bit underdone, but I hadn't given that much thought when I'd polished off seven of them while I conducted my cathartic writing exercise. But then the salmonella or whatever funk was festering in those brownies hit me, and I scrambled off to the bathroom, where I was violently ill several times before I managed to drag myself to bed.

I awoke sometime before dawn, thirsty and still queasy, to my phone ringing. I let it go to voicemail while I rubbed my eyes and went to the sink for some water.

A few moments later, a text alert dinged.

What have you done, Violet??

What was Kyra talking about? I wondered. I ran through the events of the evening. Ashleigh must've told Kyra that I'd bailed on Bunco after shouting and knocking over a chair and stealing a bottle of wine. All that was pretty bad, gossip fodder for months, but not dramatic enough to warrant a pre-sunrise call from Kyra, especially a post-*Riverdance* one. Had it been worse than I thought?

I decided not to listen to her message and to call Kyra instead.

"I love you, but you are testing me," she snapped when she answered.

"What?" I said, my tongue still cottony. "Did Ashleigh tell you I stole her brownies? I did those ladies a favor."

"Are you trashed?"

"I feel like trash, but no, I'm not drunk. I think I have food poisoning. Ashleigh should not be allowed to bake."

"Oh Jesus Christ, I can't even talk to you."

"Sorry," I said. I dropped onto the sofa. "I'm sorry. It was a bad, *bad* night. I ate some undercooked brownies that made me throw up. I feel like crap."

"I had two and a half hours of sheer joy watching those Riverdancers tear it up, slept like a baby until Harriet wet the bed, and then I make the mistake of looking at my phone and see that you've posted a fake letter from Sam's mistress on your online column. I had to get a babysitter for Harriet last night; I didn't know that I needed one for you too. That post was up for a full three hours and twenty-two minutes after you posted it, Violet, before I yanked it. Do you have any idea what can happen in that amount of time?"

I shook my head, trying to clear the lingering fog of sickness and sleep before I headed downstairs. I'd thrown away the wine—drinking was clearly not the answer—and settled for chocolate instead. It was a superfood! It had antioxidants!

The sun was just cresting over the horizon, setting the kitchen ablaze with an orange-red glow. I went to the kitchen table, where my laptop sat, closed. I opened it. There it was. The interface we used to post on the online edition.

I rubbed my eyes in case they were full of sleep or I'd finally cracked and was hallucinating. All of these options seemed more plausible than me posting a fake column I'd written only for myself. "I—"

I wanted to tell her I didn't remember writing it. But I did.

What I did not remember was posting it.

I'd finished typing and been about to delete it, then I'd run to the bathroom to puke. Right? Could I have hit the wrong button?

Kyra cleared her throat. "I'm starting to think an intervention might be in order. But first, I've got to figure out how to do damage control. I was going to make French toast and have a game of Chutes and Ladders with Harriet before I dropped her off at preschool. That's out the window now, with your good sense. God, you really fucked up this time, Violet."

"I swear, Kyra, I di—"

"Don't. Just go back to bed. We'll talk later when I don't want to hurl you into the sun."

I sat at the table, staring at my phone for a few minutes after she'd hung up. Then I turned my attention back to my laptop. The post on the web edition wasn't there—Kyra pulled it, I surmised—but by then it had already taken on a life of its own, having been shared and reposted *thousands* of times. I was frozen, watching the slow-motion car wreck unfold as I sipped ginger ale and a gossip mag picked up the story and kept the comments section open in their repost.

While there were a fair amount of nasty messages directed toward me—something I'm not entirely sure I didn't deserve—plenty of people seemed to believe that Shelby had actually written me and that she was an evil, conniving, husband-thieving bitch, direct quote, and that wasn't even the worst one. People knew who I was now, so it wasn't a stretch for them to figure out who Shelby was as well . . . especially since I'd used her real name.

What had I done?

Oh dammit. Sam might have been in the wrong, but now I was too. This was bad.

· Thirty-Three ·

I DECIDED TO CALL IN sick. It seemed the reasonable thing to do, since Kyra was spitting mad and the food poisoning had moved on and was now wreaking havoc on my lower gastrointestinal tract. I spent the day sipping Gatorade and watching romantic comedies, feeling alternatively contrite and very sorry for myself, while Kyra cooled off (fingers crossed).

On Tuesday, I rose before the sun, French braided my hair into pigtails, put on a green blouse, a pair of tailored navy slacks, and platform boat shoes—a look that I hoped conveyed innocence and professionalism—and then I baked a batch of cranberry white chocolate chip oatmeal cookies, Kyra's favorite, before heading into work. I dangled the bag of cookies from my outstretched arm through her office door before I tried to go in.

"What's that?" she asked.

"A peace offering," I said, a bit sheepishly.

"Oh?" Kyra's tone was clipped.

"Oatmeal chocolate chip," I singsonged. "With cranberries." God, even *I* was starting to hate myself.

Kyra let out a laugh. It was not, I registered, her normal laugh, which was always full and melodic and infectious. This one was decidedly tighter and more subdued, but beggars can't be choosers, so I dropped onto the office couch in relief. "Still warm," I added for extra measure.

Kyra shook her head. "You really have no idea of the shitstorm you've created, do you? I mean, nice braids, Mary Anne."

I folded. "I'm sorry. I don't know what I was thinking. I honestly never meant for anyone to see it. Like I said, I don't even remember posting it."

"I hope that's true and that you just need to get your divorce drinking under control, because the alternative is, to be frank, pretty concerning."

"Okay," I said, trying to keep the irritation out of my voice. I didn't like being chastised, even if I deserved it. Kyra was understandably furious with me. "First, I wasn't drunk. You're right, my divorce drinking was not cool, and I'm reining that in. Honestly, I was only venting to myself. It was like a diary entry. I guess I was trying to be more real about my feelings. I was ambushed at Bunco . . . Shelby came and people started asking her about who she was dating and if she wanted kids and I just, I flipped out. I ran out of there, and then I was back at the house with my thoughts and some really bad brownies. I should've done something, gone to bed, anything else . . . but I couldn't talk to anyone. All I could do was write. Didn't *you* say that great writing comes from rage?"

Kyra cocked her head. "Wait. You're actually trying to pin this on me? Do you have any sense of responsibility?" She rubbed her forehead. "You know what? I'm not even going to venture to unpack that right now. You know as well as I do that that monstrosity wasn't great writing. Not even close. That was the writing equivalent of taking a tire iron to Nancy Kerrigan before the Olympics."

"I think it was a collapsible baton, actually."

"Oh yeah? Look at the memory on you. As *I* recall, that didn't work out too well for Tonya. How's your left hook, Violet? Because you might need to start working on it when you end up having to get a new career."

I opened my mouth to respond, but instead found myself sipping air like a fish flopping around on Kyra's couch. I'd watched that Tonya Harding documentary, and truth be told, after my twenty-four-hour stomach pyrotechnics, quitting boot camp, and eating all those brownies, I was certain that if I ended up in has-been boxing, I was getting my ass kicked.

Kyra was not finished. She pointed a pen at me. "You *do* realize you're not the only person impacted by that cheap shot, don't you? Did it ever occur to you how this would make the paper look, or *me*, for that matter? I am personally responsible for what's published in this newspaper, in all its formats, whether I'm aware or not."

I swallowed. I hadn't considered that, not for a second. Initially, I'd been consumed with sick, dark, painful anger, but in the end, I'd just wanted to get all of that negative emotion out. I'd wanted to express how much Shelby's actions had hurt me—not hurt her. And definitely not hurt Kyra. She was my best friend. She was also my boss. Maybe I'd conflated the two a bit, but I'd never intentionally done anything to put her in jeopardy.

"Look." She let out a sigh. "I know this whole thing with Sam has been hard on you. It was brutal. I get that you've been struggling. That Bunco business sounds like a terrible thing to have to sit through, and if I'd been there, I'd probably have smashed that plate of brownies in that woman's face. But, Jesus, you went really low with this—Michelle Obama would be ashamed of you—and that makes us all look bad. And while you may bounce back just fine from this exercise in pettiness and supreme stupidity, maybe—I'm not even sure that's true—not everyone will. Did you think about what people will do to Shelby? Yes, she snuck in on you and Sam, she sucks, but she's still a human being . . . and you tossed her to the wolves. And at the end of the day, you left me holding the bag. I'm not saying you don't have problems, but you float through life without having to consider the fallout of your own behavior. I don't have that luxury. I am a woman of color, Violet, in charge of a newspaper. You have no idea what it took for me to get here, or what it takes for me to stay. I don't get a hundred chances to get it right. I get one. Do you know how many people don't think that I should be in charge, that I even deserve to be here at all, even though I have earned it a thousand times over? No matter how hard I work or how good I am, there's still a bunch of people just waiting for the tiniest slipup to pounce on. I won't get a do-over like you."

I bit the inside of my lip very hard. "I didn't realize. I guess on some level I—"

"Yeah, well, ignorance is bliss. It's also a choice."

I nodded. Kyra was right. I knew well enough that while I was painting my face and squatting it out and pretending like I wasn't angry or sad or whatever because I didn't want anyone to leave me, she was constantly under a microscope, with an entirely different lens. Even if I never intended to do anything to Kyra, intent was meaningless when you harmed someone. I should've known that. Sam probably never meant to destroy me when he fell for Shelby, but he had.

I wanted to tell her that I would fix everything, but there was no point bullshitting Kyra. I'd messed up, and nothing made a situation worse than a bunch of lip service. If I wanted to make things better, I needed to get my ass in gear and actually do something. What, I hadn't the faintest idea, but I knew better than to shoot off my mouth.

"Go home," she told me in a flat, distant voice that filled me with shame. "You're on probation."

I left Kyra's office with three things:

The newfound knowledge that I was vying for both *Most Self-Absorbed* and *Worst Friend in the World* awards.

A burning desire to cry (I didn't—thanks again, Mom, for that lesson) and a firm conviction that I would rectify this once I figured out how.

The cookies. Kyra didn't want them, as it turned out.

Thirty-Four

I HEADED HOME AFTER I turned in my column, a rather sedate etiquette response to a question about kids' birthday party invites, and found Dez sitting on my front porch.

"Hi," I said, ascending the stairs.

"I was just writing you a note," he said. "How've you been?"

I shrugged, fiddling with my keys to avoid his eyes. "You want to come in? I made some cookies."

"Yeah, okay."

He followed me inside, waiting while I kicked off my shoes in the foyer before we headed toward the kitchen.

He leaned against the counter while I took the cookies from the bag and removed the plastic wrap.

"It's been a bit," he said. "I thought I might hear from you after the beach."

"Sorry. I haven't been in the best place the past day or two. Things went a little sideways after we got back. You want milk?"

He nodded. "You could've called. I'm pretty good at handling things going sideways."

"I know, but I don't always want to broadcast my problems." I got a glass and filled it. "You really want to know? I'm basically one step away from losing my job. My best friend isn't speaking to me." I let out a sigh. "I've created a pretty colossal mess. That is not the kind of stuff I like to share. I read about people's problems all day long, and I am acutely aware that the novelty wears off from that real quick. So, I appreciate the offer, but some things I think are better if I just handle them my own way."

"What way is that?"

"I haven't gotten that far yet. First, I need to cry it out in the bathroom alone."

He shoved his hands in his pockets and nodded, but he didn't meet my eyes. I put the glass of milk down in front of him and placed two cookies on a plate. Dez didn't make a move toward them.

"Did you see it?" I asked quietly.

He shook his head. "I heard about it, but no, I didn't see it. I generally avoid that kind of thing."

"That's it?"

He reached for a cookie and took a bite.

I reached reflexively to smooth my hair, forgetting it was in braids. "I promise you, there's nothing you're going to say to me that I haven't already said to myself. I know I screwed up." I leaned against the refrigerator, my arms crossed in front of me.

Dez finished eating his cookie. I watched his jaw work, the bob of his Adam's apple as he swallowed. Finally, he said, "You know someone keyed Shelby's car, right?"

That glacier feeling was back; it started in my fingertips and spread, rapidly, until I was frozen. My heart seemed to flutter, encased in that ice. What did he mean? I steadied myself on the oven door, accidentally opening it a little. The hard metal smarted against my lower back.

"No, I didn't know," I said tentatively, my mind flashing to the comments on the post.

That wasn't a lie. I wasn't aware that her car had been vandalized, but I was acutely aware of the things people were saying about her online. They'd done it all, within hours of the post. My original column was gone, but the damage had been done.

A muscle in his jaw twitched. "Yeah, the whole side is trashed with the word *whore* in giant letters." He pushed a crumb around on his plate with his finger before he met my eyes again.

"I didn't do that."

"I know."

Relief washed over me. I hadn't been wrong about him; he saw me.

"They caught the guy using doorbell camera footage." Dez fell silent, but I could tell that he had something more to say. Something that wouldn't make me feel better. "What happened that made you post that? It doesn't seem like you."

I shook my head. "It was some kind of accident. Yes, I wrote a post. But it was never meant to go online. As soon as I found out what happened, I issued a statement asking people to leave her alone. What else could I do?" I pressed my lips together tightly and closed my eyes for a moment. "I would never want people to go after someone like that." I was many things, and very, very flawed—I knew that—but I wasn't cruel.

He sniffed. "People are capable of doing a lot of things when they're in pain." He looked up, his expression clouded with emotion. I felt too visible and betrayed.

"She's not innocent, you know. And anyway, what would you know about people doing stuff because they're in pain? You have no clue. I mean, if we're being honest, you don't know me."

"That's not true."

There was a tremor in my voice when I spoke, but I couldn't stop the words that were rushing out. "No. You don't, Dez. And you don't know what it's like to have everyone know that you've been made a fool of, and then have the person who did that, who ruined your whole life, show up at your game night in front of all of your friends and right to your face say they can't wait to fill a whole house with babies, with your husband, presumably." My voice cracked. *Shut up, Violet*, I told myself, but I was already off to the races. "I should be glad for Sam. He wanted a family so bad, and she can give him one. It's great." My cheeks were slick now. I hadn't even realized that I was crying, but I wasn't cold anymore. I'd melted into salt water like the decimated ice caps. I took a step; I had to get away. I didn't want him to see me like this. But Dez clasped my wrist and reeled me in to him. He wrapped his arms around me and pressed his cheek into my hair. I wanted him to let go, to leave—the dread of what happens after you say too much, of being so exposed, was more than I could bear—but he held tight, and after a few moments my breathing returned to normal.

"I just wanted to write the things I couldn't say. For myself. Punish her a little, make her embarrassed and feel a shred of the hurt that she inflicted on me. To get it out of my system. But I swear, I never intended for anyone to read it. And now I'm crying in front of you, and I don't do that."

"Okay," Dez said, still holding me. "I know. It's okay."

"I really didn't mean it. I am sorry, though. I'm sorry that people saw something that wasn't meant to be seen. I'm sorry if she read those hurtful comments. I'm sorry that someone vandalized her car. But I'm not going to feel sorry *for* her." He released his arms and I fled into the living room to sit down. He sat in a chair across from me, bracing his elbows on his knees. His hands were folded in front of him as if in prayer.

"It wasn't an indictment, you know. I do know something about pain," he said. "It's not the same as yours, but I know it."

I swiped at my eyes and waited.

"I never told you why I moved here."

I shook my head. "I don't think so."

"Ben," he said. "My best friend back in Baltimore. We grew up together, even went to the academy together. Then we worked on the same crew for years." Dez shifted in the seat. "One night, we were called out to this apartment fire and . . . there was a kid. He was hiding. We got him out, but—we didn't get there in time."

He fell silent. I swallowed.

Dez folded his hands together. "It tore us all up, but Ben, he took it the worst. He's the one that found him, and he felt responsible. I knew something was wrong. He told us all that he was okay, but I knew, I knew he wasn't. He didn't sleep most nights; he started drinking. A lot. He'd call me up, rambling. One time he showed up to work with a black eye."

I was afraid to breathe, because I felt something bad coming, something worse. Another breath seemed to pull the words closer to us.

"One day he didn't show up for his shift. I was going to go looking for him, but we got a call. Motor vehicle accident." His voice caught a little. "He'd gotten drunk and tried to drive himself home; flipped his truck on the freeway."

I couldn't speak. I wanted to comfort Dez, but I didn't know how.

He shrugged; his eyes were full of tears when he finally looked up at me. "There was nothing I could do. I just, I wished I'd done something, you know, earlier, when there was still something I *could* do. I didn't want to be there after that. It was too hard. I didn't even know who I was without Ben around. You asked about my tattoo the other day—I got it for him."

I blew out a shaky breath and nodded. It *wasn't* the same; he was right about that. Because Dez's friend was dead, and Sam was still very much alive, but grief is grief, and it's work to endure, and it sucks, and it makes home feel like a place you can't be anymore. So you run or you burn home to the ground because the alternative, *feeling* that pain and loss, living and swimming in it every moment, is just a bit more than I think humans were designed to bear. It was,

I'm sure, more than I was made to bear. In Dez's case, it seemed he'd boxed up what remained of his pain and left it cluttering his house. I should have noticed, but I was too caught up in my own problems.

I crossed the room, put my hand on Dez's back, and rubbed it gently over the taut muscles there. I didn't say a word, because I knew that sometimes the best thing to do was to just be there. Sometimes there wasn't anything you could say to make it better and you could only sit with someone in their experience so they didn't have to be alone. "I'm sorry," I said. "So sorry, Dez."

"He was asking for help, when he did those things—calling me up drunk or getting into fights—he was screaming at us all that he was not okay. And I dropped the ball." He turned his face toward me. "So I gotta ask you, Violet. Should I be worried about you? 'Cause it seems to me that you've been doing a bit of screaming too, and not just on the fair ride."

I knelt down in front of him and took his face in my hands. I shook my head. "No," I told him. "Not anymore. I've made a mess of things, that's for certain, but I can set it right." I pressed my lips to his forehead, and then his cheeks, one and then the other. I hesitated by his mouth.

"Good," he said.

I nodded, pushing down the worry that said, *Is this just me doing another wrong thing?* "You don't have to worry about me," I said. "Don't give it another thought."

"But I do. I think about you all the time." He reached out and cupped my cheek. "You never need to cry in the bathroom alone again," he said.

I pressed my lips to his, a small, soft kiss. Tender. Followed by another. And then one more, the last one, I told myself. But I'd gone too far to stop. I didn't want to. He'd come to life against me, pulling me toward him, nipping my bottom lip. I climbed onto his lap, and he tangled his hands in my hair. My hands fumbled for the button of his jeans and he pulled off my shirt. I clung to him, my skin against his, searing hot, and he stood and walked with me to the couch. He was strong against me, his expression full of desire and heat, but now I saw the sorrow there, beneath the surface, the wanting to feel something else. I knew that feeling so well. I wanted to cauterize Dez's wounds, seal them with my mouth and my hands, with all of me. He made me feel safe and cared for. Dez made my sadness recede and filled my dark spaces with light; he made me feel like I would be happy and whole again, and I wanted to do the same for him.

AFTERWARD, I RESTED MY head on his chest, savoring the slow, steady rhythm of his heart. It soothed my racing mind. With Dez holding me, I was protected and warm instead of wounded and angry. Had I done that for him too? I hoped I had. We'd bared our deepest wounds and held on to each other. I leaned close to his ear. "Dez," I whispered.

"Mmhmm," he said. He was twirling a strand of my hair around his finger.

"I think I might—"

The screech of an alarm interrupted my words and Dez sat up fast, grabbing for his phone and nearly dumping me from the couch onto the floor. He yanked up his pants. A voice crackled and Dez put a finger to his lips while he pulled on a sneaker, listening carefully to the voice.

"Damn," he said. "I gotta go, Vi. There was a gas main explosion in Holly Springs. It's all hands on deck."

He kissed me on the forehead, and I handed him his T-shirt. He yanked it over his head and pushed his foot into his other shoe. *It's just as well I didn't get to say what I've been thinking,* I told myself.

"Be careful," I called.

"You too," he hollered back as he sprinted out the door.

Thirty-Five

Positive transformation is not easy. I knew I had some big changes to make, but I wanted to do the work. I wanted to be the kind of person Dez seemed to think I was and the kind of friend Kyra deserved. I wanted to be braver, realer, more giving. The necessary changes were daunting, though. I decided to take my own advice for once from a column I'd written a year before to a woman who was trying to make over her whole life but kept getting overwhelmed and ended up doing nothing. Do the small changes first, I'd suggested. The low-hanging fruit. Once you get past the inertia, the bigger things will be easier.

I moped for most of the week, and then on Friday I sucked it up and made a list.

- Take responsibility and make sure that Kyra doesn't take any heat for my recklessness.
- Come clean with my mother.
- Make things right with my readers.
- Atone for what I've done to Shelby and Sam in my column, somehow.

All of that felt monumental, so I started with the front door and a can of cherry-red paint that had caused the man at Home Depot to ask, "Are you sure?" when I handed him the swatch and asked for one gallon of exterior paint in gloss. "Yeah," I said. And I was. Because even though I hadn't written myself on the list, I hadn't treated myself very well either . . . not for a long time.

I started on Saturday morning, tying a bandana over my hair, laying the drop cloth, stirring the paint with a stick, brushing on the red in smooth, long strokes. My arms burned from the effort. I grew tired. The strong Carolina sun seared the exposed skin on the back of my neck.

"Did you get that approved by the homeowners association?" Cindy Willis asked when she came outside to get the mail.

I resisted the urge to flip her the bird and ask her if those hideous leggings with the turkeys on them had been approved by the HOA. There were, in fact, eight other houses in our whole neighborhood with red doors. Maybe not this exact hue of cherry red, but red nonetheless. I went back to work. Two coats later, I stepped back to the sidewalk and took it all in.

I'd always wanted a bright red door. Sam had thought it would look awful and had shot down the idea the first time I'd suggested it. I hadn't tried to plead my case. Now, I smiled at the door. A scarlet door was exactly what I wanted, and it made me happy. It was the first time I realized I actually felt relieved that Sam was gone. I'd made a decision without him, one that had nothing to do with him, and it felt really good.

Hannah walked by then, stopping near the azaleas where her golden retriever was sniffing something with the kind of exuberance only a golden retriever could muster.

"Hey, Hannah," I said. "How are you?"

She looked surprised, but her grip on the leash relaxed. "I'm doing well, thanks. I like the door. Great color."

The dog lifted his leg and sprayed the mailbox post. "Bodhi!" she scolded. "I'm sorry, Violet. His manners could use some work."

"Don't be sorry. He's a dog. Where else is he supposed to go?"

A surprised "Oh" slipped from her lips.

I shielded my eyes from the sun and took a step toward her. "I've been meaning to tell you, I'm sorry I didn't reach out to you after the Bunco thing. I actually stormed out even more epically at the last one, so if anyone is going down in infamy, it's not you."

"It's okay. I was avoiding you a bit too. Everyone, actually. I don't regret calling Belinda out, but my delivery could've used some work."

"At least you said something; I was too weak back then to even try. You got the important bit, I'm not sure the delivery matters. Anyway, I'm starting to think humans aren't designed to handle things well. You know, I think what you said made Belinda think, though she wouldn't admit it. Maybe there's hope for her yet, as long as people keep calling her out. It's good you spoke up."

She shrugged, twisting the dog's leash in her hands. "It probably would've been better if I'd stayed and had a conversation about what was so wrong with what she said instead of running off. Maybe next time I could make my point with a tad less rage."

Couldn't we all, I thought. But then again, sometimes rage was justified, *appropriate* even, and as Kyra had taught me, good things could come of it. "Hey, would you want to grab a coffee sometime? Or maybe I could join you on a walk?"

"Sure. We head over to the dog park every Saturday. Would you want to join us sometime?"

"I'd like that," I said.

After she and Bodhi moved on to the next mailbox that caught his fancy, I took one last look at the red door before heading inside. Sometimes change was good.

I went to the kitchen and cleared all the alcohol, except the rum I used for cooking, out of the house, dumping it down the drain and putting the empties in the recycling bin. Afterward, I took a shower and scrubbed the stray drops of dried paint from my hands, then combed my fingers through my sopping hair. In the closet, I stood in a towel, dripping wet, and moved my clothes so that my shirts were where Sam's used to be. Then I got a couple of empty plastic bins and neatly folded his remaining clothes in one. I tucked the lingering items in the other: a signed basketball that I had been tempted to plunge a knife in many times since I'd found out about the affair, his bow tie collection, and his signed books by Jonathan Franzen, which I noted he'd never read. In one of his drawers next to a neat stack of pocket squares, there was a pink-and-white-striped baseball jersey. It was doll-sized and said *Daddy's Girl* in pink embroidery on the back. I stared at it for a moment before laying it neatly on top.

I lugged the bins down to the garage and called Sam.

"Hi," I said. "It's Violet."

"I know. Caller ID."

"Oh. Yeah, I forgot about that, I guess."

"You okay?"

I crumpled a little. "Me? I'm fine. Are you? Okay, I mean?"

"Sure. What do you want?"

"I'm just calling to let you know that I, um, packed up your things in bins and you can come by anytime to pick them up. They're in the garage. I'll leave the side door unlocked so you don't need to call or anything."

"Alright. That it?"

"I guess so," I said. "Take care."

After I'd cleaned house and called Sam, I made a batch of bananas

Foster. I used the last of the rum and didn't even take a sip, which I felt was a major victory in and of itself. Instead, I watched the blue flame of the dark rum dance in the pan, caramelizing the bananas that I would use in the pudding. I set it in the fridge to cool. Tomorrow was Sunday dinner and I didn't want to disappoint Mom this time. She'd need something sweet and smooth when I finally confessed to her that she'd pinned her hopes on me and I'd let her down.

Thirty-Six

"YOU BROUGHT THE BANANA pudding this time," Mom said, taking the bowl from my hands and giving me a kiss on the cheek in one smooth motion. "So, where should we start?" she asked over her shoulder as she glided toward the kitchen. "We have so much to catch up on—there's the separation and your column going . . . well, I'm not quite sure how to put that one diplomatically . . . going to hell in a handbasket seems appropriate, if not just a bit coarse for my liking."

She swiveled around and I looked away. I traced a dark vein in the marble of the breakfast bar. "And here I was hoping we weren't going to have to talk about that until at least dessert."

"By 'that' you mean the Sam-shaped elephant that's *not* in the room?" she said. She slid the pudding into the refrigerator and then turned to a cake pan that was sitting on top of the stove. She slid it into the oven. "I didn't know you were bringing dessert, so I made a berry cobbler."

"I always bring dessert."

"You didn't last time. And I think we can both agree that your communication lately has been less than ideal overall. But back to the dissolution of your marriage. It was a little shocking to learn it from a newspaper column."

"I'm sorry."

"Especially since you told me everything was fine."

"Never let 'em see you sweat, right?" I said weakly.

"Violet Alice!" Mom admonished. I cringed and braced for the tongue-lashing I was about to get. I'd made a fool of myself, and worse, I'd made a fool out of her, publicly. "That's not meant for your mother," she said a moment later. "That's for outsiders and jerks—people who want to beat you down. Not family . . . Well, unless we're talking about Aunt Jean. Old gossip."

Mom picked up a platter full of steaming-hot, golden-fried chicken. "Grab the potato salad, will you?"

At the table, Mom said grace and then we dug in. I wasn't that hungry, but I knew better than to refuse food that someone had worked hard on.

"Was that really what happened, what you wrote in the column?" she asked. "You found them together?"

I nodded, trying not to flash back to the scene. I'd been making progress.

She shook her head and pulled a piece of crispy coating from the chicken breast she'd selected. She tossed it into her mouth. "How did you leave things?"

"Honestly, I didn't leave things any way. It's pretty simple. He left me. You know, I think he might actually be in love with her. After I found them, he told me he wanted some time to be free and see where things go, and as it turns out she wants lots of babies, so there's that. I packed up his stuff and he's gonna come by and get it. The last time we spoke before that, he said he might sue me for defamation. The newspaper's lawyer is pretty confident that there's no case there, but my marriage is over, and I'm fairly certain my career is too, and basically I'm screwed."

"Well, alright then. But watch your language." My mother was quiet for a long time, which made me think that she was about to spout something really good, and I needed it. She dabbed the corners of her mouth and smoothed her napkin back on her lap.

"That absolute shit," she said.

"*Mom.* You just told me not swear and I said *screwed*, which isn't even technically a swear. Aren't you being a bit of a hypocrite?"

"It's vulgar. True. But Sam *is* a shit. There's just no way around it. There's a special place in hell reserved for husbands who cheat . . . and people who own tigers as pets."

I opened my mouth to speak. But she pointed at me with her fork. "Don't you even try to defend him. He had my girl. The sweetest, kindest, most perfect girl in the world, and he—"

"I'm not perfect. I don't think I ever was, but definitely I am not now. In fact, I didn't even tell you the half of it. Last time I came for dinner, I rear-ended Lillian's new Mercedes on purpose when she came to collect his things." I was on a roll. Mom never swore and she'd called Sam a shit, and it had emboldened me. I waited for her to chastise me again. *We do not treat guests that way. I raised you to be a courteous lady. All those cotillion lesson wasted for you to take the low road.* But she didn't. Instead, she giggled a little. It chortled out of her and seemed to build, bubbling out of her mouth, bigger and bigger, as if someone had put regular soap in the dishwasher. I laughed with her at first, big hysterical guffaws, my whole body shaking, but inexplicably, something shifted, and I found myself sobbing at the dinner table over my plate of fried chicken. The smoke alarm went off then.

"The cobbler!" Mom yelped. She ran to the kitchen to recover it from the oven, leaving me to cry on my own.

When she returned, she was back to the woman I knew. Collected. She sat in her seat, fixed her napkin again. She returned to the choreographed dance of taking a small bite of food, dabbing her mouth, smoothing her napkin.

"What about the cobbler?" I asked.

She finished her sip of sweet tea and looked at me. "Some things are beyond saving," she said. "Besides, who wants some burnt, thrown-together cobbler when there's gourmet banana pudding to be had?"

"How did you do it, Mom?" I asked.

"Do what, darlin'?"

"Keep it together after Dad? You never let it get to you. You were always perfectly calm and collected and graceful. The picture of poise. No matter how hard I try, I can't seem to get even close to that. I just keep making it worse."

Mom's smooth brow furrowed. "You really don't remember," she said, sounding puzzled. She took another sip of her drink. "Maybe it's for the best; it wasn't a pretty time for me, for our family."

I racked my brain, trying to remember what my mother was talking about. It was an unpleasant affair, no doubt, but she'd never let it turn ugly.

"I held it in," she said. "Trouble with that is, eventually, it had to come out somewhere. The night of the charity dinner, I drank too much. He brought her—maybe you recall some of this. She was right there with us the whole night, like we were some kind of shameful harem. I was utterly humiliated. Lord knows how much I had. I did that a lot back then. It was easier if I was just a little bit drunk; it numbed things, I guess, made them a bit more tolerable. Not that night. I drank so much I blacked out and nearly drowned in the pool. I don't actually remember the incident—but Delilah was there. She told me. It was bad, but it could have been much worse."

I had the faintest memory of my mother's best friend, Delilah, on her knees beside our pool, the sequins on her dress glinting in the moonlight. I was watching from above, clad in a cotton nightgown. I couldn't quite grasp it. Every time I got close, something pulled me away from that window.

"I saw you," I said, pulling at a thread in my place mat. "I heard noises and peeked out my window. You looked like a strange set of sea creatures next to the pool. Delilah was yelling at Dad, telling him that it was all his fault. You were on the ground. I remember I ran out to be near you—I thought you were dying and I needed to save you—but Daddy yanked me away and ushered me back to the house."

My mother's face paled. She rubbed the fragile skin on her neck.

"He kept saying, 'She's fine, princess.' And I had this funny thought. I didn't want to be his princess anymore. I'd rather have been a poisonous dart frog, the kind I'd read about in elementary school, with neon patches and venom. I waited in my room, crying. I was so scared. But then Delilah came in."

"What did she say?"

"She told me that you would be okay. She said, 'Your father's going to say your mother had too much to drink and slipped and fell in the pool. And maybe that describes the events of the evening. But it isn't the whole story, understand? You want to know what happened to your mother, Violet? *He* happened. You hear me? When you grow up and fall in love, make sure it's love you're falling in, not some lying bastard's pool.'"

Mom reached out and ran her fingertips over a strand of my hair that had fallen over my shoulder.

"I didn't really take her advice, did I?" I said.

"You realize, sweetie"—my mother's voice tore me away from the memory—"that you are not me and Sam is not your father. I know that moment left a mark. But your relationship isn't the same; it's not ours, it's *yours*. Daddy and I made our own mistakes, and I own mine. You don't."

"I've made plenty of mistakes too," I said. "My column got out of hand. I burned Sam's stuff in the street."

"And?" She took a sip of her drink.

I sighed. "I've been casually sleeping with a firefighter. Actually, I'm not sure it *is* casual. If I'm being completely honest, I think I might be falling for him. That's not smart, Mom. I'm a disaster—I shouldn't be jumping into a new relationship already."

Mom stayed quiet, until I couldn't take it anymore.

"Aren't you going to say something to me?" I asked.

"Like what? I'm hoping that at this juncture I don't need to tell you about venereal diseases."

"You don't care that I'm sleeping around?"

"There are others? I thought you just said firefighter." She drew out the singular ending.

"Jeez, Mom. That's not what I meant. I'm not divorced yet."

"Please, don't be so naive, Violet. I've had my fair share of lovers. I'm not a nun, and neither are you. And anyhow, humans are messy. They can be horrible. Some more horrible than others, but we all have our moments. I certainly didn't intend to teach you that you had to be flawless. That's a battle you'll never win." She paused to examine my face. "You and Sam are no longer together. Correct? And as for the rest of it . . . are you trying?"

"I'm trying so hard."

"Then that's all you can do."

I swallowed hard and watched my mother. She fetched the banana pudding and set it down between us. She plunged a big silver spoon into it and served us both a healthy helping.

"I thought you'd be angry with me," I confessed. "Even Kyra's mad at me, and rightly so. I've been the queen of bad choices lately, and I put her in a tough spot."

"Oh, good grief, Violet." She sucked a smear of pudding from her thumb. "For all of my commentary, you are a grown woman. What does it matter what I think? It matters what you think." She said that last sentence slowly, like she wanted to make sure I got that message loud and clear. "If Kyra's mad at you, figure out how to make it better. Delilah and I have had plenty of rough patches over the years, but we worked them out. We always do. You want to know what I've learned? Romance comes and goes, but friends, well, if you've got a friend like Kyra, you put in the work for that. I'm sure there's a way to fix it."

"But I posted that column and—"

"It's not like you ran over Kyra with your car like you did Lillian."

"I didn't actually run her over with my car. It was just a tap."

"Pity," she said.

"Mom!"

"I'm just kidding . . . well, mostly. That pissant had it coming to her. Like philandering Sam is God's gift."

"Oh."

"Pudding's delicious, by the way." She reached across the table and gave my hand a squeeze. "Now let's figure out what you can do to make things better with Kyra, and then I want to hear about this firefighter. There must be a reason they're in half my Harlequins!"

"Mom!" I flushed and shoved a spoonful of pudding into my mouth.

Thirty-Seven

Dear Sweetie,

I have a problem, a problem named [redacted], and I need advice only you can give. [Redacted] is on the PTA with me, and before that, we were great friends. Our children grew up together, playing on playgrounds and splash pads while we talked about how hard motherhood is and shared our struggles and our strategies for extending nap time. Then her son bit mine in kindergarten, on three separate occasions, so hard he broke the skin each time. I was angry about it, but I didn't blame her or the little boy. The weird thing is, even though I let the school handle the whole thing, you would've thought the entire episode was my fault from the way [redacted] treated me afterward. She not only stopped talking to me, but she turned all of our mutual friends against me. Then she ran for my position in the PTA and basically launched a massive smear campaign to beat me. The worst part is that she knew that being active in the school was the only thing that made me feel like I was doing something important. Now, meetings get scheduled at times I've indicated I'm not available, and I get all the worst jobs. Every time

I walk up to a group of PTA moms, they get real quiet, like they were talking about me. It's a nightmare. I am the victim here. I did nothing to her. In fact, I think I went above and beyond to preserve our relationship even when her kid went Cujo on mine, and yet I'm the one being punished. Here's where I need you. I want justice. I want to even the score. [Redacted] is the one who was in the wrong, so she should be paying the price. I don't want to be a doormat anymore. I'm furious. I'm ready to stand up for myself and take my revenge. So, I need your advice. What should I do?

Sincerely,
PTA Pariah

••

Dear PTA Pariah,

A few things jumped out at me after reading your letter.

1) Your child was hurt.
2) You lost a good friend.
3) You were ostracized from your peers and something you enjoyed is not enjoyable anymore.
4) All of these things are extremely painful and hard.
5) I have given some bad advice lately if people who are hurting are reaching out to me asking how to get revenge.

Let me be clear: all this is not to say that what this person did and continues to do to you is okay. She is being a bully, plain and simple, and that is unacceptable. It's not that surprising that she also seems to be raising a bully. I'm not a parent, so I'm no expert here, but from everything I've heard and read: children are just that, children, and sometimes they hurt each other, but they also learn behavior from their parents. I imagine that your former friend, a term I'm using loosely here (I'll get to that in a bit), was probably ashamed and embarrassed about what happened, but instead of being vulnerable and contrite, she lashed out. If you think about it, there seems to be a pattern of lashing out in that family, but that's for a family counselor to parse out, not a humble advice columnist. I told you I was using the term *friend* loosely, and I was, because friends don't treat each other this way. When you mess up and hurt a friend, you apologize. Examine your behavior. Make amends and set it right if you can. You do better in the future. I know it hurts to lose someone you're close to, but it sounds like you didn't lose much with this one. Not a real friend anyway.

If you can take some comfort in the situation, isn't there some to be had in the fact that you did nothing wrong? You may walk into these rooms where people are spreading mistruths about you, but you can still hold your head high knowing the real truth. That's something no one can take from you. But if you take revenge, aren't you just as bad as her? Aren't you literally the embodiment of all the negative things people are saying about you? Listen, I am never an advocate of letting the bullies win. It is completely okay to walk away from things that aren't good for you if you need to, if you can't take it anymore, but if you can stick it out, things have a way of working themselves out, and now that this individual is no longer in your life, there's space for real friends, rewarding relationships that can survive a test or a mistake.

I've made a lot of poor choices lately, on and off the page. I've advocated for revenge and I've taken it, and honestly, I can say: I don't feel better. I feel ashamed and sorry. I'm not some vigilante fighting for a noble cause or against injustice like I thought. I was so wrapped up in my own petty problems that I failed to notice the fallout. Take it from me and the wise words of my very best friend: walk away from the tire iron. Going low never did anybody any favors. Yes, you're struggling, and it hurts, but you don't have to hang your head, and she does. She knows it. That's why she's doing all this. And at the end of the day, that's something to hold on to while you ride this one out, honey cakes. So, my advice is to hang on. You'll find your real friends, who don't buy any of the BS that [redacted] is spreading about you, who listen and call you out when you're about to make a bad choice. Find them and do whatever you can to hang on to them. Be the kind of person your son can look up to. Teach him how to treat others. Help him see the difference between standing up for what's right and taking a cheap shot. Show him that we're all stronger than we think; we're resilient and brave, if we give ourselves the chance.

I have faith in you. I know this probably isn't the advice you were looking for, but I'm trying to do better and set a few things right myself, and so I'm hoping that even though it wasn't the advice you wanted, it is the advice you need.

Sincerely,
Sweetie

....

· Thirty-Eight ·

I EMAILED MY NEW COLUMN to Kyra after I'd gotten home from dinner at Mom's house and it'd poured out of me. I'd wanted to give good advice, rational and honest advice, but I'd also wanted to let Kyra know that I knew I'd been wrong and that I would do anything to set things right and to avoid making the same mistakes over again. We'd been friends since before I'd even met Sam. In fact, other than my mom, Kyra was my longest relationship.

Then there was my other relationship, if I was ready to call it that (was he? I wondered). He had just sent me a text that read:

> **The new door looks amazing. There was a scheduling mix-up so I'm off tonight. You want to sit on the porch and have a nightcap and piss off your judgy neighbor?**

I smiled.

> **Sure. Come on over. Pissing off my neighbor is what I do best.**

Dez was there in less than ten minutes, clad in a pair of sweatpants and a tight University of Maryland T-shirt, with two coffees.

"They're decaf," he said when I eyed them.

He looked like a very tall, very delicious snack. Actually, he looked a bit like a hero on the front of a modern romance novel, with those broad shoulders, biceps, and roped forearms, the cut of his sharp jaw, and the fact that he kept showing up for me again and again. I really wanted to deserve that.

"Thanks," I said, taking one from his hand. He sat in one of the rocking chairs and I settled into the other beside him. "How are you?"

"Good. I had a nice day; got in a workout, watched a documentary about the lost city of Atlantis, even did some laundry—"

I laughed.

"I figured you'd be impressed. How was yours?" he asked.

"Pretty good. I had dinner with my mother, which went better than expected."

He took a drink. "That's good."

"I wrote a column that I'm almost proud of for once."

"Sounds like a pretty great day."

"It was. It's not the beach, but I feel better, which is monumental compared to where I was a few days ago. Does that make sense?"

"Yeah. It does. Sorry I had to run off on you the other day, by the way. I would've stayed."

I fiddled with the cardboard sleeve on the coffee. "It was fine."

"You were trying to tell me something. It felt . . . I don't know . . . kind of like it might be important."

My heart paced faster. I *had* been about to say something important, but that moment had passed, and I wasn't entirely sure that I hadn't sort of dodged a bullet there in not saying what I'd been about to. The feelings behind it were still there, but the new Violet was not impulsive; she was careful. I shook my head.

He turned his chair so that he was facing me; his knees brushed against mine. "You said I don't know you very well, Violet." He reached out and stroked his thumb over my cheek. "I do know that I like you a lot, more than I should probably. I want to know you better."

I hadn't been expecting that. I took a gulp of coffee to give myself time to think. I could feel his gaze on me.

"I think maybe I was too hard on you the other day," he said.

I shook my head. "It's fine. I'm not as fragile as I seem, and I don't want everyone to think they have to go easy on me."

"What I mean is, you didn't tell me the whole story about why you were so upset about the baby thing, did you? There was more to it. And instead of sitting with you in that, I told you about Ben and you tried to make me feel better. I got thinking about it after we got that gas main fire out. I feel like a real dick."

I eyed Dez in the dim light. "You shouldn't."

"But I'm right."

There are some things that you push down because they're too painful to talk about. I wasn't sure that I could hold that much hurt if I brought it to the surface. I was barely hanging in there from the pain of losing my marriage . . . Talking about Bridie seemed like something that might break me so badly I couldn't put myself back together again.

Dez was eyeing me. There was a fine stubble starting on his jaw. I fixed my attention on it so I wouldn't feel the weight of his gaze. What happened then still felt like my fault somehow, even though I knew better than to think that. It was a burden that only some people understood, and having experienced it, I knew it was a wonder anyone ever becomes a mother.

"Sam and I weren't able to have a family," I said slowly, skirting the edges, like testing the ice on a pond so you don't plunge through.

Dez stayed quiet, his hand lightly gripping my leg. The weight of it anchored me.

"I got pregnant, after a long time trying, a couple of times." I shrugged. "I lost them all."

As soon as I said it, my eyes filled with tears, but I still tried to squeeze a smile. No one likes to see a person cry. The smile was meant to make it seem less significant, like the losses were just things that happened and I wasn't opening some deep, painful hollow inside of me.

"I'm sorry," he said, his voice low.

I shook my head. "Don't be, it was a while ago."

He tipped his head. "Violet, can I ask you something else?"

Against my better judgment, I nodded.

"Why do you do that?"

"Do what?" I gave a tight laugh.

"Make your feelings insignificant."

I scrambled for an answer, the perfect denial, but instead I said, "Nobody wants the whole story. They want the one they can handle."

"I think I want whatever story *you* can handle. I don't want you to open your wounds for me, but I don't want you to edit yourself either. If it helps to talk, if you need to lean on me, then lean. I want to be that person for you."

I retracted from him, folded my legs up to my chest in the chair, and wrapped my arms around my knees. Would it help to talk about it, really talk? I wondered. I hadn't with anyone. Even Sam and I had barely discussed it; it was too hard.

I don't know how long I was quiet, but Dez waited.

"Bridie," I said finally. "It was my grandmother's name. I just knew, I knew she would be a girl. I promised myself that I wouldn't get my hopes up, but I'd been making a Pinterest board of nursery ideas and painting little watercolor pictures of animals to hang on the walls. I'd bought a bunch of board books. *But Not the Hippopotamus* and *Sheep in a Jeep*. Everything was fine, and then she was gone. I couldn't try anymore after that. I wanted to, but I just couldn't go through that again. Some things simply aren't meant to be, I guess."

Dez reached down and wrapped his hand around the handle of my rocking chair. He pulled it toward him until we were only inches away from each other. His arm encircled me, pulled me toward him, up out of my chair to his chest.

"Bridie's a beautiful name," he said, his voice vibrating through me. I let my head dip to his shoulder and rested it there while I soaked the T-shirt he was wearing. "I'm sorry that you've been hurt so much, Violet."

"Cindy Willis said that it's a good thing Sam and I didn't have any children," I whispered. "Maybe she's right. I probably would've been a terrible mother."

His whole body tensed. "When'd she say that?"

"The day I had the panic attack. She gave me some burnt cookies and essentially called me a slut. It wasn't the best day I've had."

He smoothed a hand over my hair.

"That's what I get for letting my guard down."

He shook his head. "Nah. I think letting your guard down was a good thing. You're just surrounded by a lot of assholes. Screw Cindy Willis and her piss-poor attempt to shame you."

"Well, were it not for misogyny, she'd be shaming you too, so I guess it's good that your views are so different from hers."

"Extremely different. Let's just say that I'm very cool with it. Not the double standard, to be clear, but the other part." The corner of his mouth twitched a little.

"What?"

"Nothing. I was just thinking that it'd be kind of fun to show Cindy just how slutty we can be on your porch. A rocking chair seems like it could work to our advantage."

I smiled a little in spite of myself, but I shook my head. "I don't think that's a great idea."

"Alright then. It's your call. But will you do something for me?"

"Depends what it is."

"Keep that guard down, Vi. I can see how maybe not everything about lowering it has gone exactly to plan, but it hasn't all been disastrous, has it?" He reached over and pulled me out of my chair and onto his lap.

I looked at him, and that thing I'd been about to say when he'd been called away for the gas main started to rise up again. I bit my lip and I took a deep breath through my nose, letting the smell of Dez's detergent and Speed Stick and the faintest trace of smoke that seemed to float around him fill my senses. This didn't feel disastrous, but nothing ever starts out that way. I was getting a little too comfortable with Dez—when things had imploded at Bunco, he was the only person I really wanted to talk to—and that felt dangerous. And now I'd gone and told him about my biggest love, my deepest hurt. I tried to push those things out of my mind. Dez was tracing a path from my throat to my collarbone with soft kisses and I was thinking how easy it would be give in to temptation right there on the porch and how afterward he would hold me to him until the world seemed to disappear and I would revel in that. I would never want him to let go.

"No," I finally admitted.

"Do you have plans for Thanksgiving?" he asked.

"I don't think so," I said. "Why?"

"My crew is doing a big thing at the firehouse with families invited, and I wanted to ask if you would be my person."

"Oh."

His person. He leaned in and kissed me, a slow, languid kiss that dissolved my resistance. "Okay," I said. "I will be your person for Thanksgiving. But are you free the Saturday after next? Because I could use a plus-one for a very difficult kid's birthday party I have to attend."

Be careful, Violet, I could hear my mother saying. *Having fun is great. Just don't get in over your head.*

It's just a onetime thing, I rationalized, shushing the warning. I couldn't be Dez's person, not really, at least not yet, and I needed to make sure that I didn't start expecting him to be mine. Already, I was leaning on him too much, resting my head on his shoulder, trusting him with my bone-deep wounds. Now I had committed to Thanksgiving, a holiday that I hated, for more than just the fact that it was used as a fairy tale about the settlers when really the history of our country was a macabre robbery and more of the land and the Indigenous people who lived on it. Spending a holiday with someone was major.

"Absolutely," he said, tracing a path up my thigh under my cotton skirt while he brushed his lips over the nape of my neck. "I'll do anything for . . . cake."

Contrary to Cindy Willis's beliefs, I didn't have much experience in the romance department, but I was pretty sure that if you weren't serious about someone you wouldn't agree to the torment of a child's birthday party for the mere promise of cake. I'd also wager that you wouldn't plan to spend a holiday in a fire station in front of an entire crew unless you really cared about the firefighter who'd asked you to come. I was certain of one thing, though, despite my inexperience: you definitely were not supposed to put your heart in someone else's hands before it was healed. No matter how safe those hands seemed.

Thirty-Nine

Dez called me from the station the morning of the birthday party, deeply apologetic, over the screaming of the station alarm.

"Vi, I'm so sorry. I meant to phone you earlier, but we've been on nonstop calls. Hence the background noise—sorry about that. The next shift's lieutenant fell off a ladder cleaning his gutters before last night's storm. The other lieutenant just finished a twenty-four-hour shift, so there's only me. I can't go to the party with you. I'm so sorry, baby. I know this is going to be a tough one and I really want to be there, but I don't have a choice."

"That's okay," I said. "It's not like you're a banker or something. Go save some people. I can fend for myself."

"Yeah, you can." The way he said it, it almost made me believe he was right.

"Be safe," I said.

"You too."

I was working on being authentic and in touch with my emotions, but that didn't mean I needed to tell Dez that I didn't want to go alone or that I wanted to cry about the idea of doing so. It also did not preclude me from spending three hours picking the perfect outfit and makeup look for a preschooler's birthday party as if it were the Oscars. I might have been showing up alone, but I was going to look fabulous, dammit.

The event was the trifecta of trauma. A kid's birthday party was hard enough. Bonus points for the friends who were still mad at me, and my estranged husband and probably his very fit, very fertile mistress, who were also going to be in attendance. I stopped at Drybar on my way over and got a blowout and then I spent way more than I should've on a gift from the quaint little children's boutique in Waverly Place that sold Scandinavian toys and embroidered lovies and overpriced choking hazards. The last time I'd seen Tristan he'd claimed his favorite food was boogers, so I was pretty sure he'd be happy with a box of crayons and a pack of Play-Doh, but that didn't stop me from spending $114 on books, a stuffed bear with a set of ensembles you could swap out depending on the weather, and wooden discs painted with different shades of glow-in-the-dark paint that fit together into modern art sculptures. I had the items placed into a giant gift box with a massive gold bow that I couldn't see over.

Over the years, I'd answered countless letters about handling uncomfortable social situations. I'd told my readers that everyone else in the room is just as nervous as you. (Not likely. Not even close.) Show up on time with a killer gift. Fake it 'til you make it. The perfect little black dress. Touchstone in your pocket. None of those seemed to cover the situation I was walking into. When I checked the Evite, Sam had indicated he'd be there, as had Kyra, who still wasn't speaking to me if it wasn't essential. I also hadn't seen Ashleigh since the Bunco incident, and then there was also the joy of ass-grabbing Mark, on his own turf this time. Basically, it was an emotional minefield with cake.

I parked the Jeep at the end of Ashleigh and Mark's driveway, checked my makeup in the rearview, and then climbed carefully out. I made my way up the walk with the giant box in front of me, like a ridiculous shiny shield. The front door was open, but I could hear everyone around the back. I pushed through the gate with my knee and headed to the patio. Even in November, it was warm enough for an outdoor party. The air barely had a tinge of crispness; I wasn't sure I'd even need the jean jacket I was wearing over my grass-green Swiss-dot dress. This was North Carolina, after all, but it was a look, and I was going to sweat in it if I needed to.

"Hey, Violet," Mark said when he saw me. "Let me take that off your hands. Box's practically bigger than you, girl. What you got in here? A Peloton bike?" He took the present out of my hands and set it on a table that was already full of gifts. I took some delight in the fact that my box was the biggest. Ashleigh came over and put her hand on Mark's back. "You didn't need to bring anything, Violet," she said. "This is just too much."

"You only turn four once," I said. "Where is the birthday boy, anyway?"

"Oh, he's on the trampoline with some of his little buddies from gymnastics." Sure enough, there was Tristan in khaki shorts, a chambray shirt, and an honest-to-goodness bow tie. He was standing in the middle of the trampoline picking his nose with gusto. I felt relieved by this. Ashleigh was visibly horrified. "Mark, you want to do something about that?" she muttered.

"Sure thing, babe," he said. "Have some food, Violet. The pig's on the other side of the house."

When Mark was out of earshot, Ashleigh turned to me. "We had to move it into the side yard because Tristan had a massive meltdown when he saw it. You missed it. All the kids were screaming. That little girl in the pink dress?"

"With the bows?" I said.

"Yeah, she called us murderers. Apparently, Madison is vegan. She's three."

I shook my head and decided to take the opportunity to do a little reconnaissance.

"Sam's not here yet," Ashleigh said, "if you were wondering."

"He probably had to stop and get a gift at Target on the way," I said. "I always bought the presents." I forced a smile on my face. "This is really nice," I added. There was a rainbow fish piñata hanging from a massive magnolia branch, and different-colored paper lanterns were swaying from the trees. Acoustic children's music that actually wasn't unpleasant to listen to came from speakers that were hidden in rocks. There were some wooden picnic tables set up and a small table close to the ground with piles of pillows for the kids. Bubbles were coming from a machine and floating around the yard.

"Thanks." Ashleigh was wearing a tennis dress, a pair of navy-blue shimmery Toms, and a strand of pearls. It seemed like the perfect thing for a kid's birthday party with a lot of fancy adults, yet she looked uncomfortable.

"Have you seen Kyra?" I asked, trying to sound neutral. I'd spotted Harriet on the trampoline, so I figured that either Roxy or Kyra must be nearby.

"She's here somewhere. You know how it is at these things . . . you see everyone for a second and then it's over and you realize that you haven't eaten and the whole thing's a blur, like a wedding."

I did not know.

Behind Ashleigh, the gate opened and in strode Sam. His polo shirt was wrinkled and he needed a haircut. He was carrying a Target bag that he'd folded closed as if the bullseye pattern were actually wrapping paper. I narrowed my eyes. Of course he couldn't have been bothered to just buy a gift bag from the Dollar Spot. He shook hands with Mark.

"Hey, bud," he said. "How've you been?"

"Good," Mark said. "How 'bout yourself?"

"Amazing."

Ashleigh fiddled with her pearls for a moment. "Can we talk inside?" she asked. "I was going to get myself some sweet tea if you want one."

"Sure." Thankful for the well-timed escape route, I followed her into the house and sat down at the kitchen table.

"Excuse the mess. This was my staging area for all the snacks and dessert."

"It's fine." I took the tea from her. "Thanks." Through the window, I could see the back of Sam's head as he nodded along to something that Mark and his cronies were talking about. Beyond the all-male clump near the deck, Kyra, Roxy, and Tyler stood on the patio—the newspaper faction. Roxy was watching Harriet bounce, but Kyra was turned toward the house, glaring directly at Sam . . . or me, I supposed, since I was probably visible behind him.

"I found Kyra," I said, trying to sound light. "I guess everyone's accounted for."

"Can I show you something?" Ashleigh asked.

"Sure." She went to the desk and pulled something from a drawer. When she returned she handed me a sheet of paper.

. . . .

Dear Sweetie,

I did something terrible to a friend. At a Labor Day party at her house, I saw my husband grab her butt. I should've asked her about it, but I kept quiet and stewed. I've been assuming the worst since that day. Anyway, I came up with a plan to ruin things for her at work. I know—it's bad. I just wanted her to feel how I felt. Now I see that actually my husband is kind of a prick who grabs women without their consent, and that's his problem, not hers. But I don't know how to begin to try and make amends for what I did to her, or what he did, for that matter.

I'm really sorry.
Ashleigh

....

I looked up from the note. Ashleigh was sitting at the kitchen table across from me, twisting her long fingers, her emerald-cut ring glinting in the afternoon sun. Her manicure was perfect, but her cuticles were a shredded mess.

"I'm not sure how to respond," I said. "This obviously isn't meant for the column. It's meant for me?"

"I didn't know what to say to you," Ashleigh said. "I've been feeling absolutely horrid about the whole thing ever since I did it."

I rubbed my forehead, where a migraine was beginning to bloom. "What exactly *did* you do? I mean, my career has been kind of a mess, but that was my own doing."

"The fan at the club, the one who revealed your identity on the internet?"

"That was you?"

"Well, not quite. I didn't get my hands dirty, if that's what you mean. That was Tristan's old nanny, Gemma. I paid her to be at the club and to take the pictures and post the stuff."

"Oh." The glass of sweet tea was starting to sweat. I watched a rivulet drip down and pool on the tabletop.

"I was so angry. I thought you were trying to come between Mark and me. But then you told me in the bathroom about what happened with Sam and . . . I tried to call it off, but stupid Gemma, she was already drunk and on autopilot; she totally ignored all of my signals. Plus, Mark showed up and he seemed gleeful almost about you and

Sam splitting up; it sort of fired me up again." Ashleigh stopped twisting her hands together, but I noticed that the hand she'd rested on the table was trembling.

I let her words absorb for an uncomfortably long time.

"Is that all?"

Ashleigh squirmed. She grabbed a piece of cuticle and pulled. "The night of Bunco, I did something awful."

My thoughts drifted back to that horrendous evening. "You mean asking Shelby about her love life while I was trapped at a table with you two?"

"No." She shook her head. "I didn't know she was the one that Sam was sleeping with. I didn't realize until . . . well, I stopped by your place to check on you before I went home. You'd been acting so weird. I saw the letter on your laptop and put two and two together. I figured I could kill two birds with one stone."

My eyes widened at the revelation. "*You* posted that letter?"

"I know it was wrong. As soon as I got home, I tried to take it down, but I couldn't log in to your account, and my account didn't have privileges to change your content."

I nodded. So my not remembering hadn't been because I'd been violently ill and didn't remember the night clearly. I hadn't done it in the first place. Not that it mattered to Shelby, or to Kyra. I shouldn't have written what I had, regardless of my intent. My words had come from a place of destruction. That was the thing I was starting to understand. Yes, good writing and change could come from rage, but when it came from a place with no control, no hope, no vision for things being better, that led to worse things. If it hadn't existed in the first place, Ashleigh wouldn't have been able to post it.

"All this time, you knew what happened on Labor Day?"

She nodded. "I got the wrong idea. Mark and I finally had it out at counseling a few weeks ago. Turns out, he'd figured out that Sam was running around on you and he was pissed. He's always had a kind of fondness for you, I guess, in a little sister sort of way, at least that's how he put it. He got the other guys to throw those firecrackers at Sam and then he purposely grabbed you in front of him, hoping to piss him off. It was a shitty thing for him to do . . . I'm not trying to make excuses for him. Mark needs to keep his hands to himself, and he's a bit of a misogynist, which would make a lot of sense if you met his dad, but anyway, we're covering that in therapy, don't you worry."

"Oh." Labor Day had been so long ago and Sam had already been with Shelby then. My throat was dry. I took a sip of the sweet tea.

"I blamed you for the problems in my marriage, and there are plenty of them. You were an easy target. I'm really sorry. I'll understand if you don't forgive me," Ashleigh said.

I wiped the condensation from my glass before I looked at her. "Stupider, meaner things have been done on behalf of a hurting heart," I said. "I should know. I'm not completely innocent. Truth is, I wanted to post that letter myself. It was easy enough for me to believe that I'd done it. I wanted to punish Shelby for stealing my husband, like if she hadn't run by looking all wonderful, he'd still be here and we'd be happy . . . but the truth is, we had our issues long before he even met her. Just between you and me, I'm not sure we *were* happy."

"I made it worse."

I held up my hand. "I don't have space or the energy to hold any more anger or resentment. Let's just say that next time we'll talk to each other and clear things up before we hatch any secret revenge plots."

Ashleigh nodded. When she smiled a tear spilled over and traced a path down her cheek. It left a pale streak in its wake where it washed away her foundation. I squeezed her hand. "I'm honestly a little impressed," I told her. "I had no idea you were secretly an evil mastermind."

"We all have our hidden talents. I mean, look at you."

I shook my head. "Going rogue and imploding on the page for the world to read is not a secret skill."

She tipped her head. "Oh, I don't know about that. I heard through the grapevine that you're going to be published in *Gloss*! That's next level. And, look, I know that we were raised to be quiet and nonconfrontational—we had to be careful not to say the wrong thing. But maybe saying something, even the wrong thing, is more important and better than being quiet or right or whatever. I mean, none of this would've happened if I'd just said something to you."

"You've got a point," I admitted. "But there is such a thing as going too far."

"Well, good thing you're an advice columnist. It seems like you are the perfect person to figure out exactly what you need to do to make things better."

My chest felt a little lighter after that, even though I knew better than most that knowing a lot about something only makes you acutely aware that you really know close to nothing. Still. Honesty with a positive goal—it seemed like a starting point at least, and it didn't make me want to shrivel up with shame.

"On that note," I said, "your brownies were awful and made me projectile vomit. Next time, try Duncan Hines and the toothpick test."

Forty

I LEFT ASHLEIGH AT THE kitchen table, where she was finishing moving some kid-friendly vegetable sushi to a tray to bring outside, and made my way over to the piñata, where little Tristan was swinging a stick nowhere near the candy-filled creature. A very small piece of me hoped that he would nail either Mark or Sam in the nuts like one of those viral videos. I watched Ashleigh deposit the veggie rolls on a table. Then she approached Kyra and explained what had happened while she tested the strength of that strand of pearls with her nervous fidgeting. Kyra glanced over at me and I quickly turned my attention back to the perilous swinging. Tristan actually made good contact, but the piñata must have been made out of concrete or something, because nothing happened. The other kids each took several turns whacking it with the stick, unblindfolded no less, without busting the thing open. Tristan's face screwed up like he was about to cry. "Daddy, we want candy!"

Mark disappeared into the garage and returned with a metal baseball bat I recognized as the one that he used in the firm's softball league. He hit that piñata so hard, it went flying over the fence into their neighbor's yard, raining down candy as it arced through the air.

"Shit, man," Sam said.

Mark gave him a glare and a hands-out gesture that plainly read, *Dude, there's kids around*. Fourth birthday, the day Tristan learned the word *shit*.

"Shit!" Tristan giggled. "Shit! Shit! Shit!"

Ashleigh came running. "That's not a nice word, Tristan."

"It's not? But Mr. Sam said it."

"Mr. Sam can say it, but we don't. We say *poo-poo*."

I pressed my lips together to try and suppress a laugh.

"Shit is poo-poo?"

"Oh good Lord, Ashleigh," Kyra said. "Let the poor kid say *shit*. It's bad enough you made him wear the bow tie."

"Sorry about that," Sam said. He was blushing.

"Shit, poo-poo. Shit, poo-poo," Tristan sang. The other kids joined in. Some of them were dancing around. "Let's go jump," Tristan said, and they all ran back to the trampoline screaming about defecation.

I couldn't contain my laughter anymore. The giggles gurgled out until I was laughing so hard that I couldn't hear those adorable little potty mouths anymore. Occasionally, Sam would say, "Again, I apologize."

"He was bound to learn it sometime," I said finally.

Sam eyed me. "I hope that's true. I'm running short on people who are still speaking to me, so I'd like to keep Mark from disowning me."

I nodded. I could feel him watching me, but I was too busy looking at Kyra, who had moved back to the trampoline and was reenacting the entire swearing scene for Roxy.

"You two okay?" Sam asked.

"Who?"

He lifted his chin. "You and Kyra. Since when are you not attached at the hip?"

"It's a misunderstanding." I fell silent for several unbearable seconds. "About the online post."

"Oh."

"For the record, I didn't post that. I've been having a hard time, even I admit I haven't been on my best behavior, but I hope you know that I would never do anything to harm—"

He shook his head. "You don't have to—"

"I just want to be clear."

"I know you wouldn't do that. I never thought that you did. You're a good, kindhearted person, Violet. Even if you did set my stuff on fire and scream in my face."

I turned to him, my eyebrows arched. "I thought you were going to sue me?"

"Look, I shouldn't have said that. I've been going through some stuff at work and I was already wound up when your column came out. I was way out of line. And, you scared the"—he lowered his voice—"*shit* out of me."

The panic attack. "Believe me, *I* scared me too."

He pushed a rock with the toe of his loafer. "My gift was dumb, I think. Some Play-Doh ice cream factory thing."

"That's not dumb. Tristan will probably love it."

Sam shrugged. "What do I know about kids?"

"Me either."

We stood next to each other in silent solidarity for a long time. Even though so much had happened between us, pulled us apart, we had that shared pain. Birthday parties were hard.

"You didn't bring her," I said.

"She didn't want to come."

"Oh."

I wasn't sure if I felt grateful or guilty. Sam did not elaborate. Was that mercy or was there more to his withholding? "Thank you, by the way, for saving some of my stuff at least. I was running pretty short on clothes. And I know you think they're dumb, but the Star Wars stuff, well, Dad bought me that, so I'm real relieved you didn't sell them."

"No problem."

His elbow brushed against mine. It was just a moment, but it made my throat tighten. I squeezed my eyes shut. I needed to break that moment, somehow, before his knuckles grazed mine.

"You look nice. Green always was a good color on you."

Shit poo-poo. My heart thudded in my chest.

"I spent over a hundred dollars on a present," I blurted.

Sam blinked. I wasn't sure if it was my shouting or if it was the fact that I'd spent so much that threw him—Sam always did have a thing about money; miserly, my mother called him. *At least when you're retired you can live in style*, she'd say.

Kyra swooped in. "Remind me to make sure you're invited to Harriet's birthday party then, Auntie Violet. She really wants the Power Wheels Barbie Dream Camper." She put an arm around me. "I heard Ashleigh made those Oreo truffle thingies that she brings to the holiday party every year. Want to go truffle hunting with me?"

"Bye, Sam," I said, waving as Kyra dragged me away.

"You okay?" Kyra asked when we were out of earshot.

I stopped. "I don't know."

"What'd he say to you?"

"He told me I looked nice."

"That's it. I'm going to punch his face."

"I think Tristan's learned enough lessons today. Let's save the ass kicking for his fifth birthday."

"What an asshole," she said. "I can't believe he's toying with your emotions like that."

"It didn't seem like he was playing," I said. "I think he's just trying to be nice."

She shook her head. "You know what I think? I think he's tired of Little Miss Hot Pants. He didn't bring her."

"He said she didn't want to come. Can you blame her after what happened? She probably thinks I'd try to poison her cupcake."

Kyra's mouth squirreled up. "Ashleigh spoke to me about that."

"Yeah, she told me too."

"You're not totally off the hook. If you hadn't written that in the online portal, she wouldn't have had anything to post. But maybe I was a bit more reactive than I could have been."

"Don't. I'm glad that you yelled at me. Honestly. It wasn't particularly fun, but I hadn't realized what work is like for you. I feel pretty stupid that I didn't notice. I'm glad that you shared it with me. I wish you hadn't needed to, but now that I'm aware, I'm going to try to better support you."

"I appreciate that," she said.

"Can you forgive me for being a shitty friend who's obsessed with her own problems?" I asked.

"Only if you can forgive me for not trusting you and for biting your head off."

"Hey, you didn't fire me," I said.

"That's true. I thought about it, but I did not."

"Very magnanimous of you."

"Now that's a column for you. Being the bigger person." She squeezed her arm around my shoulders. "Now, back to your problems," she said. She cast a glance back at where Sam stood under the magnolia tree. "Careful there."

Forty-One

Dear Sweetie,

I used to be a woman who had it all, and now I've got nothing but troubles. I was deeply in love with someone who left me behind with no explanation. The pain of that heartbreak was so immense that I numbed it with pills and did a lot of stupid things. I got a DUI and lost my medical license. My family tried to intervene, but I felt so attacked by their efforts to pull me out of my drugged despair that I treated them viciously. I used my sister's prescription pad to write opiate scripts for myself. I stole money for drugs from my parents when the painkillers weren't enough anymore. I lost my house. My friends. My family. I abused their trust and ruined everything, and they severed all ties with me. So when I say I truly have nothing left, I mean it. I feel awful all the time. The only time I feel anything other than pain or hopelessness or shame is when I am high. I don't know what to do. I know this isn't the kind of thing you usually have in your columns, but I don't have anywhere else to turn. I feel completely worthless and alone.

Hopeless

Dear Hopeless,

I can feel your anguish in every word. And I want to tell you that you are not worthless, you are brave. You reached out and asked for help, and that is the hardest, most courageous thing you could do. I know it may not seem this way, because hopelessness lies to us, but so many more of us than we could ever know are facing a similar struggle. We're walking around in pain, feeling empty or miserable, and we numb those feelings, or we do things, stupid things, bad things, risky things, to fill ourselves with new feelings, with feelings we can bear. Because the alternative feels intolerable. Insurmountable.

You are not alone in making mistakes or abusing the trust of the people who love you. And you are not alone in thinking that this is all just a bit more than you were made to handle.

I've stood in similar shoes. Mine have kitten heels and betrayal, and of course I can never truly know your experience, or anybody's for that matter. But I will admit that I've been deeply hurt and felt a shocking pain that I didn't believe I'd be able to bear. I too have harmed the people around me, pulled away from them, not thought about how the consequences of my actions would impact them. My own survival mode might have taken on a slightly different shape of self-destruction than yours, but it left a mark just the same.

Through this I have learned a couple of things, and I share them with you in the hope that my words will give you some comfort.

You can be broken and still be whole. You can break things and still be loved. Life is full of second chances and thirds and sometimes fourths. Take them, but use them wisely. Look for the helpers—Mr. Rogers was way better at giving advice than I am—they're out there . . . those people who want to help; take them up on it. You're going to need support. Know that those hard truths you don't want to hear come from a place of love. Find a program. I'm going to list some at the bottom of this column, for you and all the many other people who need some support.

I hope that this initial, brave, big step is the first in a walk that will bring you to a better place. Know that I am cheering you on, even when you fall, even if you're crawling on your knees. You don't travel alone.

Sincerely,
Sweetie

Substance Abuse and Mental Health Services Administration SAMHSA.gov/find-help/national-helpline

Alcoholics Anonymous aa.org

NC Region of Narcotics Anonymous ncregion-na.org

....

· Forty-Two ·

I did not show up on Monday morning with freshly baked cookies or an innocence-themed outfit. I wore jeans and a simple black sweater with pearls and a pair of old Vans, and went straight to my desk, where I got to work.

Ashleigh stopped by on her way to her desk. "Tristan loved the bear you bought him. Once he came down from all that sugar, he decided he was going to be a meteorologist and spent the entire weekend changing its clothes and making Mark film his weather reports." She laughed. "Look, here's one of the videos." She handed me her phone to watch. There was little Tristan in a raincoat and rain boots, with that ridiculous bear tucked under his arm. "It's gonna be a wet one, folks. You're gunna need a 'brella for sure."

"He's so cute," I told her, and I meant it, even though my heart squeezed the words out of me. "I'm glad he liked the present."

"I'm pretty sure no one will ever come close to topping it. You're officially his auntie number one. Don't tell Mark's sister." She winked.

"I have to admit, I was a little stressed about the whole thing."

"Of course you were! But it worked out fine . . . except for the part where Sam taught all the kids their first swear. I could've done without that portion of the festivities."

I cracked a smile. "Sorry about that."

"Why are you apologizing? You're not responsible for his bad behavior . . . any of it."

"Thanks." I handed her phone back and she squeezed my hand.

"I missed this," she said.

"Me too."

She glanced at the time. "I gotta run. I have this tip on something big with a selectman in Holly Springs and I want to make sure I don't get scooped."

I leaned back. "A tip?" Ashleigh's tips tended to be about fashion and beauty, not necessarily something I associated with town selectmen.

"Something about misappropriation of that park bond money." My face must've not been as neutral as I thought, because she added, "I'm like Shrek, I've got layers. And I'm hoping that if I do a good enough job blowing this scandal wide open, Kyra might let me do a little investigative reporting."

"Well, look at you," I said, and grinned at her. "With all of your glorious layers."

"Are we talking croissants or cake?" Kyra said.

"I think we're talking about souls," I said, "but don't quote me on it."

Ashleigh waved and walked off fast enough to avoid any follow-up questions. "Let's chat in my office," Kyra said.

I followed her and shut the door behind me. "I had a talk with Ed and we both agree that there need to be better protocols about posting things in the online edition. Ashleigh's stunt highlighted how vulnerable we are in terms of security protocols. If someone's password got stolen, we could be in a real tough situation. That being said, you are officially off probation, so we can stop running your old hits and you can start writing your column again. Just—do both of us a favor and think carefully about what you're writing. I can smooth a lot of things over, but I can't pretend that you aren't under a microscope now."

I nodded. "I know. I talked to him."

"You did?"

"Look, I'll be the first to admit that I've been wrapped up in my own problems lately. But I am trying to do better and not be so selfish. I wanted to make sure that Ed knew this wasn't your fault in any way, shape, or form."

"It wasn't exactly your fault either," she said.

I lifted my shoulders. The conversation with Ed had been tense. While he was a decent person, he also was like one of those old-school high school football coaches who relished punishing the whole team for the misdeeds of the wide receiver. My article in *Gloss* was hitting newsstands any day now, which gave me the extra confidence I'd needed to face him. I'd assured him that if there was any blowback on the paper that I would step down, immediately and without protest. He'd seemed satisfied by that. Also, it turned out that Ed really liked cookies, and sometimes baking *can* help smooth things over.

"Maybe that's true," I said, "but I haven't exactly been thinking things through, and to a certain extent I forgot about the people I was supposed to be helping. I won't make that mistake again."

She nodded and tapped a pencil eraser on her desk. "So about the syndication . . ."

"It's fine. I'm not deluding myself into thinking that there's still a chance of that."

"There could be," she said. "What's needed here is a strategic pivot. You've gotten a lot of publicity from some of these viral columns, and yes, it wasn't all positive, but a well-timed interview and a couple of heartfelt columns and we're back in the game."

"Do you get paid extra for the optimism?"

"Did you really just ask me if I get paid extra? I thought you said you weren't delusional."

"Sorry."

"It's fine. I'll let you buy me lunch. How about Dalat over in Mission Valley? Invite the crew."

We left the office at eleven thirty to beat the lunchtime rush. Over pineapple fried rice and vermicelli buns, we chatted.

"I can't remember the last time the four of us went out together," Tyler said.

"The club?" Ashleigh said.

Kyra shook her head. "I wasn't there, y'all. I think things might have gone a bit differently if I had been. For one thing, I would definitely have kept your middle-aged ass off the dance floor. And you"—she turned her attention to Ashleigh—"let's just say that the little nanny-fan stunt would not have made it past me."

"Sorry," Ashleigh said. Her cheeks were pink as she spooned some pho into her mouth.

"I'm teasing," Kyra said. "Also, the last time the four of us went out was last year, the week after Thanksgiving."

"Thanksgiving," Tyler groaned. "God, I hate the holidays. This year I made up an excuse about having to work." He raised his glass in a toast to Kyra.

"Why?" I asked.

He lifted his shoulders. "It's kind of hard to have a meal with a bunch of people who claim to love you but also don't accept you. I can't bring Daniel. I have to sit there basically pretending to be someone I'm not, and it's exhausting to have to perform. I want to be able to share my life with them . . . and I can't."

Kyra was nodding.

"They don't support you?" I asked.

"I mean, my brother does. I think. He sometimes asks me if I'm seeing anyone or whatever. My mom said she loves me, but every time I say anything about my love life, she starts weeping. It's not like I expected her to start wearing rainbow socks or anything, but it would be great if she wouldn't act like me being gay was a tragedy."

I did not understand what it must feel like to have a mother who wept about a fundamental part of who I was, but I did know how unpleasant it was to feel like you had to perform.

"What are you going to do?" Ashleigh asked. "I wouldn't go. They don't deserve you."

"You can come to ours," Kyra said. "Rox and I put on one hell of a Thanksgiving. None of that Whole Foods premade— Sorry, Violet."

"It was a defense maneuver," I said. "Lillian criticized everything I ever made."

"You're all welcome to come. This year, we're planning to eat at Rox's new restaurant space on the patio, so there's plenty of room."

"That would be great," Ashleigh said. "I don't really feel like Mark and I are ready for the pressure of our parents at Thanksgiving quite yet. We're getting there, but if his dad pinches my butt, we may have to file for divorce." Ashleigh flushed again and gave me a contrite grimace, but she didn't apologize, which I appreciated.

I waved a hand. "It's fine. Actually, I have an invite. I just don't know if I'm going to take it."

The three of them all leaned in. I turned my attention to a very captivating piece of pineapple on my plate.

"An invite?" Kyra said, her voice dripping with incredulity. "Your mom told me that she's going to be in Puerto Vallarta on Thanksgiving, so who is this invite from?"

I cleared my throat. "Ah, Dez," I said, my voice barely a whisper. I took a long sip of my sweet tea through a straw.

"Firefighter Dez?"

"Who is Firefighter Dez?" Tyler said, his eyes twinkling with mischief.

"He's Violet's gentleman friend."

I let out a sigh of relief that Ashleigh had answered first, because Kyra, who delighted in watching me blush, wouldn't have been so tactful. She'd probably even have used the term—

"Sexual sage. She called him that." Kyra slapped the table.

"You mean like he's wise and all knowing? I want one of those. Daniel is wonderful, I mean, he's a pediatric surgeon, but sexual sage he is not . . . yet."

"I meant like clearing the bad energy out of the house," I said, although the latter interpretation was also undeniably true. Dez was wise and all knowing about a lot of things.

"It must be a bit more than energy clearing"—Tyler laughed and shook his head at the last word before he went on—"if you're having Thanksgiving together."

I shook my head. "Not together, really. He invited me to eat with his crew at the firehouse. Apparently, they're on shift that day."

"Hold on. He invited you to have Thanksgiving at the *firehouse*? Shoot, Violet. That's bigger than just the two of you, or even family, if you think about it," Kyra said.

I frowned. "How do you figure?"

"How often do you put your life on the line with your family?"

Point taken.

"That crew is probably like his coworkers, plus best friends and family, rolled into one."

"Are you *so* nervous?" Tyler asked.

I hadn't been. Okay, I had been, but not like this. A tiny tide of panic started to rise up within me. Maybe I should tell Dez that I couldn't make it and go to Kyra and Rox's instead?

"I can see you doing the mental gymnastics to weasel your way out of it," Kyra said. "What would Sweetie say? If only we had some of her wisdom available right now."

"Right!" Ashleigh chimed in. "Like in print."

Tyler did a little drumroll on the table and then all at once, Kyra and Ashleigh produced copies of the brand-new December edition of *Gloss*. Tyler stopped drumming and procured the copy he'd been hiding under his napkin.

"Congratulations, Violet! You're in a magazine!" they chorused.

I beamed.

"I am so proud of you," Kyra said. She leaned toward me. "It's good, Vi. It's real good."

"Really?" I asked. "I was worried."

Kyra shook her head and took a sip of water. "You know, I seem to remember Sweetie saying in one of her columns that we should all learn to trust our instincts. Seems like good advice to me. From this, I'd say you've got some great ones."

Forty-Three

Sweetie already had about twenty-six emails in her inbox regarding Thanksgiving issues. Family feuds. Football rivalries. Food allergies. Lumpy gravy. Place settings. Tofurkeys. The aftermath of a turkey fryer explosion and forgiveness. After I'd read through them all, I'd decided that I was lucky to have an invite to Thanksgiving and that dinner at the firehouse was just that and I needed to calm the heck down. I wasn't meeting Dez's mother or sisters. These were his coworkers and it was supposed to be casual and informal and no matter how it went, it was better than facing Lillian or sitting by myself all day in a swamp of regret and loss thinking about that one awful Thanksgiving when I'd lost Bridie and everything had changed. I didn't want to have to wonder if Sam and Shelby were hand-feeding each other crescent rolls or coating each other with whipped cream from a can and licking it off the way I'd suggested early in our marriage—Sam had thought we'd end up with ants, but he probably would've gone for it with Shelby, or maybe she wouldn't have asked, she would've just presented herself as a human pie.

Nope. Those thoughts were a sign of a truly troubled human being, and I wasn't one of those anymore. I was a woman with normal problems, like not knowing quite what to bring. I didn't want to seem like I was trying too hard, and Dez had already told me that they had the turkey and dressing covered. A salad was low-key, but no one ever seemed to eat them on Thanksgiving. That was how I found myself wandering around a crowded Whole Foods after work on the Tuesday before Thanksgiving, pushing a cart through a sea of very aggressive and stressed-out people. My phone buzzed.

"Mom, can I call you back? I'm in the nightmare of pre-holiday Whole Foods," I said.

"Why?"

"I need a pie for firehouse Thanksgiving. What do you reckon? Chocolate bourbon pecan? Does all the alcohol get cooked off, I wonder? What if they get a call or something? The only pumpkin pies left have broken crusts. Maybe they have more in the back."

"You're buying a pie."

"I always buy a pie."

"Why on earth would you buy a pie when you already are capable of making the world's best dessert?"

A woman with short light brown hair wearing running tights, headphones, and a shirt that said *Namaste, bitch!* rammed me in the thigh with her cart.

I stopped to rub the sore spot and to give her the chance to apologize, but she didn't.

"Huh? Hang on a second."

I abandoned my cart and tapped the woman on the shoulder. She swiveled around. "Pardon me," I said, as sweetly as I could. "I know it's crowded in here, but—"

She turned toward the kombucha selection, bobbing her head a little to the music. I reached out and gave her earbud a tug.

That got her attention.

"Hey!" she snapped.

"I just need a moment of your attention," I said. "Not sure you noticed, but you rammed me with your cart back there. You really should look out for other people. Nice shirt, by the way." I let the sarcasm hang in the air for a moment, and then I walked away before she had a chance to say anything.

"Mom? You still there?"

"Did you just accost someone at the grocery store?"

"I'm a little proud of myself. What were you saying about dessert? Did you have a verdict on which pie?"

"Those pies are a tad dry for my tastes. The pecan one is okay, but the last pumpkin one you bought had a crust that tasted like pressed wood shavings. No, I was saying banana pudding," Mom announced. "You should bring your banana pudding. Just make sure you burn off all of the alcohol or leave it out altogether," she said.

TWO DAYS LATER, I stood in front of the door to the firehouse holding a large disposable aluminum tray filled to the brim with banana pudding. There was a chill in the air, finally, and I'd donned a thick gray cardigan sweater. I hesitated before going inside, but a car pulled in as I was contemplating fleeing and a couple of small children and a man with a baby in a carrier got out. The children were gleeful, mesmerizing, and they ran past me and pulled the heavy door as a team effort. I held the door for the man wrangling the infant car seat.

"Thanks," he said. "Are you here for Thanksgiving?"

It seemed like a simple enough question. "I am," I said.

"Well, c'mon in then. This crew doesn't like to wait to eat." He laughed.

I followed him down a corridor, where the woman I recognized as Eva was standing with the two adorable children I'd seen in the parking lot sliding down her legs like fire poles.

"Nice to see you again," she said.

"Aw, thanks, honey," the man said, kissing her on the cheek.

"I wasn't talking to you, Eric Park." She leaned around him. "It's Violet, right?"

Heat rose in my cheeks. I'd met Eva more than once. The first time had been when I'd cut my hand the night of the Lillian incident. The second time, I'd been sure I was having a heart attack. I found myself wishing I'd been more decisive at the door and high-tailed it out of there, but since that hadn't been the case, I now found myself saying a silent plea that some sort of alarm would start ringing and I could flee while everyone was running for the trucks.

"Everybody's in the kitchen."

"So, Violet," Eric said, extracting a chubby-cheeked baby from the car seat, "who do you belong to?"

"Uh . . . I . . ." I stammered. Would it have been bad if I'd thrown the pudding up in the air as a distraction and run?

"Dez," Eva called back over her shoulder. "Violet is with Dez. Babe, did you bring the diaper bag?"

"Great guy," Eric said, grinning. "I've got the diaper bag right here. I even remembered to put the diapers in it this time."

"It's a Thanksgiving miracle," she said, but her tone was light and she winked at him.

The long corridor had a couple of doors that seemed like they were bunks where the on-shift crew must sleep. There was a locker room on the left, and then we finally arrived at the kitchen. It was a large, open space, with four side-by-side refrigerators lining one wall and an island with a massive stainless-steel hood in the middle of the room. The island was covered with food, including what looked to be the world's largest turkey. From my quick head count, we were going to need it. There were six firefighters on Dez's crew, and it seemed everyone had someone there.

Dez and I spotted each other at the same time. His face lit up and he abandoned something he'd been stirring on the stove to cross the room.

"Where should I put this?" I asked, holding out the pan of pudding.

A tall man with red hair and a fair, freckled complexion swooped in and lifted the tray out of my hands. "I'll just take that. I'm Andy, by the way."

"Violet," I said. "Nice to meet you."

Now that I'd lost my dessert shield, Dez enveloped me in a bear hug and kissed the top of my head. "I was starting to think you weren't going to make it," he said.

"Eric made his short ribs," Eva announced.

The firefighters starting clapping. "Eva's husband Eric's an amazing chef; he owns this great Korean place in Morrisville called Comet. Everything on the menu's good, but the short ribs are to die for. Sometimes he takes pity on us and brings some. Looks like today's our lucky day."

"Dez's a real sweet talker, but I guess you already knew that," Eric said, and laughed.

I flushed again. "My best friend's wife is a chef too. Roxy Sinclair, maybe you know her?"

Eric nodded. "Yeah, I know Rox. Eva and I went to her restaurant last year for our anniversary. She's great."

"Her wife, Kyra, was my college roommate," I said, relieved that we had something in common. "I'm their daughter's godmother."

"Very cool," Eric said. "Let me just get the food squared away and we can talk more." He winked at Dez.

Eva was bouncing the baby, and her two other children—who had abandoned their posts at her legs—were chasing around a set of similar-aged children who all looked exactly alike. Dez leaned over to me. "The triplets belong to Carlos. That's him next to his wife,

Annabelle—the very blonde woman currently on gravy duty. She's a complete saint. You already met Andy, the guy who took your food. His boyfriend, Mike, is a paramedic in Raleigh, and unfortunately, he's on shift today too, so he's not here. The big guy is Jerry. He's married to Michelle—she's a district attorney—and they have a new baby, Rosie."

I looked over to where Jerry stood manning the mashed potatoes that Dez had abandoned. His wife was petite, with short-cropped black hair and radiant brown skin. She was cradling a baby wearing a little pink hat and a long-sleeved onesie with kittens on it. Despite the happy noise in the room, the baby appeared to be out cold. I watched, mesmerized by the gentle sway of Michelle as she twisted side to side.

"Everyone brought somebody?" I asked.

"Ronnie's our newest probie. The girl over there with the maroon hair in the ponytail? She was going to bring her mom, but it was her brother's year so she's on her own. Doesn't matter anyway, we're pretty much all family here. C'mon, I'll introduce you."

"We better eat before someone blows up their turkey fryer and sets the living room on fire," Jerry said. He pulled out a chair for Michelle and proceeded to make her a plate. Everyone followed suit. I sat next to Dez, across from Carlos and Annabelle.

"So," Annabelle said, "Dez was telling us all that you're an advice columnist."

I swallowed a bite of turkey. "Um, yeah, I write Dear Sweetie."

Michelle turned to me. "No way. I love that column. The one about burning the bridge to protect the daughter-in-law from that vicious mother-in-law was priceless."

"What you got against my mom?" Jerry asked.

"Nothing, baby. It was just a funny column. It's not like I wrote the letter."

"What else has Dez told you all about me?" I asked, trying to keep the nervousness out of my voice.

They exchanged looks around the table and I turned to him, eyebrows raised, and gave him a knock with my knee beneath the table. He squeezed my leg in return and leaned in. "It's probably more embarrassing for me than you," he whispered in my ear.

"Well, you are sort of famous around here," Andy said.

"Famous?" I choked out.

I watched in abject horror as they exchanged a series of looks that seemed to carry in them an entire conversation. Dez took a bite of cranberry walnut bread, but the corners of his lips twitched. I shifted in my seat.

"Towanda!" Jerry shouted, and everyone laughed.

My cheeks burned, and I turned to Dez fully prepared to glare at him, but then I saw the way he was looking at me.

No one had ever looked at me like that.

He was leaning back in his seat, arms crossed, and he shook his head a little as he leaned forward. I might have thought he disapproved, but his wide grin, which carved out a dimple in each of his cheeks, said the opposite. He looked straight at me, his brown eyes soft and familiar, and brushed his fingertips over my knuckles.

"You heard it," he said, talking to the table, but not breaking eye contact with me. "Nobody messes with my girl."

I gulped. We'd never had that conversation, but so far in one afternoon, I'd been clearly linked with Dez—twice. He brushed his lips against my cheek. I liked it. The kiss, the Thanksgiving, being called his girl, all of it. But I couldn't shake that cold, scared feeling that seemed to lurk below the surface. Liking things, depending on them, was risky territory. Still, I was at a firehouse, I reminded myself. Was there a safer place than one that housed people whose literal job was saving *other* people? I pushed the worry down and took a bite of one of the short ribs Eric had brought.

"What do you think?" Eva asked. "Good, right?"

I glanced around the table at Dez, with his dimples and his declarations, and the whole raucous crew who loved him, and my heart squeezed with such intensity I thought it might burst. "So good."

· Forty-Four ·

Everyone must've gotten the memo about not frying their turkeys near their houses, because it was a quiet afternoon call-wise, according to Dez. They had one short call for an oven fire, which gave me a chance to do the dishes with Annabelle while Eric and Michelle were on baby duty.

"How long have you and Dez been together?" she asked.

"I don't really know," I said. "I guess a couple of months. To be honest, we haven't had an official conversation about it. How about you and Jerry?"

"Forever," she said. "We met in eighth grade. I know, it's kind of weird, right?"

"No. I actually think that's pretty amazing."

She shrugged and shook some soap suds off her hands. "When you know, you know."

I picked up a dish towel and dried the few things that wouldn't fit in the dishwasher. Was it really that easy? I wondered. We finished setting out the desserts—a homemade pumpkin pie, brownies, my obnoxiously giant pan of pudding—just as the crew poured back into the kitchen.

"Yes! Dessert time," Carlos said, slinging an arm around Annabelle. Dez went to the kitchen and washed his hands. Then he went over to Michelle.

"I think there's some sugar over there with your name on it," he said. "Why don't I take this little cutie off your hands so you can sit with your husband?" Michelle flashed an appreciative smile and then she passed the infant into Dez's arms. The way he cradled that baby, it was so natural, so easy, he looked like an obstetrician who'd held thousands of babies. I took a small serving of each of the desserts on a plate and went over to where he was swaying with a slumbering Rosie.

"Hi," I said in a whisper.

"Hey," he said. "What you got there?"

"Sustenance," I said, lifting the plate. "How about you?"

"I've got a Rosie. Isn't she the cutest? She looks like she's made out of marzipan."

I didn't really want to look at a baby, let alone a perfect, new baby who looked like she was made out of sweets, but I couldn't help myself. I peered down at her perfect little face, her soft cheeks, her perfect little rosebud lips, and my heart squeezed so hard that I almost dropped the plate.

"You're pretty good at that," I said, recovering.

"I've delivered my fair share of babies," he said. "I've got a real soft spot for kids."

I forced a smile so hard that my cheeks hurt. "That looks good," Dez said, nodding at the plate.

"Which one?" I asked.

"The one you brought."

I scooped some up on a spoon and held it out for him. "Ah, you read my mind," he said, and then greedily sucked the pudding from the spoon. "Oh, wow. And here I was thinking you couldn't be any more wonderful, and then you go and make the world's best dessert."

I pressed my lips together. The baby made a cute little squawking sound and pushed a fist up in the air.

"What?" Dez said, glancing between me and the baby. "I feel like I'm missing something here."

"It's nothing," I told him. "It's just that's exactly what my mom says about it. I'd actually planned on buying a pie, and she was not having it."

He presented his finger, and baby Rosie wrapped her tiny fingers around it. "Great minds," he said. "I'd like to meet this mother of yours sometime. What do you think about that, Rosie?"

Here's the thing about perfection. Sometimes there are moments that are so perfect that they can't possibly be real. Like when the man you've been sleeping with, the one who pulled you from the depths of despair and made you feel a little more alive and a little less alone and very, very good, invites you to Thanksgiving, and his people are nice and welcoming, and he thinks your pudding is the best, and looks at you like no one ever has, and you think *Maybe he loves me*, and then he's holding a baby and . . . you just can't. That's not a column. That's what happened. Dez and I were standing there, me holding the spoon and him holding Rosie, and I just couldn't. It was perfect. It was something I knew I could never have, which ruined it.

I ruined it.

"I, ah, actually I need to go. I forgot about something."

"Oh, okay," Dez said. Rosie scrunched up her face and let out a shaky wail. "Hang on, I'll walk you out."

"It's okay," I told him. "Have dessert. I'll leave the pudding." His brow furrowed. I turned to the table where everyone was eating. "It was really nice to meet y'all," I said. "Sorry I have to take off."

Michelle came over and scooped Rosie up from Dez. "Somebody's hungry," she said. "Thanks for the break, Dez. I had two pieces of pie and a coffee. It was magic."

I took the chance to hurry down the corridor that led to the exit, but Dez caught me before I reached the door.

"What's wrong, Violet?"

I shook my head. "Nothing. This was great. Thank you for having me."

"Was it because I said that thing about meeting your mom? I'm sorry. I got caught up in the moment."

That made two of us.

"No, that's—"

"I know your situation is complicated. I didn't mean to push things."

I looked down at my feet for a moment, collecting myself, before I met his eyes. His face was just as earnest, as handsome and open, as I'd expected. I wanted to reach out and smooth my fingertips over the scar on his chin from the high wire, but I twisted my fingers together instead. I'd gotten too comfortable next to him.

"Tell me I didn't ruin this," he said, his voice low and taut.

I pulled in a shaky breath. "You didn't," I told him. "I did. I always ruin Thanksgiving."

I yanked open the door and left him standing there.

Forty-Five

THE FOLLOWING WEEK, WHEN sleep eluded me, I wanted to call Dez, to nestle my head into the crook of his elbow, letting the weight of his other arm over my hip soothe me and ground me into slumber, but it was a Wednesday, when he normally was on shift, and anyway, after Thanksgiving, it seemed best to keep my distance for a while. I left my phone on silent until my mother showed up at my house to let me know that if I didn't answer for days again, she'd call the fire department to check on me—which was the exact opposite of what I wanted—so I turned the ringer back on and ignored the two calls and the handful of texts that came from Dez.

I didn't know what to say to him, so I rudely left him hanging. I can't say that it was easy for me. I tossed and turned and pictured the look on his face while he'd cradled little Rosie in his arms, swaying gently, so gently, her little tiny fist wrapped around his finger. He'd been all lit up from the inside. And that light was a problem. First, I couldn't give him that, and second, the fact that I even was contemplating whether I could or could not light him up from the inside, especially in *that* way, was worse. Because, truth be told, maybe I was a little lit up by him, and well, that could lead to ultimate heart destruction, and mine was currently pieced together with nail polish and dried pudding. I wasn't sure it was up for the challenge. Basically, I was in way over my head here.

My phone buzzed on the nightstand. I thought about leaving it. Dez often texted me when he was bored on shift—stories from his day, things he thought would make me laugh or interest me. Occasionally, he'd tell me in elaborate and blush-inducing detail about his plans for when he was able to come over here and get his hands on me. Other times, he'd tell me about his firehouse family. Their amazing save, the cute puppy they brought by, the fact that he was worried about their health. Those conversations were dangerous too. I found myself looking forward to them, smiling, and listening attentively, and now I knew those people—I liked them. So even though I'd promised myself I was going to create a bit more space between me and him—a safety buffer—I picked up the phone to glance at the message anyway, hoping that it was him.

It wasn't Dez.

The ID read *Lying Bastard*—I'd changed it after Sam threatened to sue me. The doctor said to manage my stress, and changing *Sam Covington* to *Lying Bastard* in my phone's contacts was stress relieving at the time. The message was brief.

I'm sorry that I hurt you, Vi.

I stared at the screen. The phone buzzed again in my hand.

Are you there?

I bit my lip. *I'm sorry that I hurt you*, Sam had written. Now, of all times. I debated whether I should text him back and tell him not to bother, that his apology, especially now, wasn't worth much, or if I should just ignore him altogether. I started to type *No*, when the phone rang.

He'd seen those little dots, no doubt. I couldn't ignore him. Dez's contact had tapered off, respecting my boundaries, I supposed, but Sam had always been a persistent person. It made him a good lawyer, but it also meant that ignoring his calls right now wasn't an option.

"Hello?" I said, trying to sound like I'd been sleeping.

"Violet, hey."

"What do you want, Sam? I'm tired." It wasn't a lie. I was full of nervous energy about the *Gloss* article and my confusing feelings, which at least in some small part still had to do with him (I hadn't forgotten that moment at the birthday, when our elbows touched and he liked my green dress), but I *was* tired. I was tired of being in limbo. Of caring so much.

"Sorry, it's late, I know." His voice was rough. "I just, I was thinking about you."

"Where's Shelby?" My tone didn't sound sharp, exactly, but it was close, like a butter knife.

"I'm at the hotel." His voice sounded thick, and I wondered if he'd been drinking.

"I really should get some sleep," I said.

"Wait."

And as things always went with Sam, I did. He said wait, and I thought, *How long?*

Finally, he said, "Do you ever think that if we'd just made a few different turns here and there, we'd still be together and happy?"

I scrunched up my entire face and pushed my hand back through my hair. "I can't have this conversation with you," I said.

"Please, just answer the question, Vi. Then I'll go. I won't bother you anymore."

I was quiet for a long time. I took one deep breath and let it out. "Do I think if we'd done some things differently, we would still be together? Sure. I guess if you hadn't abandoned me and screwed another woman behind my back, then yeah, we might still be together. But happy, Sam? I have no idea. And honestly, the fact that you'd call me up in the middle of the night and ask me that when you're supposedly in love with another woman, a woman that you left me for, makes me think that *no*, Sam, we *wouldn't* be happy."

I hung up.

I desperately wanted to talk to Dez. I wanted to call him so bad. But that seemed selfish and unfair, like something Sam would do, blow someone off and then call them in the middle of the night, so I rang Kyra instead.

"This better be good," she grumbled when she answered.

"Sam just called me."

"Who's that, babe?" I heard Roxy in the background.

"It's Violet. Sam called her."

"Oh, damn. Put her on speaker."

There was some shuffling and then came Roxy's and Kyra's voices in unison: "Spill."

"He said he was thinking about me and then he asked if I ever wondered if things had been different if we'd still be together and happy. Can you believe that?" I exclaimed. "I mean, the nerve!"

"Yeah, I can believe it," Kyra said. "I told you to be careful at Tristan's birthday."

"He did resemble a man who was having regrets," Roxy chimed in. "It was obvious. His shirt looked like he'd pulled it out of the bottom of the bed. And his messed-up hair—that is the hair of a man who's thinking he should have stayed with his wife."

I shook my head. "No. No, he's not."

"He didn't bring *her*," Kyra said.

"That's probably because of the incident. Would you want to go to a party where you knew the woman who had outed you on the internet and whose husband you got entangled with—"

"Entangled? Who are you . . . Jada Pinkett Smith? They had a full-fledged affair in your house. Call a snake a snake, that's all."

"Thanks for that, Rox," Kyra said. "Real sensitive. Go on, Violet."

"Well, it makes sense that she wouldn't go to the party, that's all I was saying. It doesn't mean there's trouble in paradise."

"Okay, fine, believe what you want, but it doesn't mean there isn't trouble either," Roxy said.

"What'd you say?" Kyra asked.

"I told him I was tired. And probably not."

"Is that true?"

"The tired part was. My feelings about my estranged husband are a bit more challenging to puzzle out."

"What about Firefighter Dez?" Kyra asked.

I sighed. "I think I need to end it. It was supposed to be just a fling. It's not like you sage your house forever."

I expected Kyra to agree. She was practical, and as much as she'd cheered on me sowing my wild oats instead of sliding into a deep depressive state, I knew she thought I was being a bit of an idiot, so it caught me off guard when she asked, "Do you want to?"

I was quiet for a while. I was . . . torn.

"She doesn't want to," Roxy interjected. "*What?* If she did, she would've answered right away. You both know I'm right. Let's look at the facts. He's nice. He shows up. The sex is an upgrade, isn't it?"

"I mean, yeah, that part is pretty great. It's all great. But . . ."

Kyra and Roxy were both silent, and I started to consider the most realistic way to fake a bad connection and end the call.

"Violet." Kyra's school principal tone sent a chill down my spine.

"Yes?" I said tentatively. I squirmed lower under the covers.

"Did you do something really stupid?"

"Maayybee . . ." I squeaked. "Depends on what you mean by stupid?"

"Did you get emotionally attached to your sexual sage?"

That was one way of putting it. I'd been so moved that I had to flee after watching him hold a baby.

"When I told you to be careful, that was a blanket statement!" she yelled.

"Kyra, you're going to wake Harriet up with that hollering," Roxy said.

"You're right," I said. "I let this go way too far. I need to tell him it's over. Officially."

"If that's what you need to do, then do it," Kyra said. "But first, maybe you should ask yourself why you're so eager to put an end to something that, as far as you've been letting us all believe, never even got off the ground. And then, try to get some rest."

"Alright, boss."

"I'm serious. A producer at *Carolina Sunrise* called after you left yesterday. They've been following you for a while now and they saw the *Gloss* article and loved it. They want to do an interview with you the day after tomorrow. Makeup starts at four thirty a.m., so you're going to need your beauty sleep."

After I said good night, I squeezed my eyes shut and fluffed my pillow, but I couldn't quiet my racing mind. Kyra wanted me to think it over; lot of good that would do. My heart and my head were diametrically opposed. *Just get it over with*, I chided myself, and snatched my phone off the nightstand. *This has been great, but I think it'd be best if we both went our separate ways*, I composed in my head, while my finger hovered above the screen. I closed my eyes, trying to find my resolve. I couldn't bring myself to do it. Breaking up by text is tacky, and Dez deserved the truth. I tapped out a quick message to

Dez—**Sweet dreams**—and hit send before I could change my mind. A moment later, a tone sounded a reply from him, because he never would leave *my* messages unanswered.

> **I'll be dreaming of that pudding you brought to Thanksgiving. It was the best thing I've ever tasted. Sweet dreams to you too, Violet.**

I considered responding.

Good night.

I'm sorry I ran off.

I miss you.

But instead I crushed a pillow over my head and let out a muffled wail of frustration.

Forty-Six

I spent the next twenty-four hours trying to put a lot of things out of my mind—the interview, what I was going to do about Dez, and how much I would miss him if I ended things—and failing miserably at it all. I picked a reasonably safe column from an elementary school mom who was asking if it was okay to name an expected donation amount for holiday teacher gifts, and then Mom took me shopping for an interview outfit at Crabtree Valley Mall.

I held up a striped boatneck blouse.

Mom shook her head. "Horizontal stripes, Violet? Have I taught you nothing?"

"Okay." I hung the blouse back on the rack.

"What about this?" Mom pulled a navy blue sheath dress off a display. It was very sophisticated and neutral. The navy would probably look nice with my skin tone and blue eyes, but it didn't feel like me.

"It's very flattering," she said. I tried to smile, but it came out pained.

"It's okay," I said. "Not really me."

Mom stopped. She put a hand on a hip. "Alright, Violet. What's going on? You're not yourself. You should be over the moon about this opportunity, but instead you're moping like a sullen teenager."

"Nothing. I'm good. A little nervous. I'm going to look over there," I told her, gesturing to a display for a designer I'd never heard of.

I crossed the aisle, glad to put some distance between me and my mother. I didn't want to start talking at this point, even though we'd agreed to be more open with each other after the dinner when we'd really talked. No one said these things were easy. And so far, they hadn't been.

There was a magenta shell that would look nice with a pair of high-waisted black slacks I already owned. I held it up in front of a mirror to see how it looked.

"That's a winner," a woman's voice said.

I swiveled around, expecting a salesperson, and found Eva with an armful of clothes, grinning at me. "If you haven't hit the sales racks back there," she said, "you really should. This sweater is nine bucks."

"How are you?" I asked.

"Good. Eric took the kids to the zoo and his mom is watching the baby, so I'm shopping for the first time in, gosh, I can't even remember. I'm not sure what to do with myself. How about you?"

"I'm doing well, thanks. Do you like the magenta? It's for a television interview . . . so I'm not sure."

"A television interview? That's big-time. Wear the magenta for sure. It'll look fantastic on you."

I turned back to the mirror.

"You think?"

She nodded. "When's the interview?"

"Tomorrow at the crack of dawn. It's for *Carolina Sunrise*."

"I watch that all the time! That's so cool. What's the interview about?"

"Um, about the column . . . work stuff. How're things at the station?"

"Okay. The usual. It was nice seeing you at Thanksgiving. Don't tell Dez I told you, but we were all really glad that he's got someone. He had a rough time when he first moved down here . . . losing his brother and all."

I frowned. "Wait, what? You mean Ben? I didn't realize they were related."

"I guess not *technically*. Ben was Dez's foster brother. They were family."

"Oh, I didn't mean . . . I get it, a foster brother *is* a brother, it's just that Dez called him a close friend. I didn't know."

Eva tried to hide her surprise. "Well, it's a tough thing to talk about. I imagine he didn't want to trouble you with it. It's kind of a big thing for a new relationship."

"Yeah." *Why didn't he tell me?*

"Don't read too much into it," Eva said. "He's crazy about you. You guys are great together. We were basking in your glow."

"I hadn't even considered pink, but that shade's perfect," Mom said. Her timing always was impeccable. She extended a hand, and Eva shook it from under her pile of clothes.

"I'm Wynne," she said. "Violet's mother."

"I'm Eva."

"Oh, do you work at the paper?"

"No. Actually, I work for the fire department."

My mother arched one of her perfectly groomed eyebrows. She turned to me, feigning surprise. "A firefighter? Well now, that's an important job."

"I think so," Eva said.

"It takes a special kind of a person to do that," Mom said.

"I should go pay for this," I told them. "It was nice to see you, Eva."

I left Mom and Eva standing in the middle of the clothes, hoping that the conversation wasn't going to go where I thought it might.

AFTER EVA HAD MOVED on to the kids' department and I'd bought a pair of black pumps that Mom deemed "suitable enough," we headed home.

"I liked your friend Eva," she said. "She seems like a lovely person."

"She is." I'd been running the conversation over in my mind. Dez had told me he'd had a hard time, but he made it seem in the past. The unpacked boxes. It made both perfect sense and no sense at all. Why hadn't he told me the whole truth?

"I can't even imagine how hard it must be to be a firefighter with three kids and a husband who's a chef with his own restaurant. It's a good thing both their families live nearby."

I nodded, sensing that Mom was steering us down two roads at the same time—one that led back to my house and one that hit way too close to home.

"You never told me how Thanksgiving with the firefighter—"

"Dez," I interjected.

"Right, Dez. Well, how was it? I gather you two must be getting close if you're spending holidays with each other."

I gave her a look. She returned it with lifted brows that held such a refined challenge, I caved. "I don't know. We haven't hung out since then."

"Why? I thought you told me you liked him, and lately you've seemed happier, more relaxed than usual . . . today excluded, of course. I expected shopping to be a fun outing. You wouldn't even look at the polka dots."

"I'm sorry, Mom," I said. "Next time I'll consider the polka dots more carefully. I've just got a lot on my mind." I scanned my memories. My mother wasn't wrong. I *had* been happier. I felt more like me than I had in a long while. And at Thanksgiving, I'd been having the best time, until the doubts about our situation settled in. I gave a shrug. "Did you ever have that feeling when something that makes you happy also makes you indescribably sad? Like you're on the edge of something big and it's just too much."

Mom popped open the compartment that held her sunglasses and put them on. She cleared her throat. "I feel that sometimes with you."

"You do?"

"'Course. Imagine lovin' someone more than anything and watching that person suffer. It's overwhelming."

"You mean after Sam left?"

Mom's lips turned pale as she pressed them into a tight line. "Before, sweets. You've been carrying around this sadness for a long time now. I would catch a glimpse of it underneath the surface from time to time, when you thought no one was looking. I wanted to say something, to help, but I didn't know how. You're such a strong person, and I didn't want to overstep. I'm sorry."

Tears pricked at my eyes. All that time, I'd felt completely alone. I'd been so preoccupied with trying to keep myself together, it never occurred to me that anyone had noticed. "I didn't realize," I told her. "Caring is rough."

Mom took a hand off of the steering wheel and patted mine. "That's the thing about caring. Sometimes it hurts, but that doesn't make it not worth it. Understand?"

I nodded. I understood enough. I also knew about wishful thinking, though. I cared about Dez. There was no denying that my heart beat a little faster and my smiles came easier when he was around, or the way I thought about him, the little things he did, the kindness he showed me and everyone else all the time, while asking nothing in return. But thinking about a future with him and what that might mean for us felt a little like standing at the edge of a canyon at dawn. The changing sky, orange and pink, warm sun golden on your face, is so promising and lovely, but there's still a void lurking in the shadows below, a long, dangerous drop. Letting things between us continue seemed reckless, no matter how wonderful he was.

What if I fell? Or worse, what if *he* did? What if I let him down?

My mother's fingers squeezed mine. "You'll work it out," she said. "In the meantime, try not to furrow your brow quite so much, Violet. You're starting to wrinkle."

I let out a short laugh. There she is, ladies and gentlemen, my mother; she contains multitudes. I thought back to Dez and his love of yoga and rugby and musicals, his detective novels, and the fact that he was messy and always appeared with snacks.

"Do you think we could make a stop before you drop me home?" I asked.

"Sure thing. Where?"

"There's this little café near the house. It's new. They make amazing filled croissants and I want to pick some up. How about I treat you to a cappuccino to make up for being a bad shopping companion?"

My mother can't resist a cappuccino, especially the kind with pretty designs in the foam, so she agreed immediately. While the woman behind the counter carefully packed up four croissants, two almond and two chocolate, Mom and I sat at a table by the window. Mom was delighted by the leaf design and praised the rich body of the coffee beans, but I'd never seen her savor a beverage less. She downed the drink in less than a minute and was already up and heading back to the car before I'd even finished putting the change back in my wallet. She didn't ask who the croissants were for, God love her. I think she knew.

After she left, I walked them over to Dez's house. *They're just croissants,* I told myself, *not my heart.* Still, I was too nervous to ring the doorbell. I placed the box carefully on the welcome mat and scampered off before he could see me.

Forty-Seven

I SAT IN FRONT OF the bright lighted mirror while the makeup artist dusted my face with setting powder.

"Alright," she said, "you're all set. Love the blouse, by the way. It'll look great on camera."

A production assistant came by with a clipboard. "You can follow me, Mrs. Covington. Jimmy over here is going to get you all mic'd up and then we'll start the segment in about ten minutes."

I swallowed and nodded, more nervous than ever. *Was it necessary to call me Mrs. Covington?* I had some idea of the things they planned to ask me based on a list of topics that they'd sent to Kyra to help me prepare. My marriage was fair game. I knew that. I'd put it out there in the first place, and the affair had been the catalyst that had driven me to change my approach anyway. After Jimmy had placed a portable microphone pack into the waistband of my pants and clipped the tiny bulb to my collar, I followed the PA to a small armchair. Miranda Hollingsworth was sitting in an identical chair opposite a small glass coffee table.

"You want coffee?" the PA asked.

"Sure," I said. It seemed like people drank coffee on morning shows. I was afraid of spilling on myself, but I figured the likelihood of my mouth going dry was higher.

"Just pretend the cameras aren't here," Miranda said, sensing my nervousness. "We're just two strangers having a chat."

I nodded.

The coffee arrived and the segment started.

"I'm so excited to introduce our special guest today, Violet Covington. You all probably know her better as Dear Sweetie from the *Raleigh Times*." She turned to me. "Thank you so much for joining us today, Violet!"

"Thank you for having me." I wondered if it was too soon to take a sip of the coffee.

"It's not often that we have a newspaper columnist on our show. But then again, it's not often that an advice columnist makes her own headlines."

I smiled and decided to go for the coffee.

"For those of you who don't know Violet—should I call you that, or do you go by Sweetie?"

"Violet's fine," I said. "Honestly, until two months ago, no one knew I was Sweetie. I worked pretty hard to stay anonymous."

"And why was that? To keep out of the limelight?"

"Some of it was about that. I'm a private person. Mostly, it was to protect me from people who were angry that their advice wasn't what they wanted to hear, or people who wrote for advice and I didn't respond."

Miranda nodded. "Right, not every letter is meant for the newspaper."

"You'd be surprised, some of the questions I get."

"Will you tell us about some of them? What's the wildest letter you ever received?"

I thought about it for a second. "There's a couple that come to mind. One time I got a letter about a man who had mistaken his neighbor's pet chicken for one of his own and his wife had made it for dinner. He wanted to know if he should tell the neighbor, who was still putting up posters of Henrietta everywhere around town, what had happened. Another time, I got a note about a woman who had a crush on a cartoon character. That was very awkward."

"Oh my," Miranda said. "How do you even begin to come up with your responses?"

"Some of it comes from my own experiences—not the cartoon crush, but other things. I also have a great support system that I consult, because the truth is, I'm not anything special. I have no qualifications. I'm not a psychologist or a parent. I was a communications major. And I will be the first to admit that I don't always have the answers. But I genuinely care about the people who write me, and I think that's the first step to giving good advice."

"I bet you must get a lot of questions about romance."

"Definitely. Of course, I get lots of simple questions about etiquette and that sort of thing, but most of my letters are about relationships."

Miranda set her coffee cup down. "You have some experience with complicated relationships yourself, don't you, Violet?"

"You could say that."

Miranda faced the camera. "Readers of Dear Sweetie probably already know by some of her recent responses that Violet recently suffered through an episode of infidelity in her marriage."

I pulled in a breath through my nose so that I could keep my smile frozen in place. It wasn't the woman's words as much as her sickly sweet tone that made me want to strangle her with my microphone wire.

"Can you tell us a little bit about that?"

"There's not much to say that I haven't already published in the paper. I was married to my husband for twelve years. I came home a few months ago and found him with another woman. It's not quite as dramatic as it sounds."

"It *does* sound quite dramatic." She shifted in her seat. "That must have been devastating."

I picked my coffee cup back up with two hands. "It was very difficult."

"But you chose an interesting way to process your emotions. Will you share with us what you did?"

"Well, I suppose I should preface this by saying that I don't recommend the actions I took. They weren't healthy. It's kind of a *do as I say, not as I do* situation. I suppose I went a little wild. I read through these letters that I related to in a different way, being wounded as I was, and I just felt very angry and sad, and I gave some very candid advice."

"Candid is one way of putting it," Miranda said, laughing. She pulled out a piece of paper. "You describe having the strength to tear your husband limb from limb, burning bridges between daughters- and mothers-in-law, and then there was an entire analogy that indicated that people everywhere were faking orgasms . . ."

I wondered if my cheeks were the same shade of pink as my shirt on camera.

"But there are moments in your letters that really resonate. Where you've really hit the nail on the head in these relationships. I mean, I have friends that cheered when they read that you called that mean mother-in-law a villain. And I think for many people it was freeing to see someone write about their personal experiences so authentically."

"I never intended to use the column as therapy. I wanted to be honest, and I found I had very strong reactions to some of the letters that I received. At the time, when I wrote some of them, I still had the expectation of anonymity. I didn't realize that there would be collateral damage."

"Were people angry?"

"Of course. There was definitely some fallout, but that was a good thing, I think, because it helped me understand that my words have power and that I get to choose how I'm going to wield them. Do I want to call others out, or do I want to use my experiences to let people know that they aren't alone or to help try to foster empathy?"

"We actually spoke to a few of the people who put your advice into practice. Would you like to see what one of them said?"

Miranda swiveled in her seat to face a giant screen. I mirrored her. They hadn't mentioned this. A woman came into view, larger than life. Her face was drawn and her hair had been bleached within an inch of its life. There was a tiny smudge of mascara beneath her left eye that was magnified on the screen. I cringed a little for her.

"I followed Dear Sweetie's advice and it ruined my life," she said.

My hand flew to my mouth.

"I wrote to her about how everyone was expecting my husband and me to have a baby, and she told me to just tell him that I didn't want to. Easy, right? She suggested getting a dog. I was honest with him about how I felt and then I went out and adopted a puppy that proceeded to pee all over our brand-new carpeting and eat the bottom of my wedding dress . . . through the box. I guess none of that matters much now. Shortly after, my husband asked for a separation. And now he's divorcing me." She dissolved into tears. "I'm stuck in a house that smells like urine and my marriage is over. I've lost him and I'm stuck with a devil dog."

"Oh," I said.

"Do you stand by your advice, even if this is the outcome?" Miranda said, gesturing at the screen like Vanna White.

I pulled in a breath, steadying myself. "I don't regret advising honesty," I said after a moment. "I am terribly sorry that this reader is suffering because of it."

"But you admit, you were a bit cavalier before with your advice."

I nodded. "I never meant to be reckless. I care a lot about the people who write in to my column. I really relate to them and hope for the best, but the thing is, no matter how hard I try to give the best advice I can, there's no guarantee. I guess life imitates advice in that sense. Nothing is ever guaranteed to turn out the way we want it to."

"There's definitely a discernable shift in your newer responses. They do feel more relatable, more vulnerable. I think we all feel that change. The recent one where you wrote to the woman experiencing infertility was particularly poignant. Did you feel a connection there?"

My coffee cup trembled a little as I tried to set it down. I looked at Miranda, who was waiting expectantly for an answer. No one likes dead air, Mom had warned me the previous day.

"I do, actually," I said. "I've struggled with pregnancy loss and infertility. Before our marriage ended, my husband and I had tried for years to have a baby. I'm sorry—" I broke off. "It's still hard for me to talk about."

"That's understandable."

"I think it's something that people don't discuss. It feels very personal and heavy. There's so much expectation around pregnancy. How often are newly married women asked when they're starting a family or how many children they want? People experience a lot of judgment and shame as well. Personally, I felt like I'd failed, like somehow it was my fault. Talking about it brought that all to the surface, but I also felt like maybe other people were blaming me too. So I didn't talk about it."

"Mmm. What changed?"

"Part of it was me feeling like I needed to use my own experiences to do some good. But a big piece of it was that I realized other people felt the same exact way I did, and knowing how that felt, I had a unique opportunity to give that person the kind of support I'd craved when I was going through that terrible time. I knew the right words, or I hope at least the kind of words that cause more good than harm, because they were the ones I had needed to hear."

"Moving stuff. And how about now, Violet? You've struggled with infertility and infidelity. Are things better now? What does your future look like?"

"At this point, I'm trying to take life day by day. Some are better than others. I'm hopeful though that maybe good things could happen to me. I'm open to them."

"Okay, great! Last question: if you had one piece of advice to give that everyone could use, or that you've learned from this experience, what would it be?"

"I think being vulnerable, letting people see your pain or your anger and asking for help, is not easy; it's uncomfortable. It goes against what we're taught. But sometimes that discomfort is exactly what we need to get through something."

"Great stuff," she said. "Well, thanks so much for joining us, Violet. And for you folks who haven't read her column, Dear Sweetie, it's definitely worth checking out. She's also featured in this month's *Gloss* magazine with her take on how to get over heartbreak. I absolutely devoured that article, and I can't wait to read more from you about moving on."

"I'll keep that in mind," I said. "Thank you for having me."

Once we went to commercial break and I was ushered backstage to have my mic removed, I took a deep breath of relief. The producer smiled at me. "Good job," she said. "You come across really well on camera. It's a shame you're in the newspaper business and not TV."

"I appreciate that," I said. "I was really nervous."

"You couldn't tell. Your editor told me that you're up for syndication."

I nodded.

"It would probably be a good idea to tie your next column in with this . . . maybe see if you get any letters like Miranda mentioned that are about getting over heartbreak. You'll get more exposure that way, and it's a nice tie-in to your magazine piece."

"Thanks for the advice," I said. "I'm hoping *Gloss* decides to make it monthly, but who knows. If this fall has taught me anything, it's that nothing is guaranteed."

"Well, if it doesn't work out or you're looking for a change, give me a call. While you were up there, I found myself picturing a weekly segment with you and Miranda answering viewer questions. It could be great."

"Thanks! I just might."

Forty-Eight

The following day was Saturday. Hannah and Bodhi met me out in front of my house. The sun was shining and the sky was a brilliant azure and cloudless, but there was a chill in the air, and I found myself wishing I'd put on a coat instead of a sweatshirt.

"We usually take the greenway over to the dog park," Hannah said. "That okay?"

I nodded, acutely aware of the fact that the greenway entrance was nestled into a patch of trees that stood a couple of houses down from Dez's house. We headed in that direction and I tried to ignore the way my pulse sped up.

"I like the decorations on this one," Hannah said, gesturing to a house with a wooden scene from *A Charlie Brown Christmas* set up on their lawn.

"Me too," I confessed. "I'm going to vote for them in the contest. The classic candle house on Wisteria Drive has won two years in a row. It's lovely, but where's the creativity? Change can be good." I stopped for a moment to admire the hand-painted details. That's when I saw Dez. He was dressed casually in warm-up pants and a half-zip fleece and was carrying what looked like a yoga mat. On the way to his truck, he paused. My heart ricocheted around in my chest.

He was headed this way. But then he stopped in front of his neighbor's house, where he leaned down and then set an inflatable Mickey Mouse in a Santa suit upright. It must've fallen over in the wind the night before. My knees buckled a little. He did see me then, because he waved and started toward me.

"I'll be right back," I told Hannah. I met him halfway.

"Hi, stranger," he said. "It's been a while."

"It's nice to see you," I said. Nice and wonderful and absolutely heart-wrenching.

He tipped his head while he looked me over. "Are you alright?"

"I'm getting there."

"Listen, I have so much I want to say to you, but I'm teaching a class and I can't be late. Can we talk later?"

"Sure," I said, nodding. "Soon."

He reached out and I thought he was going to smooth my hair the way he often had all those times just before he'd pressed his lips to my forehead, but now he retracted his hand. "I gotta go."

I stood beside the massive blue spruce, smoothing my own hair down in the sharp wind, watching him walk away from me. I felt each step like a paper cut on the surface of my heart.

"Ready?" Hannah asked. "That path's right over here."

We ducked into the woods and onto the greenway. The dappled light coming through the pine trees was beautiful and soft. Birds were chirping. Bodhi sniffed grass with unbridled enthusiasm and gleefully dragged Hannah after a squirrel.

"It must be nice to be a dog," I said.

"Maybe. Then again, they sniff each other's butts to say hello."

I laughed. "Fair point. They don't get divorced though, so if you ask me, it's kind of a toss-up."

"I guess you're right about that. Bodhi and I are both loving the single life. But I don't know much about it. I always thought I would meet someone during grad school or afterward at work, but that never happened, and at some point I realized I actually like being on my own. I go out on dates occasionally, but that's mostly for free food." She laughed.

"Well, my someone changed his mind, so maybe you're better off. Free food is a safe bet." Except when it's someone bringing you croissants and he's perfect and you're a disaster.

"Why do I sense there's more to the story, Violet?"

I groaned. "Probably 'cause there is. That guy I was talking to just now—"

"The super cute one?"

"Yeah. That's Dez. He's the best, and I can't seem to figure out how to make it work. God, I feel like such a failure. Story of my life."

"I don't know about that. In my opinion, failing just means you tried. We have this saying in the lab: research is ninety-nine percent failure. That's where all the real lessons are. Easy answers aren't usually the important ones. Of course, that could be some bullshit we use to console ourselves so we can keep trying when all of our experiments aren't working, but there is some validity to it."

"I like that," I said.

"Maybe you can use it in a column." She laughed, sending a cloud of breath into the air. "I can't believe Christmas is almost here. I don't love it. I spend my holidays alone or at work, so I'm not counting down the days or anything. Then again, I do look forward to your Ritz Cracker bark."

My face contorted reflexively. The idea of another holiday in an empty house felt so emotionally daunting. I had a sudden vision of myself covered in caramel, cracker crumbs stuck to my skin, with all of my neighbors banging on the door. I shivered.

"You're really pale, Violet. Are you okay?"

I shook my head. "Just stressed. Can I ask you something kind of personal?"

"Sure."

"Have you ever been to therapy?" I asked.

"Of course. I go once a week."

"Really? It wasn't because of the Bunco thing, was it?"

She shook her head. "Not at all. You don't need a reason to go; it's just nice to have someone to talk through things with. I think of my appointments as mental health maintenance, and if something comes up, I have support in place."

"I never thought of it that way," I said. Bodhi trotted over and licked my hand. I recalled the psychologist referrals that the ER doctor had given me. I'd thrown them away.

Hannah opened the gate to the dog park and stooped to let Bodhi off his leash. "I can give you the contact info for mine if you want. She's amazing."

She procured a tennis ball from her jacket pocket and launched it. Bodhi raced after it, and a couple of other dogs fell in behind him in the high-speed chase.

I took a deep breath. "Actually, that would be great," I said. "Thank you."

"What are friends for?"

"This is really nice," I told her, and I wasn't just saying that. Hannah had a soothing aura, and I liked her company. I enjoyed watching Bodhi bound around with such lust for life. "We should do it again sometime."

HANNAH'S THERAPIST TURNED OUT to be warm and a good listener. I was hesitant to say much at first, but by the end of our first session

I'd told her about Sam, and my fertility struggles, and how sometimes when I got scared or overwhelmed I turned cold and couldn't get warm. I still wasn't ready to tell Dez, or anyone for that matter, but I reminded myself of Kyra's words of wisdom from back when we'd done a daily walking challenge with the *Charlotte Observer*—*even little steps count as steps.* Nobody says you've got to go out and run a marathon.

The counselor told me she was glad I'd come and gave me a card for a bereavement group one of her colleagues ran in a community center in Cary. Even though I'd talked about support groups in my columns, I never thought of myself as someone who deserved to be there. It's so easy to tell other people to be gentle with themselves, to take care, or to be brave. In practice, it's hard. Dez had quoted Glennon Doyle to me once, telling me, *we can do hard things*, and I repeated it like a mantra when I went despite my desire to bolt in the opposite direction. My hands trembled; I barely got out a "Hi, I'm Violet" before I burst into tears. But those other people who'd lost someone they cared about sat with me and let me cry, and some of them cried too . . . and it helped. I didn't feel better, but there was the promise that someday maybe I could. And I certainly felt less alone. Remembering that hurt and pulling it to the surface was painful and draining, but it was a relief too. Nobody said my feelings weren't valid. Or that my loss was probably for the best. Or even that it would all work out. These people knew better than that.

I left the community center and I knew I'd go back the following week, and the week after that. I was like those boxes in Dez's house, full of things neglected and shoved in a corner. I needed to unpack and sort through my feelings before I could really move forward, and I wanted to.

While I worked on myself, Sam was doing work of his own, including trying to make amends with both me and my mother. Even though I'd made it clear I didn't want to get back together, he kept reaching out, insisting he wanted to cook a meal for me and her at the house to show how sorry he was. He'd sent her a note on good linen paper. My new therapist seemed to think talking wasn't an entirely bad idea, suggesting that it might bring some much-needed closure.

"I'm doing this for you," Mom said when we talked a few days later. The stationery had gotten to her.

"You don't want us to reconcile, do you?"

"I want you to be okay. What okay looks like is your call. I sincerely hope that you're in a good enough place to not let someone who doesn't deserve you back into your heart, but your life is your life, not mine. Put it this way . . . I'm just there for moral support, and food. It better be a fine meal. That's all I'm saying. A little gastronomic groveling never hurt anyone."

The following Sunday afternoon Sam showed up early to cook us dinner. I answered the doorbell, and there he was, arms full of grocery bags, Oxford shirt untucked but not overtly wrinkled, with the start of a beard on his jaw and a wild look in his eyes.

"Hey, Vi," he said, leaning in for a kiss.

I turned my cheek, but he seemed to take it in stride, depositing a bag of groceries into my unprepared hands and walking past me into the kitchen like he'd never left.

"You look great," he said.

I touched the hair I'd spent close to an hour flat-ironing as if I were prepping for battle and stood for a moment in stunned silence. Sam was already in the kitchen, opening drawers, pulling out pots. What the hell was going on here? He was supposed to be atoning, not making himself at home.

I brought the groceries I was holding into the kitchen. "Just set them anywhere," Sam said. He held up an apron he'd bought me years ago. It was black and had a huge pair of red lips on the front, beneath which read *Kiss the Chef* in white script. He put it on. I curled my fingers into fists until I felt my gel manicure digging into my palms.

While Sam had been gone, I'd rearranged things. My coffeemaker, which had been relegated to a little stand in the corner previously, had a new home on the counter next to the sink. It made it easier to refill. He frowned at it.

"Let's put you back over here," he said, displacing a jade plant Kyra had given me as a *sorry your husband is an asshole* gift and putting the coffeemaker back where it'd been.

"Oh," I said, to myself mostly.

"What's that?" Sam said, over his shoulder. He slapped a chicken breast down on the granite and I shuddered.

"It's nothing," I answered. "I just liked it next to the sink. It's convenient."

"Yeah, I get it, babe. But it eats up so much counter space."

I sighed. "Sure, but I prefer it there."

"Okay . . ."

"Put it back, please."

His brow furrowed, but he complied before he returned his attention to the chicken.

"You want a cutting board?" I asked.

"Nah," he said, "I'm good. Go relax. It's all under control." I decided to pick my battles and headed toward the living room. Just because I was letting him use the kitchen didn't mean I had to watch him desecrate it. Olivia—aka my new editor(!) at *Gloss*—had emailed me hours earlier to tell me that the response to the article had been fantastic. She wanted to hear my pitches for next month and beyond—I could work on those maybe.

Not so long ago, I would have been bursting with excitement and plotting how I could reveal the news to Sam, but I didn't even feel like mentioning it to him now. I stopped in the doorway to glance back. Sam was slicing the meat on the counter, whistling away in my apron. It was the strangest thing. He'd never made dinner, or worn an apron, or whistled before. It felt performative, like he wanted all the bells and whistles to scream he was a changed man. The same way I slathered on makeup when I felt my worst. I glanced at the coffeemaker he'd tried to exile. Underneath the apron, it seemed like Sam hadn't changed at all.

Mom arrived at six o'clock on the dot. She had flowers and a warm loaf of French bread that she'd picked up from La Farm Bakery on her way over.

"Perfect taste, as usual, Wynne," Sam said. "I've made coq au vin. This will go great with it."

"How nice," she said, her voice light. When he turned away, she raised an eyebrow. I tried to smile. I wondered if she could see how much effort it took to lift the corners of my lips.

"It should be ready in a few minutes," Sam said, fiddling with the stove. "Vi, how about you set the table?"

I reached for the stoneware plates we kept in the cabinet drawers, but Sam shook his head. "Let's use the nice china," he said.

He meant our wedding china, which I'd packed up for the thrift store weeks ago. "You don't have to be fancy for me," my mom said, jumping in and saving the day. "I'll help."

The three of us sat down together. Sam took everyone's dish in turn, serving Mom first, then me, and himself last.

"I want to let you know—" Sam began.

"How are things at work, Sam?" she interrupted.

I stabbed a piece of chicken with a fork.

"Oh fine, fine. Getting very close to partner, I think. It's all good from there."

"Violet's been doing quite well at her job too," she said. She still hadn't touched her food. Good thing too, since the chicken was saltier than the Oregon Inlet. I took a gulp of water.

Sam wiped his mouth with a napkin. "So I've heard. Her little column's been the talk of the town."

Mom reached down and extracted a copy of *Gloss* from her purse. She tossed it in front of Sam. "I wouldn't call it little—her last online advice post for the *Raleigh Times* had 1.2 million shares. Everyone reads Dear Sweetie. And now Violet is the newest featured columnist for *Gloss*, or hadn't you heard? Her article is fantastic. You really should read it."

My eyes grew moist—I loved that Mom was carrying around a copy in her purse.

"I actually heard today that they want me to be a monthly contributor," I said.

"That's absolutely wonderful, baby cakes," Mom said. I was so happy I was able to share it with her, but there was someone else I wished I could tell, and I'd pushed him away. *Stellar work, Violet.*

"Wow," Sam said, sounding genuinely surprised. "I'm really proud of her." He reached across the table and squeezed my fingers. His hand was a little clammy and I felt almost sorry for him when I pulled mine away.

"As am I," my mom said. "It's an interesting word, 'proud.' Are you *proud* of what you've done, Sam?"

I choked and had to take another sip of water.

I saw a flash of something nasty in Sam's expression, but he smoothed it out in an instant. "Not really, ma'am, no. I admit I made a grave error in judgment and morality. But believe me, all that is behind me. I won't make that mistake twice."

"In my experience, most men say that, but they nearly always do."

"Not me," Sam said. "I love Violet. And I'm committed to doing whatever it takes to make it up to her."

My mother's brow was perfectly smooth. She might as well have been discussing place settings; she adjusted a stem in the vase where I'd put her flowers in water, the slightest flare of her nostril the only tell of her lingering fury. But I knew better. If Sam were a car parked ahead of her in the driveway, her foot was hovering just above her own vehicle's accelerator.

"We forgot to put out the wonderful bread you brought," I cried, trying desperately to cut the tension. "Hold on." I started to rise, but my mother smiled.

"I'll get it, dear. I've said my piece. What happens next is between the two of you."

Sam looked at me expectantly; so did Mom.

The thing is, sometimes you decide what happens next. And sometimes what happens is decided by fate, or by a pool of white wine your estranged husband spilled on the floor by the stove and didn't bother to wipe up. Sam reached for my hand yet again, his fingertips touching down on and tracing a line along a vein I was particularly self-conscious of.

"What do you say, Violet? You can see that I'm serious, right? I'm really giving it my all here. Once we get past this rough patch, we can go back to the way we were before."

I frowned. "This isn't a rough patch," I said. "You said you were here to show how sorry you were. That you respected my decision. The decision I *already* made." I pulled in a deep breath. I wanted to scream at him, but I'd done that. I said in a low voice, "I had hoped maybe you'd apologize for all the things you did over the years that whittled me away—the way you let your mother treat me, the way you pushed me when I was so broken. I can't remember the last time you defended me or put me first. You made me feel alone."

"Violet, listen—"

"You said *you're* different, that you wanted to make amends, but you haven't changed at all. You're still bulldozing me the way you always have. You say you care about my feelings, but you don't; I'm not sure you ever did. So no, Sam, I'll say it again. And I hope you hear me this time. I don't want to go back to the way we were before. I never want to go back. I deserve better than you."

Sam opened his mouth; his face looked like I'd struck him. I was about to say something more, something about how I knew the difference between love and a swimming pool, when my mother cried out. The bread she'd retrieved from the counter flew up in the air, and so did she, as her foot slipped in the wine and went out from under her. I watched in horror as she seemed to take flight and then crashed down in a heap in front of the stove.

"Mom!" I raced over to her.

I could've counted the number of times I'd witnessed my mother cry on one hand, maybe not even a whole hand, so the sounds of her tortured moans, her displaced mascara, cheeks wet with tears, was unsettling.

"Are you okay?" I asked. "Do you think you can get up?"

She bit her lip and tried to sit up, but she yelped. She shook her head. "I can't, Violet." She pulled in a jagged series of shaking breaths. Her hands were trembling.

Sam hovered above us. "Call 911," I told him.

His brow furrowed. "I don't know how that happened," he said. "When I was cooking, I distinctly remember setting the wine bottle back on the counter with the cork in it."

"Sam," I lowered my voice. "This is serious. Mom has osteopenia—she takes something for it. I need you to call an ambulance right now."

"Is that necessary? I'm sure she's okay."

I snatched my phone off the counter and called the emergency line.

"Hello? My mother slipped and fell. I think she may have broken something. We need an ambulance, please, quick as you can."

The man on the line took my address and some other information.

Sam was pacing. I crouched down and took my mom's hand. "They're sending some help, okay, Mom? Try to hang in there." I stroked her forehead.

"Violet," Sam said, his voice plaintive. "I swear this wasn't my fault."

"No one said it was. Just wait at the door for the paramedic."

He shoved his hands into his pockets and skulked off to wait on the porch. I looked down at my mother. Her face was scrunched up and paler than I'd ever seen it. She looked so small, so fragile, my chest ached.

I smoothed her hair with my free hand until I heard the sirens. "Everything's going to be okay," I said.

She shook her head. "It hurts," she said in between sobs.

"You're doing so great, Mom. It won't be much longer, I promise. And they'll make it stop hurting. They'll fix it, okay?"

"Oh, I'm such a mess," she said in between shaky breaths. "I'm so embarrassed."

"You are not a mess, and you know what? We're all messes. And that's okay. I know you're scared, Mom, but it'll be alright."

"How do you know, Violet? What if it isn't?"

The door opened and I heard fast footsteps, familiar ones. I looked up and there was Dez.

"Because *he's* here," I said, tears of relief pooling in my eyes. "My mom is hurt," I told him. "She had a bad fall."

Dez crouched down. "Hi there, Violet's mom. My name is Dez, and I'm going to take real good care of you. I just need to check a couple of things and then we'll give you a ride to the hospital. Andy over there is an amazing driver, could've won NASCAR, I swear. He'll get you there as quickly and safely as he can. I know this is scary and you're in a lot of pain, but I've got you, okay?"

My mom took her hand and wrapped it around his. Eyes shining with tears, she nodded.

Thank you, I mouthed. He gave me a nod, but he was focused on my mom, and even though I felt a tiny pang that he didn't say anything to me, I was glad he was here to help her.

Forty-Nine

Dez and I didn't speak on the ride to the emergency room. He was focused, moving efficiently, placing an IV, pushing some morphine to ease Mom's agony. She squeezed my hand and I reassured her.

"Is it broken?" she asked Dez when her pain had subsided enough that she was coherent.

"I can't say for sure," he answered. "But Dr. Orji is on call tonight, and you couldn't ask for a better orthopedist. She's one of the best."

"Oh, what am I going to do?" she moaned. "The Chakraborty wedding is next week; this is a disaster. I'm alone, how am I going to—"

"Don't you worry about that, Mom. You are not alone; you have me. I'll take care of you. I'll take care of everything."

The ambulance slowed. "We're here, ma'am," Dez said. "I'll try to make this transition easy for you." The ambulance doors flung open. "Extra gentle," he said in a low voice to Andy. Together they eased the gurney down to the pavement and then rolled it through the automatic doors.

I followed them, clutching both my mother's purse and my own.

Once Dez had briefed the hospital staff, they took my mother for X-rays. "We'll call you once we've got her in an exam room," a nurse said. "You can wait out here in the lobby for the moment and then we'll do some paperwork."

I nodded. I considered sitting in one of the open chairs, but I was too worried about Mom to sit still. No, what I needed to do was pace, especially because the waiting room was cold and my anxiety was turning me to goose-bump-covered ice.

"She's in good hands," Dez said.

I nodded, rubbing my arms. "Is it bad?" I asked.

"It could be her hip. That amount of pain . . . But it's hard to say. The good news is that everything else was fine and she didn't hit her head. Your mom seems like a very strong woman." He reached out and grabbed a disposable cup, then filled it with hot water.

"I'm sorry I haven't called," I said.

Dez handed me the hot water. He shook his head. "No problem. You're under no obligation to call me. This should warm you up a bit."

Oh.

I twisted the cup in my hands. "How have you been?"

Dez's jaw tensed. "Is that a real question?" He ran his hand over his hair. "Honestly, not great. I was trying to give you your space. I really missed you, but I told myself that it was the right thing, to respect your boundaries. I figured at some point you'd come back when you were ready. You left those croissants, right? I thought you were telling me to hang on. But then after we saw each other on the street . . . nothing."

I bit my lip. When I looked up again, his gaze was so intense I forgot to breathe.

"I like to think I'm a pretty secure guy, Violet." The space between us tingled with electricity, and I took a small sip of the charged air. I wanted to breathe him in. He was so close. "But I'm not going to wait around for someone who doesn't want to be with me."

It should've been so easy to tell him the truth. They were just words. A handful of syllables, a single lungful of air. *I* do *want you. I'm just afraid. I want to be better so we have a real chance, and I'm not there yet.* Simple as that, and still I couldn't form the words. His eyes searched mine, and whatever tiny shred of bravery I maintained dissipated, bringing about the kind of rapid temperature drop that comes with an impending storm. I broke the eye contact.

Dez tossed his empty cup and shoved his hands in his pockets. "I always knew there was a chance that this thing between us was temporary. I accepted that. You were worth that risk to me. I just never thought you'd get back with . . . *him*."

I shook my head. "Wait." He thought I'd reconciled with Sam? "I didn't. Sam and I are not together. That ship has left the harbor. In fact, that ship belongs at the bottom of the Atlantic."

Dez's expression softened. There he was again, that sweet, kind man I knew. "When I saw him at the house tonight, I thought—"

"Yeah, I think he thought so too. You know that ass moved my coffeemaker without asking?"

The corner of Dez's mouth lifted. "Big mistake," he said. "I know how strongly you feel about coffee."

"Yeah."

"Croissants too."

I remembered the day he first appeared at my front door, before I'd known what it felt like to be cherished, before I'd stood up for myself and painted it red. I'd been such a disaster then, devastated and full of rage, and there he stood, like a sign from the universe that I would get through it.

I wanted so desperately to reach out for him that my hands ached.

"Look, I'm just going to go ahead and say it. You're so great at answering people's questions . . . you know, I'm hoping you can answer this one for me."

My whole body tensed. I lost my balance a bit and bumped my hip against the water cooler. The liquid sloshed, and I felt similar as it spilled—unsettled and shaken. Vulnerable. I held the jug in place with my free hand to keep it from toppling over.

Dez took a sideways step toward me. "What I want to ask is, do you love me?" His voice was so quiet that for a moment I thought I'd imagined it.

I looked up at him. At his lower lip, full and soft, the one that made me shiver when it touched the skin at the nape of my neck and illuminated my whole world when it stretched into a smile. At his eyes, their dark honey hue that seemed to hold the history of the universe within their depths. I took several breaths. I cared so much about him. He made me laugh and feel safe. He was the person I first wanted to share my good news about the magazine with. But more important than any of that, he made me want to be a better person, and simultaneously convinced me that such a thing was actually possible.

Love always seemed to mean hurt and disappointment, at least for me, and I knew that I didn't want that for either of us, no matter how much I wanted him.

I fought the tears that were threatening to spill, and I was losing; between Mom and this emotionally charged encounter, it's a wonder I wasn't crumpled in a corner.

"I know we haven't known each other all that long, and maybe this was never supposed to be anything long-term. You were feeling bad, and I was okay being a fun distraction in the beginning, but you have to admit there's more to us than that now." He stepped toward me again, closing the space between us. I leaned back until the wall railing pressed into my back. His thumb rubbed the edge of my jaw. "I'm in love with you, Violet. I have been for a while now."

Dez dipped his head and brought his lips to mine. I let him kiss me. There was no point in resisting. My whole body was crying out for him, for his hands in my hair, on the small of my back, for his heat. He pulled back, smoothing my hair gently away from my face.

"I want to deserve that," I said, "but I don't. I knew I was a mess, and I got involved with you anyway. I didn't think about what that would mean for you. You can do way better than me."

Dez sighed. "That's ridiculous. Stop talking like that, Violet."

I shook my head. "No. It's not ridiculous. You're being nice because, well, you *are* nice. You're like the nicest. Think about it. I've been so wrapped up in myself that I've basically pulled you into this disaster. I've been selfish and unfair."

He tucked a finger under my chin and lifted it so that I finally had to meet his gaze again. "I think you're being hard on yourself. You have lots of redeeming qualities, and you're a good person."

"*You're* a good person. You risk your life to save people, and you keep rescuing me."

"And you have a job that is literally all about helping people."

"Who have I helped? Tonight, with my mom, this was all my fault. If I hadn't agreed to this dumb dinner, she never would've fallen in the kitchen. She's really hurt. And I did this interview and it turns out that my advice injured people, ruined their relationships, and caused them harm. Not just Shelby with her car, but other people, a couple whose marriage is falling apart . . . because of me. I even put Kyra's career at risk with my stupid thoughtlessness."

"Nobody's perfect, Violet. I'm not sure why you think you should be. If you don't like how you've been acting, then change. You get to decide who you are going to be. Those days you were hurt and angry and your advice came from that place, but you were rising out of that. I saw it. Everyone did. And you can choose to write from a different place today, an even better place."

"I'm working on that," I said.

He shrugged. "I like to think I know a little about your heart, Violet. And deep down under all that bullshit refinement and layers of self-protection, it's a pretty good one. You'll get there."

"You make it sound so easy."

"Nah. It's right. Right and easy don't always equate."

I wanted to twine myself around him like one of those trumpet vines or kudzu. But those vines later choked the life of the trees they grew around, and I wasn't absolutely sure I wouldn't do the same to him. And the thing was, I had an answer, even if I couldn't bring myself to say it aloud. I loved him. He was bright and wonderful and saved people. He'd saved me when I couldn't pick myself up. He'd filled me with hope and replaced my hurt with light and laughter. He'd taught me to trust. I knew I could love again, more than I ever had before, because being with Dez was like nothing I'd ever experienced. I was myself, messy and flawed, and he loved me anyway. He wanted to be my everything. But I didn't think I could be his, not yet. And it wasn't fair to ask him to wait.

"Do you have an answer?" he asked.

I ran my fingertips over his jaw and brought my lips to his, savoring the taste of him, the feel of his strong arms encircling my waist, his smell; I was memorizing him. I broke away breathless, turning away from him so he wouldn't see the tears in my eyes.

"Sorry," I said. "I need to go see if my mom is out of X-ray."

"Violet, don't."

"Don't be a hero, okay?" I said, failing to keep the tremor out of my voice. "Thank you for being there for us today. I was really glad it was you."

A year ago, almost to the day, I'd written a column in response to a man who was a walking disaster. He had a gambling problem and was a compulsive liar who would do almost anything to get money to bet. He'd lost his house, his job, and his car. His girlfriend had two small children from a previous marriage, and he adored her. But he was always hurting her. Always letting her down. He'd steal her tips. Take the money for rent and lose it. Sell the jewelry she'd inherited from her mother. She always took him back.

I'd told him that sometimes, if you really love someone and you're toxic to them, you have to let them go. You have to sacrifice your own happiness for the sake of theirs. Now, I told myself that that's what I was doing. I was one of those invasive vines who would steal all the sun and rain and oxygen and snuff Dez out if I was with him before I was really ready. But there was a tiny voice within me screaming, *Coward—you're just afraid you'll get hurt again.* What was the truth? I didn't know.

I was only sure of two things. One: Dez and I—we loved each other. Two: one of us was definitely getting hurt. It was just a matter of when and who. So I chose. *Right now.*

"Violet," Dez said again, clasping my hand in his. "C'mon."

I pulled it out of his grasp.

"Dez . . . goodbye."

Me.

Dear Sweetie,

I wasn't sure about writing this letter. Honestly, your column's been a little wild these past few months, but I'm in a challenging situation and don't know what to do. I'm a single dad of a sixteen-year-old daughter. She's always been on the right path: honor student, great athlete, hard worker, responsible. The other day, I knocked over the trashcan in her bathroom and found a positive pregnancy test. I could barely breathe. I just can't believe this is happening. I worked so hard to raise her right, and now her whole life could be ruined. She told me that she wants to keep the baby and is working out a plan to continue with school. I'm not sure what to do or how to talk to her about it, especially when I'm so shocked and angry. What do I do?

Sincerely,
Disappointed Dad

Dear Disappointed Dad,

Your daughter sounds like an amazing young person, and getting pregnant doesn't do anything to change that. The only thing that can diminish her worth is what happens next. It seems to me that she is doing her best in this difficult situation, and what she needs is for her father to support her. Make sure she knows that she has options and that you will love her no matter what she decides. Let her know that it's okay for her to be worried and scared and to come to you with anything, because you're going to be there for her. Because what we all need in this world is someone who accepts us for exactly who we are and doesn't run away or flinch when we really need them. You have been a great father so far, and now is your moment when you show your mettle. Don't be disappointed; be supportive and loving and resolute. Be unwavering. If you can do that and you face this by her side? I can't promise it will be easy, but it will be okay in the end.

Sincerely,
Sweetie

Fifty-One

I PULLED ON A PAIR of running tights and laced up my sneakers. It was cold enough that I pulled on a sweatshirt before I headed outside. My breath formed clouds in front of me. I started off slow, one foot in front of the other, but once my muscles were warm and awake, I picked up speed. I headed out of the subdivision and turned right past the fire station. The doors were shut. I cut down past the nature park and through some trails there before I started to get tired and thirsty and decided to head home. There were Canada geese floating on the lake, and when I crossed over the bridge they honked at me. Someone told me once that Canada geese mate for life. Were they happy, I wondered, floating together? What about the ones who were alone?

I turned up my music on the way back, trying to drown out the burning in my thighs. *Bear would be proud*, I thought as I powered up the hill home. I was proud, and that was even better. I pulled my phone out and changed the song.

"Watch out!" a voice called.

It wasn't enough of a warning. I ran straight into the woman. We tangled together and rolled down an embankment, where a bunch of blackberry bushes, their leaves long turned and fallen, berries picked away by birds, tore at our limbs. We landed in a heap at the bottom in the cold, wet soil. I propped myself up slowly on an elbow, my ribs and hips aching. I didn't think anything was broken. I looked ahead of me and there was Shelby. She was wearing black shorts and a tight, long-sleeved fleece. Her perfect ponytail had a rotten brown leaf stuck in it.

"I didn't see you," I said.

"I should've moved," she said.

"I shouldn't have been looking at my phone."

We both fell silent.

"How's Sam?" she asked, after a long pause.

"I don't know."

"Oh, I thought he went back."

"He did," I said. "But I didn't. I mean, I stayed in the house, but we're not getting back together."

She extracted the leaf from her hair and shredded it between her muddy fingers. "I owe you an apology. I wanted to talk a long time ago, but Sam told me that I should stay away from you. I never meant to be this kind of person, you know, the kind of woman who goes after someone's husband. I thought that you guys were separated. At least that's what Sam told me."

"Well, I'm sure you've figured out by now that Sam is kind of a liar."

"I'm starting to." She shifted her weight to get up and fell back. "Oww."

"Are you hurt?"

She shook her head. "It's fine. I must've twisted my ankle. I deserve it."

I reached out to help her up. "I think you've been punished more than enough. My mother says none of us is immune to making mistakes. I've definitely proved that point over the past couple of months."

She hopped on one foot, balancing on my arm. "Right. Well, anyway, I'm still really sorry, Violet, for what we did to you."

I shrugged. "It's in the past. Here, I'll help you back to your house. You'll want to put some ice on that ankle before it swells."

She nodded. "I'm not an awful person," she said.

"I never thought you were awful." I glanced over at her. "Okay, maybe I did think you were *kind of* awful. I hated you for a bit there, like I really loathed you. Not enough to actually post that thing that went up online about you, but I did write it. I'm sorry about your car."

"Actually, it turns out those things weren't related. That was a guy from my gym. I seem to attract the wrong type of guys. But it did kind of get me thinking."

Sam was the wrong type of guy. He was a liar and a cheat who put his own needs before everyone else. And a dude who keyed *whore* into someone's car was definitely a bad seed.

"There's good ones out there," I said. I meant it. I had proof. I'd met one. Dez. I'd messed it all up, but for a little while there, I'd had someone good and kind and wonderful, and I'd been happy when I hadn't been caught up in what I thought I was supposed to have.

I took Shelby's arm and looped it over my shoulders. "C'mon, I'll help you. You can lean on me."

"Thanks. You know, it's funny . . . Sam always said that you hated running with a passion. But you were really motoring there, like a woman on a mission. Where were you headed?"

I glanced back over my shoulder at the firehouse. I'd tried to be a noble person and let Dez go, since his life would be better without me messing it up all the time. It was pretty pathetic that I couldn't really do it completely and had taken to jogging by like some kind of obsessed schoolgirl with a crush, hoping to catch a glimpse of him.

"Nowhere."

After I'd deposited Shelby in a chair on her porch, I walked home.

I was done running. Lot of good it had done me anyway. My phone buzzed. I pulled it out of my sweatshirt pocket and answered.

"Hello?"

"Hey, you," Kyra said. "Harriet and I are going to Roxy's for brunch. She's trying out a new menu, want to come?"

"Okay," I said. "I need to change first, though. I'm covered in sweat."

"Spicy? Why, may I ask, are you sweat covered? And please tell me you didn't go back to Bear. Your booty is fine as it is."

"I ran into Shelby on a run and had to practically carry her home."

"Say what?"

"Like I literally ran into her and sent her flying into a ditch. She twisted her ankle, so I helped her home."

"Oh, juicy. Did you do it on purpose?"

"Nope. It's fine. She's okay."

"That must've been awkward."

"Actually, she apologized."

"She did? And what did you do?"

"What could I do . . . I said I also was sorry about what I wrote, and her car, and that it was all in the past."

"How very magnanimous of you."

"Not really," I said. "That ditch was full of poison oak, and Shelby wears those short-shorts year-round."

"Now that's the Violet I know and love. I'll pick you up in twenty. Wear your chicken-and-waffle-eating pants."

Fifty-Two

Dear Sweetie,

I am a straight-A student. Captain of the soccer team and the lead in the school play. I've never messed up or gotten in trouble. And yet, last summer, my dad left. He has a new family now and barely has time for me. I really miss him, but I don't understand. What did I do wrong? How can I get him to want to be my dad again? And if being perfect wasn't enough, then what will be?

Sincerely,
Missing Out

Dear Missing Out,

I had to take a couple of deep breaths when I read your letter. Because between the lines of your listed accomplishments (and they are big accomplishments; well done, you) there is a palpable sadness. You're trying so hard and feel you're still not enough. My dad left too, when I was a girl. For some people, nothing will ever be enough . . . but that has nothing to do with you, honey cakes. I'm so sorry that your dad left you. I know how much that hurts. It's brutal and heartbreaking. It's easy to think it was because of you. Please believe me when I tell you that this is one hundred percent about his deficiencies and has nothing to do with yours. A daughter shouldn't have to be perfect to deserve love. Humans are flawed. We're going to make mistakes and fall down and fail. And none of those things are a reason why a parent should leave. Parents—even if they don't stay together—should be there. They should pick us up when we fall down. Brush us off and tell us that it will be okay, that we will fall again and they will love us anyway. Love's about many things, but never about perfection. It's about sticking.

Have you told your dad how much you miss him? Have you told him how his neglect makes you feel? I think you owe it to yourself to try. If he doesn't change, then you know and you can move on. If that happens, then he is the one who's missing out.

We can't control who we get as parents. But we can control who we let into our lives. We choose the stories we tell ourselves. I told myself a story for a long time—that I had to be perfect to be worthy of love. Maybe it all started with my parents, but it didn't end there. I hid my sadness and anger from the world, from my husband, from everyone. I slathered on lipstick and a smile and I tolerated things I never should have. I wasn't genuine or vulnerable, and all I got was unhappiness. When my whole world fell apart and got messy . . . that was when I found my true friends and my true self. I'm not happy all the time, but I wasn't before either. I just looked like it.

Your story can be that you are wonderful and enough and your dad has some work to do. It can be whatever you want, as long as it's real.

Sincerely,
Sweetie

· ·

Fifty-Three

EVERY ONCE IN A while, I write a column and it turns out that the advice I'd given was the exact thing someone else needed to hear. In the case of the disappearing dad letter, it turned out that the person who needed that advice was me.

Despite his persistent efforts, even after the disastrous dinner, Sam never got a second chance with me. I think that's fair. I didn't want to end up at the bottom of a pool in a beautiful gown because I couldn't drown my sorrows, and even though I cared about our shared history, I didn't love him anymore. He gave me the house and I gave him my word that I would keep his name out of the paper, unless he actually runs for office someday, in which case, all bets are off.

Kyra's and my friendship came back stronger than ever, and forgiving Ashleigh turned out to be the right call, because we grew closer. Yes, it was awkward that her husband had grabbed my ass and I had thought I was doing the right thing by not making waves and saying nothing, but I've learned there's a time and a place for standing up and speaking up about bullshit. What she did that night at the club that led to revealing my identity sucked, but it turned out she did me a favor. I never would have been able to be so authentic if I hadn't been forced to claim my identity by that "fan."

"So," Ashleigh asked, picking up a slice of crunchy roll with her chopsticks, "have you decided what you're writing about for next month's *Gloss*?"

"I'm working on a piece about the wonders of therapy, but I'm always open to ideas."

"Oh yes, I like that! I do have an idea for you to think about though. Maybe you could do a column on what you're going to do about the firefighter?"

"We're going to make an investigative reporter out of you yet, Ashleigh. Right straight to the point. And good topic. I know I'm personally very interested in hearing more on that subject." Kyra fixed me with one of her stares.

After the holidays, Kyra, Ashleigh, and Tyler started having lunch together once a week to catch up, but I'd missed several of the get-togethers when I was working from home while I took care of my mom. I cleared my throat and contemplated shoving a giant shrimp tempura in my mouth to buy some time, but Kyra blocked my chopsticks with hers. "Nuh-uh," she scolded. "You are not pulling that trick."

"I'm pretty sure it's over," I said.

"Why?" Ashleigh said.

"Because he asked me if I loved him and I didn't say yes."

"Do you?"

"That's not the point. I need to finish working out my issues."

"I didn't realize that was a thing. Seems to me if we all waited until we had no issues every single human would be alone until the end of time."

Ashleigh clinked glasses with Kyra.

"Fine, point taken. Even if I were ready and the right person for him, and I'm not saying I am, at the end of the day he wants a family, and the whole world knows I can't give him one."

I looked up and found Kyra, Ashleigh, and Tyler all staring at me with the same eyebrow raises. I knocked Kyra's block out of the way and grabbed the shrimp tempura. I forced it into my mouth before I could say anything else.

Tyler tipped his head. "I can only speak for myself here, but that seems like a really stupid reason to throw away a perfectly good relationship. I mean, Daniel and I can't get pregnant either, but that's not stopping us. Who says you need a working uterus to have a family? It's 2018 now. That notion's a little antiquated, even for you, Ms. Sweetie."

"He's got a point," Kyra said. "Plus, aren't you getting a little ahead of yourself? You're not even divorced yet, and who knows, a few months down the road you might decide that maybe you'd rather be single. A family is a huge commitment."

Ashleigh nodded along as she grabbed another piece of sushi and soaked it in soy sauce.

Kyra squinted at me. I tried to act like I was engrossed in fixing my napkin.

"Unless . . ."

Ashleigh smiled at me.

"What?"

"You are in love with him," Tyler said.

I shook my head. "No. He was . . . a coping mechanism for me. A very kind, sexy coping mechanism. I might have thought I was in love with him. But all the divorce websites say that a rebound relationship is an unhealthy crutch, not real feelings."

"Sexual sage," Kyra offered.

"Exactly," I said.

"Sure, honey," Tyler said. "You keep telling yourself that. I can't believe you of all people bought into something you read on, what . . . Gentleman's Guide to Divorce or whatever."

"What's your therapist say?" Krya asked.

"We're focused on dealing with my unresolved issues with my dad at the moment." I lifted my shoulders. "But she did tell me I should trust my own instincts."

"And what do your instincts say?"

"That I'm too late."

Tyler poured more sake into my cup. "Kind of telling that you care about the timing. And you look like a pathetic puppy."

I took the shot. Just one, because I wasn't going overboard anymore.

"Okay, you're right. I admit it, I'm a puppy. A scared little lovesick puppy. What should I do?" I asked.

"It's too bad we don't know anyone who's good at advice," Ashleigh said.

"A damn shame," Kyra added. "Who wants fried ice cream?"

"Me," Tyler said.

"You know," Kyra said, after she'd ordered us all fried ice cream, "I seem to remember reading a column the other day, what was it that it said . . . hmmm . . . something about how if you miss someone you should just tell them."

She crossed her arms and assaulted me with her eyebrows. Ashleigh caught on and matched the expression. I looked at Tyler for solidarity, but he shook his head. "Violet, I say this with love: it's three against one. Get it together, Sweetie."

I sat frozen in place, my skin tingling with realization. All this time I'd been so worried, about disappointing Dez, about breaking his heart or my own. I'd been focused on the wrong thing. I couldn't control what happened. I could try my best to give us a good shot at happiness, but at the end of the day, it only mattered if I was brave enough to risk those things. The man I loved was. I'd asked him once when we were lying together in the hammock in my backyard, looking up at the stars, if he felt scared when he ran into a fire, and he'd told me that it was part of the job, knowing the risk and doing it anyway.

What I was about to do was a risk. A big one. But love made me brave enough to take it.

I picked up my purse, pulled some bills out of my wallet, and left them next to my water glass. The waitress arrived with our ice cream and I took the bowl from her.

"I'm taking this to go," I said.

"That's not a take-out container," she said.

"Sorry," I called over my shoulder. "It's an emergency."

Fifty-Four

"I WROTE A COLUMN FOR you," I said to him, standing beside a ladder truck, my voice faltering a little. I twisted my hands together so he wouldn't see them trembling, but then I thought better of it, because he was Dez and he'd seen me at my absolute worst and if he was the man that I knew he was, he wouldn't care that my hands were shaking. "Did you read it? It doesn't matter."

I took a breath. "I'm just going to say it. Dez, I love you. I should've told you in the hospital. I should've told you a million times since then. But the thing is, I thought it was too soon, and I worried about the future," I said. "I know it's crazy to even talk about this; it's ridiculous. We've never even been on an official date. But I saw the way you looked when you were holding Rosie, and I didn't want to keep you from having everything that you want. And that's not all. I'm vengeful and I lose my temper. I get extremely messy when I drink. Though, I'm trying not to overindulge these days. I did have a sake earlier at lunch. I'm still working through some stuff."

"You love me." The corner of Dez's mouth twitched.

In my peripheral vision, I could see the rest of the firefighters in their navy blue T-shirts and pants. They flanked us. Maybe I should have given my grand gesture a little more thought. As soon as I knew what I wanted to do, I drove straight to the firehouse . . . I'd wasted too much time already, letting Dez think that my answer to his question at the hospital would have been no . . . I just hadn't considered having an audience.

"Yeah, I do, but it's not that simple. I'm going to screw up. Probably a lot. I panic. I'm definitely impulsive. Case in point: I rammed an old lady's car and committed arso—"

Dez pressed his finger to my lips, but his expression was soft and his touch was warm and tender.

"Shhh . . ." he said, leaning down to whisper in my ear. "I know exactly who you are, Violet, and what you've done, but probably best if you didn't tell everyone about that last bit . . ."

I looked down. *Oh.* I breathed out all of my hope and enthusiasm in one long sigh. He stroked his thumb over my cheek and tucked it under my chin, raising it just enough that I met his eyes again.

"See, you said you love me, and *I* love you, so much, and I'd like for you to be able to come see me here whenever, and if you drop the A-word in this place, in front of all of these firefighters, it might get kind of awkward." He grinned. "Besides, I don't love you in spite of those things. I love you because of them."

I bit my lip. Then I asked, "Are you sure? I only ask because I'm done trying to be perfect now. My therapist says it's an unhealthy pattern. I tried yin yoga the other day and fell asleep right after we finished talking about self-acceptance before we'd even gotten to our second pose. But I got the message; I need to accept that I'm kind of a hot mess."

He was still wearing his turnout gear, so when he grabbed me, I was met with a wall of yellow fabric. "Good thing I'm trained at handling hot messes."

The instant his mouth met mine, the firehouse erupted with noise. A long wolf whistle, a trill that sounded distinctly like Eva, some whoops. In the past, I would've been embarrassed. PDAs were rude and inconsiderate. Unladylike. But that was the old Violet. The real Violet didn't care what anyone thought, not about this. The real Violet's heart had burst like a piñata and was spilling out confetti all over that firehouse. I was happy. I was in Dez's arms. I really wanted him to take me on top of that fire truck and—

"Let's get out of here," he whispered in my ear. "Or I'll never hear the end of this."

He stepped out of his gear, stowed it away. Eva tossed him his duffel and he shouldered it. He wrapped his free arm around my shoulders and we headed home.

"Are you sure you really want to be with me?" I asked when we were outside. "I did put you on the spot there, grand gesture and all that."

He shook his head. "I want to be with you. Here, in there—" He gestured back over his shoulder to the firehouse. "Now. Tomorrow. Ten years from now."

My eyebrows raised. I wasn't sure he'd understood what I'd meant about whether he wanted a family, since I'd been rambling so fast that it was all sort of a blur. "Even if it might only be you and me?"

"I knew about that, you know. You told me, remember. And truly, it changes nothing. If we decide we want that, there's lots of ways to make a family, Violet. You know that. You wrote about it in a column last September."

I stopped. "Wait. I didn't know you read my column."

"Please. I couldn't be a bigger fan if I had a binder of your columns."

"*Do* you have a binder? Was there a box in your house that we didn't unpack?"

He narrowed his eyes at me and slid his hands around my waist. "Stay on the subject, please," he teased.

"Alright. September 2017."

Dez nodded. "A woman wrote in about how she couldn't have a baby and she wanted a family so badly. And you told her that there were countless ways to make a family. Some big and some small. Some were born and others found. You said the only thing a family requires is love."

I remembered that column. I'd just lost Bridie and grief was pulling at me like a rip current. I'd wanted to give that woman the hope that I was missing so desperately. Swim parallel to the shore, I'd been trying to say. Sam had hated it. Kyra called it one of my best.

"I remembered it because my parents were foster parents and they used to tell us all that we were supposed to find each other."

I nodded. "You didn't tell me."

"I don't talk about it that much. It seems normal to me. And then after Ben died, I didn't want to talk about it. It felt too hard. But before that, it was just how my family was. I'm lucky. I have a big, vibrant family. I have four sisters, you know that, two of whom are adopted, and I had Ben. I read your words in that column and thought, this lady gets it. And then you set that fire in the street and . . ."

I shook my head. "It was so stupid. I was just . . . lost."

"That's not what I was going to say. What I was going to say is that you set that fire and brought me to you."

"I thought that fire was a bad thing."

He stopped and wrapped his arms around me. "Not always. Sure, sometimes it burns the house down, but sometimes it's the light that guides you home."

Fifty-Five

Dear Readers,

A few months ago, I had a breakdown . . . maybe some of you were there. I had a snow globe life—you know, the kind that looks pretty and perfect from the outside, through all that glass and water and fake snow. And then it fell off the shelf and shattered into a pile of plastic debris and sharp glass. For a long time, all I could think about was the fact that the man I thought I loved had shoved it off the shelf we'd perched it on with one thoughtless sweep . . . But maybe it was already teetering and it wasn't real anyway. Only I didn't get it then, and so I went a little wild. I was angry. I set a fire and trashed my ex in the newspaper, in this very column, and I gave people a lot of questionable advice about how to handle their own problems. Reader, Dear Sweetie went rogue. But I learned a few things, and if you're still reading at this point, then I want to share these lessons with you, my brave and persistent friends.

I learned that you can't be in a marriage by yourself. A mother-in-law who constantly criticizes her daughter-in-law needs a hobby and isn't kind, but the husband who stands by and says nothing while she's doing it, well, he's an ass. If you burn your cheating spouse's stuff in the street, jump into a new relationship, and write some embarrassing stuff and then your friends use your lowest moments as party fodder, then they aren't real friends—not the kind you want, anyway. The ones you want, the real ones . . . they'll tell you when you step out of line, and they'll be there to guide you back. And when you do all these things, you maybe feel ashamed, and you lock that away, slick on a smile or your signature lipstick, and pretend everything's fine, while you throb with loathing and hurt and mortification. You hate these people who hurt you, and you hate yourself. You don't want to look at yourself in the mirror.

Do it anyway.

Look hard. You were never perfect. Or always right. You made mistakes. You hurt people and yourself.

You were vengeful.

You drank too much.

You moved too fast.

You were thoughtless.

And that's okay. You can forgive yourself and you can ask for forgiveness. The ugly parts don't make you any less beautiful.

You are flawed, but you're still worthy of love.

And maybe that fire kept you warm and gave you some light in the darkest time of your life. Maybe it seemed like a bad decision, but maybe it brought you something, or someone, good. Maybe that mistake all of your "friends" have been teasing you about was the most authentic, best decision you've made in a very long time. And those columns that perhaps shouldn't have seen the light of day, maybe the person who put them out there, who stood by quietly knowing that you needed to go a little wild and that your journey could be something other people needed too . . . well, that's a real friend. A best friend. That's the kind of friend you cling to. And the guy who put out the flames but lit something inside of you, who accepted you and all your mess—well, dear reader, don't ever let him go. Unless he really doesn't want you back, because, well, then you'd be a stalker, and despite me not really having a lot of answers or the perfect judgment, I do know that stalking's not cool.

Love,
Violet

· Epilogue ·

My mother is phenomenal at planning parties, even now. She's finally retired from the wedding planning business—a good thing after the accident, since her hip isn't like it used to be. Turns out that planning was her crutch, just like perfection was mine—so she's learning to enjoy doing things for herself. She did organize this one though, and in my estimation it's the best party she's ever thrown (I am, admittedly, a bit biased). She wanted to plan the wedding too, but Dez and I decided that we wanted a simple affair at the justice of the peace and a little shindig with close friends at home. That didn't stop his crew from driving the fire trucks with full lights and sirens through downtown on the way to the reception. We had a pig pickin' and a giant bonfire (with all the proper permits, of course) and danced under the stars long after everyone had left. Our honeymoon was a week in a little beach bungalow, full of sunsets and kite-flying and late mornings in bed.

Those events were wonderful. But this party outshines them all. It's nothing momentous, just a big backyard barbecue for the Fourth of July . . . but everyone I love is here. This morning I made my pudding—Dez's favorite. Mom helps me carry it outside and we set it on the stars-and-stripes tablecloth. Ashleigh waves from the gate. Mark is carrying a pitcher of sweet tea.

"Hey, girl!" Ashleigh says, and wraps me in a hug.

"Where should I put this?" Mark asks.

"I'll show you," Mom says. "Wait until you see the buffet. We've got Eric's famous short ribs, and Dez's oldest sister brought the best-looking fruit salad I've ever seen in a watermelon basket."

Ashleigh's smiling. She gives Mark a little wave as my mother ushers him away from us. He grins back at her. They were able to work things out after lots and lots of counseling, which I think is good. He apologized to me a few months ago about the ass-grabbing incident, and I decided to let it go. It was extremely out of line, but I'm confident that he won't ever do it again, and not because I would punch his lights out, but because he's faced his toxic masculinity and now actually respects female autonomy. Besides, Ashleigh would bury him and I'd bring a shovel.

"I'm going to find Toby," Tristan says, and takes off running.

Just to be clear, I did not get pregnant. But I am an aunt. Dez's sisters—all four of them—have a total of six kids, ranging in age from one to fifteen, so I get to flex my birthday present muscles and give makeup tips pretty regularly. In fact, a couple of months ago Dez's youngest sister, Rhiannon, moved into his old house with her son, Toby. We are only too happy to help her out while she goes to nursing school at Carolina. I don't know if we will ever have kids, but I've learned that we're never going to have all the answers and that's okay. What I *do* know? Dez meant what he said that day at the fire station when I bared my whole heart, with all of its scars and fears. We'll figure it out in our own way when we're both ready, and we'll do it together.

Tristan and Toby are the same age and became fast friends over a shared love of Durham Bulls baseball and mischief making. Thankfully, Tristan stopped picking his nose last year at Christmastime, thanks to a message from an Elf on the Shelf regarding Santa's disdain for booger foraging, so I didn't have to worry about him being a bad influence. The boys find each other on the other side of the yard, and before I know it, Mark and Dez are taking them on in a game of Wiffle ball. From the looks of it, the boys, who are both athletically gifted and blatant cheats, are whupping the men pretty heartily, and I am here for it.

"Look at that move," I say, as Tristan grabs on to his dad's Bermuda shorts to keep him from rounding a shrub they're using as a makeshift third base.

"That's my boy!" Ashleigh hollers. She turns to me. "I just hope he doesn't pull them down too far."

"I'm prepared. I'm trying to be more easygoing. Things go wrong at parties . . . it's like a law," I said. "Fortunately, Toby already knows the word *shit*, so we won't have a repeat of that incident."

The gate creaks and Kyra and Harriet burst through. Roxy does not burst through—she's waddling behind them and promptly settles into a papasan chair in the shade to doze off—which is a relief because she is several days overdue with their second baby, and although I am prepared for party mishaps, I don't really want the kids to be traumatized by the miracle of birth in the backyard.

Kyra squeezes me hard. "God, I miss you!" she says. "Tyler and I go to Krispy Kreme, but it's not the same. He always wants to talk about wedding stationery and whether it would be weird if he and Daniel wore the same exact brand and cut of tuxedo, and he's got his life so together. There's nothing for me to do."

"Okay, first, I miss you too. Second, I have everything together . . . mostly," I tell her, squeezing back. "Listen, when you're on maternity leave, we'll have to make the best of it. I'll visit you every day as soon as I'm done shooting."

"See how she does that?" Kyra says, turning to Ashleigh.

"What?" I say.

"It's like every little chance she gets she has to remind us."

Ashleigh nods along. "I know exactly what you mean. Listen, Violet, we all know you're a big star now, not some lowly newspaper columnist, there's no need to keep rubbing it in."

They're teasing me, I realize at the sight of their dual grins. They were there when Hastings let me and Kyra know that the board wasn't sure they liked the direction I'd taken with my column and I could either tone it down or be replaced. They probably wondered if I was going to sit down to my computer and type out a fake Dear Sweetie letter about handling disappointment or burn down the office, but I did not. I shuffled off to the bathroom for a couple of sniffles and called Dez—because he'd made good on his promise to never let me cry in a bathroom alone ever again—and after some commiseration and a pep talk, I had an idea. I didn't get syndication. Maybe I got something better.

I got myself.

I've kept the monthly feature at *Gloss*, though it's evolved to focus more on women's well-being—I wanted other people to know it's okay to not be fine. Yes, the right shade of lipstick is great, but it won't solve your problems for you. I also landed my own daytime television show, which is perfect because as long as I don't make the FCC mad, I can be my authentic self, plus these days I walk Toby to the bus every morning and say a cool hello to Cindy Willis and then on the days that Dez is working, I stop by to say hi on my way to the studio. Once a week I talk to Ruth, Dez's mom, on the drive into Raleigh. She's like him, kind and funny, the sort of person who builds people up and makes them feel at home. At our wedding, she told me she always wanted five daughters and she was so excited that

I was part of their family now. She and Dez's dad, Roger, even got some sort of premium cable package so they could watch my show.

Toby hits a home run now, whacks the heck out of the ball and sends it flying. We all stop and watch it careen through the air and over the fence into the neighbor's yard. Then he and Dez turn around at the exact same moment, their bright smiles shining, bathing me in the light of their incandescent happiness. I wave my arm over my head.

"Hey, Bill," I call out to our neighbor, "could you toss that ball back? Thanks!"

I turn back to the boys. Dez scoops Toby up and runs the bases with him held high in the air like baby Simba.

"I love you!" I shout, feeling like I might burst into bits.

And then Bill returns the ball. It thwacks me right in the face.

"Dang," Kyra says, trying to contain a laugh.

"That's going to leave a mark," Ashleigh says, wincing.

"Oh well," I say. I stoop to pick up the ball. Then I toss it to the waiting players.

Dez isn't with them though. True to form, he's already loping over to me, checking for damage, asking if I want a cold pack, planting a gentle kiss on my temple.

"Are you okay?" he asks.

I look up at him—this good man, who I brought to me with a poorly thought-out bonfire, who stayed by my side and always will—and smile. I press the back of my hand beneath my nose to check for blood. "Never better, babe," I tell him, and pull him back down for a firework kind of kiss that lights up my heart like the sky.

Mom shrieks and we all turn to see the commotion. "Well shoot!" she says. "Bodhi ate all the hot dogs . . . every single one!" The dog runs through the yard, a golden streak, and the boys take chase. Even though Mom has her arms up and she's muttering about not having enough burgers for everyone, the rest of us can't help but laugh.

"No worries," Dez says. "I'll order some pizzas."

It's not perfect, this life. But it's pretty darn close; it's full and real and sweet, and—most importantly—it's all mine, and that, dear reader, is more than enough.

Acknowledgments

Y'all, I'll be real. Writing a second book is scary, and I wrote this one during a pandemic while I was working a new job, my kids were home, and I was worrying about everything. I am so thankful for my husband, Tom, who is an absolute rock star. Whether it's collecting coffee mugs or listening to my woes or every other thing you do for our family, none of this would have been possible without you.

My mom is my first reader, and her support and endless patience while I worked things out on the phone got me through the points when I didn't think I could finish. Mom, you are my touchstone, and in many ways, I wrote this one for you.

To my little realist and my little optimist, I love you both more than I thought was humanly possible. You've taught me so much about what hearts are capable of.

I am eternally grateful for the support of my wonderful editor at Berkley, Kerry Donovan. Working on books with you is a joy, and your notes are always exactly what I need to find my way in a story, plus you're always spot-on about the need to add another date. The entire team at Berkley is amazing, especially Bridget O'Toole, Brittanie Black, and Stephanie Felty—you work so hard to help my books find their way to readers, send me the nicest emails, and don't mind my overuse of exclamation points—as well as the brilliant artists and creative team, including Daniel Brount and Vikki Chu, who create the most beautiful covers and art for my books.

Writing can be a solitary act, but I am blessed to walk this path surrounded by many kind and wonderfully talented authors. To the fabulous Berkletes—I am so thankful you exist! Your kindness, humor, caring, and friendship have been such a source of joy and comfort. To the upperclassmen authors who have been so welcoming and supportive, I'm truly indebted and wowed by you. Jen DeLuca, Denise Williams, Rachel Lynn Solomon, Priscilla Oliveras, Samantha Young, Virginia Kantra, Sonya Lalli, thank you for your kind words and your generosity!

To my agent, Sharon Pelletier, you've been there since the beginning and I could not ask for a better partner. Your steadiness, savvy, insight, and unwavering support are beyond compare. Thank you for everything. Thank you also to Lauren Abramo, Kemi Faderin, and Andrew Dugan at Dystel, Goderich & Bourret for your continued support.

To my coworkers, I may only see you on video, but your caring, intelligence, and enthusiasm is awesome, and I'm glad I get to do my other writing with you. To Karen, I was lucky to have a boss who not only taught me so much but who supported my creative endeavors so wholeheartedly. You are a gem.

I've lived in North Carolina longer than I've lived anywhere, so the list of people I need to thank there is long, and my love for them is wide. To my NC State toxicology crew, we grew up together and I will always love you all. Alyson and the Bitches Who Book, you are my lifeline; you taught me that it is okay to be vulnerable. My neighbors—whether it's saying hi over the fence, inviting me to Bunco when I was brand-new in the neighborhood, making sure my kids get home safe when I get stuck in a meeting and can't make it to the bus stop, helping chase my Labrador when he escapes, sharing your excitement about seeing my book at Target, chatting in the cul-de-sac, or raising my children's best friends, you have shown me what a community can be. As a person who moved around a lot as a kid, I treasure that.

Finally, I want to thank my amazing readers. When I was writing *Meet Me in Paradise*, it never occurred to me that someday strangers would pick it up and read it. That was too far outside the realm of possibility for me to even dream about. When I wrote *If You Ask Me*, you, dear readers, were always on my mind. I wanted to write a book you would love, that would make you laugh, move you, fill you with hope. While I'm not always able to respond to your messages and photos, they've done exactly that for me . . . inspired me to keep going. Thank you from the bottom of my heart.

Keep reading for a special preview of

Play For Me

Coming out in Spring 2023!

I LOST EVERYTHING I LOVED in the span of twenty-four hours. Well, nearly everything, since Dad was still safely tucked away in Sommerset Meadows, but that's a different story. Heartbreak comes in all forms.

Baseball went first.

Boston and cannoli from Vitales in the North End quickly followed.

I was eating my feelings in the form of a chocolate chip cannoli when a man holding a sheet cake paused to look me over and, upon recognizing me, promptly spit in my face. He was wearing an autographed Big Papi jersey and an expression that can only be described as murderous. They say hell hath no fury like a woman scorned . . . well, a woman scorned has nothing on a Red Sox fan who just stumbled upon the trainer responsible for ruining the team's World Series run, stuffing her face with pastry in an Italian bakery.

"That's for benching Iwasaki!" he hollered. "You cost us the series!"

The rabid fan couldn't have known only two hours earlier I'd been forced to resign in front of a room full of middle-aged men in ill-fitting polo shirts. He wouldn't have seen me sitting on the T next to a cardboard box full of my things, willing myself not to cry. And he definitely had no earthly notion that I'd arrived home to find the rest of my worldly possessions packed away in a matching luggage set my boyfriend, Patrick, had bought for me to use on our trip to Zurich in January. He'd said it was for our four-year anniversary. I'd been so excited to go abroad, picturing us finally reconnecting in front of a crackling fire in a Swiss chalet, clad in matching Fair Isle sweaters after a long day of skiing. I'd been about to book tickets for the Sound of Music Tour when he confessed that he'd be busy most of the time at the International Conference on Orthopedics and Sports Medicine. Work came first. As the team doctor, he hadn't taken kindly to having his medical judgment called into question, especially by me. We were supposed to be a *team*. He'd carved me out of our shared brownstone and life with speed and surgical precision.

I didn't fault any of them for being angry, even this guy. I was a fan, after all; the agony of defeat had rocked me to my core more than once. On a different day, I'd have taken the vitriol with a smile and mustered up a joke to diffuse the situation. But I wasn't at my best, and my cheek was damp with spittle, which is probably why I exploded out of my chair, knocked the cake box out of the man's hand, and smashed my half-eaten cannoli into his face.

"I'd do it again!" I yelled. Cake splattered on the floor around us. It was completely out of character and bad choice—the aggression, I mean, not the thing that had brought me to that moment; still, I meant what I said. At only twenty-two, Iwasaki was already the kind of pitcher that comes along every hundred years. He'd had an ulnar ligament sprain that the medical team had been treating with stem cells and plasma injections, but it wasn't ready. I could see it in his face, the way he grimaced and guarded his arm when no one else was looking. Just hours before the game, he'd been drenched with sweat after throwing a couple of easy pitches.

"How bad is it?" I'd asked him.

He'd shook his head. "Not bad," he'd said. "Just nerves." As if the league's best pitcher had ever been nervous a day in his life. I gave him a look. "I'm good," he lied.

What ensued was a series of fights with what felt like everyone in the organization from Patrick to the GM, but in the end, Iwasaki went back on the injured list, and I went on a list too—one that started with *black* and ended with *balled*. "It'll be fine," I'd assured everyone. "Morano is one hundred percent and he's looking great."

The backup pitcher, Morano, was solid. The pitching coach agreed, and everyone conceded; no problem, I thought. I am an optimist.

Morano choked. Epically.

The Phillies hadn't just beaten us, they'd humiliated us in Fenway Park.

The man who'd been on the receiving end of my cannoli was screaming, a strangled, animal sound that didn't seem to equate with getting a bunch of sweetened ricotta in the face. Espresso cups stilled. Around us, the bakery patrons fell silent. There were no shouting spectators here, egging us on. A woman with a small child cowered, shielding the toddler's small form with her body. The worker behind the counter who had winked at me when he handed my food now picked up a phone to make a call. I retreated, accidentally placing my shoe directly in the middle of a chunk of cake. I slipped on the mass of buttercream and nearly fell. Frantically, my arms windmilled, and I grabbed for anything to keep myself upright. I caught the man's shirt again. A button popped off and thwacked against my forehead.

I looked up. The man's screaming ceased. He reached up and wiped the cream from his face while the skin beneath turned purple. A glop of frosting landed in my hair. I had a sudden, sickening realization that there was no team behind me, ready to get in the mix, and there never would be again. I was on my own, and my life in baseball—and my favorite bakery—was over.

There's no bullpen in the North End, no dugout to get sent to to cool off, and since, as I learned later, the delectable flaky pastry scratched the man's cornea, I spent the better part of the afternoon in a holding cell in the Boston District A-1 police station.

I WAS FRENCH BRAIDING the shiny red hair of a habitual reckless driver named Wanda Rose and trying to work out how I was going to tell my dad about my fall from grace when my best friend Astrid appeared, looking like a cross between a blonde bombshell with a foul mouth and a glorious angel. She was wearing oversized black sunglasses, ripped high-waisted jeans, and a tube top with puffed sleeves that revealed her pale midriff. She might have been the only person over the age of thirty who could pull off a look like that. Astrid was warm and disarming, and at the sight of her, relief pooled in me and that feeling of utter loneliness dissipated.

She tossed her blonde waves over her shoulder and removed her sunglasses.

"In all our years of friendship, I never once envisioned having to bail you out of jail," she said, tucking the glasses into her purse. "I feel like we've reached a whole new level of closeness."

"Thank you for coming." I smiled; I couldn't help it. "Bye, Wanda Rose. It was great chatting with you."

"Thanks, doll," she said. "You keep teaching men a lesson with baked goods."

A cop unlocked the door and gestured for me to get out with a quick jerk of her head.

"It better be a good story," Astrid said, folding me in her long arms. "Was it a pervert? I love it when a perv gets what's coming to him."

I grimaced. "I *was* defending my honor. Sort of." I eyed the room. From the glares I was getting, the police were also Red Sox fans. It was Dunkin' Donuts with a side of dirty looks in here. "I didn't mean to hurt him."

"Let's get you out of here," Astrid said. "I know everyone loves Iwasaki, but jeez." She raised her voice. "It's just a game."

"Astrid, shhh. Don't antagonize them." She slung one arm around my shoulders, and together we speed walked toward the exit.

"So, where to?" Astrid asked once we were outside beneath the old blue station sign, standing in the shadow of the brick behemoth. "Home?"

"About that . . . Patrick's pretty mad." I glanced up at the brick behemoth. The architect must've had a mandate to put as few windows as possible.

Astrid's eyes narrowed. "How mad?"

"'I can't be with someone who would question me at work. It's over' mad. At least that's what he wrote in his note."

"Wait, he left a note?"

"It was taped to my suitcase."

"You've been together for what . . . four years? I know you said things had kind of cooled off a bit, but that's beyond cold. Okay, well . . . I never liked him anyway. His nurse was an extra with me on *ShadowWorld* back in March, and she said he's a dick to all the office staff."

"You're just telling me this now?"

"Yeah, game night's been wicked awkward."

Astrid was trying to cheer me up, so I obliged her, but the laugh I managed to conjure was paper thin. My stomach swirled. I wasn't sure whether I was going to burst into tears or throw up, but some kind of emotion was threatening to surface.

"Could I stay with you for a bit?" I asked.

"I would love to be your roommate again, Soph, but I'm headed to Toronto in two days for that film I told you about. Since I'll be gone for a while, I sublet the place to a family of four. You should see the baby. Cheeks for days. Anyway, you can crash until they arrive on Thursday, but after that, you'll have to figure something else out."

"Okay, no problem. Two days is fine. It's great, actually. I'm sure I can figure out something. How hard could it be to find a new place and a new job, right? I mean, this is Boston, the land of opportunity."

Astrid wrinkled her nose. "Especially now that you've been fired and charged with assault."

"I don't think I was actually charged. It's all kind of a blur."

Dad always calls me his little sunshine, his sunny Sophie, the girl who could light up a room, but I wasn't feeling very bright . . . *panicked* was probably a more apt descriptor.

"I think I know exactly what this situation calls for," Astrid said.

I peeked up at her. "You do?"

"Yup, I do. I'm going to feed you and get you really drunk."

"Seriously? That's your brilliant solution? I don't think that's the best idea."

"Good thing I'm in charge now, because you need to drown your sorrows, and I do my optimal thinking when I'm hammered."

I opened my mouth to argue, but Astrid's legs were longer than mine, and she was already several steps ahead of me. "Let's go, Cannoli Kid," she called over her shoulder. "I promise you, by the time I leave for Toronto, we'll have this sorted out."

ASTRID'S IDEAS FOR SORTING things out were generally questionable, even in the best of times. But lobster rolls from Neptune Oyster and unlimited Sam Adams Porch Rocker in the rooftop garden with a view of the Charles River felt like an inspired choice, even if she'd claimed to have selected lobster rolls because they were soft in the event my temper flared again. It was a beautiful evening: we couldn't see the stars, but the lights of our beloved city blinked on and the air turned cooler. The beer and the buttery lobster smoothed out my horrible day.

Astrid leaned forward in her lounge chair. "What about another team?" she said. "The Lowell Spinners, maybe?"

I shook my head. "The Spinners have Ricky Phillips as their trainer, and he's fantastic. Besides, there's no point deluding myself; I'm tainted goods right now. A job in pro baseball isn't going to happen. At least not until everyone forgets about this. *If* they forget, or some kind of miracle takes place."

"It's such bullshit," Astrid said, slamming her beer down. "You said if he pitched, he probably would have blown out his elbow completely. You were just doing your job. It's not your fault Morano had a bad night. Did they fire *him*?"

"I see the point you're trying to make, and I love you for it, but I'm sure Morano's getting his fair share of abuse right now. And it happens. The pressure he was under was immense. Everyone forgets that at the end of the day, athletes are people too." I pulled at the label on my bottle.

"I know! Morano is *definitely* a person. A fine person. I enjoyed watching him wind up for every terrible pitch he threw last night," Astrid said, mischief twinkling in her light eyes. "How about this? Maybe you could come to Toronto with me. I could be your sugar mommy."

I squinted at Astrid and took a long draw from my beer. "You are an angel, but you're not really my type."

She flipped her hair over one shoulder and batted her eyelashes at me. "I thought I was everyone's type."

"You're too beautiful."

"That's fair."

We opened new bottles and clinked them together, then fell into a comfortable silence that only longtime friends could have.

"Besides, I can't leave Dad without a visitor for that long. But I do think you're onto something. It might be nice to get out of the city for a bit," I said. "A girl can only be spit on so many times before she needs a change of scene . . . and a new bakery. And by so many, I mean one. Once was one time too many. Plus, I'm pretty sure I'm banned from Vitales until the end of time. And the idea of running into Patrick at Trader Joe's is not appealing."

Astrid grabbed another lobster roll and took a bite.

"I've got it," she said, her mouth still half-full. I waited for her to swallow. "Where's the perfect place to hide away and reinvent yourself?"

"Is that supposed to mean something to me?"

Astrid narrowed her eyes.

I held my hands up. "Okay. I don't know, Vegas?"

"That's ridiculous. Vegas is where you go to see a Britney Spears concert and somehow wake up married and broke. No. The place you go to hide is New Hampshire."

"How many of these beers have you had?" I asked. "You go to New Hampshire to hike and buy stuff without sales tax. It's not exactly transformative."

"Not true. And also, not enough beers. But that's beside the point." She pulled out another bottle and used the side of the farmhouse table to thwack the cap off in one smooth and slightly vicious motion. "Remember how I got into some trouble junior year?"

"Yeah?" How could I forget? Astrid's parents went through a brutal divorce when she was sixteen, and her coping strategy had been her mother's painkillers and a pretty bad shoplifting habit that had culminated in an actual chase scene, through Faneuil Hall of all places. Her parents had shipped her off to boarding school in New Hampshire for the rest of high school. At the time, I'd been devastated and braced myself for what was sure to be the loneliest two years of my life, but Dad let me borrow his car about a month after she'd left to meet her in Concord at Bread & Chocolate, and sitting across from her, I could see that she was happier, more herself than she'd been in a long time. So I'd hugged her and driven home, thankful and contented, eager for the day when we could go to college together and be roommates.

While I'd been lost in memory, Astrid had fiddled with her phone. She thrust it in front of my face.

I squinted at the bright screen until the words *The Monadanoc School* and a mountain scene came into focus. "The boarding school you went to? I'm not following."

"I donate a boatload of money every year to the theater department, so I get all the emails. I remember seeing one recently that they had a position open for a trainer for the school year that's already underway."

"Isn't it an arts school?"

"They have sports teams. They're just not very good."

"Not good? What does that mean?"

"They suck, okay, but that's not important. This is the answer."

"I feel like I'm missing something. How does a training job at a school in New Hampshire solve my problems?"

"Boarding school," Astrid corrected.

"And?"

"And everyone on staff at a boarding school gets housing, smartass." Astrid leaned back in the Adirondack chair she was sitting in, a smug smile spreading across her face.

It took a few more beers before I was convinced. While dancing around the rooftop, Astrid waxed poetic about how much she'd loved it there. The nature, the community, the fresh mountain air, the hours of therapy with the school's psychologist. It had changed her life, she said. She'd gotten clean, made a handful of lifelong friendships, and fostered her love of the arts, which had led her to an amazing career as an actress. The kind of career that got you a rooftop garden with the view we were currently enjoying. Acting was what Astrid was put on this earth to do. Kind of like me and working for the Red Sox. God, Astrid was compelling. No wonder people loved seeing her on-screen. The way she spoke about the school, I started to wonder whether it might change my off-course life too. Also, truth be told, the beers were going down a little too easily, and since I'm not a big drinker to begin with, they were hitting pretty hard.

"I'm a distinguished alumna," Astrid said, energized by the drinks and doing something that looked like a cross between a runway pose and an arabesque. "With me as a reference, you'd be a shoo-in."

"Okay," I replied, trying not to slur my words.

"Really?"

I nodded. "I'll do it. How do I apply?"

"I can just email them from my phone. They'll probably want your CV or something later."

I thought maybe that should wait until morning, but Astrid was already pecking away.

"I told you I could solve the problem!" she said, triumphant.

"I never doubted you for a minute."

I woke in the morning, sore from sleeping on a small love seat and sticky hot. The sun had crested orange over the horizon, and I had to shield my eyes. The evening had been exactly what I needed to feel better about the state of things, save for the severe hangover I was going to have to nurse.

Across from me, Astrid was splayed out on a sectional, her hair fanned out around her like a halo, a single pool of drool at the corner of her mouth. My stomach grumbled.

"Hey, Astrid," I whispered. "Want a bagel sandwich? I can go get us Dunkins."

She sat up. "Best roommate ever," she said. "I need an iced coffee. Extra cream, extra sugar. And I want bacon on my sandwich."

Her phone pinged and she looked at the screen. "Guess what, buttercup," she said, stifling a yawn. "The job is yours if you want it."

Did I want it? I didn't know. In the car, I pulled up the school's website on my phone. A glance at the athletic program page was enough to make me question what on earth I'd been thinking letting Astrid even plant this seed, but by the time I'd finished my breakfast, I was pretty sure I was going to take it despite my ambivalence. Things usually worked themselves out—maybe I could turn their lackluster athletic program into something special or take the opportunity to do some cool research that would put me back in the big leagues. Plus, there weren't any other viable options unless I wanted to crash on the tiny love seat in Dad's room at Sommerset Meadows. There was nothing left for me here. At least, not now, not until I could stage some sort of comeback, and I would. I didn't know how, but I'd figure it out. I always did. In the meantime, fresh mountain air and a free apartment couldn't hurt, *and*—you gotta love a good silver lining—I was already packed.

Photo by Thomas Hubscher

Libby Hubscher is an author and scientist. She studied biology at Bowdoin College in Brunswick, Maine, and holds a doctor of philosophy in molecular toxicology from North Carolina State University. Her work has appeared online and in textbooks, scientific journals, and literary journals. Her short story "The Unwelcome Guest" was long-listed for the Wigleaf Top 50 in 2018. She lives in North Carolina with her husband, two young children, and a menagerie of pets.

CONNECT ONLINE

LibbyHubscher.com
EMHubscher
LibbyHubscher
LibbyHubscher